Triple Threat

Triple Threat

ISHA RAYA

MICHAEL JOSEPH

PENGUIN MICHAEL JOSEPH

UK | USA | Canada | Ireland | Australia
India | New Zealand | South Africa

Penguin Michael Joseph is part of the Penguin Random House group of companies whose addresses can be found at global.penguinrandomhouse.com

Penguin Random House UK,
One Embassy Gardens, 8 Viaduct Gardens, London SW11 7BW

penguin.co.uk

First published in the United States of America as *You'll Never Forget Me* by Bantam Books, an imprint of Penguin Random House LLC 2026
First published in Great Britain by Penguin Michael Joseph 2026
001

Book design by Diane Hobbing
Set in 13.5/16pt Garamond MT Std
Typeset by Six Red Marbles UK, Thetford, Norfolk
Printed and bound in Great Britain by Clays Ltd, Elcograf S.p.A.

The authorized representative in the EEA is Penguin Random House Ireland, Morrison Chambers, 32 Nassau Street, Dublin D02 YH68

A CIP catalogue record for this book is available from the British Library

HARDBACK ISBN: 978–0–241–73768–2
TRADE PAPERBACK ISBN: 978–0–241–73769–9

Penguin Random House is committed to a sustainable future for our business, our readers and our planet. This book is made from Forest Stewardship Council® certified paper.

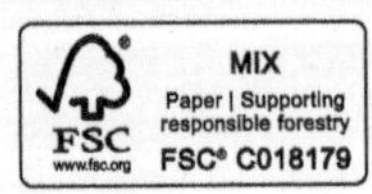

For the reader: May you always be famous.

ACT I

Emergence

I

January 23, 2026

A party commemorated the death of Dimple Kapoor's career.

Attendees paid no mind to the expansive grounds of the Singhs' Beverly Hills mansion, cramming together as close as they could physically manage. Amateurs and seasoned actors alike had one common goal: to brush shoulders with a director sober enough to remember an introduction or drunk enough to hire on the spot. It was never that easy, though, as Dimple Kapoor knew better than anyone.

Tonight, she had the unfortunate, irrevocable gift of perspective. The party in question was a celebration of her latest addition to a long string of losses. That wasn't to say that these events weren't fun. They were, but only in retrospect. The ability to boldly proclaim, *I was there,* when the gossip mill ran rampant in subsequent weeks. In the moment, though, Dimple was having about as much fun as the sole sober individual could have in a loud, sweaty gathering of drunk people.

Her gold bangles clinked together as she tipped back the last of her soda water. Across the room, the band played music reminiscent of vintage Hollywood. They'd managed to get the microphone just crackly enough, the singer's voice shaking with vibrato. This was meticulously planned. Dimple had personally witnessed the staff at the door refusing entry to those who dared dress out of theme.

Now she watched as colorful pills swapped between

hands. Those were not historically accurate, but Irene Singh had never cared much on that front. Cliques born of status were beginning to mingle into one big congregation as the band's trumpet player, sensing this, began belting out shrill tones that made Dimple's heartbeat pick up in speed.

A girl to her right shrieked at the sight of someone vaguely famous. Nobody spared so much as a fleeting glance in Dimple's direction. She couldn't take another second of it. The crowd was dense, but when she wielded her elbows as weapons, they parted automatically for her. Sometimes Dimple liked to pretend they were making way out of reverence alone, but then an ungainly drunkard would brush up against her and dash her fantasy back into the delusion it was.

'Drink?' someone shouted over the music.

She startled at the voice so close to her ear. They were the first words anyone had spoken to her all night. Judging by the dimly lit name tag, the waiter's name was *Isaac.* He was lanky, although shorter than her, and dressed in an ill-fitting black suit. The drinks on his silver tray were strong enough to make Dimple flinch and shake her head.

'Are you sure?' the waiter asked, looking pointedly at the empty glass in her hands.

He leaned closer, the fumes sending Dimple's stomach twisting, and she pushed him away instinctually. The offended look he shot her was enough to induce a flash of horror. She usually had better control than this.

'No thank you.' She fished out a twenty-dollar bill from her pocket and held it out between two fingers. The motion was clumsy, given the pair of elbow-length gloves she was wearing. Isaac accepted the note but continued to stare.

'Do I know you from somewhere?' he asked, sending Dimple's heart thudding for another reason altogether.

On the rare occasion it happened, being recognized was always an out-of-body experience. She felt bigger than herself, straightening her shoulders and holding her chin higher to account for the disparity. The last movie she'd been in – *Horrorville 3* – had been a horrendous flop, but people were talking about it and that had to count for something. The first two *Horrorville*s had made enough money to warrant a third, even if the majority of reviewers were convinced money-laundering had to be involved.

'You work for Irene Singh, don't you?' Isaac asked. 'I bet you've got some wild stories.'

Her heart sank. She'd never worked *for* Irene, only *with* her – and even then, very rarely – but clearly Dimple looked as out of place as she felt. She caught her reflection in the silver of his tray, cheeks flushed in humiliation, and set her empty glass down to block her view of it. There was nothing she could say in response that would save her any shred of dignity.

She turned away. If she weren't so eager to escape, she might've noticed him trailing behind her.

Blurred faces, the shrill tone of a trumpet. The early stages of a migraine beat an irregular rhythm against her temple. Suddenly, Dimple was grateful to be so invisible. Nobody seemed to notice her spiraling, several unbothered attendees bumping into her as she fought her way through the crowd.

The main foyer was just as crowded when she pushed her way through the double doors, the music only the slightest bit muffled through the walls. A passing duo gossiped about the party's host, who had yet to show her face.

'I heard she's going to Paris Fashion Week.'

'So what? She gets invited every year.'

'Yeah, but this time as a *model*.'

It didn't take long for Dimple to realize that she felt no

better out here than she did in there. If she was miserable either way, she might as well go back inside, where at least the glitter and color and opulence lived. But with a dying career that had been mediocre at its peak, there was little her presence had to offer. Five years of booking nothing but commercial failures meant that even her manager, Julie, who'd been there since her first audition, was considering dropping her as a client. The world Dimple had fought so hard to cling to was slipping through her gloved fingers and there was nothing she could do about it.

The music faded until it was gone, replaced by the clicking of her heels over white marble.

Peace, at last.

If there was one thing Dimple could appreciate about the Singhs, it was that they were connoisseurs of the arts in all its forms. Oil paintings on the walls, stone sculptures on display. Several kingdoms lived within this mansion. Lands of glittering temples and vast palaces.

Out here, Dimple was alone. Perhaps there was some irony in the fact that Hollywood's newest generation of artists had more desire to self-medicate behind closed doors than to appreciate the finer things. The very things that had paved the way for the art they created on-screen.

She came to a stop in front of a young woman's likeness fashioned in stone. Her fingers darted out, tracing the dips and curves of her nose, her cheeks, trying to vicariously understand what it was to be immortalized. The statue was beautiful, with an arched nose and thick brows. This – the touching – was surely not allowed amongst such precious artifacts, but there wasn't so much as a security camera in sight.

Such was the folly of the rich. To let their wealth speak for them. *Look at our jewels, see how little we care what happens to them.*

Take it, break it if you dare. We will buy hundreds more to replace it. It sent a thrill down Dimple's spine.

There was something fascinating in art, inverse to that of life. Wherein women in this business lost value with age, this stone woman would only grow in value as time went on. The statue would be remembered exactly like this – young and beautiful, forever. Unlike Dimple. As of now, nothing of hers would stand the test of time. And neither would she.

Dimple pressed her palm against the statue, contemplating pushing. Smashing it to pieces on the ground. Subjecting it to the same fate she couldn't seem to escape; to be discarded, forgotten. But it wasn't a fate she would wish upon anyone. Not even stone.

She dropped her hand.

There was a grand staircase at the center of the mansion, stark white in comparison to its blood-red runner and just as ostentatious as the chandelier that hung above it. Dimple scanned the empty balcony of the second floor. The difference in popularity between the two stories was evident; Irene Singh did not allow people upstairs, where her family's rooms were.

As she climbed, Dimple could almost pretend she was the star of this event. A crowd staring up at her as though she were holier than the sun. Camera shutters and blinding flashes vying for her attention. Perhaps this was how Irene felt every day.

Dimple reached the second-story landing, heart stuttering as she took in the unforgiving marble from her new vantage point. A twenty-foot drop, the police reports would later confirm.

The sound of another pair of heels had her stiffening, fantasies dashed yet again. She braced herself, putting on her most somber face. It felt oddly as though she'd been caught amidst committing some sort of misdeed.

'Hello, Irene,' she greeted the owner of the mansion before turning to face her.

They assessed each other at the top of the grand staircase. Irene Singh was, of course, dressed entirely in the exclusive fashion brand Salomé. Dimple had never once been offered the opportunity to don one of their gowns, let alone one as beautiful and expensive as Irene's velvet black number.

'What are you doing up here?' Irene's smile was polite, but the sharpness of her gaze was anything but.

'I could ask you the same question,' Dimple replied.

'I live here,' she said, which was fair. 'You on the other hand – well, I'm surprised you showed up at all.'

'How could I say no to a personal invitation?'

'The last thing I'd want is for you to feel left out,' Irene said, false pity overtaking her soft features. 'But just because I have reason to celebrate doesn't mean you have to put on a brave face.'

'I'm not –'

'I know how hard you work. If only it paid off,' she said, sickeningly sweet.

Any amount of calm Dimple had managed of herself had been for naught. Irene was talented in many things; acting was not one of them, but irritating Dimple certainly was.

She loathed admitting it, but it was because they were so similar that they were constantly competing for roles. And not just in their long brown hair and golden skin. Both Dimple and her manager had thought the sweet, doe-eyed girl-next-door in real life contrasted with the intense horror actress on-screen would be a unique niche for her. And then came Irene.

Dimple couldn't help the way her jaw clenched in annoyance. 'Speaking of,' she said pleasantly, 'congratulations.'

As though unable to hold herself back any longer, Irene

reached forward and clasped both of Dimple's hands in her own, shaking them with excitement. Dimple instinctively took a step back, heartbeat jumping to her throat. Irene's breath carried whatever she'd been drinking and Dimple couldn't help feeling like easy prey.

'You have no idea how hard it's been to keep this a secret! You're the only one who knows.'

She said it like it was something to be proud of, something exclusive between close friends. Dimple knew about the role Irene had landed only because it had almost been hers. The invitation to this party had come less than an hour after the call that she hadn't booked it. The tears on her cheeks hadn't the time to dry before sending the RSVP.

Dimple bit back a scowl and pulled away, but judging by her smirk, Irene didn't miss the resentment that had snuck into Dimple's expression. Blood rushed in her ears. As much as Irene claimed a desire to forge her own path, she had her family name backing her. Singh Sr was so often pictured in magazines playing golf with the rest of Hollywood's biggest producers, Dimple wondered if he did anything else.

Irene had stepped into the spotlight years after her, but it wasn't long before they were glaring daggers at each other outside audition rooms. It was impossible not to see each other as competition with how often they were mistakenly called the other's name. The difference was that after every failed audition, Irene went home to her mansion.

Sometimes, a lost role still left a chance to be cast as a minor character if she made a good enough impression on the director. But if Irene was cast, Dimple looked far too similar to be given any other role, no matter how small. The same was true vice versa. Directors had joked that the only way they'd both make it in the industry was if they trained in stunt work so they could substitute for each other. The constant passive aggressive barbs didn't help either. Irene had won the first victory, and so she'd been the one to start that tradition.

And now she'd be the one to end it. Irene had landed her breakout lead role, and just like that, Dimple had lost their short-lived cold war. Considering that Irene was only the latest of many actresses who had beat her to the finish line, Dimple figured there had to come a point where she accepted that her career had died before it had even begun.

'You might think you want this, Dimple, but it's hard always being in the spotlight,' Irene said, eyes shining. She looked out forlornly over her mansion. 'You don't realize how lucky you are.'

'I appreciate the advice from such a seasoned actress as yourself.' Nobody could claim that Dimple didn't at least attempt pleasantries.

Irene laughed. 'Seasoned? That's a little much. I mean, you're older than I am!'

Dimple snapped her jaw shut so hard her teeth began to ache. She couldn't account for what she would say if she opened her mouth, so she bit the inside of her cheek hard enough to draw blood.

Irene turned back, seemingly to continue her barrage, but something else caught her attention. 'What happened to your dress?'

Dimple looked down and froze. There was a glaring stain at the center of her stomach, dark enough to stand out against the cheap polyester red of her gown. It almost looked like blood. She wasn't sure what it was or how long it had been there, and felt her face heat at the thought of everyone who'd seen it. Did they laugh behind her back? Tomorrow, would she find herself in an article, '*Top Ten Worst Dressed People at*

Irene Singh's Party,' not even notable enough to be mentioned by name?

The humiliation was familiar – the same as a child who'd come back from playing with dirtied clothes. Dimple never noticed her dishevelment until there was an open palm smacking her for it.

Raised voices, the smell of alcohol on her aunt and uncle's breath as they berated her for ruining the clothes they'd worked so hard to buy. They appeared in front of her again now, the world around her melting away. Once, these waking nightmares had terrified her. They'd left her sick to her stomach, unable to sift through reality and fabrication. Eight years later, in place of her guardians was something blurry, out of focus, an afterthought of a face. These phantoms were mere imitations of the real thing.

Of course they were – Dimple's aunt and uncle had long since burned. It hadn't been difficult to stage the accident, not when notoriously careless drunkards were involved. It was entirely believable that they'd left the stove on, that they'd never replaced the batteries in their smoke detectors. *I'm so sorry, but your family didn't make it,* the doctors had told her afterward. What a joke. It was difficult to think of them as *family* other than in terms of blood, and they'd never treated her as more than a burden. Dimple touched the cold plastic of the lighter tucked securely in her dress pocket. Usually this – some reminder of reality – would be enough to snap her out of the nightmare.

But the potent smell of alcohol was entirely too strong to be a memory. A phantom hand darted toward her, sending panic through her veins. This was all wrong. They weren't supposed to be able to touch her. Dimple flinched, her hands moving faster than she could think. She pushed with strength she'd never had as a child.

And connected with something solid.

It was no apparition. Both the hand reaching toward Dimple and the smell of liquor were attached to Irene. The gasp she let out sent chills down Dimple's spine. Irene's feet slipped out from under her, arm still outstretched. Their fingers pressed together for a fleeting moment, and Dimple tried to grab ahold of her – to take it back – but she was still wearing her slippery elbow-length gloves. The personification of old Hollywood that the party's theme had called for.

Fabric tore, loud as a gunshot, and Irene plunged down the grand staircase in slow motion. It felt halfway between a dream and a movie. Dimple was almost certain that she'd seen this exact scene in one of Irene's films. They'd probably competed for that role as well.

There was a sickening crunch as Irene's body hit the stairs neck-first and all the breath in her lungs expelled itself. She tumbled the rest of the way down, dress twisting, all pretenses of grace lost somewhere between the first step and the tenth.

When Irene finally reached the bottom, long brown hair fanning around her like a crown, she was as motionless as a statue.

2

January 26, 2026

By the time the police got to Irene's mansion, gossip was already circulating, spurred on by the loquacious nature of those present. Irene had fallen and Dimple had run. Like a fool, she hadn't bothered to check if anyone else was around. Although agitated, the crowd Dimple had assimilated into seemed unaware of what had transpired. Only a few people had managed to catch a glimpse of Irene motionless at the bottom of the grand staircase, a sight Dimple hadn't been able to get out of her mind.

The rest made do with what they had: rumors. There was nothing people wouldn't give to be a part of the hive mind that operated Hollywood. As soon as the next day, gossip sites were already posting articles about rumored overdoses, fights, and other raunchy misdeeds resulting in the police being called to the Singhs' Beverly Hills mansion. The party had been the number one trending topic since it ended. Dimple thought Irene would've rather enjoyed that, were she there to see it.

Irene's normally overactive social media presence, on the other hand, had shifted to an eerie silence. Half of the world was convinced she was hospitalized, the other half oscillated back and forth between kidnapped and jailed. Death, it seemed, was not at all within the realm of possibility.

But this was a good thing. It gave Dimple the time to get her story straight. The police had been almost comically out of their depth when they arrived at a crime scene brimming with hundreds of inebriated low-level celebrities. They'd spent a good few hours collecting the contact information of everyone present before sending them home with a stern warning to keep quiet.

And now, over forty-eight hours after the party, Dimple had yet to sleep. She had yet to do much of anything other than sit on her couch, wrapped tightly in a blanket as she went over the events of Friday night. Getting a lawyer would only look suspicious. Not to mention expensive.

No, it would be detrimental to act rashly. Instead, she worked her brain until she herself could hardly remember which aspects of her cover were reality and which weren't.

Dimple Kapoor had been with the rest of the crowd for the entirety of the function. Like the others, she hadn't caught a glimpse of Irene Singh all night. And she'd been drinking – which was why her memory wasn't the clearest.

Becoming someone else was Dimple's specialty, something she'd always savored, like slipping into her favorite coat. Eight years ago, she'd been sent home early from school to find that her childhood home had burned to the ground. Part of her had been sad to miss it. Fire was a fleeting beauty, and Dimple only had the chance to bear witness to the ash that was its calling card. It shouldn't have shocked her, but nothing she'd done to put an end to the abuse had ever worked before. Her aunt, who'd never stopped grieving the sister she lost due to childbirth, could never love the child that had taken her from the world. Her uncle, who'd never wanted kids in the first place and resented Dimple's father's ability to walk out with such ease, found solace in inebriation. Both had burned. For how intently Dimple had studied the silent film actors on her mother's old VHS tapes, it hadn't been difficult to play up her innocence to anyone who'd asked.

People always seemed untouchable until they died. Years after the fire and sometimes even now, Dimple would hold her breath and listen for their footsteps at night. Just in case it hadn't worked after all. She'd flick her lighter to life, comforted by the knowledge that the flame could consume anything, even her.

It wasn't until she remembered that today was Monday and that she had work to do that Dimple finally dragged herself from the couch and got dressed for the day. She'd spent nearly thirty minutes staring at the wall, debating whether she should give her assistant another day off or fire her altogether. On one hand, she could barely afford hiring Priyal in the first place. Her manager had insisted on it given Dimple's aversion to social media, but now that Julie was likely to drop her anyway, it would be prudent to save the money instead. Barely three months of employing the girl and it was already eating into Dimple's meager savings. She ended up giving her assistant the rest of the week off.

The bell rang and Dimple frowned. Perhaps Priyal had already been on the way. Dimple cleared her throat, testing her voice, before swinging her apartment door open.

She stopped short when she realized she didn't recognize the two men standing on her welcome mat: one olive-toned and the other with skin a deep umber. A glance back at the clock reminded her that it was a bit too early for Priyal's shift; she was always late regardless. Part of Dimple was relieved – she still didn't know how best to deal with her assistant.

By now, several seconds had passed and neither of her visitors had offered up so much as a greeting. Dimple hadn't ordered delivery or called for maintenance. And police officers didn't wear suits nice enough that she could recognize them by brand.

The men, however, seemed content to stand there and

stare at her, unblinking, as she gave them a cool once-over. Dimple glanced up at the security camera above her head. Their gazes followed hers, just as she'd hoped, but instead of leaving in a panic, they laughed.

'I'm Eli Taylor,' the shorter of the two said, though he still loomed considerably over Dimple. Which was saying a lot, as she was nearly six feet. 'And this is Atlas Andino. We're private investigators with Andino and Taylor Private Eye. Ever heard of us?'

When he smiled, his teeth shone brightly. Dimple's heart dropped.

The other man – Atlas – handed Dimple a black, gold-embossed business card etched with both of their names. She attempted to take it, but he held steadfastly on, a strange expression on his face. It was only when Eli cleared his throat pointedly that Atlas finally let go. Now neither of them would look at her.

The business card didn't lack in quality, made from an expensive card stock, and he did seem to have a thick stack of them in his wallet; all signs that they were telling the truth. Dimple pretended to read over it as she continued to study the investigators in her periphery. They seemed comfortable standing next to each other, complementary even. Atlas's scowl, Eli's grin. One green-eyed and the other dark brown.

Her sweaty hand slipped on the doorknob, drawing Eli's scrutiny. His pleasant expression didn't falter, but it was clear that he was paying closer attention now. Could he tell, somehow? She couldn't help but worry that a drop of Irene's blood might've made its way onto her skin. Would it be incriminating to check?

'Apologies, but do you carry identification?' Dimple asked.

The men exchanged vaguely surprised looks, but Dimple

figured it wasn't too out of character for a woman living on her own.

'I'm guessing you haven't heard of us, then,' Eli said.

She'd been half hoping the request alone would send them on their way but, albeit hesitantly, the two of them produced a pair of California driver's licenses. Dimple didn't have one of her own, so she couldn't speak for authenticity, but all the information seemed to match. It was the best she could hope for.

'I'm sure you're a very busy woman, but I promise this won't take up too much of your time. Can we come in?' Eli asked, tucking his wallet away and taking a step forward.

Dimple took half a second to collect herself. She reminded herself that she'd been mentally preparing for this since the party ended. Just because she'd been expecting the police rather than private investigators didn't mean there was any reason to panic. This was better, in some ways. These men had no authority over the law. They couldn't arrest her, which meant there was no concrete evidence against Dimple. Not yet, at least.

'You may,' she said with shakiness that she didn't have to fake. She opened the door wider, an invitation. 'Can I get you anything? Coffee? Tea?'

'No –'

'I'll have a tea –'

Atlas and Eli spoke at the same time, neither seeming particularly moved by her show of hospitality. Dimple acquiesced, making her way into the kitchen, and trying not to mind the way the two immediately began sleuthing around her apartment.

'Thanks.' Eli accepted the mug, exhaustion evident in his tone. 'We have so many of these interviews, I hardly have the time to breathe between them.'

So she wasn't the only suspect. Unless it was a bluff to lure Dimple into a false sense of security.

Even though she'd given them plenty of time to get settled before she sat down in an armchair, the men took their time getting comfortable, organizing their folders and fluffing the couch cushions. Where her apartment was colorful and mismatched, the men were twin voids of blandness attempting ineffectively to blend in.

Dimple wasn't a fool; she could recognize a tactic when she saw one. They were waiting for her to speak first, to willingly give up information on her own. More than that, they were destroying her carefully curated pillow placement. Atlas's gelled brown hair didn't move an inch – that was more unnerving than anything else. Every bone in Dimple's body was hardwired to rise to the challenge, to refuse to give in, but she couldn't afford to do that now. Not when she actually had something to hide.

'Is this about Irene's party?' she managed to grit her teeth and ask when the silence reached its most unnerving peak.

'It is,' Atlas said, suddenly perfectly comfortable. Eli, however, continued to squirm for an additional moment before settling down.

'Do you mind if we record?' Eli asked.

He held out a silver device and when she shook her head, he pressed a button and set it down at the center of her coffee table. A light in the corner blinked red. Not so dissimilar to a ticking bomb.

'What do you remember from that night?' Atlas asked. He stared straight down at the notebook open in his lap.

Dimple wrung her hands together. The character she was portraying – Innocent Dimple Kapoor – would be anxious in a setting like this, she decided. Because Innocent Dimple wouldn't have been expecting anyone at her doorstep. While she would've noticed strange behavior and unrest at Irene's party, she hadn't seen the body and thus had no idea as to the severity of the situation.

With the story fresh on her mind, the words came easily. 'I got there around eleven, I believe. It was the usual drinking and dancing – at least until the police arrived. I'm not quite sure when that was, but I didn't get home until about five in the morning.'

As she spoke, the sound of Atlas's pen scratching paper filled the room. Another tactic. Dimple would bet anything he wasn't inking down more than meaningless squiggles. There was no point, they were already recording the conversation.

'Do you know why the police were called that night?' Eli asked.

Dimple furrowed her brows in thought. 'I've only heard the rumors.' She began smoothing out an invisible wrinkle in her sundress, the picture of innocence. 'I think I saw an ambulance?'

'You think?' Atlas prodded.

'I don't know. It was late and I was drunk,' she said, closing in on herself.

'We completely understand,' Eli said placatingly, shooting Atlas a look. The poor guy actually seemed remorseful.

After a beat, Atlas shut his notebook with a snap. 'Listen, the story's gonna break soon whether we like it or not, so we might as well tell you,' he said, still not meeting her gaze. 'The reason the cops showed up that night is because Irene Singh is dead.'

Dimple didn't have to fake the way she froze at their words. It was a strange thing to so suddenly confront the information she'd been keeping tucked away in a corner of her mind. Her hands fisted in the fabric of her dress. Before this, a small part of her had still held on to the delusional hope that it had been nothing more than a nightmare. Now it was cemented into reality. Irene Singh was dead, and Dimple Kapoor was the only person who knew why.

'What?' Dimple asked softly. Her voice broke unintentionally, but that only played into the characterization.

She'd thought perhaps a little too much about how she should react to this news. It wasn't the first time she'd come to the realization that Irene was dead, but it felt like it, nonetheless.

Because she couldn't be dead. This was *the* Irene Singh. As much as they had irritated each other, Irene had always seemed untouchable. How could it be possible that after standing in Dimple's path for so long, she could disappear just like that? Dimple would never be invited to one of her extravagant parties again. Along with Irene died the only connection she had to the glittering, opulent, star-studded side of Hollywood.

But Irene would live on in the minds of her admirers. In her wildly successful modeling career and her budding acting debut. Whereas it would make no difference if Dimple were to drop dead right here and now, not if there was nobody left to remember her. She would end up just like her aunt and uncle; insignificant. All the pain she'd gone through culminating in nothing at all. Living a pointless life, in many ways, was much worse than death.

Every one of Dimple's nerves ignited when Eli coughed. She could feel every ridge, dip, and crevice in the fabric of her armchair. 'How?' she asked breathlessly.

'There was an accident,' Eli explained.

'She was found at the bottom of a staircase with her head cracked open,' Atlas said.

Dimple flinched, the horrifying sound of Irene's neck slamming to the stairs ringing in her ears. The picture of

Irene in her mind felt even more vivid now than it had at the scene of the crime. There was an itch deep under her skin that she tried to scratch, but to no avail.

'If it was an accident, then why are you here?' she challenged, swallowing around the urge to vomit.

The two of them seemed to have an entire conversation with just their eyes. Briefly, Dimple wondered what that was like – to know someone so well, you didn't even need words to speak to them.

'That was my mistake – I was referring to the fact that the police ruled it an accidental death,' Eli said. 'Of course, as far as we're concerned, this is still an open investigation. Irene's parents hired us to look into it and we plan to do so to the best of our ability.'

Eli's expression was nothing more than a practiced calm, but Atlas's gave away far more than he probably realized. It was likely they both agreed with the police's initial thoughts. Dimple wondered if she could push it further, to see how much they were willing to give away.

'I see,' Dimple replied, the tension in her shoulders loosening. 'And what do you think?'

Instead of answering, Eli said, 'We've determined the time of death to be between the hours of twelve thirty and two thirty A.M. Do you have anyone who could confirm your whereabouts during that time?'

Dimple did have someone who could do that. The only problem was that person was now dead. She imagined that Atlas and Eli assumed she had several alibis lined up – and after a long night of socializing, she definitely should have.

'I tend to let myself go more than I should at these things,' Dimple admitted, trying not to gag when her mind helpfully conjured up the vile taste of alcohol. 'I can hardly remember the night, let alone who all I spoke to.'

Atlas sighed and rubbed his temple as though her response was unsurprising. It was exactly what Dimple had been counting on. Who stayed sober at one of Irene's parties? It was unheard of, blasphemous even.

Eli picked up the recording device and deactivated the blinking red light. Atlas clicked his pen sharply, slipping it into his coat pocket. And then they stood up in unison. Eli gave a perfunctory, 'Thank you very much, Ms Kapoor. You've been a great help.'

'Is that all?' Dimple asked, following their example.

'Unless you have something to add?' Eli prompted.

She shook her head and tried not to seem too relieved. 'Let me know if there's anything else I can do to help.'

They were both halfway out of the apartment when Atlas suddenly turned back, pinning Dimple with an intense expression she couldn't place. It was the first time he'd looked at her all morning. Dimple attempted to remain calm even as fear seized her. Instead of throwing out an accusation, though, Atlas wordlessly held out his notebook and pen.

'Yes?' she asked hesitantly.

'Could you –' he mimed a sweeping motion in the air with his hand.

It took a good few seconds frozen in place to comprehend what exactly he was asking for. Even then, Dimple was certain she'd misunderstood.

'I've seen all your movies,' he muttered in awe, as though she were the sun.

Eli muttered something about professionalism that Dimple didn't quite catch. Her face heated. She didn't think she'd been in anything that could constitute as *her* movie. Nor had she done any work that would warrant signing an autograph. And yet, when she closed her hands around Atlas's notebook and pen, they didn't dissolve into a specter.

She laughed and it left her feeling light. 'Of course.'

The signature she penned into the crisp white paper was one she'd practiced since she was a child but had never had the opportunity to use. She'd never felt so real. Dimple almost wanted to keep it for herself as a memento. Because this felt like the start of something bigger than herself. Something that could outlive her.

'Thanks,' Atlas muttered.

Eli only shook his head.

Dimple gave them a small wave, watching them go. It wasn't until they disappeared inside the elevator that the full force of the morning's proceedings knocked the air out of her lungs. She slammed the door shut behind her, sliding to her knees. Only the hum of kitchen appliances and the thud of her heartbeat were there to keep her company.

3

January 27, 2026

A phone call marked the beginning of Saffi Mirai Iyer's descent into madness.

Two days ago, she'd been minding her own business in a café in Paris when the name of an old colleague flashed across her phone screen. She'd been too shocked to react at first, painful nostalgia washing over her. And then dread. And finally, begrudgingly, a touch of warmth.

'An heiress is dead? That's why you're calling?' Saffi had finally picked up after the sixth missed call, mistakenly assuming that such an incessant bid for her attention implied there would be something interesting to share.

'The Singhs hired us because we've helped out a few people in their circle, but that was with insurance fraud and divorce cases,' Eli Taylor said. 'This is our firm's first murder investigation.'

This alarmed Saffi. Not because of the death – she'd seen plenty of that – but at the fact that it had landed in the laps of Andino and Taylor Private Eye. She felt horrible for it, especially when Taylor sounded so anxious.

'So throw a party,' she deadpanned, taking a sip of bitter coffee. She couldn't understand for the life of her why this exchange couldn't have been accomplished via email. It would've saved her this turbulent cocktail of emotions that hearing Taylor's voice again stirred up.

'I think I'm more worried than excited,' Taylor said. 'I bet it would be different for you, though. We've heard all about the cases you've solved abroad –'

'Get to the point, Taylor,' Saffi bit out. She could already see where this was going, and she didn't like the sound of it.

'Well,' he started. 'We were thinking, if you're interested, that you might want to help us?'

For a moment, there was only static between them.

'You could finally visit the office.' Taylor, who'd never been a fan of silence, continued, 'We could show you around Los Angeles. You've never been, have you?'

Saffi found herself astonished that Taylor had the gall to ask this of her. 'You know why I can't come back to America.'

In fact, other than her, they were the only people who knew. It wasn't just her reputation on the line. Her father had recently been appointed to his second term as Arizona's senator. If word of the last American murder investigation she'd been assigned got out – or worse, if she got herself tangled in another lawsuit – it would be his last term. He'd never forgive her.

The other end of the line had no response for that. So he hadn't forgotten.

'I wouldn't ask if it wasn't important,' Taylor said solemnly. 'The police have already written this case off as an accident, and Atlas is willing to go with their judgment. But Saffi, you should've seen the Singhs' faces. They're convinced their daughter was murdered. What if they're right? I want a second opinion before we make a mistake we can't take back.'

'There are plenty of private investigators in America,' Saffi said. 'Ask one of them.'

There was no reason this needed to be her burden. Besides, Saffi was finally starting to build an international reputation for the quality of her work. The days were tedious, sure, but she was much better at her job now than she was five years ago – that was undeniable. She was in a good place: The botched murder investigation in Arizona was no longer haunting her. The last thing she needed was to rehash everything in America and risk tarnishing her reputation for good. Still, she couldn't deny how gratifying it felt that her old friend was seeking out her help specifically.

'It'll be different this time. California isn't like Arizona. There's a moratorium on the death penalty.' Nothing that Saffi didn't already know. 'You're the only one I'd trust with this,' Taylor said in that earnest tone of his. That was one thing that hadn't changed in five years.

And that was how Saffi found herself standing in the Los Angeles International Airport two days later, her every possession packed into the duffel bag strapped across her shoulders.

As she stood over polished white flooring, watching the others rush to baggage claim, she felt no pull toward her destination. She took in the arched ceilings, the stifling air, the migraine-inducing fluorescent lights. It couldn't be more different, and yet this airport felt exactly the same as the one in Phoenix.

This prescribed meaning was nothing more than a trick of her mind, she knew that, but she couldn't slash through the mental block as easily as usual. Five years ago, standing in such a similar place, she'd had the stupid notion that she'd been about to experience something momentous.

Saffi hadn't told anyone that she was planning on leaving. Still, she'd thought that she'd turn around in the TSA line and there would be Andino and Taylor begging her not to go. Or maybe as the crackling voice at her gate announced the last call for boarding, she would get a coincidental message from her parents to convince her otherwise.

Five years later, Saffi had come to recognize that momentous occasions never occurred when you expected them to. The only person waiting for Saffi at TSA had been a security officer shouting at her to take her shoes off. The only person who called her at her gate had been the announcement for boarding. The feeling she'd been left with afterward was awfully similar to that of someone forgetting her birthday. Childish and overall inconsequential, yes, but still painful.

It was no different after she left either. Investigations across the ocean weren't all murder mysteries and scandal – at least not with the few connections Saffi had started out with. There was still the same boring paperwork to get through, there just wasn't anyone to keep her company while she did it. Her parents had contacted her, but the number of calls quickly diminished when they realized the filial daughter they thought they knew had fled, leaving a shell of a person in her place. Andino and Taylor had tried calling too, but she'd declined until eventually they stopped trying. Saffi didn't know what she'd been expecting – just *more.*

Then came the first birthday card.

It took several years of maturing to recognize that nobody had betrayed Saffi. If anything, she'd been the betrayer. But leaving had been good for her. Saffi never would've been able to grow – in her confidence, in her knowledge – had she never left in the first place. But now that she'd done all she could, it was time to go back.

She hailed a cab and tried not to think too much about where she was going.

'So, where'd you fly in from?' the cabdriver asked in that distinctly West Coast drawl.

She responded in a flurry of French, enough to make him give up on the prospect of a conversation.

When she finally arrived at the PI agency, even though

some part of her still expected a grand reunion, fireworks and all, she knew better now than to be disappointed when the building was dark. She paid the driver and stepped out of the cab into the chilly night.

'Are you sure this is the right address?' he asked.

Saffi didn't bother with a reply, crossing the empty parking lot with the overconfidence of an ignorant tourist. It was after-work hours, which meant there wasn't a single car in the parking lot. Double-checking over her shoulder that the cab was gone, she removed a bobby pin from her hair and began picking the lock. It didn't take long. She'd have to speak to Andino and Taylor about that. The security system inside the entryway was a nice touch, though, even if they were using the same code as the one at their old PI agency.

She locked the door behind her, taking a moment to adjust to the dark. Goosebumps prickled under her suit jacket – she'd forgotten how much she missed American air-conditioning.

The office was clean, but cluttered, all warm tones. A small waiting room with two couches greeted her immediately inside, but she bypassed it for the hallway. There were two open doors to her right, leading into what looked like a conference room and a break room. To her left were four doors: three shut and one wide open.

All three seemed to be offices, so Saffi claimed the open one for herself – her new home for however long the investigation would last. There was no use checking in to a hotel if she'd be spending most of her nights here anyway. Besides, Andino and Taylor wouldn't mind.

She'd spent the entire plane ride poring over the preliminary information she'd been sent, so she was glad to find case files and a silver recording device already waiting for her on the desk. Saffi shrugged off her suit jacket and draped it over the back of her chair. Unlike Andino and Taylor, she had made murder investigations her bread and butter. Saffi almost felt bad for the culprit, who had likely grown used to running circles around the law enforcement here. But now that Saffi was in America again, this killer's days were numbered. It would only be a matter of time before they realized it.

4

January 27, 2026

It was early in the morning when the pounding at Dimple's door began. Anxiety crept up her throat, making it difficult to breathe. Her phone clattered to the ground behind her.

'Dimple?' a familiar voice rang out.

She exhaled. It was Priyal. Who had she been expecting? Irene? Dimple would've laughed if her heart wasn't still threatening to beat out of her chest. Slowly, she grasped the cool steel of the doorknob.

With several excuses prepared on the tip of her tongue as to why she hadn't replied to anyone in days, Dimple swung the door open. But instead of confronting her, Priyal hurried inside, round cheeks flushed with effort. Short and lively and always in a rush. That was Priyal Tiwari.

'I thought I gave you the week off,' Dimple said.

'I'm so sorry to barge in unannounced like this,' she exclaimed, brushing her bangs out of her eyes.

Priyal pressed a lukewarm coffee cup into Dimple's hands as she made herself at home in the otherwise still apartment. A canvas bag tossed over the back of the couch, feet propped up on the coffee table, she looked even more exhausted than Dimple felt.

Somewhat mechanically, Dimple appraised the paper cup. *Something with matcha* was her guess. Priyal was always in a matcha mood during winter. She took a tentative sip, inhaling a mouthful of grass. A matcha latte – she'd been right.

Definitely not the iced coffee that Dimple always asked for, but Priyal's temperamental memory was no reason to waste a ten-dollar drink.

'It's lovely, thank you, Priyal,' she said, setting it down on her coffee table.

'So?' Priyal prompted.

'So what?'

'Did you hear the news?'

Dimple's heart sank. The story of Irene's death must've broken just like the investigators had said it would. Although, perhaps talking about this would put off the inevitable conversation Dimple had to have with Priyal about her termination.

'I can hardly believe it,' she replied solemnly.

'You better believe it.' Priyal grinned. 'Because it's true!'

Dimple paused, considering her tone.

'You got the lead!' Priyal said impatiently. 'In *Insomnia*!'

Dimple's breath caught in her throat, a chill running down her spine. That – the starring role – had originally belonged to Irene. The very thing that was supposed to slingshot her into stardom and subject Dimple to a pointless existence. It hadn't even occurred to her that Irene was no longer around to do it.

One star snuffed out, the other beginning to flicker.

'But they went with someone else . . .' Dimple mumbled absently.

'Apparently, they changed their mind. Scheduling conflicts with the previous actor, you know how it is. They want you now,' Priyal said. 'Julie's been trying to get ahold of you all day – that's why I'm here. You would know all of this if you ever checked your phone.'

Priyal and Julie had been bombarding Dimple with texts and calls, but she'd ignored them. There was no telling what she might've said, given her fragile state of mind.

Dimple and Irene both knew that Irene had been given the leading role prior to her death, but there was one other person Dimple had forgotten to consider: the man who'd cast her. *Insomnia*'s director, Jerome Bardoux. Irene's death hadn't been publicized, yet somehow he already knew about it. And upon learning this, he'd immediately turned around and offered the role to runner-up Dimple Kapoor. This man was attempting to lock her into a contract before Innocent Dimple could realize she'd been offered a dead woman's job. It was despicable.

And what did it say about Dimple that she was actually considering going through with it?

If she was going to do this, she needed someone who could corroborate Jerome's manipulations and her innocence. Her word alone would count for nothing if news got out that she'd knowingly poached a job postmortem from the beloved Irene Singh.

'The role was supposed to be Irene's,' Dimple found herself saying.

Priyal's expression softened. 'That's why you were so devastated when you didn't get it.' She hadn't worked for Dimple for long, but even she'd come to realize how deep the threads of this rivalry extended. 'Don't think of this as them going with the second-best option,' Priyal told her, picking up on what was bothering Dimple in the way only a fellow actress could. 'Think of this as the universe telling you that the role was meant to be yours all along.'

Dimple felt herself smile. Priyal was right. Irene had forfeited her claim over this role with her last breath. Even if Dimple didn't take it, it would just go to someone else. At least she could do it justice.

Taking Priyal's advice, she found her phone on the ground and turned it on. The poor thing began overheating the second the screen brightened, chiming with dozens of messages and voicemails. Dimple clicked through them all with Priyal hovering on her tiptoes over her shoulder.

The offer was official. Julie had confirmed it. There was a contract waiting for review in her inbox. Thanks to Hollywood secrecy and NDAs, the general public had no idea that Irene had been offered the role first. Hell, given how big of a book and how recent this was, Dimple doubted any of Irene's friends or family knew either. Especially not if the director was planning on moving forward with filming regardless of Irene's passing.

Dimple caught her reflection in the small mirror hanging beside her bookshelf. She thought of a stone sculpture fashioned in her honor. One with the thick arch of her brow and the deep hollow of her dimples, immortalized through time. She thought of Atlas Andino. Of people who were too blinded by her stardom to care about any of the imperfections that lay underneath. Of her mother, who Dimple could barely remember despite being the only thing left of her legacy.

She called her manager back. Whoever it was judging her from above, whether it was some omnipotent deity or Irene Singh herself, Dimple hoped they could understand.

Later that same night, looking through some old photos, Dimple came across something startling deep in her camera roll. It was so late, her eyes burning with lack of sleep, she was at first certain she was hallucinating. But it was real: a photo from one of the rare instances she and Irene had been working on the same film. The director had asked the cast for behind-the-scenes promotional content, and Irene, ever eager, had pressed their cheeks together and snapped the shot before Dimple could protest. Perhaps her surprise was why, from certain angles, the two of them almost looked like they got along.

It had never been posted, but Dimple had saved it anyway. She'd forgotten about it until now.

Looking at this, the version of Irene bleeding from her skull, neck bent at an unnatural angle, didn't immediately snap to the forefront of her mind. Instead, she felt an intense wave of sadness that left her heart heavy. The woman standing next to Irene didn't look like someone who'd killed her. She looked like a friend. Someone who had a right to mourn her.

Dimple couldn't remember posting it. She must've done so in a fit of delirium because she couldn't remember falling asleep either. And by the next morning, the news had broken just like Atlas and Eli had said it would.

Two contentious revelations were unleashed upon the world. First, that Irene Singh was dead. And second, that Dimple Kapoor and Irene Singh had once been the best of friends.

5
February 2, 2026

It seemed Jerome Bardoux, the director of *Insomnia,* was just as eager to get Dimple on set as she was to be there. There was no time to waste before throwing herself into preparations, writing journal entries as her character until her wrist ached and reciting lines until her voice went hoarse. It was the only way to build the muscle memory in her brain that would allow her to call upon this fictitious woman as though she was a fragment of Dimple's subconscious.

It didn't scare Dimple how easily she adopted the mentality of a woman losing her mind. She herself had never been better. There could be no nightmares if Dimple dreamed of nothing but her own face, immortalized on the silver screen. There would be no time to ruminate in guilt if she worked herself until she passed out from exhaustion.

Dark circles were easy to conceal. Bloodstained hands, less so.

She'd been so fixated on her preparations that she hadn't realized *Insomnia*'s cast had been released to the public until she met up with Priyal one week after accepting the role. It was her first day on set and her last day of peace. Priyal trailed behind her through the maze of what was easily the biggest and busiest studio Dimple had ever seen, an unusual stiffness in her steps. Dimple pulled her aside where there wasn't anyone around to overhear.

'You seem upset,' Dimple remarked.

'Not at all,' Priyal said, her tone clipped. 'I'm really happy for you.'

'If this is your best performance, I have a few notes.'

Priyal sighed. 'I'm sorry. I just hate that you have to work with Bardoux after he manipulated you like that.'

With the news of Irene Singh's death also came the inevitable revelation that Dimple had been coerced into accepting this role under false pretenses and Priyal was beyond livid on her behalf. Dimple had known all along that 'scheduling conflicts' couldn't have been the true reason she'd been offered the job, but Jerome Bardoux didn't need to know that. If news that she'd taken a dead woman's role leaked, Dimple's career would never recover. But, then again, neither would that of Bardoux's. It was at least reassuring that their interests lined up, but Dimple wasn't satisfied leaving it at that.

While the rest of the world began the long process of mourning Irene Singh, Dimple was busy setting the stage of her innocence. Priyal had been standing anxiously over her shoulder as she wrote out the email. The response she'd gotten would be enough to solidify her position as a victim of Jerome's manipulations if the other shoe were to drop.

Dear Ms Kapoor,

While I am touched by your concern for the late actress, Irene Singh, she has nothing to do with our production. It would do you good to keep this in mind. Please understand that a project of this scope cannot be halted on such short notice. There are investors and people's jobs to consider, yours and mine included.

The stipulations in your contract are clear. So long as we can trust each other, know that there is not much we cannot achieve.

See you on set.
J. Bardoux

For now, it would sit in Dimple's inbox for her to revisit as needed. Still, knowing how smug Bardoux must be weighed heavy on her mind. Even if she hadn't been the one who'd killed Irene, she still would've ended up tangled in this mess, thanks to him.

'Can I ask you a question?' When Priyal nodded, Dimple continued, 'How does one win in a world that favors the cruel?'

Priyal seemed taken aback – their conversations had rarely ventured beyond the general film industry and Dimple already regretted asking. She was so young, of course she hadn't thought about something like that. But instead of brushing the question aside, Priyal had a thoughtful expression on her face that Dimple couldn't bring herself to interrupt.

'You can't,' she said eventually. 'You just have to make sure you can live with yourself.'

It was an answer, but not to her question, and it betrayed Priyal's naivete. That wasn't how you won, it was how you survived. Dimple would know better than most – she'd been pushing through, just trying to make it one more day for the better part of twenty-six years. She was the same age now that her mother had been when she'd died in labor. It seemed an insult to waste the life that had been gifted to her.

'Then maybe I shouldn't be doing this –'

'That's not what I meant,' Priyal said immediately. She chewed her lip before deflating. 'I'm sorry. I'm being horrible, aren't I? This is your big moment.'

'How can you be so certain this is the right thing to do?'

'Because you know that if you quit, they'll just give the role to someone else. And you and I both know nobody else can do it as well as you can.' Dimple stiffened. That was almost exactly what she'd been thinking days prior. As far as signs from the universe went, this felt like a big one. Especially when Priyal added, 'You have to do it for Irene.'

Dimple felt something churning deep in the cavern of her heart, but it wasn't as simple as guilt anymore.

'Let's go. I'm done sulking,' Priyal said, looping her arm through Dimple's. 'Did I tell you how many new followers you have now?'

Dimple didn't know – nor care – what the baseline was, so she nodded absentmindedly. Everyone revered the *Mona Lisa,* but what did they care what Da Vinci had done in his spare time?

Movie sets were always chaotic, and yet everyone looked up when Dimple approached. Almost as if they could sense her presence. Her days of floating through a room unnoticed, half-certain they'd all forgotten about her, were long gone.

Priyal stifled a yawn into her fist and Dimple gave her an amused sidelong glance. 'I'm sorry, is this boring you?'

She'd expected Priyal to be a bit more excited, having never been on a movie set before. It was just three months ago that Julie suggested Dimple hire the girl, so she'd only ever accompanied her to auditions and commercial shoots thus far. If Dimple was going to be carrying a latte instead of her usual iced coffee to the most important day of her life, Priyal could stand to be a little more reactive.

'Sorry,' the girl said sheepishly. 'I've been up all night replying to your new fans.'

Dimple frowned. 'You don't have to do that.'

She didn't know much about social media, but she did know that she wouldn't have bothered had she been in Priyal's shoes. No matter how much she was being paid. It felt a bit egotistical to talk to strangers as though they were friends – or even worse, fans. Dimple had always subscribed to the idea that her work should speak for itself. Although, that was why Julie had implored Dimple to hire Priyal in the first place.

'Of course I did. Your newest fans are the most temperamental,' Priyal insisted. 'We need to keep them engaged at least until the trailer comes out or they'll get bored.'

Before Dimple could respond, something in the expansive hustle and bustle of the studio seemed to catch Priyal's eye. She practically dove toward a table stocked with food, leaving Dimple to trail after her. Admittedly, the craft services setup left even Dimple feeling impressed. It was odd to see fresh fruit and sandwiches laid out with aesthetics in mind rather than granola bars thrown haphazardly across the most atrocious tablecloth.

'Is all of this for us?' Priyal asked, leaning closer to inspect her options.

Someone perusing the fruit selection shot her a look. 'For actors, actually,' he said, making Priyal flush and retract her hand.

He was blond, muscular, and a few inches shorter than Dimple. It didn't take long to place him as her co-star and on-screen love interest, Chris Porter. If he recognized Dimple, he didn't show it. Thankfully, he left this interaction much less obtrusively than he arrived. Apple in hand, whistling to himself as he went.

Having been on-screen since he was a child, Chris was the only truly well-known name among *Insomnia*'s cast. Dimple didn't even want to know what he was being paid to be here. Her compensation was surely pennies in comparison, despite being a co-lead.

The lanky man working the craft table gave Priyal an apologetic look and Dimple had a sudden inkling that she'd seen him somewhere before as well. He turned to Dimple, giving her such an intense stare, it was a wonder she didn't burst into flames. Was he expecting her to say something? She looked down for a name tag and found none. It was all

Dimple could do to turn away and pray he didn't attempt to strike up a conversation.

She could still remember her first day on a film set, terrified of being kicked off for breathing wrong. Actors often had egos far bigger than the quality of their work warranted. Some took it out on anyone they deemed lesser than. Dimple's version of Chris Porter had been a bit older, perpetually upset he was no longer the heartthrob of the era. Under the guise of mentoring, he'd nitpicked all of the extras' work even more than the director. But none more so than Dimple's. Perhaps it had been because the others had broken long before her, all clenched fists and hastily dried tears. But Dimple wasn't so easy. In the end, it was the acting he'd called stiff, the nose he'd called distracting, the expressions he'd called dead, that had landed her this role. Priyal needed to see that too – that it would be worth it in the end.

'Take whatever you'd like,' Dimple whispered, low enough for only Priyal to hear. 'If anyone says anything, tell them it's for me.' Priyal nodded like a soldier accepting orders and snatched three sandwiches before Dimple could pull her away.

As Priyal exchanged cheery greetings with everyone they passed, Dimple tried to reconcile with the fact that this wasn't a dream. Her assistant stomping on her toe by accident helped to solidify the moment, if only a little, but it wasn't until someone stopped Dimple to point her in the direction of her trailer that it began to sink in.

Dimple had waited her whole life for this and yet she couldn't help dragging her feet on the way there. She was half afraid this would all dissolve into a mirage. The other half was convinced she didn't deserve it. This was supposed to be Irene's role. Irene's trailer.

They stepped outside, heels crunching across the gravel.

A cool breeze had her hair standing on end – although that could've been nerves. The aforementioned trailer didn't look like anything special on the outside. Taped to the door, though, was a paper with Dimple's full name printed on it, the corners ticking up with the force of the wind.

Her name, not Irene's.

It was a bit of a shock when she firmly grasped the icy metal of the door handle and it didn't fade away. However she'd gotten this role, she had worked for it. She'd spent her whole life thinking she was at the lowest point she could possibly be and then sinking even lower. All to hope that, by some stroke of luck, she'd end up here one day. And that was exactly what had happened. Dimple swung the door open with all her might, holding her breath. She wasn't sure if she or Priyal gasped louder.

'Oh wow,' Priyal breathed.

The trailer was bigger and nicer than Dimple's first LA apartment. It was temperature controlled, whereas her first apartment had always been swelteringly hot in the summer and freezing cold in the winter, with no hot water. Smooth brown hardwood and the smell of lemon cleaning product compared to ambiguously stained carpet and a lingering sour smell. From community plays to acting classes, Dimple had scrambled for any opportunity to be onstage. All of them exhilarating, but none of them paid. Not at first, at least. There were several weeks she'd come home bone-tired and convinced she'd made a mistake packing her bags and moving to Los Angeles.

But Dimple had persevered, if only for a taste of the same feeling she got in the middle of the night in her childhood home, watching silent films on the old VHS tapes her mother had left behind. She could turn the sound all the way off and still understand the story, the simple black and white of the screen subtle enough not to awaken her aunt and uncle. At times it felt like her mother was right there beside her. And Hollywood *was* beautiful, but it was the kind of beauty you had to work for. Dimple could see that now more than ever, standing in the trailer she could call her own.

'I can't believe all of this is yours,' Priyal said, poking her head into the empty cabinets.

Hers. It felt right. Dimple's fingertips danced across the countertop. She didn't have Irene's money or connections. Ultimately, it was Dimple's talents and her talents alone that had gotten her to second place. If everyone else had something extra to bolster them to first, then why couldn't she have the same?

For the first time in a long while, she felt completely at home.

After a long first day of filming, the sun having set hours ago, Dimple had never felt more confident in her choice to take this role. Her co-lead, Chris Porter, while an utter buffoon, was a much more capable actor than he appeared. His character was serious and he adapted to it well, years of experience translating into confidence on set. And Jerome Bardoux was just as ruthless and ambitious as she'd expected. They were already running ahead of schedule, and she had never felt so fulfilled after a single day's work.

Priyal had gone home earlier in the day. She wasn't technically supposed to be on set in the first place – Jerome ruled his kingdom with an iron fist – but Dimple hadn't seen the harm in letting the girl sit in on a bit of the process. She was an aspiring actress, after all.

Not that Priyal had told Dimple of her aspirations so explicitly, but other than to break into the industry, there was little reason for someone in their early twenties to move to LA and work as a personal assistant, of all things.

She wrenched her trailer door open to collect her belongings. Usually, this level of bone-tiredness alone would be enough to knock her out, but the adrenaline thrumming under her skin kept her from rest. The familiar – but never any less unsettling – image of Irene's motionless corpse flashed across the back of her eyelids every time she blinked. As though her brain had simply bookmarked it for later.

Dimple forced herself to move through a budding migraine and burning eyes until something caught her attention. Any other day, she would've ignored it. Today, she was on edge and desperate for a distraction.

There it was – something blue stuck to her mirror. Probably a note from the assistant director. Snatching it from the glass, Dimple held it up to the light. It left behind a faint sticky residue and that only worsened her mood, but she was too busy trying to make out the messy handwriting to focus on that.

I know you pushed her, and I have proof. If you don't want me going to the police, make the call.

6

February 2, 2026

Monday found Saffi alone in the office. Andino and Taylor must be working from home. She didn't bother informing them of her arrival, figuring she'd wait until she had something of substance to discuss.

The case had not officially been closed, but the general consensus was that Irene had slipped. It seemed that even the Singhs were beginning to buy into this narrative. Apparently, they were in the process of suing the fashion brand Salomé. The claim itself was ridiculous – that the shoes their daughter had been wearing were what caused her to fall – but Saffi supposed they had the funds to rewrite the narrative however they desired. It was as easy as finding a new target to bear the brunt of their ever-shifting blame.

It didn't take long for Saffi to realize that her former associates' shortsightedness was due to a chronic lack of imagination. On the surface, the victim had no boyfriend, no crazy exes, not so much as a filed restraining order. Those were the most cliché suspects: jealous, violent men. But the men whom Singh had been connected to in the past had alibis for the night. And her friends and family couldn't name any recent trysts. The textbook that Andino and Taylor worked from only held so many chapters. It wasn't their fault they were used to the usual scam artists and cheating spouses.

Really, it was impossible to know for sure if Singh hadn't encountered a man who took rejection too personally. Or, hell, even a stalker. While Saffi couldn't rule out a crime of that nature, men like that usually weren't satisfied with something as tame as a push down the stairs. Irene Singh was an heiress and a rising Hollywood star who'd died at a party she'd thrown for herself. If she'd been killed, it was most likely at the hands of an invited guest. Given that this was a party featuring the pinnacle of Hollywood's diet-elite, the culprit had to be a peer. Another actress. Saffi had always privately held the association that the best killers were the theatrical ones. Jealousy and competition were the first things that came to mind. Someone who'd finally snapped. Someone who'd stand to gain from her death. Surely an heiress had no shortage of resentful competitors.

The toxicology report they'd provided Saffi showed evidence the victim had at most two drinks. She was not at all inebriated enough to explain a stumble to her death. Let alone a stumble down a staircase in a house she'd lived in for over a decade.

Photos revealed a tear in the dress – in the back. Saffi could see it clear as day, Irene Singh taking a step back onto the fabric and stumbling. A loud rip as her heel tore into the material. And then falling.

The rip meant she'd likely fallen backwards – facing away from the staircase. Chances were, she'd been speaking to someone. Someone who hadn't come forward to reveal this information. Maybe the person had pushed her. Maybe they were aware that it would look like they'd pushed her if they did. Guilt or fear, whatever it was – Saffi found herself intrigued.

Disturbing the threads of an industry so closely interwoven might've intimidated any lesser investigator but, maybe because she was of spinster age, Saffi was a big fan of gossip. It fueled most of her investigative theories. Coming across gossip was like discovering a gold mine. Separating the good from the bad, however, was similar to mining for said gold. Which was to say: dangerous and often disappointing.

For this case, Saffi got her fix of gossip from the C-tier actors who were in attendance at Irene Singh's party on January twenty-third. The lesser-known celebrities were easy to contact and far too eager to show off their insider knowledge. After suffering through several tedious phone calls and needlessly lengthy email threads, Saffi concluded that there were a few names that kept coming up in conversation. Shyla Patel, for example, was a strong contender.

There was one name, though, that made itself known most of all. Dimple Kapoor.

Once she started looking into it, Saffi found she couldn't stop. She'd probably clicked through every mention of the actress online. Apparently, Kapoor had been recently named the lead in a highly anticipated movie coming out next year. Saffi couldn't quite comprehend why, especially considering that nearly all of the actress's past films had flopped. Not to mention how suspicious the timing was. To announce the casting of such an anticipated movie the same week as a beloved heiress's death – Saffi knew next to nothing about public relations and yet even she could recognize that it was strange. Regardless, every question led back to Dimple Kapoor.

'Who would you say was Irene Singh's greatest rival in the industry?'

'Dimple Kapoor.'

'Who would you say was Irene Singh's closest friend in the industry?'

'Dimple Kapoor.'

Saffi had yet to find a scandal in relation to Kapoor, but she'd unearthed enough of them from her father's political opponents to know that there was something lurking underneath the surface. Kapoor's interview with Andino and Taylor was one of the more predictable ones. A bit like an actor delivering a dramatic monologue. For someone who'd supposedly been drunk, she didn't take longer than a second to recall the events of the night. Almost as though she'd been anticipating Andino and Taylor's questions.

The pictures Saffi had looked up online made it clear that she was a carbon copy of the victim – she'd be more shocked if Singh and Kapoor *hadn't* held any resentment for each other. There were some differences, of course. The most notable being that Kapoor's hair was longer, her skin a deeper brown. And, obviously, her trademark dimples.

For someone who came up so often in conversation, however, Dimple Kapoor hadn't warranted a single mention in any of Irene Singh's interviews, photos, or social media accounts. There was only one photo in existence of these two supposed friends, standing side by side, cheeks smushed together almost painfully. As though the closer they were, the more convincing their facade. Although, it wasn't Irene Singh who'd posted it – it was Dimple Kapoor.

There were a few reasons she might've done so. It could've been that the rivalry was played up for media attention. Maybe they braided each other's hair and made friendship bracelets off camera. But the only people who got along with their doppelgängers were those conditioned at birth to do so, like twins and triplets. And even then, sometimes not. And especially not in an industry so focused on image.

Another reason could be that Kapoor had posted the photo to capitalize on the attention surrounding the victim's death. There were plenty of celebrities who had done the same, but those had all been professional photographs coupled with a long, thoughtful PR-approved message. The standard. This, on the other hand, was blurry and captionless, extremely out of place in Kapoor's carefully curated feed. It felt raw. Not to mention that it had been posted before the official news had broken.

The last reason was one Saffi hoped to be true purely because of how interesting it was. That Dimple Kapoor had posted this picture as a manifestation of guilt after killing Irene Singh.

Saffi managed to get ahold of the casting directors responsible for Irene's most recent films. They were all too eager to chat when Saffi revealed she was working on a high-profile murder investigation. Gossip was a two-way street, after all. It turned out, every major role Singh had auditioned for recently had been in competition with Kapoor. And she'd won the vast majority of them. Maybe that was why Kapoor would want Irene dead.

Could she really have done it?

The innocent, doe-eyed woman off camera said, *No, never.* The actress on-screen in the thrillers said, *Yes, of course.* And Saffi found herself wondering just how far this woman would go for her ambitions.

7
February 2, 2026

There was a thud as Dimple's bag fell to the pristine, polished hardwood, but she barely registered the noise through the ringing in her ears. A phone number with a California area code was listed below the message in the same terrible penmanship. She pressed her fingers harshly into the note, sending a spiderweb of crinkles throughout.

Dimple attempted to think rationally through the panic, through the metallic tang of blood in her mouth where she'd bitten her cheek. She leaned against the cool granite countertop, blinking rapidly into the yellow light. Her skin crawled at the thought that someone had so easily invaded her space. Had they kicked their feet up on her couch? Drank from her sink? The paper displayed on the front of the trailer, the one printed with her name, was fragile, all things considered. A harsh gust of wind could blow it away. The granite countertop she leaned against felt seconds away from cracking under her weight, the sticky residue left behind on the mirror taunting her. None of this was permanent and none of it was really hers.

And yet the granite remained unmoving beneath her. A damp napkin was all it took to wipe away the residue on the mirror. Dimple left the water running for a moment, watching it swirl down the drain as though washing away the impurities the intruder had left behind. The sign on the front of the trailer could rip to shreds, it didn't change the fact that for the duration of the shoot, this space belonged to Dimple. It was her right.

She'd just learned that the Singhs were in the process of suing Salomé for their daughter's death. Freedom from this nightmare was within sight – within grasp. Dimple's entire life up until now had been endured with survival in mind. Finally, she was beginning to live – truly live. The person who'd left this note was the only one capable of taking this from her. They would have to claw it from her cold, dead hands.

Whoever this was, they wanted something. The phone call, should she choose to make it, would end in a list of demands. And an actress only had two things that people desired – money and fame.

It was possible they were bluffing about this so-called *proof,* but regardless, they knew what Dimple had done. That was dangerous enough on its own. Her knees gave out and she collapsed painfully to the ground next to her bag.

This was the worst kind of person – someone who knew an opportunity when they saw one and wasn't afraid of taking it. Someone like Dimple. If they were smart, they would hold on to whatever evidence they had even if she complied with all of their demands. And if they were bluffing, they would continue to do so until they'd extorted everything they possibly could from her.

Dimple listened to the hum of the air conditioner, counting down from ten and then thirty and then fifty. Just like she had following Irene's fall, she painstakingly pieced herself back together. It wouldn't do her any good if she looked as frantic as she felt.

She was able to catch the last few crew members before they left, but they were of no help. No one had noticed any strange visitors.

As she stepped outside again, the night breeze cooled

Dimple's sweat-slicked skin, inducing a shiver. In a sense, she was relieved. The way things were going so smoothly since Irene's party had unnerved her. At least now it didn't feel too good to be true.

This was nothing more than another decision to make.

Dimple followed the sidewalk to the back of the studio building, where she knew a phone booth sat. She remembered it because someone had spray-painted *smile* onto one side and it felt too ironic to be real. Up close, the chipped paint and cracked glass grounded it firmly in reality.

She gave the handle a curious tug, and the door swung wide open with only a modicum of effort. A cloud of dust exploded from within, and Dimple waited patiently for it to disperse before stepping inside. The glass was so dirty it was translucent, the threads of an abandoned cobweb swaying in one corner. Thankfully, the dial tone that graced her ears when she lifted the phone indicated that it was still in operation.

Dimple punched in the number from the note and waited with bated breath as the line rang once, twice, thrice. She looked around again to make sure no one was watching. Her blackmailer answered after the fourth ring.

'Hello?' They had the audacity to sound irritated.

'Hello,' Dimple replied. The voice was familiar, but she couldn't pinpoint where she'd heard it.

'Who is this? I'm not interested in buying any –'

'Who do you think?' Dimple asked with a slight edge.

A pause. Then, 'Oh. Dimple Kapoor.' In a tone of disbelief, as though they hadn't been expecting her to call. Undeniably amateur, but she couldn't hang up now. The fact that she'd responded to the threat was an admission of guilt in and of itself.

'How impolite of you not to introduce yourself,' Dimple commented.

'I'm just a waiter,' he said. 'You probably don't remember

me, none of you do, but that's fine. I remember you. Next time you push someone down the stairs, better make sure no one is watching.'

'I'm not sure I know what you're referring to,' she replied smoothly.

'Really?' he asked, sounding amused. 'Then why did you call?'

Dimple had no response for that, but she could practically hear him laughing at her. 'What can I do for you?' she asked, her tone sickly sweet.

'I'll be reasonable,' he said. 'One hundred grand. If you can get me that much, I'll delete the video and you'll never hear from me again.'

The video. It was worse than she'd thought.

'Are you out of your mind?' Dimple hissed. 'Who has that kind of money just lying around?'

'I'm not an idiot,' he said. 'I know how much they're paying you. It should be no problem.'

'And how would you propose I get such a large sum of money to you without raising several questions?'

'Leave that to me,' he said. 'I'll forward you the details and you handle the rest.'

'And if I don't?'

'Then I won't just send the evidence to the police, I'll post it online too. Good luck beating those allegations.'

Dimple felt sick to her stomach. How would people react? Kind words turned cruel – or worse, apathetic. She'd never book a role again. Hell, she'd never see the light of day again, locked up in some criminal penitentiary. Now that she'd had a taste of fame, sweet on the tip of her tongue, the bitterness of obscurity was no longer palatable.

'I need time,' Dimple said.

'You have until tomorrow.' And the line went dead.

8

February 2, 2026

Seven blocks from the film studio on a street illuminated only by dim moonlight, Dimple hailed a cab. She adjusted the wig she'd borrowed from the set. The light brown was cut to shoulder-length, rather than down to her waist like her natural dark brown hair. It was cold enough to warrant a light scarf, which Dimple used to cover the lower half of her face, and the gloves were swiped, funnily enough, from craft services.

Not even her own mother would be able to recognize Dimple now. Though, that was a terrible example. Her mother had never gotten to see what Dimple looked like.

The taxi dropped her off a block away from her blackmailer's apartment, which, as she approached, seemed much nicer than what most people in the heart of Los Angeles could afford on a waiter's salary alone. Open-air corridors with everything but the apartments exposed to the elements, black railings gating every floor.

In a way, life itself was a movie set. Everyone was constantly performing and even if they didn't do it for the cameras, those too were everywhere. This constant documentation meant that much of the world's knowledge was readily available if one only knew where to look.

The waiter hadn't been stupid enough to give away any incriminating information, but Dimple knew the catering company he'd been working for the same night Irene died. It took no longer than an hour of browsing through the company's database of employees on networking sites to stumble across a familiar face. The waiter she'd bumped into at Irene's party. It was the same man who'd been working craft services on set. No wonder his voice had sounded familiar. From there, Dimple had access to where he went to high school, the names of his closest friends and family, and even his job history. And it became clear that on the grand stage of life, his role was infinitesimal.

Isaac Klossner was an aspiring – or rather, failing – actor who split his time between working as a waiter for a local catering company and crafting services on film sets. His career was even worse than Dimple's, his only credit being an extra in some flop of an action film three years ago.

Dimple skipped the elevator and the unavoidable cameras in them, choosing to climb the stairs instead. Every step had her too-small shoes pinching her heel, but these would make it more difficult to trace any footprints back to her. She ducked her head out of view of the visible cameras. Once she reached Isaac's floor, she scanned the walls until she found what she was looking for – the placard for room 422. She peeked into the spyhole. It was impossible to make out anything specific, but Dimple was looking for signs of life. Lights turned on or the brightness of a television screen, nothing more. She found none but decided to double-check anyway.

Raising a fist, Dimple knocked very lightly on the door. Loud enough to alert a conscious person, but soft enough not to wake someone from a heavy slumber. It was two in the morning now and Isaac's work schedule said he was supposed to come in at six, so he should already be deep into a REM cycle. As expected, nothing within the apartment so much as stirred.

Being locked in her room as a child for days on end meant Dimple had no choice but to become very adept at lockpicking. And without waking her guardians, at that. Though she hadn't done so in many years, it came back to her at once. Like riding a bike, or so she imagined.

The door clicked open.

Dimple let out a breath of relief. She did a quick survey of the space, examining trash that hadn't been taken out in what had to be months. A quick glance to the open room to her right revealed a bed with a man-shaped lump atop it. Dimple stepped across so she was no longer in his line of sight.

In place of where a television might go, three expensive monitors emitted a soft glow in Isaac's living room. And on the desk, a stack of blue sticky notes. This was also the only corner of the apartment that his selective cleanliness seemed to extend to, not so much as a speck of dirt in sight.

Dimple jostled the mouse and squinted when the monitor came to life. The resulting password prompt was not unexpected. Given all the research she'd conducted, it was easy enough to bypass with his mother's maiden name.

All at once, Dimple had access to every one of Isaac's saved files. None of these contained what she was looking for, but that in itself was not discouraging. Even an amateur wouldn't make it that easy.

It was curiosity that brought her to a window still open in Isaac's browser. There she was met with a candid photo she vaguely remembered Priyal sending to her for review. Dimple's frown deepened, dread settling in her stomach as she traversed through several open tabs of her own social media accounts.

He was following them all, had liked all of the photos. On one of them – a post announcing that she would be playing the lead in *Insomnia* – he'd even commented.

ik_1204: when does filming start?
|_ dimplekapoor: @ik_1204 feb 2nd! :)

A shiver ran down her spine as she closed every tab as fast as she could, uncaring of how the clicks sounded like gunshots in the stillness of the apartment. But it was the last one that she'd been waiting for.

An online drive full of various celebrities caught in compromising situations. From fights to drugs to nude photographs, there was a little bit of everything. Isaac was not one to discriminate when it came to his victims. Dozens of people, from Dimple's coworkers to those far her superior. Everyone the public adored, this man had something on them all. And there was clearly a market for them. Isaac would get paid – either through the blackmail or through the publications willing to buy these stories. Perhaps he was the type to take the money and then sell the photos anyway, given that most of these looked familiar. She'd underestimated him.

Not a single movie open on his computer, not so much as a DVD on his shelf or a poster on his wall; this was what Isaac Klossner chose to devote his life to. There was a reason people like him never made it in this industry. It was because they did not know what art was. To them, art was what made them money. But true art was remembrance. The careers of each and every one of these people had eventually recovered, and most of the public couldn't recall the details of their controversies. Nor could they recall a man named Isaac Klossner.

It was one thing to break the law. Dimple had done her fair share for survival. But this was perverse. Part of her wondered if Isaac gained some kind of sick pleasure from seeing successful artistry – something he could never himself achieve – at its lowest.

A video at the bottom of the page was the most recent entry. For all his shortcomings, Isaac Klossner was not a liar. Hands shaking in anticipation, Dimple muted the volume and pressed play.

The camerawork was shoddy, taken from behind a pillar on the ground floor. Dimple's throat dried when Irene's face took up the screen. The woman's innocent shock as a hand pushed her – as *Dimple's* hand pushed her – was palpable. The memory of acting out a scene was never quite the same as seeing it on-screen for the first time. Dimple had replayed this moment so many times in her mind, yet it was so vastly different from the real thing. Irene's expression wasn't as exaggerated. She seemed more frozen and uncomprehending than betrayed. She'd barely gasped, so why could Dimple hear her screams so vividly in her mind?

Dimple paused half a second before Irene's neck hit the staircase, as though that could save this pixelated version of the actress from her inevitable fate. And there, in the last few frames, this naïve version of herself had turned unknowingly to face the camera, blank incomprehension clouding her features. From the beauty mark at the corner of her mouth to the stain on her polyester red gown, her likeness was unmistakable. The evidence was worse than damning. Her blood boiled. She deleted the entire folder, but it wasn't enough. Isaac Klossner had seen everything.

There was a loud thud as Dimple ripped the keyboard from its wires and threw it against the hardwood. Keys clattered across the ground, scattering in every direction. Another thud and there was subsequent scrambling from the bedroom.

'Who's there?' Isaac Klossner came barreling out of his room.

He looked exactly as she remembered from the party – exactly as the photos online depicted him. Lanky and pale. His clothes were ill-fitting, his hair untrimmed. It was easy to see why someone like him could never understand true artistry.

Isaac came to stand in front of the open door, his attention landing first on the broken keyboard and then on her. Dimple lifted her chin so he could get a better look at her face. It wasn't until her cheeks hurt that she realized she'd been smiling this entire time. In some ways, she'd been craving this. The same fear he'd instilled in her now reflected in him.

For a moment, the world slowed to a standstill and Dimple stopped to consider what she was about to do. Isaac couldn't be taller than five-eight and Dimple had a few inches on him still. She probably weighed more too. There was no one else around. And in a few hours, she would be due on set.

There was a flash of too-light hair in Isaac's glasses – Dimple's reflection. This too was nothing more than a role she was playing. What kind of actress would she be if she didn't give it her all?

Isaac finally broke from his trance, expression contorting in horror and recognition. 'It's you? You fucking creep! I'm calling the police –'

Dimple cut off the tail end of his sentence, barreling into him and pushing with all her strength. It was unclear whether it was Dimple or the universe who had a sick sense of humor, because when Isaac Klossner was pushed out of his apartment and sent tumbling backward over the fourth-story railing, free-falling, all Dimple could think about was the irony that this was happening again.

Isaac wasn't like Irene, though. There was no beauty in his death. An ugly shout worked its way from his throat. Still, the sound when his head connected with concrete below was hauntingly familiar.

Isaac took longer to die – that was another difference. Irene's neck had snapped cleanly, but he was a gasping mess for what felt like an eternity. Slowly losing consciousness as his head injury bled out. Dimple knew it was over when she was left with only the still night sky to keep her company.

She wrapped her arms around herself, suddenly aware of how cold it had become, although that could've been the adrenaline winding down. She looked up because it was safer than looking down, trying to pinpoint stars in the polluted sky. There were none.

The fact that none of the other residents seemed to stir gave Dimple a sense of satisfaction. Perhaps everyone had heard and hated Isaac enough to disregard it. Or perhaps this was the universe's way of telling her that she'd done the right thing.

As Dimple peered over the railing, it turned out that Isaac was not entirely dissimilar to Irene. Head bent at an unnatural angle, blood leaking from his skull. His eyes, however, were wide open and unblinking, marking his end. Isaac Klossner would torment no one else ever again.

At least, no one but Dimple.

9

February 3, 2026

As the sun began to rise, Saffi concluded that there wasn't much additional information to be found in the paperwork.

Most of the knowledge she had now were things she could have – and had – already guessed. In her early years, this would've made her impatient. And that meant making mistakes. Now, however, she only felt excitement – the kind she hadn't felt for a case in half a decade. Saffi was still getting to know the major players and the setting that brought this mystery to life. This was the calm before the first breakthrough. The building itch under her skin that reminded her that she was on the precipice of something big. It never lasted long, so she tried to savor it while it did. Regardless, now that she had something to discuss, she'd finally let Andino and Taylor know she was taking up residence in their office building.

For the first time since stepping foot in it, Saffi took in the space. The interior design started and stopped with an antiquated ticking clock on the wall, but the furniture was new and the appliances fully functional. A mounted television she hadn't immediately noticed stared down at her. She felt a pang of something foreign. Perhaps a reminder of what could've been hers in another life.

It was ridiculous. Saffi wasn't the type to stick around long enough to build a foundation. She'd never wanted that in the first place. But she might as well set it to her liking for as long as she was here.

Someone knocked on the door, but Saffi, in the middle of pushing her desk closer to the window, didn't answer. She opened the shutters, allowing in daylight. Despite not hearing a reply, Taylor pushed the door open and stepped inside, Andino shuffling in behind him with crossed arms and a scowl. It suddenly struck her how familiar this was, as though she'd never left at all.

The emotions hit her all at once: relief, comfort, fear. Andino and Taylor's looks held five years' worth of questions that Saffi didn't have the mental capacity to decode. She was saved from speaking first when both men looked away, distracted by the rearranged furniture.

It may have felt like no time had passed, but the years gone by were evident in their faces. They'd all been in their early twenties when she left, and now they were closer to thirty. Taylor had the beginning traces of smile lines etched into his dark skin, Saffi was glad to see, whereas Andino was developing an eyebrow crease and frown lines across his pale forehead. Taylor's hair had been shaved short, but Andino still styled his with copious amounts of gel.

Similar, but different.

'I see you didn't waste any time making yourself at home,' Andino said.

That was when she realized *Andino was wearing a suit.* It hadn't struck her as odd because of how at home he looked in it. Before, it was all casual wear, which was at times synonymous with what he wore to the gym. Neither she nor Taylor had ever been able to get away with that. Whether Taylor had finally worn him down or he'd grown up at last, things were different now. Owning a business must've played a part in it.

'Have you eaten?' Taylor asked. That was when she noticed the take-out containers he was holding.

'No,' she said. 'Have you?'

Taylor distributed the meals, Saffi on one side of her desk while the men took an armchair each on the other. The packaging screamed overpriced touristy spot. For a smug moment she wondered if they were trying to show off, to prove that they'd made it big too. It was unnecessary – Saffi was well aware they were doing well for themselves. The fact that none of their furniture had any missing legs was proof enough.

Saffi took a bite of her food – vegetarian. They'd remembered.

Back in Arizona when they were interns, still in college, the three of them had worked together at a single cramped desk. Chipped tiles, broken furniture, and flickering lightbulbs had been the extent of their interior design. Every day was a comfort and a chaos: fist-fighting over who had to go pick up lunch, heated debates over far-fetched theories, consuming lethal doses of caffeine. It had been home once.

Saffi had been the first of the three to obtain her license and be offered the full-time private investigator position. She'd been so smug at the time. Andino and Taylor had been promoted together a few months later – they always did things in pairs. But even once they'd gotten their own offices, the three of them still spent their lunch breaks – or rather, their one-of-them-remembered-they-needed-to-eat-to-survive breaks – poring over case files together.

And then Saffi had fucked up and left the country and Andino and Taylor started their own PI agency not long after. A few years later, when Saffi had grown curious – and perhaps a little drunk and lonely – she'd looked up their old workplace. Stronghold Private Eye in Arizona.

It didn't surprise her to find that it had been shut down, but it did catch her off guard. A similar feeling to misplacing your birth certificate.

Taylor cleared his throat awkwardly when they were finished eating. 'So,' he began, 'how've you been?'

'Busy,' Saffi replied. 'You?'

'Good, good,' Taylor said, nodding.

He gave Andino a look, elbowing him in the side when he didn't respond. The fact that he thought she wouldn't catch the motion, especially when five years ago she was the one who'd invented the game of secretly elbowing Andino during boring meetings, was insulting.

'Um, yeah, good,' Andino said, coughing. 'Great even.'

The three of them stared at one another for a moment.

'So, what do you think?' Taylor asked, gesturing to the case files strewn across her desk.

The relief washed over her. Cases, she could manage. Small talk was another beast. 'It definitely was not an accident.'

They both stared at her. 'You know?'

That was not the reaction she'd been expecting. 'Know what?'

They exchanged glances. 'There's been another death,' Taylor said. 'Irene Singh was murdered. There is no question about it anymore.'

Saffi leaned forward in her chair, intrigued.

'At the start of the investigation, a waiter who was there the night of Irene Singh's death called in a tip. He insisted that if something happened to him sometime within the next week, then we needed to check his online drive,' Taylor explained. 'Not long after that, he fell down four stories and has since passed.'

So he died in the same way the actress had. A coincidence? It was possible, but not likely. 'I assume you checked the drive?' Saffi asked.

'It was wiped clean,' Andino said.

Saffi hummed. 'It was definitely murder. At this point,

anyone with a brain could tell you that much. Probably the same killer who got the actress. Why didn't you check his computer before he died?'

'We were getting calls like that all month. Two separate people claimed they gave birth to Irene Singh's reincarnation – *two*!' Andino said. 'It was obviously an accident; we had no reason to believe the waiter was anything more than paranoid or attention-seeking.'

'*Obviously an accident,* huh?'

'Shut up,' Andino grumbled. 'I'm still pissed off we did all those interviews for nothing. The killer probably left the premises the second the murder happened. It's what I would do.'

'Not likely,' Saffi said.

'Would you like to elaborate on that?' Andino asked, a hint of irritation poking through. Saffi had forgotten how fun he was to rile up.

'You can't control the narrative from outside the room,' she said thoughtfully. 'This person is so methodical, they killed the waiter too. They could've stopped at deleting the evidence, but that wasn't enough for them. It's about control. And they'll do anything to keep it. That's what makes them so dangerous.'

'Wait,' Andino began skeptically. 'If you didn't know about the waiter, how did you know it wasn't an accident?'

'Singh fell backward,' Saffi said, 'down the stairs in a house she's lived in for over a decade. She wasn't *that* drunk. She must've been speaking to someone. She must've been pushed.'

'How do you know she fell backward?' Andino asked.

Saffi retrieved a photo from the file and set it down on the coffee table facing the two men.

'The dress has a tear in the back,' Taylor said in understanding. 'Probably ripped it with her heel before she fell.'

Saffi leaned back in her chair. 'Our killer is someone the victim knew, but not in a positive sense. A rival, probably. And if I had to guess, I'd say the victim and the killer are very similar.'

'Why do you say that?' Taylor prompted.

'In some of the interviews it was mentioned that the second floor of the mansion is off limits. It's a well-known rule. But the perpetrator went up regardless. I doubt anyone with a lot of respect for the victim would blatantly ignore the rules like that.'

'It could've been someone she didn't know at all. A drunk person who wandered upstairs,' Taylor suggested. 'Or someone who went up there with the intent to kill.'

'An heiress wouldn't give the time of day to any drunk stranger just because they found their way upstairs. If they'd been arguing, people would've heard. If it was someone with ill intent, my guess is she would've been running away. Facing forward not backward. Or screaming for help, which, again, someone in the next room would've heard,' Saffi explained. 'Considering it's Hollywood, what's the most common reason a person might kill?'

'Jealousy,' Andino muttered.

'But Irene hasn't been cast in anything recently,' Taylor said.

'Could be a past grudge,' Andino offered.

'So that's why you think they're similar,' Taylor said, finally catching on as he turned back to Saffi.

'If they're competing for the same roles, they have to be,' Saffi said.

'So, you'll be looking into actresses who not only look like Irene Singh, but who also knew her,' Taylor said. 'That should narrow things down.'

The issue was, it didn't feel narrow enough. 'Was there

anything else with Isaac Klossner?' Saffi asked. 'Did you check his phone? His emails?'

'We just got sent this from the LAPD,' Taylor said, passing a file to Saffi over her desk.

A quick glance through revealed nothing of interest. Isaac's emails were all either work related or junk. And other than a weekly call to a contact labeled 'Mom,' those were all work related as well. Except –

'What are these?' Saffi asked, highlighting the three unknown phone numbers Isaac Klossner had gotten calls from this week.

Andino shrugged. 'We haven't gotten the chance to look into them yet. Probably telemarketers if I had to guess.'

Saffi typed the numbers into her search bar. Andino was correct for two of those cases. 'Actually, one of them is from a phone booth,' she informed them. She showed them the map she'd pulled up, pointing to direct their attention. 'There are four movie studios near this phone booth and it looks like only three of them were being used at the time of his death. While it's possible someone specifically made the trip to use it, there's an even better chance our suspect is someone who'd been filming on one of these three lots.'

'How did you find that so quickly?' Taylor asked.

'Pattern recognition,' Saffi said. 'Every outlier has the same sense of otherness to it. Once you see a few, you start getting an eye for them.'

'That's amazing,' Taylor said in awe.

'It's just a theory.' Saffi shrugged. 'If anything, it'll let me rule out some suspects.'

After all, the most exciting part about creating a hypothesis was getting the chance to disprove it.

10

February 22, 2026

'I know what you did.'

Dimple froze. She was back at Irene Singh's party, at Isaac Klossner's apartment. Everyone in the room turned to her, ants crawling under her skin. In the distance, a body thudded against the ground.

Hadn't she already put out this fire? Isaac and Irene were dead. And yet here she was again. Dimple's head was spinning.

'What –' She had just begun formulating her response when she was interrupted.

'Cut!' Jerome Bardoux said from his director's chair. 'We're moving on.'

Like a camera lens out of focus, the world tipped back into place. Dimple was on set. The man in front of her was not wearing an ill-fitting black suit. Nor did he carry a tray of alcohol. Everyone in the room was breathing, alive. Dimple inhaled deep, lies straining against the capacity of her lungs.

It was always disconcerting, coming out of such an emotionally charged scene. For how crowded movie sets were, it was difficult to think one could get swept away by a page of memorized lines. Dimple took in the bright lights and background chatter, grounding herself in reality.

'That was good,' Chris Porter said, sounding more shocked than he had any right to be. Dimple found she much preferred his somber on-screen persona to the way he presented in real life.

Insomnia followed Dimple and Chris's characters as they revisited the events of a night in their youth when everyone in their friend group except the two of them had died. The scene they'd just shot was the start of them realizing it had been their fault. They'd unknowingly slaughtered their friends in their sleep. Dimple released the breath she'd been holding.

'Why do you sound surprised?' Shyla Patel asked, coming to stand beside Dimple with her arms crossed.

If Dimple had to pick a favorite co-star, it would be Shyla. She was a bit younger – closer to Irene's age before she died – but she had a lot of talent. In *Insomnia,* she played Dimple's best friend, and their camaraderie at times transcended the screen.

'It was a compliment,' Chris scowled.

As Shyla and Chris traded barbs, as usual, Dimple came to the realization that her co-stars were impressed with her. Even Jerome Bardoux seemed pleased, though he would never admit it in so many words, but the fact that he'd moved on without even a second take for safety spoke volumes.

Only, Dimple had not been acting.

The same thing had happened a few days prior when Chris's character killed Shyla's with a push off a ledge. It was a moment of immense gravity, the start of Dimple's redemption arc, and she'd frozen then just as she had today. Ghosts awaited her at the bottom of the ledge. In place of Shyla's golden brown skin caked with dirt and blood splattered across the ground, Dimple had seen Irene lying there, motionless. The greatest performers claimed that the best acting was derived from personal experience, but surely this was too far. What would she have said, had Jerome not interrupted her? Would she have uttered a name she had no business knowing, like *Isaac Klossner*? Or would it have been an admission of guilt? Dimple closed her eyes. She needed to get ahold of herself.

Innocent Dimple Kapoor had been close friends with Irene Singh.

She'd never met Isaac Klossner.

She did not know what it was to kill.

And she was a damn good actress.

This role was even more important than the one she was playing on-screen.

'Are you okay? You seem kind of out of it,' Shyla asked, nudging Dimple with her elbow until she opened her eyes. Chris Porter had moved off to the side, discussing something with Jerome Bardoux.

'Just thinking about how her fingerprints were all over that door,' Dimple muttered.

She and Shyla had created a game of cataloging all the ways Dimple's character would've been caught in real life. It was rather fun.

Shyla laughed. 'And are you telling me there's not anyone else at that party who heard her scream?'

A flash of deleted camera footage – Irene Singh's mouth open in a soundless scream. Falling, falling.

Dimple snapped herself out of it with forced pleasantry. 'Exactly. She wouldn't stand a chance.'

11

March 1, 2026

Saffi had assumed that the additional information from Isaac Klossner's death would give her a new perspective on things, but she found herself slipping back into old habits. As rare as it was for an initial theory to be the correct one, she had never been able to restrain herself from at least looking into it. Especially one as interesting as this.

And once again, something on Kapoor's social media accounts caught Saffi's attention. A comment on a post announcing her as *Insomnia*'s lead, one that Kapoor's official account had responded to. The acting headshots posted to the commenter's profile matched the photos of Klossner that they had on file.

Kapoor had been working at a studio close to the phone booth at the time. There was a good chance she had been the one he'd been speaking to. And a few hours later, he'd been found dead. As always, every sign pointed toward Dimple Kapoor.

If Andino or Taylor were asked what to do in this situation, they'd probably advocate for confronting the suspect immediately before she got the chance to run away. Never one to be outshined, Saffi shrugged on her black suit jacket.

As she was leaving, something compelled her to pause at the office closest to hers. The door was wide open and laughter echoed down the hallway. Three desks were crammed into the small space, an intern sitting at each of them. College students getting their required work experience before they could apply for their PI licenses. Two boys and one girl. Saffi's fingers clenched in the fabric of her jacket at the sight of them. They hadn't noticed her standing there, and she turned away before they could.

The bell chimed as Saffi stepped onto the checkered tile of an upscale café, cueing a cheesy greeting from one of the staff. The air was ripe with the smell of overpriced coffee beans and underpaid workers. It didn't matter which city she was in, Saffi had never felt compelled to spend more than five dollars of her own money on a coffee.

This side of LA didn't seem to share her mindset, full of designer bags and expensive cars and people who acted more important than they were. If Saffi let the chatter of the patrons wash over her, she could almost pretend she was in any other major city in the world.

She stepped into the line that wrapped all the way around the store, staying alert. A quick glance at her watch confirmed that it was a quarter past twelve in the afternoon. Most of the city had already finished their lunch hour. There was a chance Saffi was too late to accomplish what she'd come here for. Still, she could use the caffeine.

She had yet to sleep, having stayed up all night to watch Kapoor's entire filmography. It had been for naught; she still couldn't quite admit that she understood the appeal. Saffi held steadfastly on to the belief that actors were overpaid and unjustly idolized. And for telling lies for a living. She'd locked people up for less.

When it was finally her turn, Saffi ordered a black coffee, swearing that if she came all this way for nothing, she'd sue the place for price gouging. As soon as the thought crossed her mind, the bell made a garbled half-chime, half-clunk sound as someone stumbled inside.

Every head snapped to the door. The girl's chunky glasses were askew as she leaned forward, hands on her knees, and attempted to catch her breath. She didn't seem to notice the stares. Deep brown skin, round cheeks, and short enough that her head barely reached Saffi's shoulders. It was twelve thirty on the day Saffi first met Dimple Kapoor's assistant, Priyal Tiwari.

Tiwari's presence came as no surprise. The tone of Kapoor's usual social media posts were far too chipper for the personality Saffi had assigned to the actress. Priyal Tiwari's personal account, the one credited for Dimple Kapoor's candid photos, had a suspiciously similar tone to Kapoor's. It was likely Tiwari had been the one who'd replied to Klossner's comment.

There was often a coffee cup or sandwich bag from this particular café somewhere in the background of Kapoor's photos, so it wasn't difficult to stage a meeting like this. If Andino and Taylor were in charge of this case, they would've gone to Kapoor directly – probably going so far as to knock on her door and ask outright if she was the killer. As much as Saffi was thrown off by being back in the States, emulating Andino and Taylor would do her no good, not when she'd long since developed her own tactics.

She preferred to let her suspects stew. The longer she waited, the more her targets sweated, wondering why she hadn't yet approached them. That was when the guilty made their most drastic, desperate mistakes.

As Tiwari waited in the long line, Saffi bided her time, mind sharpening with every sip of her drink. Past experience of what was to come made her slip off her suit jacket and drape it over the back of a chair for safekeeping.

The girl was just as absentminded as Saffi suspected, looking anywhere but in front of her as she walked. It was a collision course waiting to happen. Saffi would prefer anything to small talk, even surface-level burns, but thankfully Tiwari was holding two iced coffees.

The inevitable collision was underwhelming, one drink splashing onto Saffi's white button-down, the other coloring the ground. A shocked gasp from the girl. Conversation halted, scaling down into murmurs as everyone stopped to stare again. Saffi prepared her meanest glare.

'I'm so sorry!' Tiwari said, elbows pressed flat against her sides.

She looked like she was about to cry, which Saffi hadn't accounted for. She hurried to the single-occupancy bathroom, relieved to see Tiwari clambering after her, wringing her hands with nerves. With angry, stilted movements, Saffi wiped her shirt clean. She didn't actually want it to stain. Fortunately – or maybe unfortunately – she'd done this enough times to work out the best method to avoid that problem.

Guilt was a powerful bonding tactic, especially for a first meeting, but it only worked on certain types of people. Priyal Tiwari, luckily, was exactly that type of person.

'Can I do anything to help?' she asked.

The girl was trembling. She kept a very specific distance from Saffi, standing almost exactly an arm's-length away, and had left the door open behind her.

Deciding she'd let the girl wallow in misplaced guilt for long enough, Saffi braced herself to endure yet another conversation. As if the needlessly verbose dialogue with Hollywood's diet-elite hadn't been enough. The things she did for justice. Her father would be so proud.

Saffi looked up, glaring at Tiwari through the mirror. And

then she faltered. Her eyes widened as though sudden recognition had struck.

See? Acting was easy. Even Saffi could do it.

'I know you,' she said. 'You're Dimple's assistant.'

Tiwari seemed caught off guard – but not like she was about to cry again. Thank god Saffi had circumvented that potential disaster. It would've completely turned the conversation on its head, leaving her as the guilty party.

'Have we met?' Tiwari asked warily. Kapoor probably wasn't famous enough to have a rabid fanbase, but stalkers were an issue for any woman.

'I'm a friend of Dimple's,' Saffi lied, tossing the wet paper towels into the trash. There wasn't a trace of coffee left behind.

'Oh!' Tiwari said in surprise. 'I didn't know Dimple had friends.' Realization of what she'd just said seemed to dawn on her. 'I didn't mean – !'

'She shouldn't,' Saffi agreed, leaning back against the sink and crossing her arms. She resisted the urge to roll her eyes at her own performance. How actors did this and still had the gall to take themselves seriously, she couldn't fathom. 'She's always so busy, no time for anything but work.'

Tiwari laughed like it was the truest statement she'd ever heard. 'Don't be too hard on her. I've only worked for her for a few months now, but even I know how much being a lead means to her.'

'She finally did it, huh?' Saffi asked.

'With *Insomnia,* yeah! It's about time people started recognizing her talent.'

The way Tiwari said it, practically sparkling, made Saffi wonder what kind of woman inspired such devotion. Her mind began working faster than she could keep up with it. Flashes of rivalries and dead actresses at the bottom of stairs.

'Sorry,' Tiwari said, looking genuinely confused. 'How do you know her, again?'

'We worked the same temp job a few years ago,' Saffi said, figuring it was a safe bet. Most actors had side jobs.

'You're from California?' Priyal asked a bit skeptically.

It seemed that despite her best efforts, Saffi couldn't pass for a local as well as she thought she could. 'Arizona originally,' she said. It was always best to stick as close to the truth as possible.

'Oh wow, does an Arizona driver's license really have the Grand Canyon on it?'

As innocent as she seemed, Saffi knew what Priyal was trying to do. She wasn't quite as clueless as Saffi had initially thought.

'See for yourself.' Saffi flashed her license in Priyal's direction, taking care to block out most of her name and other vital information with her fingers.

Priyal relaxed at the mere sight of it. 'Oh, it does!'

No matter how suspicious, most people had a strong compulsion to believe their peers. Confirmation that Saffi had been telling the truth about a single aspect of her story was usually enough to convince them that she could be trusted. It was certainly enough for Tiwari.

'I can't believe I've never heard of you before,' Priyal said. 'Then again, Dimple doesn't really talk about herself. What am I saying – you probably know her much better than I do.'

Saffi gave her a bland smile. 'You like working for her?'

'It's the best job I've had in a while,' Priyal said without missing a beat. 'The last one stole half my tips and made me work through my breaks. I couldn't even complain because I needed the money.'

'I'm sorry.'

'Don't be,' Priyal said, laughing. 'Thanks to Dimple, I don't have to worry about that anymore.' She gestured at Saffi's shirt. 'She buys me coffee every day and lets me shadow her while she's filming.'

'Maybe I should visit her on set,' Saffi mused. 'So she can't avoid me anymore.'

Tiwari brightened with what seemed to be pleasant surprise before suddenly deflating. 'I wish you could, but today's actually their last day of filming.'

Saffi tried to act disappointed, but it fell flat. There was something here. She just needed to keep the girl talking. 'I'm sorry I missed it.'

'Me too,' Tiwari said. 'Seeing Dimple act up close is something incredible.'

'So she's doing well, then?'

'Better than ever – she's glowing. And to think she almost didn't take the role.'

'What? Why not?' Saffi asked a little too quickly.

Tiwari shuttered immediately, her whole body closing in on itself. 'Um, never mind. Please just forget I said anything.'

Saffi had just witnessed her first hint of gold. 'What do you mean?' she asked with false innocence.

'It's kind of a sensitive topic.'

This was going nowhere, but Saffi knew enough to take a chance and make a wild guess. 'It has to do with Irene, doesn't it?'

'How did you – ?'

Saffi had struck gold. She tried to temper her rising giddiness. 'Dimple's told me a little, but you know how she bottles things up. She probably doesn't want me to worry, but I do anyway,' she said, attempting to replicate a level of devotion that was still foreign to her.

Tiwari's expression softened. 'She's a good person, she really is,' she insisted. 'Dimple didn't know why they offered her the role all of a sudden. As soon as she found out, though, she tried to get out of it. But the director refused and she's under contract, so – you know how it is. But I think it still bothers her. What if people found out . . .'

Holy shit.

Saffi had just found her motive.

'You mean, if people find out that Irene had the role first?' Saffi guessed. Her voice came out breathless.

Tiwari nodded solemnly.

'When did she accept the job?' Saffi asked.

Tiwari's eyebrows furrowed, and Saffi worried she'd probed too far, but she didn't have to worry for long. The girl was deep in thought. 'I told her about it myself. The Tuesday before filming started, I think.'

'January 27th?' Saffi guessed.

Tiwari sighed in relief. 'So she did tell you. I was worried she didn't have anyone to talk to. If you're going to blame anyone, though, blame the director, he's a horrible man. He practically tricked Dimple into signing the contract.'

Saffi couldn't believe her luck. Kapoor had been interviewed by Andino and Taylor on Monday the twenty-sixth. Saffi had heard the tapes; she knew the men had explicitly told her about Singh's death. Which meant she knew exactly why she'd been offered the role. Clearly, Kapoor wasn't above lying to keep her image clean, even to those closest to her.

'How awful,' Saffi replied, this time unable to keep the sarcasm from her tone. 'Poor Dimple Kapoor.'

Tiwari didn't seem to notice her insincerity and nodded along enthusiastically.

Kapoor was a liar, that much was certain, but the question was why she'd lied. To keep her image clean or to cover up a murder? Saffi crossed her arms, staring down at Tiwari. She had no idea who she was dealing with. Then again, neither did Saffi.

12

March 1, 2026

After a long final day of filming, the crew threw a wrap party.

There was a toast at the end of the night, led by one of the producers. 'To topping the box office!' he said, punctuated with the rise of his champagne flute. They all conveyed their agreement with a chorus of cheers followed by the whole room knocking back the contents of their glasses.

It wasn't just the sparkling water that made Dimple feel like she was floating. While nobody stayed on set longer than her and Jerome, Shyla Patel was always eager to run lines and gossip in their trailers after hours. Even Chris Porter was a better scene partner than expected, adapting to improvisation with ease, ebbing and flowing with their manufactured emotions.

The hard part was over and Dimple couldn't believe it. The waking nightmares were less frequent and being the face of such an anticipated movie meant her name was gaining some traction. Julie was having a much easier time setting up opportunities for her.

A group of Dimple's co-stars chose then to approach, faces bright and mouths stretched wide with laughter. Before she knew it, she was being corralled into a photo. Shyla Patel was the ringleader. She insisted on putting the leads front and center, which Dimple good-naturedly refused a couple times before embracing it with flushed cheeks. Her co-lead, Chris Porter, swung a leaden arm over her shoulder.

'We did it, gorgeous,' he slurred.

Dimple froze under his weight, but everyone else seemed too preoccupied to notice.

This uncomfortable weight against her side reminded her of those blurry photos of Dimple on set, completely unaware of a camera tailing her. Shots of her and Chris Porter through the window of a café. They were framed in such a way to look like the two of them were alone even though the entire main cast had been there as well.

Dimple tried to avoid it at all costs. Horrid words from Chris's jealous fans always accompanied them. Insults to her appearance from a cluster of blurry photographs. Attacks on her character coming from people who'd never so much as crossed paths with her.

But there was nothing that could be done. The producers liked the implication that their two main leads were romantically involved. Apparently, it was *good publicity*. As though art had to be publicized. If it weren't for Julie, Dimple might've deleted her accounts right then and there.

Surrounded by her co-stars, the heavy arm holding her down, she was utterly trapped. The flash of the camera lens couldn't have come quick enough. She ducked away, unapologetic at the way Chris stumbled without her support. Claiming to the crowd at large that she needed a refill, Dimple fled across the room fast enough to avoid their chorus of disappointed *boo*'s. The poisonous phantom of Chris's touch lingered long after she left him.

It was ridiculous. So what if he was drunk – they'd had to *kiss* on set, for god's sake. Five takes. That was how long it took to get it right. Shyla had teased her about it for days. The entire cast had a running joke about Chris having to stand on a platform so he could appear taller than her. He was annoying and arrogant, sure, but the man had never bothered her to this extent before. Dimple watched her coworkers shriek with laughter from across the room, unreasonably angry with herself. Had she even smiled for the photograph?

It wasn't until she noticed someone approaching that she remembered to put on her best face. She affixed her brightest expression and raised an empty glass in greeting, but faltered when she noticed who it was.

Jerome Bardoux looked around to make sure no one else was listening before leaning in close. Contrary to the champagne in his hand, he seemed sober. 'I would say sorry for what it took to get you to take this job, but I'm really not.'

His words took a moment to register. When they did, Dimple was more shocked at his carelessness to say such a thing in public than at the words themselves. She tightened her grip on the stem of her glass. Other than to direct her, he'd never actually initiated a conversation with her. Not even a *hello, how are you,* or so much as a customary *good morning.* This was an interesting attempt at their first, Dimple would give him that.

'I'm sure you'll agree once you see the final product,' he continued, reaching out to pry her empty glass from her death grip and replacing it with a full one. Then, at full volume, 'We work well together, don't you think?'

Dimple stared at the clear bubbling liquid in her new glass. Raising it to her nose, she confirmed that it was indeed sparkling water. Jerome clinked glasses with her. When he pulled away, Dimple noticed he was picking his fingernail raw.

With that, the man was gone, leaving Dimple dumbstruck. She could do nothing but stare at his retreating figure, attempting to parse through mixed emotions. Jerome truly thought he'd conned her. It would be laughable if it weren't so concerning that Dimple shared such a damning secret with an idiot. If he was acting so careless already, how much worse off would he be with pressure applied? Dimple was one step closer to effective immortality through art. If Jerome ever dared to stand in the way of that, she would have no choice but to deal with him accordingly.

For now, though, perhaps their tether could work to her benefit.

A small body barreled into Dimple's side, breaking her free of her thoughts. She tightened her grip on her champagne flute at the last moment, saving it from a shattering death.

'Priyal,' she said.

'Sorry I'm late,' the girl breathed.

Dimple had invited Priyal to set after lunch, correctly assuming that the director would be far too busy to care about his more minor rules. She surmised it would be an interesting experience, getting to see up close how film projects wrapped. It was something Dimple wished she'd gotten insight on before being thrown into the deep end. However, according to the clock, it was seven in the evening. This was late, even by Priyal's standards.

'You might as well have called in,' Dimple said, raising her brows.

'I know, but I promise I got you your coffee at noon,' Priyal said.

Dimple frowned. 'And is this coffee in the room with us now?'

'No, I kind of spilled it all over your friend.'

Dimple blinked. 'My . . . friend?'

'I'm just now realizing that I never asked for her name.' Priyal said. 'You used to work together. She's from Arizona? About your height, black hair. Some kind of businesswoman, I'm guessing?' When Dimple showed no signs of recognition, Priyal continued. 'She looked pretty angry, even when she said she wasn't.'

Dimple knew no one by that description. 'Ah, yes,' she said. 'Was she all right?'

'Yeah! It was an iced coffee, so no burns, thank goodness.'

Dimple resisted the urge to pinch her brows and sigh. The one day Priyal actually bought her an iced coffee and it never made its way to her. She felt more despair toward the lost drink than she did for the con artist it ended up on.

'That doesn't explain why you're late,' Dimple said.

'Well, we got to talking and I lost track of time. And then I took her to get her shirt dry-cleaned because I felt bad,' Priyal recounted. 'And then I was hungry, so I –'

Dimple tuned out the rest of her explanation. It was possible this stranger would target her assistant again. Perhaps she needed to speak to her manager, Julie, about potential security measures. She didn't want to scare the girl, though. Especially if it was nothing. Perhaps she really did know someone by that description. Dimple wasn't exactly one for remembering people who didn't catch her interest.

'What did you talk about?' she asked.

'Mostly you,' Priyal admitted. 'You should really call her, by the way. It seems like she misses you.'

'I'm sure she does,' Dimple said dryly.

'She sends her condolences about Irene. Oh, and . . .' Priyal leaned in conspiratorially, 'she told me to tell you that she hates Jerome just as much as we do.'

Dimple's heart stuttered. It took a moment for her to find her voice. 'She told you to tell me that?'

Priyal nodded, a secretive grin stretched across her lips.

Dimple had never told another soul about anything relating to her work, Jerome, or even Irene. There was a good chance she had a new blackmailer on her hands. And so soon after she'd dealt with the last one. To make matters worse, this one seemed much smarter than Isaac Klossner. Bolder too. This would be a problem.

Priyal's phone chimed. 'Oh wow, did you hear?' Dimple hummed, half listening. 'The Singhs aren't going through with the lawsuit anymore.'

That had her attention at once.

'What?'

Priyal showed her the headline, sending Dimple's stomach twisting into knots. Either a chill had washed across the room or Dimple's heart had stopped beating altogether. The full article revealed nothing as to why the Singhs had suddenly changed their mind. It did, however, offer several quotes from the family stating that they'd been too hasty in assigning blame and that they were confident that Salomé had nothing to do with their daughter's death. But if Salomé no longer held the blame, then who did?

This coupled with the mysterious stranger who'd approached Priyal couldn't be a mere coincidence. It was never ending, this practice of setting fires only to put them out again. Dimple had already decided that from now on she wasn't just going to survive. She was not going to take the gift of her life for granted. She would make sure her likeness lived on even longer than she did. Whatever it took to break the cycle – even if it meant burning the whole world down – she'd have no choice but to do it.

Dimple reached into the shallow pocket of her dress and traced the shape of her lighter. She had enough presence of mind not to pull it out and ignite the flame like a madwoman, but knowing it was there was enough to ground her.

She had found the thing under the fridge of her first Los Angeles apartment, discarded by the previous tenants. A deep red lighter with two scratches at its base, completely out of fuel. She'd been about to toss it, but something had stopped her. Her waitressing job had kept her on her feet nearly every day of the week, dealing with entitled, angry patrons and managers with no respect for her time. And she'd still barely made rent every month. Dimple had figured she might as well get something out of her lease. So she'd kept it, refueling as soon as she was able. She'd landed her first speaking role not too long after.

No matter how far Dimple had come, though, or however far she would go, it seemed Irene Singh was determined to reclaim what should have been hers. Her role, her trailer, her wrap party. But Dimple was not willing to let it go.

13
March 2, 2026

'You look like you're having fun,' Taylor remarked, letting himself and Andino into Saffi's office.

They tended to do that, but they did also own the place, so it was technically within their right. Saffi kept meaning to lock the door, but they always brought food with them, so she didn't mind forgetting every once in a while.

'The case is more interesting than you thought it would be, isn't it?' Taylor asked, setting a take-out container on the desk in front of her and sounding entirely too happy with himself.

A quick glance up from her monitor alerted her to motion. Taylor had left the door open behind him – something that brought up a flare of annoyance so old it could only be described as nostalgic. Standing in the open doorway were the interns from before, but they ducked away as soon as they noticed Saffi looking at them.

'They still can't believe we actually know you,' Taylor said, exasperated.

'They're fans,' Andino explained, somehow making it sound like an insult.

'Of me?' Saffi asked.

'You're somewhat of a minor celebrity in the PI community,' Taylor said. 'Especially with college students. Apparently, they talk about your cases in class sometimes.'

It was the first time Saffi was hearing about this. She'd

made headlines before, but if it was regarding her PI work, it was always some variation of *Investigator Uncovers Deadly Secret.* Her name, if it showed up at all, was always toward the end of the articles. Unless it was regarding her father's career in politics, which she hadn't been connected to in five years.

'Then I better wrap this one up quick,' Saffi muttered. 'Give the professors enough time to write it into their lesson plans for next year.'

The thought of her name being printed alongside Dimple Kapoor's almost made her laugh. Surely an actress would hate having to share the spotlight like that.

'I knew we shouldn't have said anything,' Andino sighed, flopping gracelessly onto a brown armchair. 'Your ego is inflated enough as is.'

'I've already narrowed it down to one suspect. It's only a matter of proving it now,' Saffi replied, waving her hand flippantly.

When the resulting silence stretched on for too long, she looked up again, but her mood quickly diminished. She'd said it lightheartedly, but both men looked equally taken aback. Something like insecurity, disbelief, and irritation flickered in both of their faces. As though she'd done them a disservice by being good at her job. Cultures differed as did climates, but jealousy and envy were the same in every language.

It wasn't, however, supposed to be a concept in the language the three of them shared. Perhaps because they'd always been a team. Now it felt stilted to discuss the case as a group, none of them quite sure where they fit into the conversation. There was a disconnect, as where Saffi had solved dozens of murder cases worldwide, Andino and Taylor were extremely out of their depth. All three of them expected the other two to be exactly on their level, simply because that was the way it had always been. But that assumption meant they were rarely on the same page. Saffi's mind was used to jumping five paces ahead, and she found herself growing irritated at having to explain her thought process several times a day. Andino and Taylor were just as agitated that she moved so quickly, leaving them behind when the case was theirs to begin with.

'Who?' Taylor challenged.

'Doesn't matter.' She was fixed on her screen, but she could feel them exchanging looks with each other on the other side of her desk.

'It kind of does,' Andino replied. 'I'd argue it matters a lot.'

'You know what?' Saffi said. 'I think I can handle the case from here. I work better alone. Besides, don't you two have other things to worry about, running a business and all?'

She could've heard a pin drop.

'Oh.' Taylor's tone had her almost regretting she'd said anything at all. She had no trouble keeping contacts, solving cases, but there wasn't a relationship in her life that hadn't gone down in flames; platonic, familial, or romantic. It was always easier to leave someone behind than to face the inevitable weight of their disappointment. 'I guess that makes sense. You are much better equipped to handle it.'

'But –' Andino started before cutting himself off.

Curious, Saffi looked up from her computer just in time to see the warning look Taylor had shot him.

'I just thought . . . Never mind.'

His gaze flicked to Taylor, then to Saffi, and then back to Taylor, before turning away and marching out of the room. The door slammed shut behind him.

'What's his issue?' Saffi asked.

Taylor shook his head. 'You know how he is.'

His disappointment reminded Saffi too much of her

father's. She'd never been able to handle being on the receiving end of it for long. 'Minus ten for excessive arrogance,' she said in an attempt to diffuse the tension.

Andino's coined phrase. Back in college, it had irritated the two of them beyond belief. Now it brought a fondness to Taylor's expression.

Saffi attributed the start of their friendship to one late night at the library during finals week, after almost an entire semester of competing to give the best answers in class. That night, Taylor had wordlessly slipped into a seat beside Saffi and asked for help with calculus. Her annoyance quickly diminished when she realized he could help her with the introductory science class she'd been forced into. Both of them struggled with English, however, which was why when Taylor began inviting Andino to sit with them, Saffi didn't complain. Even if he did write *minus ten for excessive arrogance* at the top of all of their papers after proofreading them.

In a way, they mellowed one another out. It just made sense to stick together. And while Saffi had come to prefer working alone, she knew that when it came time to leave again, she would miss picking fights with Andino and taking peaceful walks with Taylor after lunch. Moments of domesticity were rare in the life of a private investigator.

If Saffi and Andino were the wheels of a bike, then Taylor was the chain. After she'd left, though, Saffi had felt like she'd lost the spark that had once made investigative work so fun. She'd struggled to find the meaning in any of it, especially when she started solving cases as easily as breathing. A single wheel could spin alone for an eternity, but it could never take you anywhere.

14

March 2, 2026

Dimple paced the length of her apartment. She must've been going for hours now, calves straining with effort, but she could think of nothing but the woman who'd approached Priyal. There weren't many rationalizations she could come up with. At least, not many on feasible grounds.

Explanation One: Salomé had bribed the Singhs into letting the case go.

The Singhs were unfathomably rich, however, so Dimple doubted there was any amount of money that could buy them. Especially when their precious daughter was involved. Although it was possible the company had managed to ascertain something else the Singhs desired more than money, offering them that instead. If that was the case, Dimple had no concept of what such a thing could be.

Explanation Two: The Singhs had simply given up.

But Irene was their only daughter. They had always doted on her the way parents were meant to. Moreover, the Singhs' lawsuit had been met with nothing but support from the public. Money wasn't the issue because, once again, they had that in spades. There was not a single thing, as far as Dimple could see, stopping them from moving forward.

Explanation Three: Salomé blackmailed the Singhs.

It was possible, yes, but Dimple couldn't wrap her head around it. Even those on the highest of pedestals had their downfalls, but would a fashion brand go to such lengths? *Could* they go to such lengths?

Four: The Singhs had found something or someone else to blame for Irene's death.

This was the final rationalization Dimple could invent. It was also, to her horror, the most logical. To cancel the lawsuit so publicly without utmost certainty that Salomé was not to blame would be beyond foolish. The Singhs would be made a laughingstock if they tried to sue Salomé again after this. Nor would it look good in front of a judge, especially following the comments they made in the published article.

And if the Singhs were this certain that something or someone else was to blame, that would mean that Irene's case had been undoubtedly determined a murder. Dimple took a seat at her couch, tucking her feet under her legs and pulling out a notebook. Pen pushing thoughtfully against her cheek, she drafted a timeline.

January 23, Irene Singh dies.

January 26, private investigators appear, bringing news of Irene's death.

January 27, accepted the lead role in *Insomnia*.

Morning of February 2, the Singhs announce plans to sue Salomé.

Evening of February 2, message from the blackmailer (Isaac Klossner).

Early morning of February 3, Isaac Klossner dies.

March 1, the Singh's publicly announce their decision to rescind the lawsuit against Salomé. Additionally, Priyal is approached by an unknown woman claiming to be a friend.

With the facts laid bare, it became clear that if definitive proof had been found that someone was to blame for Irene's death, it would've had to have been between February 2 and March 1. Which meant it was most likely Isaac's death that tipped them off. Dimple couldn't imagine how anyone could have managed to link the two. Perhaps someone discovered that he'd catered Irene's party the night she died, but surely there would've been no reason to look into him so closely?

It also became clear that whoever had approached Priyal could be investigating Irene's case. The thought alone made Dimple's blood run cold. This meant she was almost certainly a suspect. For a brief, hysterical moment, she wondered if the proof Isaac had on his computer had somehow not been erased. But she reminded herself that if that were the case, she would've been dragged away in handcuffs by now.

No, it wasn't possible there was anything officially linking Dimple to Irene's or Isaac's death. It was more likely she was one suspect in a pool of many. But if the investigators kept pulling at these loose threads, the entire spool would unfurl. She had to do something drastic – something to throw them off her trail entirely before they unearthed something she couldn't explain.

As she scanned the timeline once again, she found herself drawn back to the woman who'd approached Priyal. That had to be the best place to start. Dimple opened the drawer closest to her and retrieved the black embossed business card. *Andino and Taylor Private Eye.*

On the front page of their official website was a picture of

Atlas Andino looking fierce and Eli Taylor smiling brightly in front of their practice. No sign of the woman. It was possible that the Singhs had hired another company to investigate after realizing that Atlas and Eli had come to a false conclusion. Which would be a shame; the men had been all too easy to deal with.

Dimple spent the next hour researching the top private investigator agencies in California. Surely the Singhs would settle for nothing but the best. She found a few women-owned agencies, but none matching the description her assistant had given her.

Although, thinking back to it, Priyal had mentioned Arizona. Dimple typed in, *Arizona Private Investigator* and hit search.

There she was. The first photo that graced the screen, a young woman with a scowl on her face, black hair pulled into a ponytail almost as an afterthought. Dimple got the feeling she was meticulous about everything but her appearance.

The headline of the accompanying article read, *Arizona's Sweetheart: Governor Iyer's Daughter Graduates with Honors, Licensed as a Private Investigator.* It was from six years ago. Her name was Saffi Mirai Iyer and she'd worked at Stronghold Private Eye, an agency based in Arizona that had permanently shut down about a year after she'd joined.

Some more digging connected Saffi, Atlas, and Eli's names in various articles about cases they'd solved together. This had to be her, but Dimple sent a picture for Priyal to verify just in case.

When she received back a message with far too many exclamation points, Dimple knew her suspicions had been confirmed. This woman – the one who'd approached Priyal claiming to be Dimple's friend – was a private investigator. Irene's case had turned into a murder investigation and Dimple, somehow, was a suspect.

Instead of an uptick in the dread already coursing through her veins, she instead felt an inexplicable rush of an emotion she couldn't describe. One that made the hairs on the back of her neck stand upright. She had the sudden and desperate urge to meet this woman. To see who exactly she thought she was, issuing such a direct challenge.

There were some answers online, but Dimple knew better than anyone the skewed nature of public perception. Saffi's persona, however, was odd in and of itself. Usually when one looked into the children of major political figures, there were no shortage of embarrassments to sift through. Saffi, though, had only heaps of praise. From community service initiatives she'd founded to the fact that she'd gotten into Harvard and gave it up in favor of staying closer to family (thus earning her the nickname *Arizona's sweetheart*). It didn't matter that in every published photo of her she wore a scowl. Saffi clearly knew how to play the game – how to be remembered. Her interviews were as practiced as any scripted line Dimple had delivered. A fellow performer, a fellow artist, and in the investigative field, of all spaces.

That wasn't to say that Dimple couldn't read between the lines.

She eventually ran out of archives of local Arizona publications to sift through, switching to the international ones instead. Saffi Mirai Iyer was, according to several credible sources, one of the best private investigators in the world. Dimple could only imagine how tired she grew of playing the same old archetypal daughter at home. She wondered what Saffi's life had been like behind closed doors. Whether Governor Iyer ever raised his voice – or his fist. Whether he or his wife had a drinking problem. Like a true performer, though, Saffi never slipped up.

Or maybe she had, and that was why she'd left the country. The show must go on.

Knowing who her pursuer was strangely calmed Dimple. Because that meant the best private investigator in the world still had yet to gather enough evidence to bring her in. The best private investigator in the world, at the end of the day, was as human as she was.

Dimple scanned her bookshelf. The text she extracted from the lowest shelf was heavy and stiff, having been untouched for several years. She brushed her fingertips across the top, sneezing as a cloud of dust erupted.

Advanced College Physics, the title page read. Dimple flipped the paper with her timeline over to its blank side and opened the textbook to the chapter she was looking for.

It had been a long while since she'd had to use this part of her brain, but the knowledge there had never deserted her. It was simply locked away. Finding the key was the difficult part. It lay in the margins of the annotated pages she flipped between, in the relevant formulas she marked down. Soon enough, Dimple's muscle memory took over and the textbook began collecting dust again on her coffee table.

Only once she was satisfied with the scrawl of numbers, equations, and Greek characters scattered across the page did she pause. With her other hand, she ignited her lighter and watched, fascinated, as fire caught and began to consume, eating the paper alive. Ash gathered at Dimple's feet, the knowledge forever burned into her mind.

It was Dimple's turn to make a move, and she would be doing so on her own terms.

ACT II

Encounter

15

March 13, 2026

Saffi sprang violently upright from her desk at the burst of light. Taylor, the source of her disorientation, gave her a tight-lipped smile from the open doorway, looking more frantic than apologetic.

'Sorry,' he said. 'I know you don't sleep enough as it is.'

'What's going on?' she asked, already shoving her arms through the sleeves of her suit jacket and jumping to her feet. She pinched her thigh when the brain fog took longer than usual to dissipate.

'I know I'm not technically supposed to be investigating –'

'Get to the point, Taylor.' The fact that he couldn't help himself was as unsurprising as it was uninteresting. Saffi fell into step beside him and they hurried out of the office together.

'Something happened two days ago, and I think it's related to the case,' he explained. At her expression of disbelief, he added, 'It wasn't public knowledge until a couple hours ago.'

Saffi was suddenly more awake than she'd been in days. She forced her feet to move faster. 'There's been another murder?' she guessed.

'Something like that,' Taylor said vaguely, huffing as they crossed the hallway.

The perpetrator must've taken notice of Saffi's challenge and panicked. It had been quiet since she first issued her challenge almost two weeks ago, which had been worrying. But clearly it had paid off.

Saffi was so caught up in her excitement that the hollowness creeping into her chest shocked her enough to stumble. Taylor steadied her by the arm and gave her an odd look, to which she couldn't respond. Usually, the familiar heart-pounding, full-body excitement of a mystery close to its end was her favorite part of the process. But all she could think about now was how soon it would all be over. How soon she'd be on the other side of the world again with no more peace than she'd started with.

Taylor held the door for her, leaving Saffi with no choice but to swallow her hesitations and hurry after him. The late-night chill sent tingles across her cheeks, the moon bearing the greatest witness to the world's latest atrocities. Andino was already waiting for them behind the wheel, his car's engine rumbling to life quicker than they could buckle their seatbelts.

'Will one of you explain to me what's going on?' Saffi asked as the car peeled out of the parking lot.

Andino and Taylor exchanged a look, almost freakishly in sync. Saffi wondered how she'd never noticed the mirroring or the wordless, easy communication before. Maybe because, back then, it had been the three of them moving as one.

'I have reason to believe the killer struck again two days ago in Beverly Hills,' Taylor explained.

'So we're going to Beverly Hills?'

Taylor shook his head. 'We'll get the police report for that. Right now we're going to the hospital.'

Saffi was confused for half a second before she caught on, heart thumping in anticipation. 'The victim survived?'

Hospital waiting rooms, despite their best efforts, were never not the most depressing places on the planet. The walls were white, the floors gray with the occasional speck of color to give the illusion of life. The chairs lining the walls were always a simple neutral color, but somehow exceptionally comfortable. Posters either raved about what fun it was to wash your hands and eat your veggies or gave detailed depictions of various bodily systems that could put even Saffi to sleep.

Something about this made her skin crawl and it wasn't just the environment. Saffi had a high tolerance for fucked-up shit considering her line of work, but even she'd never come across something so wrong. Something so confusing it spun her mind in circles.

When they'd arrived at the hospital, it wasn't supposed to be Dimple Kapoor bleeding out in one of the patient rooms. It wasn't supposed to have been her who'd fallen two stories from the balcony of yet another celebrity Beverly Hills rager. More than anything, Saffi was horrified that she'd been the last to know.

Despite aching lethargy and a pounding migraine, she paced as she awaited her turn to visit the woman in question, fingers tapping a staccato beat against her biceps. The victim. Saffi shuddered. *Victim* and *Dimple Kapoor* didn't belong in the same sentence.

The message left behind by the killer had been even more subverting. A weathered promotional poster for the *Insomnia* movie with Dimple Kapoor's face marked out in red. On the back was a printed note that read: *Two down.* They'd been graciously sent pictures of it by the otherwise unhelpful LAPD. The real thing had been sent to the lab for DNA and fingerprint analysis, but Saffi severely doubted they would find anything of substance.

The entire thing felt like the workings of a cartoonish movie villain attempting to get their motivations out in the open before their ten-minute monologue came to a close. But Andino and Taylor ate it right up because of course they did. Hell, even Saffi was self-aware enough to realize how absurd it was to continue to suspect Dimple Kapoor now. But it couldn't be a coincidence that the moment Saffi approached Priyal Tiwari, Dimple Kapoor happened to take a nosedive off a two-story balcony.

Honestly, if all her suspicions were true, she couldn't help respecting the woman a little. Because even she was beginning to doubt herself. Who would go to such lengths? Who had such presence of mind under pressure and such intrinsic theatricality to come up with as absurd a play as this? Saffi found herself hoping that such a person existed simply because of how desperately she wanted to meet them.

'You know, it wouldn't kill you to sit down,' Taylor said.

'I'll take a break when crime does,' Saffi said.

Taylor sighed. 'I'll go ask the charge nurse how much longer it'll be.' Saffi gave him a grateful nod and the door shut softly behind him.

'So, what are you thinking?' Andino asked, his voice unnaturally loud in the small space.

'I'm thinking I'm tired and hungry.'

'About the case,' Andino said, clearly irritated. Apparently, she wasn't the only one missing out on sleep.

'I'm sorry, was I not clear enough the first time?' Saffi asked. 'I work better alone.'

'Alone – ?' Andino's face turned red. 'Eli was the one who found this lead! I drove us here!'

The reminder of her own negligence stung. 'And as much as I appreciate the help, I would've found my own way here eventually.'

'Would you have?' Andino challenged. 'Or would another innocent have to die before you can accept that you're not always the smartest person in every room?'

For a long moment, Saffi heard only her own heartbeat and the ticking of the clock.

'What,' Saffi said.

Andino visibly thought it over for a moment, but he'd never been able to help himself. 'This is Phoenix all over again.'

He must've woken up with a death wish.

'Go ahead,' she said, gesturing for him to continue. 'Finish that thought.'

She could see the way Andino's biceps tensed where they were crossed over his chest. 'I thought you'd changed, but clearly not. All you care about is yourself. Being the first or the fastest or the best.' Before she could refute, he scoffed. 'The great Saffi Mirai Iyer has never been wrong about anything.' He paused, feigning surprise. 'Oh, wait . . .'

Saffi didn't try to reply right away, her mouth so dry she knew nothing would come out even if she did. Other people's opinions had never meant anything to her – least of all Andino's – so she was at a loss for why her chest constricted so painfully when she heard it.

Still, part of her had always wondered what they'd really thought of her after she'd left. Whether they'd blamed her for their old agency shutting down. Now she had her answer.

Saffi kept her face carefully neutral as she met Andino's scrutiny. She forced a swallow, relieved when her tongue no longer stuck to the roof of her mouth. Whatever he felt brave enough to vocalize, she had long since learned how to trust herself again. Oftentimes, she was the only person she could trust.

'In case you've forgotten, I'm here as a favor to you,' Saffi said through gritted teeth. 'Even with my mistakes as a cautionary tale, you were more than happy to rule the death an accident without properly looking into it. What would you have done if the waiter hadn't been killed before you closed the case, huh? That's the kind of mistake that gets agencies shut down, in case you've forgotten. You'd have put yourself and Taylor out of a job. Then what?'

Andino had no response for that, but his rage was similar to hers. It could not be diffused; it needed an outlet. And so it remained simmering under his skin.

'Fuck you,' he spat.

'You need me here,' she said. 'Because you're in over your head and you're too much of a coward to admit it.'

'You –' Andino began.

A nurse chose that moment to burst inside, chastising them for the noise. They'd been raising their voices without even realizing it. Taylor was on her heels, ready to appease her with his charm. Andino's shoulder knocked against Saffi's as he marched right out of the waiting room, leaving the nurse even angrier in his wake.

Not that Saffi didn't trust her gut, but there was a chance she was keeping Andino and Taylor at arm's length because she was worried they'd immediately poke holes through her theories, giving weight to all of her resurfaced insecurities. Maybe Kapoor truly was innocent, and this was nothing more than Saffi's stubbornness rearing its ugly head. Maybe it was the reminder of her last mistake hanging over her head that made it so necessary for her to be right now. Maybe she *was* right. Maybe Kapoor was just as much a criminal mastermind as Saffi suspected.

Either way, the difference between the girl of five years ago and the woman of now was that she couldn't care less what Andino and Taylor thought.

The nurse, finally through chastising them, informed them that it was their turn to visit Kapoor. She'd only had four visitors: her assistant and the three private investigators.

Given how charming the actress could be on-screen and in interviews, Saffi been half prepared to fight off an entire entourage of adoring friends and family.

Taylor scratched the back of his neck awkwardly. 'So, what was that about?'

Saffi shrugged. 'Andino was being an asshole about Phoenix.'

'I'm sorry about him. He never really learned tact.'

Taylor didn't seem to grow tired of apologizing on behalf of both of them. She knew he would say the same to Andino about her. Had he been anyone else, she'd be pissed. But it had always been like this. Taylor was the only way she and Andino had any chance in hell at understanding each other.

'He's always been like that,' Saffi muttered. 'He takes everything so personally.'

Taylor gave her a look.

'What?'

'Come on, Saffi,' Taylor said, sounding exhausted. 'You and I both know this *is* personal.' Not giving her the time to be offended, he added, 'That doesn't mean whatever he said to you was okay, but you have to understand where he's coming from.'

'What are you talking about?' Saffi asked. 'It's work – how is that personal?'

Saffi had felt something underlying in Andino's words, but she no longer had the tools to uncover what it was. It was shocking to realize that she'd once understood the man in any capacity. She'd always thought that Andino was a mystery to her.

'You left without warning,' Taylor said, brows furrowed. He looked so much older than his years. 'You never reply to any of our calls or texts or emails. Then all of a sudden you pick up. And you say you're coming back. Sure, you're still cold, but we know how difficult it is for you to be back here. At least we still have the case to talk about, right? But no, you don't even want our help with that. I half believe you never would've even talked to us if we weren't assigned this case.'

It was true, but Saffi didn't dare say it out loud.

'He's not upset about Phoenix or even that you won't let us help with the investigation,' Taylor continued. 'He's upset because you're back, but you still don't seem to want anything to do with us.'

This version of Andino and Taylor were strangers to Saffi. The Taylor of her past never would've expressed his grievances so openly to her face, he would've bottled them up and suffered in silence. And Andino never would've walked away to cool off, his temper was like a loaded gun with the safety off. These were not the people Saffi knew. Despite their faults, she missed the boys she'd abandoned five years ago. And the person they missed was the girl who'd left them behind without a word.

From everything she'd seen – the resentment, the jealousy – it was beginning to look like the three of them had grown irreparably apart. If they tried to replicate the past and failed, it would hurt so much worse than never trying at all. She wouldn't risk tarnishing the good memories they had together. And even if they could fall back into what they once had, it wasn't as though Saffi could stay in America. If only for the sake of her father's reputation, she would have to leave again.

'Taylor, we're not those kids anymore,' Saffi said. 'We can't go back in time and it's unfair of Andino to hold me to his expectations of what I'm supposed to be like. We've all changed. Maybe it's time to move on.'

She regretted the words as soon as she said them, but it was for the best. Taylor's face shuttered and he turned away from her. Neither of them spoke for a moment. The ticking clock felt so loud, Saffi half expected the nurse to come back in and shout at it.

'You're right,' Taylor said eventually. She couldn't see his expression. 'I should go make sure Atlas isn't terrorizing the nurses.'

There was so much more to say, but not enough words to express it. So Saffi let him go. Instead, she allowed her mind to wander.

She wondered whether Kapoor's innocence would come across in person as well as it did behind the lens. She wondered which aspects of her were real and which were airbrushed. Which were altogether lies.

It was probably not good practice to keep a celebrity waiting.

Saffi went down the hallway toward the room number the nurse had given them. It was then that she realized how rapidly her heart was pounding. She wiped her palms against her pants, shocked to find that they were sweating. And when she raised them to her face, she realized they were trembling too. The distantly familiar full-body excitement of an unsolved case was still thrumming under her skin.

It wasn't over yet.

Saffi clenched her fists, reining it in. When she looked up, she saw someone familiar.

'Hey!' Tiwari said, surprised.

Saffi winked as they crossed paths, the corner of her mouth upturned in amusement. The assistant hesitated, opening and closing her mouth as though she had more to say but couldn't get it out in time. She was heading in the same direction Andino and Taylor had gone. Saffi almost stopped to watch the collision course, but something else compelled her.

There were exactly ten rooms in the hallway before Dimple Kapoor's. It looked like every other door, but there was a certain gravity to this one in particular. Saffi wondered if anyone walking by could feel the importance of the person waiting behind it or if it was just her imagination.

Before she could hesitate any longer, with a swift knock to announce her presence, Saffi made her entrance. The hinges didn't so much as creak.

An overwhelming floral scent greeted Saffi and the door shut behind her, feeling a lot like the conclusive snap of a coffin.

Shakespeare himself might've orchestrated the scene waiting inside. An ashen, broken woman decorated with bright flowers in the hopes that they would breathe some life into her. While the plants served to emphasize her beauty, it couldn't be helped that they also brought attention to how wilted she was in comparison. There was a certain enchantment to that.

A white bandage covered the woman's forehead and a sling was wrapped around one arm and strapped over the opposite shoulder. Her skin, which Saffi had noted to normally be a healthy bronze, was pale. The brightest things about her were her ever-red lips and that dark, intense gaze that was locked on Saffi.

Despite the weight she'd felt standing outside, she hadn't expected Dimple Kapoor to be so intimidating. Her presence was a tangible thing, filling up the room and choking the air out of even someone like Saffi – who couldn't care less about celebrities and their culture of pretension.

This, she realized, was a momentous occasion. There was no question about it. The very grandeur that the universe itself had deemed Saffi unworthy of. Perhaps there just wasn't enough to go around when people like Dimple Kapoor had it in bucketloads.

The sharp beep of a heart monitor cut through the silence and Saffi broke eye contact first, drawn instead to the machine. Seventy-one beats per minute, a perfectly normal heart rate, but Saffi could see that there had been a slight uptick around when she'd entered the room. Nothing out of the ordinary, though. Maybe she could change that.

She stepped closer, inspecting one of many floral bouquets blanketing the room. Her fingertips slipped over flower petals as she took note of the messages on the cards. A dozen *Feel better soon*s and *We love you*s. All of them gifts from fans. Her growing popularity was evident. In a flash of delirium, Saffi felt bad for not having brought anything herself.

It was with that absurd thought that she broke free from the trance, snapping back to the picture of innocence lying helplessly on the hospital bed. Excitement rose in Saffi's chest. People like this didn't evolve from nothing. She wanted to take this woman apart by hand, piece by piece, just to see how she worked. To see if anything lay underneath other than manufactured parts. Maybe it was because Saffi knew that she herself was achingly empty inside.

She finally realized what had been bothering her so much about this. It wasn't that Kapoor was such a doe-eyed sweetheart – unsuspecting suspects were nothing new. But Dimple Kapoor herself? A person Saffi couldn't look at and immediately predict their next three moves? Someone whose mind she couldn't even begin to fathom the inner workings of? That was once in a lifetime.

'Hello, Dimple Kapoor,' Saffi greeted. 'I've been dying to meet you.'

16

March 13, 2026

So this was her. Saffi Mirai Iyer, private investigator.

A predator instinct lurked underneath coal black eyes. It was Dimple who would have to be on the defensive. Otherwise, Saffi would eat her alive. She had the kind of confidence, posture relaxed and chin held high, that indicated years of experience. Dimple wondered if it was an act – overcompensation.

Look at me, she wanted to say. *Do you realize now who it is that you're dealing with?* It was difficult to read Saffi's expression, but Dimple liked to imagine she saw a touch of awe.

Despite being the one who'd orchestrated this meeting, she felt hauntingly vulnerable lying atop the hospital bed. Her mind seemed disconnected from her body and sudden movement left her nauseous and dizzy. That coupled with the dull ache in her wrist served as a reminder of her complete and utter powerlessness. The heart-rate monitor at her bedside beat a steady rhythm, reminding her to count her breaths.

Dimple had always been terrified of heights, but they had at one point ruled her life so intrinsically, she would have to be dragged, kicking and screaming, up a flight of stairs. Probably a result of one punishment too many. There were only so many times she could be brought to the edge of a balcony and threatened before she began avoiding them altogether. It was a paradox, a positive feedback loop. Her phobia resulted in the very punishment that gave her the fear in the first place.

That was why, when she finally realized that she had no choice in the matter, Dimple had learned to adapt. She pushed the fear so far back into the recesses of her mind, it only leaked out in her weakest of moments. Unsurprisingly, that same terror had reemerged when she stood on the balcony of some actor's mansion two days ago. The ever-encompassing darkness of the polluted, starless sky threatened to consume her whole as the blaring music of the party inside set her nerves on edge. It reminded her of clumsy hands threatening to push. Of the one time they'd actually gone through with the threat.

It was only when she'd smashed the vase against her own head hard enough for blood to splatter that she could stomach jumping. The calculations she'd done the night before told her everything she needed to know. She would survive. The injuries would be minimal.

But that was, of course, only a given if optimal conditions were met. With the disorientation of her head injury, Dimple couldn't stop herself from instinctively tensing her muscles and using her hand to break her fall. As a result, the wrist of her dominant hand was now swollen and throbbing, every accidental movement like lightning shooting up her arm. Eight weeks in the cast, they'd told her, and then physical therapy afterward.

It seemed Dimple was destined to collect a new nightmare every time she tried to stop her life from turning into one. Each time, she found herself thinking they couldn't possibly get worse. Now when she closed her eyes, Dimple relived that same fall. The pain in her imagination was so visceral, she found herself realizing that the actual impact had hurt far less in comparison.

At least no person in their right mind could think Dimple had done this on purpose. She could hardly believe it herself.

'*Dimple Kapoor*,' the private investigator had said, finally through inspecting the bright flowers – Dimple had *fans* now – decorating the hospital room. '*I've been dying to meet you*.'

It was a curious turn of phrase, one that Dimple was more than willing to make true. She'd already decided how to play this, but something in the woman's expression gave her pause. Saffi Mirai Iyer appeared almost excited. Had it been Atlas or Eli in the room, Dimple was sure they would've stumbled their way through a clichéd checklist of condolences first. This woman, however, seemed the type to stomp on eggshells rather than tiptoe.

'Do I know you?' Dimple asked, not bothering to hide her irritation. She could both see and feel her heartbeat pick up ever so slightly. Saffi seemed to notice as well, not bothering to hide her interest in the growing number.

'I get the feeling you know exactly who I am.' She said it challengingly, as though Dimple was supposed to know what she meant by that. When she remained tactfully quiet, it was Saffi who turned away. Somehow, it still felt like a loss.

'Saffi Mirai Iyer, private investigator.' She didn't hold out a hand to shake nor did she offer a business card.

Dimple pretended to mull it over. 'Do you work with Atlas and Eli?'

Saffi shrugged, neither in confirmation nor denial, but she seemed tense. Dimple thought back to the countless articles that connected Saffi, Atlas, and Eli. If one of their names were mentioned regarding an investigation, the other two were sure to follow. That is, until Saffi had left the country and Atlas and Eli had started their own agency without her. Curious. There was likely some history there.

'You mentioned to the police that you were pushed by

someone, but that you didn't get a good look at them?' Saffi asked, and Dimple nodded in agreement, the movement making her wince. This time when her heart rate shot up, it was due to pain.

'Did you catch them?' Dimple asked.

'Not yet,' Saffi said. 'But it's only a matter of time. Your attacker very helpfully decided to leave a little message for us on the balcony.'

'A message,' Dimple echoed, trying to keep her tone wary, yet bland. 'Yes, I believe I recall the police mentioning that.'

It was something Dimple had thought up last minute when she realized she needed the investigators to quickly link her fall to Irene's and Isaac's deaths. The workings of real-life murder investigations were a mystery to her, however. Eight years ago, she hadn't the foresight to pay attention, so all that she knew now was from research. Somehow, she doubted that *Insomnia*'s take on it was accurate, considering Dimple and Chris's characters hadn't been caught.

'Ridiculous, I know,' Saffi said, mischievous. 'But it connects your attack to Irene Singh's murder.'

'Murder? I was under the impression that Irene's passing was an accident,' Dimple said.

'Were you?' Saffi hummed. 'Well, according to the note, it wasn't.' She huffed a laugh. 'Funny. It's the kind of thing you'd expect to see in the movies, not real life.'

Dimple's blood ran cold. She could've been imagining it, but she had a feeling this woman knew more than she was letting on. But Dimple couldn't afford to panic. She forced herself to count her breaths, lungs straining with effort. The number on the heart monitor next to her bed steadily began to decline.

'I suppose,' she replied, slightly breathless. 'But I'd rather it stay on-screen.'

'It's the screen itself that seems to bring out the worst in people.'

What could Saffi possibly intend by that other than to provoke?

'You'll catch whoever it is, won't you?' Dimple Kapoor asked earnestly. Innocence was an art form she'd had a lot of practice perfecting.

'Of course I will,' Saffi replied, seemingly more interested in the vibrant roses by the bedside.

The promise did the opposite of reassure her. Dimple fought the urge to shiver – only partially because the movement would make her sick. 'Do you have any leads?'

Saffi moved closer to Dimple's bed, looking down at her from above. Her head eclipsed the bright light at the top of the room, shrouding her face in darkness. God, she really was so tall. She leaned closer, shirt collar dipping to expose neck and collarbone. It was unsettlingly reckless, this display of vulnerability. Another provocation. Saffi didn't register Dimple as a threat and wanted to make that fact known. Dimple had the brief, feral urge to sink her teeth into the unmarred flesh as a reminder of the danger she possessed. But this was a challenge that she could not meet head-on, not without upending everything she'd done to get here.

'Give it up,' Saffi said. 'This innocent act might've worked on the pigs, but it won't work on me.'

It took a moment for the words to sink in.

Panic followed next, anchoring itself in Dimple's rapidly thudding heart. All her hard work had been for nothing, the heart monitor's beeping turning shrill. She'd been sweating profusely for hours now thanks to the pain and the bright lights and the needles pumping nutrients into her veins, but never as much as she was right now. The walls felt like they were closing in, the lights glowing brighter until they supernova'd.

Dimple couldn't stomach the thought that she'd thrown herself off a balcony for nothing. Eighty-hour workweeks, earning pennies on set throughout the day and at temp jobs throughout the night, all worthless because one woman stood in her path. What would happen, truly, if she reached up and strangled Saffi right here and now? Dimple had only one good hand, but she could probably catch her by surprise.

The world was a dancing mosaic of color. It took her a second to recognize that it was the bouquets her fans had sent her. Just moments ago, Priyal had been reading each of the kind messages out loud while Dimple had let the words sink in.

She had no choice. She would have to kill Saffi just like she did Isaac and Irene.

She had to preemptively strike before the threads of her deception unraveled. The thought was quickly tempered by the fact that she would never get away with it. Forget killing her in the middle of a hospital – even if Dimple threw Saffi down a flight of stairs at some remote location, it wouldn't end well. Because who else had Saffi told about her suspicions? Who were the other suspects in this investigation? If she died immediately after confronting Dimple, there would be no question regarding Dimple's hand in the matter.

She was completely at this woman's mercy.

A hand clamped itself over Dimple's mouth and she was suddenly made aware of her own erratic breathing. The pounding in her skull. The ache in her wrist.

Saffi's shadowed face gradually phased back into view. 'Relax,' she hissed. 'Do you want the nurses barging in here with tranquilizers?'

Dimple could see her own reflection, pale and helpless, in Saffi's irises. When she finally let go of Dimple's mouth,

Dimple breathed in so fast that her lungs threatened to explode. She didn't dare look over at the heart-rate monitor.

It would be okay. This was fine. Any reasonable person would panic when met with such a direct confrontation. Even Innocent Dimple Kapoor – who'd just survived a very traumatic attempt on her life. She could still salvage this.

'What is wrong with you?' Dimple choked out, horrified. Though the artist in her couldn't help being impressed by Saffi's delivery, the buildup to the big reveal.

Saffi blinked innocently. 'What?'

'Are you suggesting I asked for this?' Dimple held up her bandaged wrist.

'I'm suggesting that there was no one for you to ask in the first place.'

She knew. If there was any question before, it was clear now.

This woman was here to fix Atlas and Eli's mistakes, and she wouldn't be making quite as many of her own. It made sense now why Saffi had left them and America behind. If only she'd stayed gone.

Still, she couldn't be all that good of an investigator if she was still at the beck and call of men so far her inferiors.

Dimple's uninjured hand clenched the scratchy fabric of her blanket. 'You'll have to understand, given where we are right now, why a statement like that might anger me.'

Saffi reached out, pinching a blood-red rose petal between her fingertips and plucking it free from the stem. 'And you'll have to understand that I don't give a shit. I didn't get into this line of work to make people happy.'

'Why did you, then?'

'I love a good puzzle,' Saffi replied flippantly.

'Is that what I am to you?'

'You're nothing to me.'

But there was something else. Something in the glint of her eyes. As though Dimple was a shiny new toy for her to play with. It was infuriating.

'If you think I'm a killer, then why not arrest me?' Dimple challenged, jaw clenched.

Saffi grinned, clearly delighted. 'I never said you were a killer, but if the shoe fits . . .'

'This feels extremely unethical,' Dimple muttered, not even having to fake the queasiness in her tone. Her head was floating somewhere above her body.

'Not illegal, though,' Saffi said. 'Can't say the same for your offenses.'

'Do you have any intention of taking my statement at all?'

'That's what the police are for.' Something must've shown on Dimple's face because Saffi adopted an insufferable tone. 'Don't give me that look. They probably ate up every word you said. It's only fair. I'm sure that's how you imagined this encounter going.' She gestured between the two of them.

'What is this, good cop, bad cop?'

Saffi seemed to consider it for a moment. 'If the police were any good at their jobs, then maybe.'

Dimple had never met anyone so antagonistic. As though reading her mind, Saffi flicked the rose petal at Dimple. It floated down in a slow arc, landing softly on her cheek.

'I should let you rest before you have another heart attack,' she said. 'We'll catch up soon, okay? This was almost fun. Don't go doing something stupid and ruin it.'

With that, she turned and left the same way she'd entered. And despite how much Dimple desired the contrary, she knew this would not be the last time they met. She sagged against her pillow, shoulders sore, and absently lifted the petal from her cheek. Soft, velvety. She crushed it within her fist. Next time, she would be much better prepared.

17

March 13, 2026

Saffi wished she could say that she'd completely forgotten about her little spat with Andino when she got back to the office later that day, but it was stuck in the back of her mind, warring for attention. She'd taken a cab back, nearly vibrating with unused energy. The entire course of her conversation with Kapoor had felt like mining for gold.

The actress spoke almost with an accent – not in a way that made her sound like she was from a different country, but as if she belonged to a different century altogether. Her voice reminded Saffi of the old Hollywood films Andino forced her and Taylor to watch.

She'd been intending to avoid the men for the foreseeable future, but when Saffi stepped into the break room for a coffee, she was met by them both at the same time. They sat across from each other at the lone rectangular table, turning to face her as soon as the door swung open. All three of them froze for a moment. The overhead light flickered. Then –

'We picked up the police files for you,' Andino said, gesturing to the unopened folders strewn across their table. He'd never been one for the silent treatment, but his voice was unexpected, nonetheless.

The tension broke and Saffi crossed the room to pour herself a coffee. 'Thanks,' she said, stilted but not unwelcoming.

'Also,' Taylor said, somewhat hesitantly, 'we ran into

Dimple's assistant at the hospital. She seems to think you and her employer are friends.'

'Obviously, I lied.' Saffi shrugged, leaning against the counter. The mention of Kapoor had her itching to pick up the files, but she held back.

'I keep telling Eli we should lie more,' Andino said.

'Yeah, Taylor,' she encouraged. 'Lie more.'

Taylor looked between the two of them incredulously. Even Andino couldn't hide his surprise.

'We agree on some things, me and this clown,' Saffi said.

'Hey!' Andino protested.

'So how was Dimple Kapoor?' Taylor asked before they could delve into yet another argument. It worked to distract Andino, who sat up straight in his chair.

To be fair, Saffi's conversation with Kapoor had ended in a stalemate. While she was even more certain now that the actress was guilty, Saffi had gained no incriminating evidence and desperately needed to figure out her next move. The good thing was that Kapoor had made a big gamble, inventing a new villain out of thin air. It would take a lot of effort on her part to keep up that charade.

But Kapoor would be on high alert around Saffi from now on, which would make it difficult to catch her slipups. Where it had been beneficial to work alone before, Saffi had a new plan in mind. One that could use Andino and Taylor's ignorance to her benefit.

'Kapoor didn't see her attacker,' she said. 'I've established that the waiter was killed because of the information he had, but other than the phone booth, anything to do with him is a dead end. I want to look into everyone involved in *Insomnia* who was also at both parties, just to cover my bases.'

Taylor seemed touched, although his brows were furrowed

in concern. 'Thanks for the update, but I meant Dimple the person, not Dimple the case. She was just targeted by a serial killer. I'd imagine she's pretty shaken up.'

Saffi rolled her eyes. 'Let her fans do the crying and fretting. She'll be fine.' As far as she had gathered, the public knew that Kapoor was in the hospital but had no idea the severity of the situation or that there was a killer at large.

'They don't know anything about her,' Andino blurted and then recoiled as though he hadn't meant to speak. 'I just meant this stuff is all surface level. None of them actually care if she's okay.'

Saffi exchanged a curious glance with Taylor, whose expression told her not to bother asking. It seemed as good a time as any to finally bite the bullet.

'So, no one saw what happened at the party?' she asked. 'No cameras?'

Both men paused, exchanging identically bewildered looks. Then, as though afraid she'd change her mind, Taylor's fingers flew across his keyboard and Andino ripped through the police files. 'I'm not sure, but we can find out pretty easily,' Taylor said.

So they'd honored her request to stay off the case. It was equal parts touching and shameful. Were Saffi in their place, the files sitting right in front of her, she wasn't sure she would've been able to resist.

It wasn't just that Andino and Taylor could be useful now. Saffi had severely underestimated Kapoor. She had no doubts that the woman could kill her and make it look like an accident. Were that to happen, there would be no one there to pick up the pieces. Unless she let them in. Well, to an extent.

'The police report says she was on the balcony by herself,' Andino confirmed. 'A few people heard her body hit the ground, though, and came running. They were the ones who called 911.'

'What are your thoughts?' Taylor asked, but it was clear that he actually meant, *What made you change your mind?* The answer he wanted was that it was their talk that did it. But she would be letting him down yet again.

'This is the first time a victim has survived,' Saffi murmured. 'It would be stupid not to use that.'

'What do you mean?' Taylor asked.

'If you attacked someone and they lived, what would you do?'

'Anything to make sure they didn't speak,' Andino said.

'Exactly,' Saffi agreed.

Taylor's eyebrows raised in understanding. 'You want to use her as bait.'

'When you put it like that, it sounds so sinister,' Saffi said. 'But, essentially, yes.'

It wasn't as cruel as it sounded; there was protocol for this. They would have to get Kapoor's consent and properly train her beforehand. This, of course, was really a means for Saffi to study the actress up close. Andino and Taylor were there to lure her into a false sense of security. As interesting as things were right now, there always came a point where Saffi began winning so thoroughly that the game bored her once again. She wanted to enjoy this while it lasted.

Taylor didn't say anything, but from the way he glanced at Andino it was clear he didn't approve. Saffi turned to Andino, expecting opposition, but he was so intently typing away at his laptop that it seemed he'd barely heard her.

'Weren't you the one begging to help with the case?' she asked, irritated.

'Please don't start another argument,' Taylor pleaded under his breath.

'Huh?' Andino said, glancing up. 'Hold on, I have something I want to show you. A suspect, but he doesn't exactly match the profile you created.'

Curiosity piqued, Saffi gestured for him to show her.

The man on Andino's screen appeared to be in his sixties, although it was very possible he looked old for his age. Pale, wrinkled skin, and a receding head of gray hair. He was tall, though, and sturdy.

'Hector Olsen,' Andino said. 'He's a big-name director in Hollywood, known for a lot of popular movies in the past couple decades. He's also known for a lot of sexual misconduct. Physical and verbal abuse too.'

'Alleged,' Taylor corrected.

'Not all of it,' Andino said.

'And?' Saffi prompted.

Andino started typing again. 'There have been rumors he wanted to direct *Insomnia,* but Bardoux got there first.'

'That's a motive against the production of the movie, but why would he take it out on the actresses instead of Bardoux or the producers?' Taylor asked.

'This is what Hector's ex-wives look like.' Andino's screen this time displayed four side-by-side pictures of young South Asian women. 'He was accused of abuse in three cases and in one of those, his ex-wife Laila Olsen claimed he pushed her down the stairs.'

'Oh,' Saffi said. 'That is alarming.'

How could she have missed him? Maybe this really was her stubbornness rearing its ugly head, too desperate to prove herself to consider any other options. Her stomach flip-flopped with guilt. But at the same time, she knew what she'd seen when she met Kapoor at the hospital. The actress's desperation was palpable.

'Was he at both parties?' Taylor asked.

'He was definitely at Irene's,' Andino said. 'I don't know about this recent one.'

Saffi remembered the interview Andino and Taylor had conducted with Olsen after Singh's death. It hadn't revealed anything of note other than the fact that he was a pompous asshole, but Saffi could've guessed that by looking at his picture.

'We need to find out if he was at that party,' she said. 'And also follow up to confirm if he really was passed up for Bardoux.'

'I'll get the interns on it,' Andino said.

Taylor grinned. 'Brings back memories, doesn't it?'

Saffi rolled her eyes and Andino groaned, but there was an undercurrent of fondness to it. The way he'd said it, Saffi almost wondered if they'd decided to hire three interns on purpose. She should've been horrified to find that all three of them were stuck in the past, tethered to one another, but there was also a comfort in that. She herself still wasn't sure if it was Andino and Taylor's presence that she'd missed or if it was the simplicity that came with being a girl in her early twenties.

And yet somehow, the three of them had managed to fall back into their old rhythm. Maybe Saffi had been too hasty in cataloging the differences their years apart had created. Maybe, at their core, they were all still the same kids with dreams too big for their bodies and freakishly compatible working styles.

Regardless, between them was the unspoken knowledge that things could never truly go back to the way they'd been. Saffi almost withdrew again, but this time she resisted. Dimple Kapoor had thrown herself off a balcony simply because she'd wanted, so desperately, to hold on to something.

An actress murdered two people in cold blood to further her career and Saffi was too afraid of rehashing things with her old colleagues to collaborate on this case with them. It was probably that absurd comparison that gave Saffi the courage to bring her laptop and files into the break room instead of going back to her office. What was the harm, really? It wouldn't kill anyone.

18

April 1, 2026

Two weeks after she had been discharged from the hospital, Dimple was torn between frustration at the limitations her injury had imposed upon her and a fear of what her thoughts would turn to if she was left alone.

'Priyal, this isn't your job,' Dimple chided exasperatedly.

'I'm your assistant,' Priyal replied, continuing to fold Dimple's laundry into a neat stack on the couch.

'That's exactly my point. I don't pay you to do household chores.'

'It's not like you have much of a schedule for me to keep track of with your wrist like that! Either I can make myself useful or you can take me off your payroll.'

Dimple sighed, thoroughly scolded, and sank deeper into the couch cushion, velvet fabric scratching lightly against her cheek. Both feet were tucked under her legs, wrist cradled to her chest. No one had ever done chores for her. It was unnerving.

'By the way, I'm great at multitasking,' Priyal said, folding a yellow sundress into a neat square. 'I've been keeping up with your social media.'

Dimple thought of a computer with several tabs open, of a keyboard clattering to the ground. 'Have you?' She reached for her phone on the coffee table and powered it on.

'There've been a lot of rumors going around after it was leaked that you were taken to the hospital. For some reason, everyone thinks you're in rehab. But Julie helped me draft a statement and I think it helped.'

Sure enough, pinned to Dimple's profile was a long string of text. It rather vaguely read that she'd been injured at a party and would be recovering for an unspecified amount of time. She should've known better than to look, but the top comment, sitting at thousands of likes, said *definitely rehab.* Which part of her was it that alluded to substance abuse? Or was it the stain of her past that she could never seem to remove?

'It's not completely terrible, I guess,' Priyal mused. 'People are curious, so your follower count keeps growing.'

Dimple screened the rest of the comments, glad to see that they were mostly thoughtful well-wishes. She tactfully ignored the ones praising her bravery for taking the steps she needed to *get better.* Dimple set her phone to the side and took a sip of the now lukewarm hot chocolate Priyal had brought her.

'What do you want for lunch?' Priyal asked. 'Should I order something for you?'

'Don't worry about it.'

The pricing of most LA restaurants wasn't worth it. Thanks to her work on *Insomnia,* for the first time in her life, Dimple had money to squander – even if hospital bills had siphoned a sizable portion of it – but she couldn't help thinking of years into the future. If *Insomnia* flopped, there was a chance she would never see a paycheck like this ever again. The last thing she wanted was to go back to the gruelling minimum wage jobs between auditions.

Her broken wrist only made it more difficult for her to get work in the meantime. It meant a month of near-total isolation – broken up only by Priyal's occasional visits – with nothing for her mind to do but conjure up nightmares. It was already spring and the two weeks that had gone by since she'd been discharged from the hospital had been hell.

With nothing else to occupy her mind, Dimple had fixated on the proverbial ax hanging above her head that was Saffi Mirai Iyer. She'd spent her free time attempting to conjure up ways to get closer to the investigation. It was the only way to shift this stalemate in her favor.

A knock sounded at the door, startling both Dimple and Priyal.

'Are you expecting someone?' Priyal asked.

Dimple shook her head, rising to join Priyal beside the door. Paranoia anticipated the police had finally come to arrest her. Delusion anticipated Irene or Isaac with a vengeance. Whoever it was knocked again impatiently. Dimple reached for the doorknob with her good hand, but Priyal beat her to it.

And there, at Dimple's doorstep, was Saffi Mirai Iyer in her signature black suit, looking as unimpressed as ever, as though Dimple had cast her straight out of the movie in her mind.

This was much worse than the police.

'Oh. It's you,' Priyal said, opening the door wider. She was still under the impression that Dimple and Saffi were old friends trying desperately to reconnect.

'Nice to see you again,' Saffi said, stepping inside at Dimple's wary beckon.

Priyal wasn't the kind to question things much. She never asked why Dimple's family hadn't visited or even called after her accident. Nor had she asked why Dimple didn't seem to have any friends or where Saffi had come from all of a sudden. She took things as they came, and it was something Dimple intensely admired. To be fair, Dimple was similar. She didn't know anything about Priyal's private life, and so she extended the courtesy and didn't ask either.

'You should be more careful,' Saffi said, glancing around Dimple's apartment. 'What if I was your attacker?'

'That's what I keep telling her,' Priyal said, completely missing the undertone of sarcasm.

'I am more than capable of taking care of myself,' Dimple said evenly.

An alarm sounded and Priyal pulled out her phone, turning it off with a sigh. 'I have to go,' she said regretfully.

'She's in good hands,' Saffi said mirthfully.

'Are you sure you don't need me to stay?' Priyal asked.

'You said you had plans.' Dimple had a feeling it was an audition, but she doubted Priyal would admit that to her current employer.

'I can cancel them!'

'I'll be fine, Priyal.'

Only the police, the investigators, and Priyal were under the impression that Dimple had been attacked. It wasn't public knowledge yet that there was a killer going around. According to law enforcement, it would cause too much widespread panic. The secrecy helped in her case, though, so Dimple gladly went along with their wishes.

'Just promise me you'll keep your phone on,' Priyal said, relenting. 'If you don't reply, I'll get worried. I might kick your door down at three in the morning.'

'Now, that I'd like to see.'

Priyal swung her bag over her shoulder and, with one last glance at Dimple, left the same way Saffi had come. And then the two of them were alone. This was the first time they'd seen each other since the hospital, but if Saffi wouldn't bother exchanging pleasantries, then neither would Dimple.

'Cute,' Saffi said. Her fingers brushed Dimple's wrist brace. Not even hard enough to jostle, but Dimple felt the phantom touch in her bones. 'You want me to sign it?'

The rough fabric wrapped tight across her wrist felt like a prison. Dimple forced politeness into her reply. 'You're a natural. We'll make an actress out of you yet.'

And then the shape of Saffi was slipping past her farther into the apartment. It was this kind of easy confidence that made her so enthralling. Taking ownership of any space as though it were her own. They plunged into a terse silence as Saffi took in Dimple's mismatched interior design, the hum of kitchen appliances just loud enough to emphasize the tension in the air.

'Don't feel the need to strangle me today?' Dimple couldn't help asking, relishing in the way Saffi turned to her, brows furrowed, before understanding dawned.

'I didn't strangle you,' Saffi said. 'I was trying to regulate your breathing.'

'By strangling me.'

'You were having a panic attack.'

'It is a blessing you never pursued a career in psychiatry,' Dimple replied dryly.

'I'm not the one who lies for a living,' Saffi said. She ran a finger along the spines of Dimple's VHS collection, pulling one free from the shelf. 'You do realize that everything is online nowadays?'

But where was the appreciation in that? Dimple had been collecting old films since her college days. Her mother's collection had been destroyed in the fire – the only thing she regretted about the incident – but she'd slowly been able to build up her catalog again.

It wasn't just technology that was left behind in the past, but also the art displayed upon it. How was it that so many people went to visit the *Mona Lisa* every day, but had completely forgotten so much of the dramatic arts? Was there no one left to appreciate the masterpieces that had been forgotten simply because they were not available to stream online? Dimple liked to imagine that she alone was keeping them alive, immortalized through time. But she didn't expect Saffi to understand that.

Dimple grasped the VHS, but Saffi held on, patiently awaiting an explanation. A childish performance of tug-of-war – it amused Dimple far more than it should have. Even more when she realized Saffi had chosen a horror film. One of her favorites.

'I like being able to hold them,' Dimple replied, which was also true. 'Is that too cliché?'

Saffi took a moment to consider before letting go. 'Kind of fitting, actually.'

That Saffi claimed to understand her to any degree almost made her laugh. Dimple returned the movie to its rightful place and took the time to study her counterpart in her periphery. Saffi dressed identical to Atlas and Eli – same expensive black suit, exuding formality. At least until she opened her mouth. But they diverged in where Atlas and Eli were twin voids, Saffi had a certain vividness to her. She seemed oddly at home amongst Dimple's mismatch of shapes and colors in the same way a flower looked more beautiful in a bouquet.

'So, how can I help you?' Dimple tried for casual.

Saffi leaned against the bookshelf, studying her. 'How would you feel about assisting with the investigation?'

Dimple's hands, which had been busy smoothing an invisible wrinkle in her dress, froze. It was the last thing she'd expected to hear. Just moments ago, she'd been trying to think of ways to infiltrate Andino and Taylor Private Eye. She'd even considered breaking and entering. But to be invited? It sounded too good to be true.

And perhaps it was. Perhaps this was Saffi's attempt at entrapping her. After all, an innocent actress like Dimple

Kapoor would have no desire to be involved in a murder investigation, especially given what had just happened to her. In all her amusement, she'd almost forgotten Saffi was just as much a performer as she was.

'I doubt I'd be of any help to you,' Dimple replied carefully. 'Besides, wouldn't that only provoke whoever it was that targeted me?'

'You don't seem that worried.'

'Pardon?'

'You haven't hired any security,' Saffi noted, gesturing around them. 'And you were practically herding your assistant out of here. Most people in your shoes would consider turning themselves in for witness protection.'

It was, infuriatingly, a good point.

'I can't afford security –'

'I know that's not true,' Saffi cut in.

'It is,' Dimple said, 'a child's notion to assume that all actors are millionaires.'

'Can we drop the pretenses for a minute?' Saffi asked, irritated.

'I wasn't aware that we were using any.'

Saffi huffed, her breath displacing a strand of hair that had come loose from her ponytail. 'Fine. Help me with the case and I'll make sure to protect you from the invisible boogeyman you invented.' She waved her hand flippantly.

She had a perpetual air of uninterest about her. Dimple could see it for what it was – rudeness. But the show woman in her saw it as a challenge. Dimple pretended to mull it over as though she hadn't already made up her mind before the conversation had begun.

'I'm not sure I feel comfortable acting as bait for you,' she said eventually.

Saffi scoffed. If she was surprised that Dimple had caught

on to her intentions so quickly, she didn't show it. '*Bait* implies there's something for you to catch.'

Neither of them were willing to give in. What was the old saying again – unstoppable force, immovable object? Their collision was inevitable, the only question was how cataclysmic the aftermath would be.

'If you're so certain I'm a killer, then why are you here alone with me?'

'I never said I was afraid of you.'

'Why not?' Dimple pressed.

Saffi raised her brows. 'What, are you disappointed?'

'If I were a killer, I'd at least want to be a talented one.'

'You can't kill me, Kapoor,' Saffi said. 'There are only two ways this ends: Either you turn yourself in now or I'll do it for you later.'

As if it would be that easy. 'If you were to kill somebody, all it would take for you to turn yourself in is someone asking you kindly?'

Saffi grinned. 'Depends on how kind they were.'

'You could stand to put in a bit more effort, in that case.'

'I guess I wouldn't know,' Saffi said. 'If I killed someone, I wouldn't be careless enough to be a suspect in the first place.'

Dimple couldn't help it, she laughed. 'You are the last person who should ever be a private investigator.'

'And yet . . .'

Every hair stood on end, the moment before a lightning strike. And then it was gone. Saffi was turning away, straightening her suit jacket. It was impossible to tell who'd won.

Just as Dimple began wondering if they were truly going to leave things like this, Saffi paused in the entryway. 'Last chance,' she said. Her arm was braced against the door, holding it open. It made her appear taller, despite them being the same height.

This was a bluff. Dimple knew Saffi needed her just as much as she needed Saffi. Their stalemate would have to come to an end one way or another. She glanced down at her phone and considered canceling her appointment.

'Ask me again later,' Dimple said pleasantly.

It was worth it for the irritated look Saffi shot her. 'Oh, I'm sorry. Are you in the middle of something, your highness?'

'A meeting with my manager.' Dimple held up her brace. 'Not much work I can accomplish while I have this on.'

Dimple used to act in community plays for free when she first moved to LA, and she'd met her manager, Julie, after one of those shows. It was apparently her charm and relentless effort that attracted Julie, who'd always claimed that Dimple treated life itself as a performance. It wasn't until recently that Dimple began to understand what she'd meant.

They were long overdue for a meeting to discuss the future of Dimple's career. She was also supposed to pick up a couple of scripts to start working on for upcoming auditions.

Saffi's brows furrowed. She did that when she was thinking, Dimple realized. 'Surely you're not strapped for cash with the feature film you just shot.'

'The starving artist is a trope for good reason.'

'Oh yeah, I could tell by the squalor you live in,' Saffi deadpanned. 'What else ails you? Was the red carpet the wrong shade for your complexion?'

Dimple didn't know why she felt such an intrinsic urge to defend herself, but the words burned deeply in her chest as she forced them down. The issue with invisible scars was that nobody ever noticed them. But once you tasted true, carnal hunger, it burned itself into your mind for an eternity. Dimple couldn't keep a stocked pantry for fear of bingeing it all to the point of sickness. When she first moved to LA, most of her meals had been expired overstock from the café next to her old apartment; she'd since had the pleasure of eating at a Michelin star restaurant downtown. One of those had been the best food she'd ever tasted in her life.

She'd had a full scholarship to a reputable university, and still she chose to drop out and leave it all behind. Dimple could still remember the day she realized watching movies in her spare time would only worsen her fear of what she knew then to be inevitable: a meaningless, forgettable existence. Just like that of her aunt and uncle. It was an insult to her mother, who'd died so Dimple could live.

That day, standing atop the grassy hill on campus, a few film students had set up a tripod to capture the sunset. Dimple had never felt a stronger compulsion to do something than she did to walk past that camera. To leave some record of her having been here. There was no academic prestige, no desk job, no amount of money in the world that would make her feel as real as when a camera was pointed at her.

Dimple laughed, a manufactured thing. 'I'm not quite what you think I am. But perhaps one day I'll live up to your expectations.'

It was the wrong thing to say.

A flash of white as Saffi bared her teeth in a grin. 'That's only if you're not behind bars before then.'

And the door slammed shut behind her.

19

April 15, 2026

Saffi didn't extend another invitation to Kapoor regarding the case until mid-April.

Andino and Taylor were treading on her very last nerve, so Saffi welcomed any distraction at that point. The two of them were under the impression that it was a good idea to go straight to Olsen. They hadn't been able to get a clear answer as to whether he'd been at the second party, so they wanted to get his statement.

Saffi, of course, didn't agree. When they found no evidence that he was guilty, like Saffi suspected they would, she doubted he would keep his mouth shut about it. A prideful man hated nothing more than to be accused of something he didn't do. Olsen's notorious temper and large following would make it infinitely more difficult to continue investigating, especially since Kapoor would then be given a heads-up about who else they were investigating.

It wasn't entirely their fault, however. Saffi still hadn't told them that Kapoor was the one she really suspected. She planned on having Andino and Taylor spend the most time with the actress, as Kapoor would likely see the men as easy targets to siphon information from. This way Saffi could keep a solid grasp on what, exactly, was being revealed to Kapoor. More than that, Saffi had the option of doctoring the flow of information, completely unbeknownst to all parties involved.

The most dangerous killers in the world were the ones who had something to lose. They tended to go to extremes to both hold on to and rationalize their wrongdoings. Considering what Kapoor had done the last time she'd been cornered, Saffi needed to play this very carefully.

Her career in film could only explain so much, though, and Dimple Kapoor's in particular was superficial in every conceivable way. Saffi found herself more interested in the woman's past, which was riddled with questions. Specifically, the year-and-a-half-long college stint. A full ride, including room and board, was many people's dream. And yet it didn't take long for Kapoor to drop out and throw herself at an uncertain future instead. It made little sense for someone so intelligent and calculating.

Saffi had been in the middle of deciphering Kapoor's college transcript when she heard an office door slam shut and a pair of footsteps darting out. That would be the Andino half of Andino and Taylor Private Eye. The man had been jittery ever since Saffi mentioned that Kapoor would be coming in. Clearly, the actress had arrived.

It was worrying what the man might do in this state, so Saffi snatched her jacket and hurried to intercept them. A concerned-looking Taylor was waiting for her when she stepped into the hallway. Together, they watched Andino attempt to balance an armful of bottled water and snacks. Dimple Kapoor stood in front of him, her heels as red as her lips, politely accepting a little bit of everything. If Saffi hadn't been looking so closely, she wouldn't have noticed the actress slipping most of it into her purse.

'Oh god,' Saffi said.

'Yeah,' Taylor agreed with a sigh.

Even the interns, who were usually unobtrusive, came out of their office to gawk at the local celebrity. Living in LA,

Saffi had assumed most of its residents would be used to this kind of thing by now. It took her a moment to realize that they were gawking just as much at her as they were at Dimple.

'Didn't take you for a fanboy, Andino,' Saffi muttered under her breath as they crossed paths.

'Fuck off,' he said, ears red.

'Thanks for coming in,' Taylor said to Dimple politely.

'I don't know how much help I'll be, but I'll do anything I can,' she said. Saffi deserved an Oscar for successfully suppressing an eye roll.

'Let's go to the meeting room,' Taylor suggested. 'It should fit all of us.'

Taylor led the way and Saffi followed last. When she heard shuffling behind her, she turned back. As she did, all three interns turned away as though they hadn't been gazing at her with forlorn expressions. It set Saffi on edge, perhaps because it reminded her so much of herself when she was their age.

More established investigators tended to take advantage of the youthful eagerness to please. How many cases had she solved without credit or compensation? At the same time, how many of those investigators had ignored her, never bothering to learn her name let alone give her the time of day?

Saffi let out a long sigh. 'Come on,' she said, holding the door open.

They seemed bewildered, as though unsure if her offer was serious, but scurried inside when Saffi made an irritated sound. Taylor gave her a curious, approving look when she joined them. Not even a full minute had passed, and she was already regretting it.

Eager not to ruin their chances, the interns stood with

their backs to the wall, holding up identical notepads and pens stamped with the agency's logo. Saffi took it back – she couldn't remember being *that* eager. She leaned against the wall behind Kapoor, facing Andino and Taylor. Early-morning sunshine illuminated the circular wooden table separating them.

Saffi had already briefed the men on exactly how much information they were allowed to disclose to Dimple Kapoor. They could discuss what she already knew, but no new information was to be revealed. They could bring up Irene's and Isaac's deaths in conjunction with her attack, but they could not inform her that they suspected Hector Olsen. Simple.

'I want to make sure you know what you're getting yourself into,' Taylor said to Kapoor. 'Your comfort is the most important thing here.'

'Wow,' Saffi muttered. 'Who died and made you head of HR?'

She didn't get a response. Kapoor's eyes did widen in surprise, however, as she seemed to catch onto the fact that Andino and Taylor didn't know she was a suspect. She glanced back at Saffi, who only raised a challenging brow in response.

'Helping us with this case might mean putting yourself into dangerous or stressful situations,' Taylor said. 'It might bring up trauma associated with your attack. Is that something you're willing to risk?'

Kapoor had both hands clasped together, her black wrist brace inconspicuous against the dark brown of the table. Ever the selfless, demure damsel, she said, 'I don't want this to happen to anyone else.'

'That's admirable,' Taylor said genuinely. 'We want the same thing.'

An intern's pen scratched eagerly across their notepad.

'If I agree to help, what would that entail?' Kapoor asked.

'There is protocol. We'll train you on the basics of undercover work,' Taylor explained.

'Which should be easy, since you're already an amazing actress,' Andino added.

Unbelievable. Saffi looked up at the ceiling and tried not to grind her teeth to dust. She was beginning to understand the appeal of throwing yourself off a two-story building.

'Right,' Taylor said after a beat. 'The goal is to get you to a point where you feel comfortable going to another party that we know for certain our suspects will be attending. We're hoping your presence might induce a reaction. They might try to get you alone or even attack you again.'

Taylor must've noticed the manufactured terror on Kapoor's face because he hastily added, 'Of course, all three of us will be there with you, ready to pull you out on the off chance something goes wrong. We'll make sure you have everything you need to ensure your safety.'

'Excuse my hesitation, but are you sure you'll be of much help? I haven't seen you carry any weapons,' Dimple said.

It was a very smart, very roundabout way of ensuring her own safety, but not in the way Taylor was made to believe. Kapoor needed to be aware of the weapons they carried – not so that they could be used to defend her, but so she could make sure they wouldn't be used *against* her.

Taylor seemed to mull it over for a moment, turning to Saffi first. He was deferring to her. They both were. She shouldn't have been surprised, but after years of working exclusively with egotistical strangers, she'd grown used to boundaries being pushed until they broke. Ultimately, she shrugged, leaving it up to his discretion. She didn't know what protective services Andino and Taylor Private Eye provided, if any, nor had she ever worked in that sector.

'We don't do a lot of security work,' Taylor admitted. 'However, Atlas and I are trained in self-defense. And we've been in this field for a long time. We're familiar with the dangers of the job.'

It was true enough. Saffi didn't have a permanent office, so she hadn't had to deal with the death threats or extremist ideals in a while, but she'd had more than enough experience back at Stronghold. The sheer volume of mail she'd seen the interns shred every day was enough to confirm that nothing had changed. Most PIs eventually became desensitized to it, but there was always the possibility that someone would follow through with their threats.

'We prefer not to carry weapons,' Taylor continued. 'We're not law enforcement. However, we are licensed in the state of California – Atlas and I, that is – so, if it would make you feel safer, one of us could bring a gun with us to the party.'

Arizona hadn't required any permits for concealed carry, so Saffi was left out of the equation. She was glad for the excuse. Even though she'd learned the basics in her home state, she hadn't ever felt the need to carry weapons. All but one of the cases they'd been assigned in Arizona had been petty crime. And it was especially unnecessary abroad. It probably should have made Saffi feel uneasy knowing that there was a gun somewhere on the premises, just out of reach of Dimple Kapoor, but firearms weren't exactly her style.

'That won't be necessary,' Kapoor said after a beat. 'I was just curious.'

'Any other concerns?' Taylor asked.

'I don't suppose you'll tell me who the suspects are?' Kapoor asked.

Again, they deferred to Saffi. She pushed off the wall and

went to sit on the table beside Kapoor, who bumped her elbow with Saffi's thigh.

'Well?' she asked the interns.

All three of them straightened. She was certain one of the boys almost saluted before thinking better of it. In the end, they stared blankly at her.

'What do you think?' she asked them. 'Should we tell her?'

One of the boys stammered out, 'Yes.'

'Why?'

'So she knows who to look out for?'

'Wrong,' Saffi replied. She didn't have to turn around to know Taylor was wincing behind her back. Judging by her shaking shoulders, Dimple Kapoor was holding back laughter. 'Any other guesses?'

The girl raised her hand.

'I'm not your teacher,' Saffi said.

'You shouldn't tell her,' she answered, notepad in a tight grip. 'Because the suspect could be innocent, for all we know. We want to induce an authentic reaction in case the real culprit is not someone we're expecting.'

'What's your name?' Saffi asked.

'Mia Martinez.'

'Gold star, Martinez. That is one reason.' Of course, the real reason was that Dimple herself was a suspect – not that Saffi expected the interns to know that.

Martinez beamed, her iron grip on her notebook relaxing. The boys seemed dejected, but disappointment was a vital part of investigative work. The best PIs had to get comfortable with it or else they'd make the same mistakes as the stubborn Saffi of her past. However, she couldn't help but give them an encouraging nod. That seemed to ease the corners of their frowns.

'I see,' Kapoor said. She'd been studying Saffi, but she

turned back to Andino and Taylor. 'And what if I go through this training and decide I don't want to do it in the end?'

'Then you'll have wasted our t –'

'That's perfectly within your right,' Taylor said, cutting Saffi off.

Kapoor took a moment to formulate a response. 'From what you've told me, this killer sounds manipulative and intelligent. I don't know if I stand a chance against them.'

'Wow, Kapoor,' Saffi muttered, leaning down and speaking low enough for only the actress to hear. 'I'm all for self-love, but this is a bit much.'

Kapoor's expression didn't so much as twitch, but there was a tenseness in her jaw that hadn't been there before. Saffi couldn't help her amusement. There was a certain thrill to be sitting in a roomful of people, winning a game that nobody but the two of them knew the rules of.

'But,' Kapoor continued, 'if there's a chance I can help, then I will.'

They finished the meeting with a tour of the building. No man had ever made paper clips and staplers sound as exciting as Andino. His chest puffed up every time Kapoor complimented something of his, cueing Saffi and Taylor to exchange unimpressed expressions. Taylor didn't seem to notice, though, that Kapoor reacted similarly whenever Andino chose to wax poetic about her work. It was minute, but the twitch of her lips gave it away.

Egomaniacs, the both of them.

The tour concluded outside the agency, where a cool breeze greeted them. Dimple paused to call a cab, which prompted Andino and Taylor to head inside, but Saffi remained. She rocked back on her heels, hands stuffed into her pockets.

'Do you hate communications or something?' she asked eventually.

When Kapoor looked up in confusion, the sunlight hit her eyes just right, igniting a kaleidoscope of brown and gold. She had extremely long, dark eyelashes that cast shadows against her skin. Saffi supposed she could see why someone might want to put her on a movie screen.

'You gave up a full ride to a great university,' she continued. 'I figured you weren't the biggest fan of your major.'

If Kapoor had been surprised by Saffi's knowledge, she didn't show it. She did, however, take her time before responding. As though considering her words carefully.

'Communications is fine,' Kapoor replied. 'Just not my passion.' She reached into her bag and held up a thick bundle of papers, the corners of which lifted with the wind. It had the weathered look of a well-loved book.

The large '[Confidential]' mark splashed in ink across the front gave away that it was a script. Nobody would give two shits about it if it were blank. Saffi wouldn't be surprised if actors stamped it themselves to be sure everyone in a twenty-mile radius noticed.

'Communications is no one's passion,' Saffi deadpanned. 'But what I don't understand is how you came to that conclusion. You hadn't taken a single communications class. Your coursework was all over the place. Organic chemistry, physics, English – hell, even computer science.' Kapoor tensed for a fraction of a second, but Saffi still caught it. The endless phone calls and trips down to the university to acquire those transcripts, while a truly harrowing experience, had been worth it.

'You've done your research,' Kapoor said. It felt vaguely mocking. 'What is there to say? I enrolled in those courses because they sounded interesting, but,' she shrugged, 'I was out of my depth. It doesn't matter how many lectures you attend if you don't retain the information.'

Saffi grinned. 'You're lying. You aced all of them, I saw your transcript.'

If she hadn't studied liars and criminals for nearly a decade, she would've thought Kapoor was completely unaware of being caught out. But the way her body stilled for a fraction of a second spoke volumes.

'Grades are nothing but ink on paper. Perhaps my true skills lie in plagiarism.'

'I don't doubt that for a second, but that doesn't explain why you would lie about it.'

But Saffi already knew why she'd lied. Kapoor was an actress, she enjoyed manipulating people's impressions of her to her liking. Maybe that was why she'd chosen the communications track. It was vague and unassuming enough, at least for those who didn't bother to look deeper at the classes she'd been enrolled in.

Saffi thought back to the shelves of VHS tapes at Kapoor's apartment, not a speck of dust on them. Or maybe it was that Kapoor had wanted to give the traditional college route an honest effort, trying a bit of everything to see what stuck. And it was her true passion that won out in the end.

This was something Saffi could understand: putting your all into a passion until it consumed you whole. But the problem with that was that it would eventually leave you hollow inside.

Saffi hadn't been expecting an answer, so it startled her when Kapoor spoke again.

'Perhaps I feel bad,' she said, looking up through dark lashes. Cars honked on the busy street nearby, but the sound faded into background noise. 'Perhaps I'm turning over a new leaf.'

'You act like I don't know you.'

Kapoor gave her a small, almost sad look in return. 'It is never a good thing to be known.' It was the first thing she'd said that sounded like the truth.

The sound of crunching gravel heralded a cab pulling into Andino and Taylor's parking lot. They put their conversation on pause, tracking the vehicle until it came to a stop in front of them. There was so much left to say, but neither of them spoke again. Saffi thought that would be it, but Kapoor stalled in closing the door, poking her head out again.

'You were right,' she said, twin dimples on either side of her face. 'This is fun. Don't ruin it.'

Saffi watched as the car peeled out of the parking lot, blending seamlessly into midday traffic. She knew better than anyone the look of a woman carrying the weight of her past. Kapoor didn't seem all that concerned that Saffi was looking into her college years, so her secrets likely didn't lie in her coursework. She did, however, seem alarmed at the level of access Saffi had managed to obtain. Saffi was on the right path, she just had to keep digging.

She didn't notice the new presence beside her until Taylor spoke. 'Sorry – have you seen a blue folder?'

Saffi nearly jumped.

'I swear it was just on my desk. It wouldn't be a big deal, but the printer's out of commission and I have to get this finished within the next half hour.' Taylor sounded haggard.

When Saffi turned to face him, he looked even worse. She took pity on him, knowing he was in a rush to leave the office.

'Kapoor's paperwork?' she asked. 'I took care of that yesterday.' There was no use in waiting when she already knew Kapoor would agree to help them.

Taylor opened his mouth, as though to reply, but nothing came out. He shut it with an audible click, brows furrowed.

'Why?' he asked eventually.

'Don't you have plans tonight? For once in your boring life, I might add.' He continued to stare at her with suspicion, so Saffi sighed and added, 'I figured I could cut you some slack on your birthday. You only turn twenty-nine once.'

Taylor blinked in surprise. 'You remembered?'

Saffi gave him a look.

'Sorry, I just figured you forgot when you said you didn't want to come out with us.'

It wasn't as though Saffi hadn't considered it. But she wouldn't fit in with Andino and Taylor's new friends, whoever they were. It wouldn't be the same as the three of them getting utterly plastered on cheap whiskey for every occasion they could come up with. And she wouldn't be able to stop herself from comparing it.

Besides, she'd been dying to get the two of them out of the office so she could finally implement a half-decent filing system.

'Thank you,' Taylor said, breaking her from her thoughts. 'I appreciate it, really.'

'Don't get used to it,' she muttered.

Infuriatingly, Taylor's smile only grew brighter. 'So, what do you make of her?' He gestured at the space where the car had just been.

Saffi shrugged. 'I'm not you. I don't make anything of anyone.'

She liked to think she was similar to her father in that regard. Her job was to gather evidence and the law would take care of the rest. It always did. Inserting too much personal bias into the narrative would only end in disaster. And Saffi did not play losing games.

Saffi bristled at the look Taylor gave her. 'What?'

'Nothing, just . . . you're not usually that antagonistic. Not even with Atlas.'

'The hell is that supposed to mean?'

A thoughtful expression crossed Taylor's features. 'I can't tell yet whether you hate her or respect her, but it's clear she gets under your skin.'

He was already heading back inside before Saffi had the chance to be properly offended.

'You coming?' he asked over his shoulder. It was his birthday; she wasn't allowed to start an argument with him today and he knew it.

Saffi almost followed him, but when the shade hit her cheeks, robbing them of their warmth, she hesitated. A kaleidoscope of brown and gold. She stepped back into the sun.

'Maybe later,' she mumbled, wondering just how much antagonism it would take to know a woman who did nothing but lie.

20

May 13, 2026

Knowing that Saffi, Atlas, and Eli had known one another for several years was one thing, but to witness it was something else altogether.

Dimple found it was much easier to pinpoint Atlas and Eli's bond. It was apparent in the way they anticipated each other's needs, passing over documents without having to ask – without even having to look. There were several instances when Dimple had been certain the two of them were on a collision course, only for them to slide past unobstructed, a hand clapping over the other's shoulder in a quick greeting to confirm that, yes, they had known the other was there the entire time.

It was slightly more challenging, however, to pinpoint where Saffi came into the picture. At first, Dimple had attributed her years abroad to the apparent chasm between her and her coworkers. But then she'd witnessed Eli handing his phone over to Saffi, his parents on the other end of the line. And how eerily similar Saffi's and Atlas's thought processes were at times. There was also the mirroring: three pairs of legs crossed at the exact same time, three nods of approval for the price of one. A casual, almost frosty intimacy.

There was also the matter of the case. Dimple had poked and prodded, but nothing. It truly seemed that Atlas and Eli had no knowledge that Dimple herself was a suspect. Either that or they were far greater actors than even she. It almost felt like a personal affront that Saffi had been able to keep up with Dimple with one arm tied behind her back.

But if no one except Saffi knew of her guilt, then Dimple had nothing holding her back from killing her. When it was done and over with, she could mourn alongside an Atlas and Eli who were none the wiser. She'd wrongly assumed that Saffi wouldn't be as careless as her coworkers had been. It might've been disappointing if she hadn't been expecting it. Of course Saffi could only keep up with her for so long.

While Dimple didn't see much of Saffi when she was in the office, the men were fascinating company when it came down to it. Where trying to glean information from Saffi was a lot like interrogating a brick wall, they were much more malleable.

Eli kept her at arm's length, but he was at least kind and had something of substance to offer. Similar to acting, confidence was key in undercover work. He taught her how to orchestrate a situation to her liking – that causing a scene could sometimes work to divert attention from herself.

'If you need a reason to speak to someone, the easiest way is to bump into them,' he'd told her. 'Literally. Spill a drink or, better yet, make them spill a drink on you. It also works if you need a distraction.'

Dimple found herself using his advice in auditions as well. Treating every scene like the conductor of a symphony. She must've been doing something right, given she'd made it through several rounds already.

Atlas, however, was helpful in another way. He stammered through explanations of pressure points that could bring a man to his knees and methods to break out of holds, but Dimple liked him for the opportunity he begot.

It presented itself in the constant tripping over air in Dimple's presence. When she would try to help him clean up his messes, he'd implore her to stay put and that he didn't want her to get dirty. When she'd try to help him up, he'd refuse her hand and scramble to his feet with red ears. She'd never been treated so preciously.

Learning the dynamic at Andino and Taylor Private Eye and, more importantly, Dimple's place in it was a precarious thing. As little as she saw of her, Dimple knew Saffi was watching her like a hawk. As a precaution, she didn't dare try anything before now.

Eight weeks after being released from the hospital, the wrist brace finally came off. Dimple felt thankful for it as the weather grew steadily warmer. And just in time for the start of *Insomnia*'s promotional season.

Still buzzing from a magazine interview earlier that day, Dimple and Atlas walked side by side to the meeting room. It had become something almost like her office, given how much time she spent there. The hallway leading up to it wasn't a very long one, revealing four more offices whose occupants she'd determined, thanks to her constant presence. All except for the one at the end of the hall left their door open. That one could belong to no one but Saffi.

Atlas, realizing Dimple had fallen behind, turned to her in confusion. 'Something wrong?' he asked. 'Do you need a break? Water?'

Dimple laughed. 'I've only just arrived.'

Atlas's ears reddened. It was that easy.

'Actually, I was hoping for a change of scenery,' she suggested.

Atlas contemplated it. 'We could go to the break room?'

Dimple shook her head apologetically. 'The lights in there give me a migraine. Sorry, I don't mean to be difficult. Let's go to the meeting room as usual.' She took one step in that direction before Atlas cut her off.

'We could go to my office?' he suggested. 'I get plenty of natural light in there.'

Almost too easy.

Dimple let her eyes grow wide. 'Really? Are you sure that's all right?' When he nodded in confirmation, she beamed. 'That would be lovely, thank you.'

He was already walking away and Dimple hurried after his long strides. As she passed Eli's office, he gave her a small wave, which Dimple returned. It was a good thing Saffi couldn't see, though, because she'd certainly clock that Dimple was up to something.

Long after Dimple stepped into Atlas's office, he lingered awkwardly in the corner, as though afraid she would bite. She took the opportunity to look around, hands clasped innocently behind her back. It was the same layout as the others Dimple had caught brief glimpses of. Desk at the center, armchairs for guests, plastic potted plants in the empty corners. She wondered if Saffi's looked the same. Somehow, she doubted it.

She scanned bookshelves of textbooks, walls of diplomas and certifications, and countless photographs, senses alert for anything of relevance. Atlas seemed to thrive on organized chaos, with files and books scattered all over the place and memos stuck to the wall at random.

'Where is this from?' Dimple asked, fingertip tracing a picture of Atlas and Eli with a mountain range in the background.

'Colorado,' he said, clearing his throat.

The question seemed to cut through the tension and Atlas took a step closer. He launched into a story about how he'd sprained a ligament while skiing not long after the picture was taken. Dimple nodded like she was listening and tried not to think of the phantom twinge in her own wrist. Sometimes when she moved too quickly, she still froze in anticipation of pain that would never come.

With her back to him, Dimple ensured Atlas had no idea she couldn't care less for his photographs. Her eyes were glued to the notes he'd scribbled on his whiteboard. In between doodles of cacti and palm trees, she could make out *Insomnia*'s production schedule and names of people who'd worked on the film. Producers, writers, even extras. Several were crossed out.

So she *wasn't* the only suspect. Dimple made a mental note of every person on the list, vowing to look into them all when she went home later that day.

Her unofficial reconnaissance mission came to a staggering halt when Dimple spotted a familiar paper pinned to the corner of the board. Jagged edges, written on by a pen nearly out of ink. She plucked it from its place and held it up to the sunlight, her fingers tracing the familiar loops of the first and only autograph she'd ever been commissioned.

'You kept it,' she said.

'Of course,' Atlas replied, as though it were that simple. That was how everything seemed to be with him – simple.

'This was the first autograph I've ever given.'

When she turned to look at him, Atlas seemed taken aback. 'Really?'

'Is it so surprising?'

'Well, yeah. You're an amazing actress.'

Dimple twisted the words in her mind, attempting to make sense of them. 'What's your favorite movie of mine?' she asked eventually.

'*Horrorville 3*,' he said without missing a beat. 'You deserve an Oscar for that performance, and I'm not just saying that.'

Dimple found herself at a loss for words. He couldn't be serious. Not even she could watch that movie without breaking into hives. It was a disgrace to cinema. Dimple didn't even like to say the title out loud for fear of inviting demons into her home.

But Atlas's expression was open and earnest. There were no signs of jest or malintent. Dimple felt incredibly powerful, as though being viewed through a camera lens.

'You truly believe that?'

'It's one of my favorite movies of all time. The terrible script and cinematography only made your performance more impressive. I could tell the other actors had given up, but not you. I don't think I've ever seen anyone deliver lines like that.' Atlas spoke so quickly, many of his sentences sounded like one word. He was breathless by the end. And then he kept going. 'My mom and I are the only ones in my family who like old Hollywood films. We used to watch them all the time when I was younger, before my parents divorced. I don't know what it is, but your acting reminds me of that.'

Dimple let out a shaky breath to collect herself. She'd liked to imagine she would've been the same, had she gotten the chance to meet her mother. They'd had the same taste in films as well.

And apparently, so did Atlas. No one else had noticed the effort Dimple had put into that role. Hours after set arguing with the director, with the writers, running lines with other actors in the hopes that it would somehow counteract everything else she couldn't control. She'd been determined to prove Julie – and the other actors, *everyone* – wrong. That one good performance could save a production. But in the end, the joke had been on her.

'Thank you,' she said, and she meant it.

He seemed to want to say something more, but Dimple wasn't sure she'd be able to handle it. It wasn't right to face such sincerity with the mask she'd donned. She shattered the moment, turning away and pinning the autograph back to the board.

Atlas could monitor Dimple more closely as she moved to his desk, so she carefully regulated her expression to one of neutrality.

There was a photo frame. A sister, a brother, and two parents standing on opposite ends. They all had the same thick eyebrows Atlas did. Taped to his computer were more photos: a white coat ceremony for his sister, another where his brother wore a Harvard Law stole. But, curiously, none of his own graduation. Moreover, he seemed extremely young compared to his siblings. Somewhat detached from the group, even amongst family.

Dimple looked down at the photo frame again. There was another picture tucked behind the same glass. Younger versions of Atlas, Eli, and Saffi. The three of them were sitting on the floor, seemingly unaware of the camera as they sifted through papers. Eli had an arm resting on Saffi's shoulder as he read the document she was holding. Atlas was leaning so close, all three of their foreheads were brushing. If Dimple hadn't known any better, she would've thought this was the family photo. She abruptly looked away. This wasn't what she was here for.

Dimple scanned the documents scattered atop the dark wood. Someone's criminal records, but she couldn't tell who was listed as the perpetrator. Dimple's history was clean, so it couldn't be her. She moved suddenly, reaching for something invisible and making a show of accidentally bumping into the mouse.

The computer screen lit up with a profile. She didn't have the time to read the name before Atlas's wide frame blocked her view of it, but she would recognize that face anywhere.

Hector Olsen.

A man difficult to forget. He'd approached her for work once in the past. On first impression, it had been beyond exciting. Back then, Dimple had neither an agent nor a manager. In fact, she had yet to land a speaking role. Yet somehow Hector had seen her in a commercial and come out personally to ask her to play the lead in a movie he was directing.

Even at twenty-one years old, Dimple hadn't been that naïve. She couldn't afford to be. There were too many questions he couldn't answer – why he wanted her or what he expected in return. She knew what predators looked like and Hector Olsen was nothing if not one. And Dimple had long since declared she would never be prey again.

She'd been careful, but not careful enough. She'd thought she had to entertain anyone in the business that was interested in her, even if she wasn't in return. She didn't think to be wary when Hector far too easily accepted the fact that she didn't drink. Or when he introduced the bartender as an old friend of his. Not even when the liquid in her glass started to leave behind a strange aftertaste.

Dimple's head was spinning. Her senses heightened, overwhelming her: the uncomfortable wooden bar seats, the patrons she'd immediately noticed to be of the older male crowd, the sticky floors.

Hector Olsen's grating laugh. *Having fun? I knew you'd change your mind once you got a taste of it.* It took her that long – him quite literally confessing what he'd done – for her to realize how much of an idiot she'd been. The sickly sweet smell of the bright pink drink he'd promised was a mocktail turned her stomach.

'Thirsty?'

Dimple flinched violently, her arm swinging up to knock the glass away. The space in front of her flickered as soon as she made contact. It was not a cocktail glass. Just water from the carafe Andino kept in his office.

'I am so –' she began, flustered.

'Don't worry about it.' Andino laughed. He'd managed to catch the glass at the last moment so only a bit of water had spilled onto the floor, which he quickly cleaned up. The back of Dimple's hand still throbbed where she'd smacked against it. 'You just looked a little pale, I didn't mean to startle you.'

Dimple was horrified. She was no stranger to her nightmares bleeding into reality, but Hector Olsen hadn't bothered her in years. As soon as she'd realized what had happened, Dimple had stumbled away to the bathroom, emptied the contents of her stomach, and pretended to sip on her drink for the rest of the night. She was careful not to make a bad enough impression that he'd blackball her and not a good enough impression to make him want her. Of all the villains in her story, Hector was nothing more than a speedbump.

'Shall we get started?' Atlas asked.

He didn't seem to suspect anything was amiss, so Dimple took that for the opportunity it was. She nodded and sat down in the armchair opposite his desk.

'So, last time we talked about headlocks . . .' Atlas paced in front of her. It sometimes seemed that he had too much energy for even his large frame to contain.

But Dimple was somewhere else entirely.

All of Hector Olsen's wives, all young brown women, were actresses who'd once worked under him. And years later, the allegations had come out, just as Dimple had suspected they would. Forget the list on Andino's whiteboard, nobody made more sense as a suspect in Irene's case than Hector Olsen. Not even Dimple herself.

Years of misconduct and the man walked free. And now the opportunity to put him behind bars had landed so perfectly in Dimple's lap. Was it not her duty to see it through?

Perhaps with this, she could bring peace to all the women who'd been hurt by him.

Hairs rising on the back of her neck, Dimple whipped around. The movement was so sudden that it startled even Atlas. But there, peeking in through the ajar door, was one of the interns. The girl – Mia, if Dimple remembered correctly. How long had she been standing there? She looked terrified. Dimple forced a pleasant smile, but it did nothing to soothe the girl. And then it hit her.

Mia knew.

So this was Saffi's plan. She hadn't confided in Atlas and Eli, choosing a girl barely out of her teens to bear that burden instead. Dimple's heart pounded. She'd been careless to assume that Saffi didn't have measures in place in the event of her death. Of course it wouldn't be that easy.

And to think she'd almost walked right into her trap.

'Sorry,' the girl stammered before disappearing down the hallway.

Head spinning, Dimple found herself fascinated. How had Saffi managed to plan so far ahead right under Atlas and Eli's noses? Although, she wouldn't be surprised if their involvement would only slow Saffi down. It was much simpler working with someone naïve and eager to please.

Atlas huffed out a laugh. 'That would be Mia. She's also a fan.'

What a performance of dramatic irony played out for Dimple's viewing pleasure. It felt like an oil painting brought to life. It felt like a gift.

As he returned to coaching her through the most effective way to knee a man in the gut, Dimple's mind wandered to burning buildings and blood-spattered staircases. She felt the familiar weight of a lighter in her pocket. The fate of a cruel man's life rested gingerly in the center of her palm.

21

May 28, 2026

The end of May marked four months in America, four months of taking up residence in her office at Andino and Taylor Private Eye, and Saffi had no choice but to face the glaring issue that was her family. She hadn't expected Dimple Kapoor to run circles around her to this extent. This was the longest she'd stayed in one place in five years, not that she missed constantly moving from hotel to hotel as the job called for. If she didn't contact her family soon, they'd begin to worry. The rational thing to do would be to make the call and explain everything. So, Saffi picked up the phone – and called in a favor from a contact in France. Her parents would get a postcard from Paris in the upcoming week and hopefully that would buy her enough time to solve this case and get the hell out of America again.

Just like that, a favor wasted. And on a fifty-cent piece of paper, no less.

Her whole life she'd been working to make her parents proud. She'd come so close five years ago, only for one mistake to ruin it all. And now she never would.

For all her research, Saffi had found nothing.

Nothing not in the sense that Dimple Kapoor lived a very boring, dull life from birth until now, but *nothing* in the sense that Dimple Kapoor didn't even seem to exist prior to her college enrollment. Of the dozens of photos and articles of her online, all of them were recent. Every time Saffi thought she was nearing a conclusion, something like this would happen to remind her that Kapoor was anything but predictable.

It didn't matter how many *Dimple*s, *Kapoor*s, and *Dimple Kapoor*s Saffi had looked into, there was no passport, no driver's license, not so much as a yearbook photo before eight years ago. But that had to be impossible. There was no way Kapoor would've been allowed to enroll in college without a proper background check and a high school transcript. Or at least her GED. Regardless, Saffi couldn't find any trace of her.

Until now.

It took meandering through the online archives of every California valedictorian the same year Kapoor would've graduated high school to finally find her. A much younger, much more timid version of Dimple Kapoor.

Her name, though, was Anya.

Saffi had been pouring herself a celebratory drink when Dimple Kapoor herself waltzed into her office. It was the first time the actress had actively sought out her company, so it left her suspicious.

Saffi moved to unroll her sleeves and put her jacket back on, but Kapoor was quicker. 'Leave it,' she said.

Struck by the unexpected nature of the request, Saffi froze, inadvertently obeying.

Kapoor's attention dropped to the whiskey. 'I don't believe I've ever seen you willingly take a break before.'

'I could say the same about you.'

With her came a strange scent that Saffi couldn't place. There was the sweet honey that seemed to follow Kapoor everywhere she went, but this time there were notes of burnt plastic.

And then there was the exposed skin of Kapoor's wrist. Saffi remembered the scratchy feel of the brace and wondered what the skin felt like underneath. Would she feel Kapoor's pulse thrumming with the beat of every lie? Saffi reached out on impulse, but her mind warned her to go slow. Her grip on Kapoor's wrist was loose and while she tensed, she didn't pull away. Saffi's thumb swiped across smooth, unmarred skin. Kapoor must've been made of fire because every point of contact burned.

'You got the brace removed,' Saffi said. Her voice sounded far away.

What was she doing?

Saffi dropped her wrist, but too late. It was as though she'd become drunk by the act of pouring alcohol alone. She half expected there to be a mark left behind when she looked down at her palm. There was nothing but a burning sensation. Curling her hand into a fist, Saffi tried to remind herself why, exactly, playing with fire was so dangerous.

'You'd know that if you visited me at all. I'm beginning to think you're avoiding me.' Kapoor was pouting, an overdramatized version of it. If anything, Saffi had been letting her stew, but that didn't mean she hadn't been keeping watch over her.

It was then that Saffi was drawn to the white bandage wrapped around her forearm. 'What's that?'

Kapoor turned away. Saffi wanted to reach out again and pull the arm free to study, but she didn't. Just to prove she hadn't completely lost it. Instead of slipping into the armchair, Kapoor sat directly on Saffi's desk, giving a clear view of her thigh as her dress rode up.

The next time their gazes met, Kapoor seemed amused. She was too observant. That was supposed to be Saffi's job. 'Are you going to inquire about all my injuries? Should I tell you about the papercut I got this morning?'

It was strange but not entirely out of character for the ever-secretive, ever-elusive Dimple Kapoor. Saffi filed the information away for later and lifted her glass of whiskey. She hadn't touched the stuff since she'd arrived in California despite how much Andino and Taylor begged her to go out with them, so this was long overdue.

Glass pressing against her lips, Saffi made inadvertent eye contact with Kapoor as she began to tip it back. The actress was staring at her, tracking every move. She would've appeared perfectly at ease, her shoulders relaxed and posture comfortable, had it not been for the slight tick in her jaw.

Saffi thought about what she'd read regarding Anya Kapoor and paused. Dropping the untouched glass to her lap, she traced the rim consideringly.

'Were your aunt and uncle alcoholics?' It hadn't been officially stated in the reports, but it would make a lot of sense.

The way Kapoor momentarily stilled was confirmation enough, even if it was gone in the next second. Her pleasant expression hadn't budged. It was terrifying how good an actress she was. Except Kapoor's magnum opus wasn't any of the work she'd done on-screen – it was the performance of her life.

'I don't know what you mean,' Kapoor said.

'You don't have to lie about everything,' Saffi replied dryly.

'I don't.' *Lie.*

'Getting me drunk won't make it any easier to kill me.' Saffi attempted to joke, but it fell flat.

'I would never harm you.' *Lie, again.* 'You fascinate me too much.'

'Well, it wouldn't be smart. We are in a PI agency.'

'There's also the factor of me not being a killer.'

'I wonder if you'll be saying the same thing when I catch you red-handed.' Saffi dropped the whiskey straight into the plastic bin beside her desk, glass and all. Some of it splashed onto the floor. Kapoor watched, at first in disbelief, and then, slowly, her mouth twisted into something wild and dangerous. Something pleased. And despite herself, Saffi felt a sense of accomplishment.

'You look especially smug lately,' Saffi said. 'Find something you were looking for? Should I be concerned?'

She was curious to test just how good of a liar Dimple Kapoor was. Thanks to Martinez, she already knew that Kapoor had figured out who the other suspects in this case were. And soon, the actress would be making her next move. Saffi was prepared.

'Of course not.' Kapoor waved off her concerns. 'You seem to be in a rather celebratory mood, though. Should *I* be concerned?'

Denial, deflection, and redirection. Impressive work. Saffi couldn't have done it better herself. Was this something Kapoor had practiced like her acting or did it come as naturally as breathing?

Saffi would bite – for now, at least. Let Kapoor think she had the upper hand.

'Of course not,' Saffi echoed. 'Kitchen fires are pretty common, after all. Not particularly unbelievable when it comes to careless drunkards like your aunt and uncle.'

Kapoor didn't so much as flinch. She did, however, pull something free from the folds of her dress – a lighter – and held it loosely in her right hand. 'I suppose so,' she said, flicking the flame to life. Saffi couldn't help it, she laughed. Even backed into a corner, Kapoor never failed to surprise her.

'Lucky Anya was at school when it happened,' Saffi said.

'One of the few times luck favored her, I'm afraid.'

Kapoor was transfixed with the flame. Orange danced in her irises, melting the dark brown into a molten gold. For a moment, there was the irrational fear that the fire would consume her, but then Kapoor blinked out of her trance and the flame died out.

'What did they do to you?' Saffi asked. *What made you want to kill them?*

'It will not help you with your case.'

Regardless, Saffi wanted to know. If she understood Kapoor better, maybe then she could finally file her away into the appropriate box and move on. 'Tell me anyway.'

'It makes no difference. They're gone.'

'You're not.'

The words seemed to surprise Kapoor. Neither of them spoke for a moment, the newscaster's voice indistinct in the background.

'Tell me why you hate California so much,' Kapoor said.

Now it was Saffi's turn to go still. Again with the surprises. It was clear Kapoor hadn't been expecting an answer because she made to stand, but Saffi spoke first.

'It's not California. It's America,' she said distantly. It was a fair exchange, trading one stalemate for another. She opened her mouth, intending to continue, but the words were stuck in her throat. It was then that she realized she'd never actually told this story out loud before.

Kapoor's eyes held nothing but utter and complete understanding. Of course. If there was anyone who could empathize, it would be her. If she were even capable of empathy, that was.

'Not today,' Kapoor said.

'Not today,' Saffi agreed, and tried not to let the relief show in her face.

Her line of work had taught her that not everyone deserved to be mourned. Sometimes, those people just so happened to be responsible for children. Maybe Kapoor's guardians were like that. Or maybe they were just an excuse. Maybe Kapoor had always been as fucked-up as she was now.

'I never would've taken you for an *Anya*,' Saffi muttered.

'Don't think you can start calling me that now.' It was a clear warning.

'Wasn't planning on it, Kapoor.'

'Well, don't call me that either,' Kapoor said thoughtfully. 'I think we're well past first-name basis by now, are we not?'

Saffi almost protested before she noticed the mirth in Kapoor's – in *Dimple's* expression. As though they were both in on the same joke. It left her restless. Her hands itched to do something other than sit here so placidly. Saffi tugged open several desk drawers, digging through them.

'Looking for something?'

'I know I have one somewhere – here.' She lifted a single wax candle from her bottommost drawer.

The *emergency drawer*, as Eli liked to call it. Inside were matches, a first-aid kit, a flashlight, and the like. Saffi held the sad, beige thing to Dimple, who accepted it with visible confusion.

'What's this for?'

'Happy Birthday,' Saffi said.

She only knew three birthdays off the top of her head: Andino's, Taylor's, and her own. Now, inadvertently, she would be adding Dimple Kapoor's to the mix. May twenty-eighth. That she'd found Anya Kapoor's birth certificate on her birthday itself felt like a cosmic coincidence – if Saffi were inclined to believe in such things.

Dimple seemed at a loss for words. She stared down at the candle as though it was the world's most confounding puzzle. Saffi felt a little ridiculous now, watching her flounder.

'Go on, light it. I know you want to, you damn pyro.'

For whatever reason, Dimple played along. She lit the

candle and closed her eyes, as though making a wish, before blowing it out.

The corners of Saffi's mouth tugged upward. 'What did you wish for?'

Dimple gave her a sly look. 'I can't tell you or it won't come true.'

Saffi had been about to retort when something on the TV caught her attention. It shouldn't have registered in her preoccupied mind, but some subconscious part of her must've been paying attention – and it was a good thing she was. The reporter said a familiar name and Saffi stood abruptly, increasing the volume.

'– warrant out for the arrest of the lead in the upcoming film *Insomnia.* Law enforcement is seeking –'

Saffi inhaled sharply. Dimple shot to her feet in her peripheral.

Impossible. No one had ever solved a case faster than her. Nobody was faster than her, period. No matter rain or shine, weekday or holiday, if Saffi wasn't awake before the sun, then she'd already fallen behind. Her father had always said that the sleeping hours were the ones most often wasted. First, she'd slept through the news of Dimple's fall and now this. Clearly, he'd been right.

Saffi turned to Dimple and was transported back to when they first met at the hospital. Her face was just as ashen as it had been then. Except this time, there were no flowers attempting to breathe life back into her. Just a dull candle and a red lighter cradled in her palms.

22

May 29, 2026

The news anchor's mouth moved rapidly, but Dimple heard only static. A picture of *Insomnia*'s cast was displayed beside the reporter's head. The one they'd taken at the wrap party. She could still feel the heat of Chris Porter's arm around her shoulders like the press of an iron. Nobody had ever picked up on her discomfort before. Nobody except for Saffi.

Saffi, who was attempting to speak to her.

'– do anything stupid. It'll be better for both of us if you remain calm,' she said. Even now she sounded matter-of-fact.

It was odd, seeing herself on television in this context. When she was a child, she'd never imagined that being on-screen could instill anything but pride in a person. She'd always told herself that if she made it, she'd have to completely reinvent herself first. That she'd be remembered as the best possible version of herself for all of time. The only role models she'd had were the actors on her black-and-white VHS tapes. But now, as Dimple watched the full-color photograph of the *Insomnia* cast displayed on the big screen, she could only see that scared little girl. Could Saffi see her as well? Was that how she'd uncovered so much of Dimple's past?

Dimple had never sunk this low before. To be caught now when she hadn't been as a child was beyond insulting. She worked through every step she'd taken before this point, wracking her memory for mistakes. Had she not deleted all of Isaac Klossner's evidence? Had she left behind some traceable piece of her – a drop of blood or an eyelash?

'– We have an update!' the reporter suddenly exclaimed. Both she and Saffi snapped to attention. 'Police have finally caught up to him – Chris Porter is now in custody. Fans are in an absolute uproar –'

Chris Porter.

Chris Porter, as in her co-lead Chris Porter.

She felt her whole world spinning, much like it did the one and only time she'd gotten drunk, and that was nearly enough to send her into another panic. The television screen flashed black for a split second before going to a commercial break, but it was enough time for Dimple to catch a glimpse of herself. Her curls coming undone, her lipstick smudged. She wiped the excess from the corner of her mouth, looking down at the red stain across her hand.

Saffi read out loud from her computer, 'Chris Porter has been charged with gross vehicular manslaughter while intoxicated after a party last weekend.'

Distantly, she marveled at the odds that both *Insomnia* leads were killers themselves. She'd never liked him and liked even less that production had leaned into the dating rumors circulating since principal photography – but to think he was a killer. As the relief began to dissipate, anxiety took over. Would all this scrutiny on him put a spotlight on her as well? Ever since the casting announcement, Dimple and Chris's names had always been mentioned in conjunction with each other. Julie had claimed that it would boost her popularity. If only Dimple could see her expression now.

A wordless understanding passed between them over Saffi's desk. It should have – and would have – been terrifying if Dimple had been in any other state of mind, but as of now she only felt resigned. Her reaction to the news had given her away, there was no getting around that. Not only had Saffi seen her reaction, she now knew Dimple's history as well. She wondered how vulnerable she must look to Saffi in this state – even more so than when she'd laid broken atop a hospital bed. Most people would be smug. Saffi seemed angry.

Dimple's hands were freezing when she set the candle down. As she crossed to the other side of the desk, reading the article over Saffi's shoulder, the door to the office burst open and Atlas and Eli erupted inside. Saffi stepped in front of Dimple, half obscuring her from view.

How would Saffi have reacted had Dimple really been the one on the news? Now Dimple was almost certain she'd imagined her anger. Because why would she be anything but glad to see her behind bars? Wasn't that the point of this all?

As soon as the thought crossed her mind, she knew it to be false. The point of this, whatever performance they were putting on, couldn't be so simple.

'Good, you already know,' Eli said, looking up at the news. 'They've got him in custody.'

'Don't bother looking into it,' Atlas added. 'Chris Porter has alibis for both parties; I had the interns check weeks ago.'

'He's done,' Dimple said softly. 'His career's over.'

A whole childhood's worth of work culminating in nothing. If Saffi had it her way, it would be Dimple in his shoes. The thought left her lightheaded. But then again, when Dimple looked up, it was Saffi's broad shoulders that were shielding her from the rest of the world.

At the sound of her voice, the men paused, craning to find Dimple over Saffi's shoulder. Atlas's face did a strange thing where it turned white, then red, and then almost purple. Eli's jaw dropped.

'Dimple – I'm so sorry. I didn't realize you were still here,' Eli said.

'I can leave?' she offered, but Eli shook his head.

'No, stay. I can't imagine how shaken up you must be.'

Saffi rolled her eyes and shifted so Dimple was in full view. 'She's not the one who got arrested, she's fine.'

'Would it kill you to not be a complete bitch all the time?' Atlas snapped.

Dimple blinked in surprise.

'It might,' Saffi replied. 'I've never tried.'

'She's a guest here, treat her with some respect.'

Saffi scoffed. 'Just because you're one of her fanboys doesn't mean you have to be her white knight too.'

Atlas tensed, face flushing in what seemed to be a combination of embarrassment and righteous fury. 'That's rich, coming from you. You don't care about anyone but yourself.'

Sensing motion, Dimple turned to catch the interns – who'd been watching from the open doorway – being herded away by Eli. It was almost adorable until Saffi and Atlas exchanged another round of loud, scathing retorts.

This was nothing at all like the closeness in the photograph Dimple had seen on Atlas's desk. Perhaps she hadn't been completely off when she'd assumed that Saffi's years away had put a strain on their relationship.

The wax candle stared at Dimple from Saffi's desk. The flame hadn't extended past the wick and yet warmth had spread across both of her palms. She missed it now as she hugged her arms tighter around herself, remembering Saffi's expression as she'd said *Happy Birthday*.

Dimple found that she rather liked the way Saffi looked at her. It was nothing like the way Atlas looked at her – not like she was the sun. Nor in the way Eli did, a mix of polite intrigue and professionalism. While the rest of the world looked at Dimple through a camera lens, Saffi was the only one who felt present. Her scene partner.

There was a beautiful shot in *Insomnia* of a campfire reflecting in Dimple's eyes that she hoped made it into the movie. Her teeth had been chattering as she warmed herself up beside it. That was what it felt like. Saffi looked at Dimple like she was that raging fire and Saffi was frozen to the bone.

'Go, run away again,' Atlas was shouting. 'At least then you can't fuck up any more investigations!'

'Fuck you,' Saffi spat.

Saffi crossed the room in a few angry steps, slamming the door shut behind her. But Dimple recognized the expression on her face the same as she did the one in her mirror. A chord struck. It became clear exactly what this performance was. Where it was all culminating. Two women weighed down by their past. One who'd faced it head-on and the other who'd run. Like this, neither of them would be free.

'Is everything all right?' Dimple asked, startled to find that it wasn't all that difficult to inject concern into her tone.

Atlas ran an angry hand through gelled hair. Now that Saffi was gone, he seemed to realize how out of hand their argument had gotten, judging by the way he refused to face Dimple. 'Sorry,' he mumbled.

It was unclear if that was aimed at Dimple or the absent Saffi. And it was too late to ask before he too was leaving the room, right as Eli was returning. Atlas couldn't seem to look at him either.

'Is it really all right to let them argue like that?' Dimple wondered aloud once she and Eli were left alone. She couldn't imagine forgiving someone who'd spoken to her the same way Atlas had just done to Saffi.

'Sorry you had to see that. I didn't mean to abandon you with them, but the interns are too nosy for their own good,' Eli replied tiredly. 'Saffi and Atlas are harmless anyway. I let them fight it out because that's the only thing that works. By tomorrow it'll be as though nothing happened.'

Nor would the root issue be solved. Eli shot her another apologetic look before hurrying after his friends. Part of her wanted to follow, curious to see whether he'd speak to Atlas or Saffi first, but that would be inappropriate. And Dimple couldn't risk not being invited back. Not when the show was just beginning.

Good thing she was perfectly capable of piecing things together on her own.

23

June 15, 2026

It seemed Dimple Kapoor was making a habit of letting herself into Saffi's office. She sat on the desk, same as before, but Saffi refused to give her the satisfaction of her attention. Instead, she continued to pace as she studied Dimple in her peripheral.

The actress always sat so properly, her shoulders squared and chin tilted up. Had she always been that way? Saffi imagined a small child holding her head up high as the weight of the world bore down on her. Discomfort pricked at her skin like ants until she banished the thought.

Saffi worried how much Dimple had figured out from the fight with Andino. It had been eating at her far more than the fallout of the fight itself, which had been inconsequential. Andino had apologized for calling Saffi a *bitch* – either Taylor's doing or of his own volition, she still wasn't sure – and things were more or less back to normal.

For the rest of the agency, at least. An unnerving hush blanketed her office now. The news was still playing at a soft volume in the corner and Saffi watched Dimple's attention draw up toward the TV. This scene was too familiar, almost eerily so.

'Can I help you with something?' Saffi asked, unable to take it any longer.

Taylor had informed her that Dimple's training was nearly complete, but Saffi still wondered how she had the time to come bother her alongside the auditions, interviews, and nefarious schemes she was surely busy with. With her brace removed and the skills she now had to safely go undercover, it was only a matter of time before their stalemate would come to an end. Dimple clearly had a plan, but so did Saffi. It would come down to who was better prepared.

'Sit down,' Dimple said, strangely gentle.

It infuriated Saffi enough to keep her standing, arms crossed, but the way Dimple laughed made her regret it.

'Even now, you always have one foot out the door,' she said.

Saffi was sitting before she'd even realized what had happened, hands fisted, nails digging crescents into her palm. The gall of this woman. She didn't know the first thing about Saffi.

'Do you always argue with Atlas?' Dimple asked, leaning closer. She was either oblivious to or uncaring of Saffi's anger.

This was somewhat expected, but the question still sent another spike of anxiety through Saffi's veins. Anxiety and defensiveness. But she would never let that show. Dimple was clearly practiced in using people's emotions against them. So she allowed a manufactured calm to settle over her features. One that her father had helped her perfect. He'd always said that Saffi's turbulent emotions would be her downfall.

'We've known each other for years,' she explained. 'It's what we would call our normal.'

'That is far from normal.'

Saffi narrowed her eyebrows. 'I don't see how that's any of your concern.'

'It isn't.' Dimple shrugged, immediately letting it go.

That was a little too easy. Now Saffi was curious where she'd been planning on going with that.

She sighed, rubbing a tired hand over her face. 'Andino knows how to irritate me better than anyone.' She almost said *He knows how to hurt me,* but that was something she would never admit. 'And I'm not much better. It's almost like a game at this point.'

'Does it ever affect your work?' Dimple asked. It seemed to be a genuine question, but it was nearly impossible to tell when the actress was hiding something. Luckily, Saffi had learned to read between the lines.

'You'd like that, wouldn't you? Unfortunately for you, I know what I'm doing. I'll catch this killer.' *I'll catch you* went unsaid.

Dimple didn't respond right away to her challenge. She seemed to be gathering her thoughts, gearing up for something big. Saffi got the feeling she was about to find out the real reason Dimple had decided to interrupt her evening. And it wasn't to gossip about her coworkers.

'If you were to catch this person,' Dimple asked slowly, 'what would happen to them?'

That was all it took to send ice through Saffi's veins. This line of questioning couldn't be a coincidence. Dimple knew, or at least had an idea, of what she had worked so hard to hide.

'Death row,' Saffi replied, voice even.

Dimple laughed humorlessly. 'Catching a killer only to kill them. How hypocritical.'

'There's a moratorium,' Saffi tried, but her resolve was beginning to crumble. 'Nobody's been executed in California since 2006. They're trying to get rid of it altogether.'

'So you don't believe in the death penalty,' Dimple said thoughtfully. 'Somehow, that's even more hypocritical.'

'What do you expect me to do?' Saffi snapped. 'I can't exactly go up to a killer and ask them to kindly kill somewhere else, preferably a place where the death penalty doesn't exist.'

Dimple's eyes glinted with understanding and Saffi grimaced, knowing she'd played right into her hands.

'Where did you live for the five years you were abroad?'

Saffi scowled. 'Don't act like you don't already know.'

'I can guess.' Dimple hummed. 'France? Norway? Hong Kong? Portugal? Anywhere without the death penalty. Am I right?'

Saffi didn't respond, which Dimple took as her answer. 'I figured it out, don't I get a reward?'

Saffi leveled Dimple with a glare. She wasn't sure if she was more humiliated or pissed off that Dimple was making such a mockery of the very thing that haunted her every waking moment.

'Oh, don't look at me like that, I'm only joking,' Dimple said. 'Why move so far away, though? There are many states that have abolished it altogether.'

There was no use denying it any longer, but Saffi couldn't help the sheer stubbornness that overpowered her, keeping her mouth shut.

That only seemed to intrigue Dimple further. 'I could guess, but I've seen how angry that makes you.'

Saffi's hands were shaking, so she crossed her arms, pressing them close to her chest.

'You needed a fresh start, I suppose that's reasonable,' Dimple said, as though she'd plucked the words right out of Saffi's mind.

How did she do that?

'It makes sense. After all, you did kill someone,' Dimple said and Saffi's shoulders stiffened. 'You were naïve. You thought you could handle it, but you were in over your head.'

'That's not true,' Saffi said. 'That case was assigned to me – I never asked for this.'

'But you wanted it, didn't you? You wanted to prove

yourself, so you cut some corners. And you might've closed the case faster than anyone else, but that just meant the wrong person got put on death row.'

'I didn't cut any corners,' Saffi snapped. 'The evidence I gathered was enough to convince an entire jury. It's not my fault the investigator in charge was such a lazy sack of shit, he wanted to take credit for a rookie's work without even fact-checking it!'

She was breathing heavily now. The outburst was supposed to wipe the smirk off Dimple's face, to show her just how subpar her investigative skills were, but the smug look on her face was not promising. Saffi's heartbeat stuttered in her chest, kicking into overdrive.

'So if you understand that none of it was your fault, then why do you keep punishing yourself for it?' Dimple asked.

She'd done this on purpose. Gotten the details wrong to infuriate Saffi into defending herself. Her father had been right – her emotions had gotten the better of her yet again.

With a sigh, Saffi pushed loose strands of hair away from her face. All of a sudden, she was too tired to feel anything but the buzz beneath her skin. The main reason she kept her past hidden was for fear of how others might view her. It was different with Dimple, though. Saffi was more worried about how she might use the information against her, which was futile since she clearly already knew most of it.

More than that, Dimple was *asking*. Not even Andino and Taylor had cared to hear her version of the events. Saffi had always wished she could explain this to someone who'd understand or could give her a valuable perspective like her father. By some strange twist of fate, maybe Dimple could be that person.

'I did kill someone,' Saffi said. The words came out like

sandpaper, but Dimple didn't so much as blink. 'An innocent woman. A mother.'

Saffi's arguments with Andino had reached a breaking point around that time. They were both so competitive and eager to please – to be seen as equals in the judgment of the senior investigators. Only Taylor had been smart enough to realize that it would never happen. Saffi had no doubt that leaving the agency behind to start their own had been his idea.

'Due to the nature of the crime, and the fact that the victims' families had more than enough money and resources to throw around, her execution had been expedited. It wasn't until months later, after she'd already been killed, that I looked into it again and realized how wrong I was,' Saffi continued. She could still remember the way her stomach had dropped. 'I went to my supervisor with the new information, but he forbade me from telling anyone. He'd taken all the credit for the case, so he would get all the backlash too. I couldn't live with myself, though, so I reported the miscarriage of justice and, like a coward, I ran. Stronghold suffered a major hit to its reputation and shut down. I was never supposed to come back.'

Dimple hummed. 'You had the wrong suspect, but Atlas and Eli – their theory ended up being right?'

'And Andino's never let me live it down.' Not that she needed the reminder. 'Don't be fooled, though. It was our first murder investigation and none of us had any idea what we were doing. I've spent the last five years learning everything I could so I'd never make the same mistake again.'

'Is that why you work so much, then?' Dimple asked thoughtfully. 'Because you're trying to make up for what happened?'

Saffi could've laughed. 'No. There's nothing I can do to

change the past. An innocent woman lost her life because of me – a child lost a mother. I can't reverse that.'

Saffi's father was possibly the only person in the world capable of giving her the answers she needed. How to repent, how to move on. When it came to crime and punishment, he always had a solution.

'Why, then?' Dimple asked.

Saffi didn't have an answer. Maybe at some point in her life, she'd had one, but it had been gradually leached from her since the day she started running.

'I see,' Dimple said.

Saffi's first instinct was to retaliate. There was no way in hell she understood. But then again, of everyone, maybe Dimple Kapoor was the only person who could.

'You don't think I'm a wicked murderer?' she deadpanned.

'No, you definitely are,' Dimple said, amused. 'But I think I like you anyway.'

Her words were cruel and inappropriate and should not have sent a flutter through Saffi's chest. The irony of it was laughable.

The corners of Saffi's mouth quirked despite her efforts to suppress it. 'What does that make you, then, I wonder.'

Saffi felt herself moving before she realized Dimple had hooked a leg under her chair, wheeling her closer. Her body cast a menacing shadow from above. It felt counterintuitive. This close, Saffi could hear the way Dimple's breath hitched with every lie. She could see the way her pupils dilated, maybe even feel the way her heartbeat picked up in speed. But maybe that was the point. Maybe this was not the time for lies.

'Tell me, Saffi,' Dimple began, 'how does one win in a world that favors the cruel?'

Saffi paused, taken aback. Not necessarily because of the

nature of the question, but because it was something that she'd asked herself several times. It was impossible not to, given her line of work.

'You have to play by their rules,' she found herself saying. 'And you have to be better at it than anyone else. Otherwise, don't bother playing at all.'

'Is that why you allow Atlas and Eli to weigh you down?' Dimple asked. 'Because you're *playing by their rules*?'

Saffi blanched. 'What?'

'Even your words aren't your own. You didn't run because you're a coward like you allow everyone to believe. And perhaps you're starting to believe it yourself. But really, you left to preserve your father's reputation,' Dimple said. 'Let me guess: No matter what you do, it never seems to be enough, does it? Not for your family, not for Atlas and Eli, not even for yourself.'

Her words felt like a blow. Was she really so easy to read? Or was Dimple Kapoor just that intuitive? Part of her felt that same, age-old instinct to flee. To give up on this investigation that was unraveling her and go back to Hong Kong or Paris. But she would never win that way against Dimple Kapoor. And oh how Saffi hated to lose.

'Being around Atlas and Eli only serves to remind you of your greatest mistake,' Dimple said. 'Haven't you seen how much more you can accomplish on your own? Because they certainly have. And it makes them feel incompetent. That's why they're always trying to tear you down.'

Saffi was at a loss for words. Dimple's expression, however, was bright. Saffi was a stranger to such a show of earnestness.

'You're reading way too much into this,' she said, but her words sounded uncertain even to herself.

And just like that, the moment was broken. Dimple leaned

away, the usual pleasant mask taking over her features. 'Perhaps. But do not presume to know what it is to take a life.'

That much was true. Saffi had never experienced the desperate state someone like Dimple would have to fall into to kill someone. What was it like, to watch the life drain from someone's body? To be the last thing they ever saw? An ice-cold chill shot down Saffi's spine. She wished she could go back in time and force herself to keep her mouth shut, to talk about anything else, to have never allowed Dimple to carve a space for herself at all.

But at least she had no right to judge Saffi.

'My childhood punishments weren't as simple as being put in a corner.'

Saffi's head snapped up at Dimple's words and she frowned in confusion, but Dimple's gaze was trained on her own feet. It took Saffi a moment to work out that she was meeting Saffi's vulnerability with some of her own. That *not today* was now.

'They'd always threatened to throw me off the balcony,' she continued. 'I don't know why I never thought they'd actually go through with it.'

Saffi's blood ran cold.

'The hitting and shouting and drinking I could handle, but living in fear is not living at all,' Dimple said softly. 'I just wanted it to be over, but bruises can be covered up until they fade, and broken bones eventually heal. I always had good grades and minded my manners. No scars meant no proof.'

And so Dimple had taken it into her own hands, Saffi realized. She tried picturing a scared young girl on death row, sickened by the picture her mind supplied. How many times had Dimple asked for help before realizing it would never come? How many people had failed her? If she were in Dimple's position, Saffi couldn't imagine herself rising to the challenge like that. If anything, she could see herself running, but as she was beginning to realize, that was not a permanent solution.

This was no use. Taylor's investigative method often relied on picturing himself in others' shoes, but Saffi had always thought it was an unfair comparison. Who was to say whether another person saw colors more vividly or felt pain more deeply? The fact of the matter was, Saffi was Saffi and she could be no one else no matter how hard she tried. This was why there was no use getting to know the characters involved in every case; it would only complicate things.

But this truth given by Dimple was paid in good merit, a reimbursement for the one Saffi had given her. In a currency only the two of them seemed to understand. Dimple Kapoor was not someone who had initially struck Saffi as caring about fairness. And the notion that Dimple could never understand her didn't coincide with why it sometimes felt like the world viewed the two of them through the same warped lens.

24

July 9, 2026

Saffi's story rattled Dimple more than it should have, now that she knew the weights of their individual guilt could balance a scale. They were connected, in a way, both haunted by accidents and a path to hell paved with all the right intentions. It didn't change the fact that they were on opposite sides of an ongoing war, but maybe they didn't have to be. Dimple had always thought that, by the end of this, either she would be on death row or Saffi would be bleeding out at the bottom of a grand staircase, but perhaps they were more alike than she'd initially thought. Alike enough to share a fate even.

Exasperated by the dead heat of summer, Dimple had her first meeting with everyone involved in *Insomnia*'s production. Save for Chris Porter, of course.

With the inclusion of the public relations and legal teams, it was excruciatingly long, fluffed up by incomprehensible jargon mentioned every five minutes. Dimple's co-stars were somber. Shyla Patel seemed to teeter between anger and holding back tears. Dimple wasn't sure what to do with herself.

By the end of the meeting, it was *strongly suggested* not to make an official statement about Chris Porter's situation. They wanted to wait and see what would come of it first. Chris wasn't to be involved in any of the promotion, but they were keeping him in the movie for now. In his place, it was suggested that Dimple take on the task of being the face of the film. On one hand, she was terrified it would all backfire on her. On the other, it was too good an opportunity to pass up.

'Are we not going to talk about it at all?' Shyla spoke up suddenly. 'He *killed* someone!'

A hush overtook the room. Somehow, that word had been avoided for the better part of three hours. Dimple watched as the executives exchanged glances.

'She has a point.' Jerome took the opportunity to speak up. He sounded contemplative, picking at his fingernail. 'It's our job to fix this. We don't want the public taking us down with him. The best thing we can do in this situation is to treat it as a learning opportunity. Chris is already working with his team. To cover our bases, I propose we donate a portion of the movie's box office proceeds to charity.'

Dimple hoped that portion would come from Chris's paycheck. Because why should they suffer for Chris's mistakes? Dimple might've done worse, but at least she hadn't been caught.

The executives put a pin on Jerome's proposition with a promise to discuss the logistics further and the meeting concluded, but not without bringing up lawyers, contracts, and NDAs to ensure everything remained among the people in the room.

Online traction, on the other hand, was on a steep upward trend. Say what you may, death was not terrible marketing for a psychological thriller. Even if the reception was as chilling as it was.

Fans were nearly split down the middle regarding Chris Porter. One side called him *murderer* and *villain,* even escalating to death threats – which Dimple found dreadfully ironic. The other claimed he was misunderstood – that he'd learned his lesson and didn't deserve to have his life ruined over a simple mistake.

Regardless, *Insomnia* had been trending worldwide since the news first broke. And while Dimple had gained several followers, most of them were only there in anticipation of what she had to say about the situation. Some even berated her for ever having dated a monster like Chris – going off baseless rumors from their early filming days. As though she'd been the one behind the wheel.

Dimple, admittedly, was no different from those so fascinated by everything going on. She'd spent every waking moment religiously monitoring the state of affairs. She was sure not even Chris Porter's lawyers were as up-to-date as she was.

Consequently, an alert heralding a new article was waiting for her when she got back to her apartment.

BREAKING: Actor Chris Porter Checks into Rehab, All Charges Dismissed

Every molecule in the room came to a standstill. Dimple didn't move, didn't breathe. She read the headline once, twice, thrice, and it didn't change.

Could it really be so easy?

Dimple scanned the article for new information, squinting as the brightness burned her retinas, but it was filled with nothing but glowing praise for the fact that Chris was getting the help he needed. No mention of the innocent he'd killed, and none in the comments either. Just like that, public perception was already shifting. Chris was being praised for the very thing Saffi had fled the country for.

Would people be so quick to forgive if it had been Dimple behind the wheel? If she'd confessed to her crimes, she knew for a fact that her career would never recover. And yet she doubted Chris even had enough time to perspire before everything was dropped as though it had never happened. When Dimple spotted her name nestled within a long paragraph, her heart nearly jumped out of her chest. The words on the page blurred and danced, morphing and changing shape.

BREAKING: Dimple Kapoor, Debut Lead Actress of 'Insomnia,' Indicted on Charges of Murder

Dimple dropped her phone like it had burned her. It landed somewhere on her rug, but it might as well have vanished. Her breathing came out short, chest constricting as the world shifted. With uncooperating legs she staggered to her knees, hands reaching haphazardly for stability and finding none. The ringing in her ears reached a fever pitch. Suddenly, it was she who was facing trial. And it was Irene Singh on the witness stand in front of her.

'Dimple Kapoor is a murderer,' she said as blood leaked steadily from her head, trickling down her face like tears.

The jury, the shadowed figures of her aunt and uncle, laughed and laughed. Dimple searched for a shred of normalcy, for the briefest glimpse of an understanding face –

'Saffi,' she breathed.

If anyone were to understand what it was to kill as a byproduct of ambition, it would be her. Saffi was unflinching, staring right into Dimple's soul.

She stepped closer and reached out just like she had back in her office. Slow, deliberate movements. Dimple almost flinched when cold fingers traced her neck, but found that she couldn't move. It hadn't been like this before. Saffi's touch had always felt electric, like the lights dimming before the start of a film.

Hands closed around Dimple's throat without warning, squeezing tight. Every scream, every wheeze, every protest died before it could be set free. She thrashed around, scratching at the hands, leaving rivers of red in her wake, but they did not relent. Saffi did not relent. It reminded Dimple of fingers brushing against her wrist brace, proof of her confinement.

Dimple, behind bars.

Dimple, heart pounding, sitting on a cold slab, waiting to die by lethal injection, then by electric chair, then by a push down a grand staircase. Each time, it was Saffi administering the punishment. Chris Porter's mocking laughter echoed in Dimple's ears, his heavy, leaden arm permanently slung across her shoulders.

Scrambling blindly for her lighter, Dimple counted backward from ten. Cold plastic against skin snapped her back to reality. She nearly passed out in relief when she confirmed that the name in the headline belonged to Chris Porter – not her.

These episodes were becoming worse. The waking nightmares had never been able to touch her before – something that happened more often than not recently.

When her breathing finally evened out and the ringing in her ears subsided, Dimple took a deep breath and felt the world gradually stop spinning around her. There was nothing she could do to put an end to the bouts of mania, but her hands itched regardless. She picked up the pages of an upcoming audition and read them over yet again.

25

August 8, 2026

Dimple had gone to five parties over the course of the past few weekends and it wasn't because she'd finally reached rock bottom. On the contrary, Dimple was working. This was the culmination of months of training. Andino and Taylor Private Eye had even provided her with an earpiece she could easily hide under her hair. She was an actress to her core, so she took her role seriously.

'Do you see anyone watching you?' Eli's staticky voice came from her ear.

This was a complicated question. Dimple leaned with her back against the wall, squinting under the dim lighting to scan the crowd once again. This function couldn't hold a candle to any of Irene's. There was something so heedless, so utterly unremarkable about the whole event. One man could wear a three-piece suit and the other shorts. One could carry a can of beer and the other a glass of wine.

There was also the telling itch under her skin of eyes trained on her. Spurred on by the dating rumors, everyone wanted Dimple's version of the events leading to her co-lead's murder investigation. She could either say that their relationship had been a publicity stunt or allow people to assume that she'd broken up with Chris. Neither was a great option, and nobody would believe that they'd never been together in the first place. She remained vague, like Julie had suggested, and suffered through the treatment. Her refusal to comment on the dropped charges, however, was a statement in and of itself. She couldn't bring herself to do it, but of the main cast, only Dimple and Shyla had failed to voice their support.

Some stared outright, some threw a few fleeting glances every now and again. They only came up to her if she was stationary for too long, mostly giving her space so long as she looked busy. These were not the stares she was on alert for.

'No one's looking,' Dimple finally replied to Eli.

Saffi and her team were growing impatient, but Dimple knew exactly who they were waiting for. She had yet to find any sign of Hector Olsen. It was exhausting, not to mention embarrassing. She was twenty-seven going out every weekend by her lonesome.

If anyone caught her speaking to herself, she was sure she'd die of humiliation.

'Still nothing?' Atlas asked.

Somehow, that spurred a round of bickering between Atlas and Saffi, which Dimple tuned out. It made her feel dreadfully lonely.

If only Dimple could speak openly about her knowledge, perhaps then she could offer more insight. She could tell them that Olsen was of an older crowd, that he didn't go out every night, that he was of a higher profile than Dimple. The parties they were both invited to rarely intersected. It would take time and patience to find him at one of these events.

A few of the partygoers closest to Dimple began whispering, as though considering approaching her. It was time for another leisurely stroll around the premises. Everyone Dimple passed turned in her direction, as though magnetized by her presence. The crowd was dense, but not enough that Dimple had to fight her way through. She caught fragments of shouted conversations as she weaved in and out. A mention of a famous actor here, a comment about cheap drinks there.

Dimple had come straight here after a final audition round for the lead role in another major film. It felt completely different from when she'd auditioned for *Insomnia* – back then she'd been terrified out of her mind. She'd spent nearly every hour of every day practicing, reciting the script in hundreds of tones and tens of accents, imploring Priyal to give her feedback on the most compelling delivery. And yet, she'd still lost the role to Irene. This time, while Dimple had prepared extensively, she hadn't been as obsessive. And the role was hers in everything but name.

'You seem so relaxed,' Priyal had told her. 'I'm glad you're starting to trust yourself more.'

Dimple didn't know how to explain to her that it was because she was more fixated on framing Hector Olsen. Auditions, even for large-budget films, paled in comparison to that challenge.

A group of friends twirled to the upbeat rhythm of the music. Dimple ducked around them. Much to her chagrin, Priyal had been unable to accompany her to these parties. The investigators had denied her this comfort for fear of her assistant getting caught in the crossfire. Dimple wished she'd pushed back more on the issue. It was incredibly isolating, standing alone in a crowd full of intersecting relationships.

But it wasn't just that. Priyal had been pestering her less and less as of late. Julie had told her it was because Priyal had finally gotten herself an agent. She was already booking minor roles and Dimple knew that it wouldn't be long before she became too busy for personal assistant work.

She was interrupted from her thoughts when she spotted a woman in the crowd. Sleek black hair to her shoulders, golden brown skin, couldn't be more than a couple inches taller than Priyal. Shyla Patel caught Dimple's attention, waving hello, which Dimple returned. That was one piece of the puzzle in place, but Dimple didn't want to get ahead of herself. Shyla had shown up to several of these parties – Hector Olsen was the more elusive of the two.

Dimple pushed her way through the masses, alert. Crowd placement at events like this was always extremely deliberate. The younger, more up-and-coming bunch tended to keep to themselves until later in the night when they had liquid courage running through their veins. Even then, only the bravest – or perhaps most foolish – dared approach the A- and B-listers.

That wasn't to say that this was a particularly exclusive party, but the most narcissistic of the elites liked to come to these because it gave them a sense of superiority. Those newer to the business clamored over one another for the opportunity to brush hands with the stars that burned brighter.

Which was why Dimple knew Hector Olsen's presence at one of these events was inevitable. He was a perverted, geriatric, washed-up has-been. Here, though, he was a god.

Just then, Dimple spotted a flash of white hair through the crowd and froze. Her heart thudded in anticipation as he turned.

It was Olsen.

The silence in her earpiece didn't give away whether or not the investigators had noticed him as well. They wouldn't tell her even if they had.

Dimple positioned herself by the bar, in his direct sight. He, however, was too busy guffawing with his friends to look over at her. This wouldn't work. Saffi, Eli, and Atlas were posted around the room, ready to intervene in case something went wrong. More than that, they could hear every word she said through her earpiece. Dimple scanned the room once again to make sure they were where she'd left them.

Instead of approaching Hector, Dimple ducked away and disappeared from the investigators' line of sight. They wouldn't question her right away, but Dimple would have to work fast before she raised suspicion. She blamed anxiety for how quickly she dismissed the hairs raising up on the back of her neck, the feeling of being watched.

There was always a dark corner of the room where party-goers got a head start on the hard drugs. The classier folks waited until the night was winding down to partake, but the junkies hardly cared about the time of day. Dimple usually never drifted so close to this corner, but she'd been scouting it out for a few weekends now. She was familiar enough to know that she could swipe a packet of whatever they were using this late in the night and they'd either be too high or too preoccupied to notice. Dimple strolled past the group, careful not to draw attention to herself as she did just that.

She held the packet tightly in her fist as she made her way over to the bar, back in the private investigators' view. Only waiters ever came by this end. Uniform black suits, silver trays piled high with drinks. Dimple's heart skipped a beat, almost thinking she caught a glimpse of a familiar scrawny man. She grasped onto the edge of the bar, nails digging into polished brown wood, forcibly reminding herself that Isaac Klossner was dead.

A waiter knocked shoulders with Dimple, paying no mind as he frantically refilled a glass with Scotch before taking off again. Dimple watched as he ducked expertly through the crowd over to Hector Olsen and his friends. Their glasses hadn't been empty for more than a second before he plucked them from their hands and replaced them with full ones. An attendant just for them.

The waiter circled back to the bar.

When Dimple checked again, she was pleased to see that it would be Olsen's turn for a refill soon.

Casually enough that it could be considered an accident, Dimple kicked at a woman's heel and slipped away. The woman shrieked as she fell, the glass in her hand shattering as it hit the ground beside her. Everyone in the vicinity turned to look. Olsen's waiter, who was the closest employee, rushed forward to help clean up the mess.

'The hell was that?' Saffi asked in her ear, alarmed. Her voice reminded Dimple of fingers digging into her throat, which she promptly shoved aside.

'Dimple, are you okay?' Eli asked. The crowd's sudden agitation meant they'd lost sight of her again.

'Fine,' Dimple replied breathlessly. 'Someone fell.'

With everyone preoccupied, nobody noticed when Dimple emptied the packet she'd swiped into the glass of Scotch sitting on the waiter's silver tray. Swirling it a few times to make sure it dissolved, Dimple set the drink down and allowed the surging crowd to swallow her up. The empty packet got lost in all the commotion, but that was of no consequence.

Mess finally dealt with, the waiter turned back to the tray and glanced up at Olsen and his friends. He did a double-take that Dimple didn't understand until she checked for herself. Both Olsen *and* one of his friends had empty glasses. She cursed under her breath. There was no telling who the drink would go to. The waiter filled another glass with Scotch, overestimating. The liquid threatened to spill, but there was no time to re-pour. He made his way to the men.

Unwilling to let her hard work go to waste, Dimple pushed her way through the dense crowd. She aimed for casual as she plucked the overfilled Scotch from the tray.

The waiter froze, but Dimple didn't give him the chance to complain as a group of rather energetic dancers surged around her.

Olsen was getting increasingly irritated as the seconds ticked by and his glass remained empty. Not many dared contribute to the discomfort of A-listers at events like these, where their presence was widely regarded as a gift. The waiter would have to decide: have Olsen complain about him slacking and lose his job, or deal with the wrath of Olsen's C-lister friend for not bringing him a refill as well.

When Dimple looked down, heart thudding, the dim light reflecting off the liquid within the glass revealed a perfect mirror image of herself. Cheeks flushed a healthy red from exertion, colorful lights glimmering in her dark gaze. Dimple had never looked better. She pawned the Scotch off on an actor she vaguely recognized and moved to where she could watch the orchestrated chaos unfold.

She looked up again just in time to see the waiter had made the smart choice. Almost in slow motion, he handed Hector the tainted glass. Olsen didn't so much as look up, let alone thank him. In fact, the only one who acknowledged the waiter's presence was the C-lister with an empty glass, berating him.

Any of Dimple's guilt, though, was quickly overshadowed by the excitement of Olsen taking a sizable sip. There was a pause as he stared deeply into his drink with a puzzled expression. Dimple waited, shoulders squared, for the accusations to come flying, but Olsen didn't so much as blink before tipping the rest back.

Not long after she watched Olsen down the liquid as though it were water, she saw his pupils blow wide, and standing up was evidently becoming an ordeal. He excused himself and began stumbling in the direction of the bathroom.

Dimple was already trailing behind him. 'Excuse me, I'll be in the restroom,' she whispered into her mic.

Saffi began to protest, but it was too late. The wiring from Dimple's ears had long since been tossed unceremoniously into a potted plant. She passed the group of older men, their amusement apparent over how quickly their friend had gotten plastered.

Hector was stumbling more than Dimple had anticipated and she found herself in the hallway ahead of the restroom before he'd taken ten steps. It was no matter; he would have to pass her on his way there. A speaker positioned strategically to her left would make conversation difficult to overhear.

It was unclear whether the investigators had noticed Olsen's presence yet, but either way, it wouldn't be long before Saffi realized Dimple was up to something. Perhaps she already had. Dimple would have to work quickly. Awaiting Hector's appearance, she scanned the crowd for Shyla Patel. The actress was quite a ways back, but still visible, and that was all Dimple needed. She only had one shot at this.

A tall, hunched figure stumbled into her line of sight. Dimple stabilized Hector Olsen by the shoulder with one hand. The other dipped into his front pocket and fished out his keys, transferring them into her own. They clinked as they settled beside her lighter. She retreated, trying to avoid his pungent, alcohol-infused breath, but it was too late – Hector reached out and grasped her arm in an unforgiving grip. Everywhere his skin came into contact with felt like a burning poison. Dimple shivered in disgust.

'Well, hello there,' he slurred. 'What's your name?'

He didn't recognize her.

'I'm married,' Dimple said instinctively, desperate to get his hands off her. 'With kids.'

For a moment, his face twisted in disgust, his grip loosening on her arm. Then it was back in full force, and he leaned even closer.

'How's that? You don't look a day over eighteen,' he purred.

Forget it, so what if he was holding on to her? It wasn't as though he could do anything in front of so many people. And Dimple was running out of time. She put on her most severe expression.

'I have the perfect actress for your next movie,' she said, struggling to be heard over the pounding bass.

'The hell?' Hector exclaimed. He shoved her and Dimple nearly fell to the ground, catching herself on the wall at the last moment. At least he wasn't touching her anymore. 'Fucking leeches, I'm not here for work. Get outa my –'

'I promise you'll love her,' Dimple tried, heart pounding as Hector continued to ignore her. She wracked her brain for something he could latch onto. 'She's beautiful –'

'I told you to fuck off!' he shouted.

Spit flew, his face inches from her own. Dimple flinched, taking an involuntary step back. A man just like him flashed through her mind, shouting at her for dropping his beer after he'd asked her to fetch it. Her hands dripping blood as she attempted to gather the broken pieces.

She had forgotten herself. Whatever delusion had made her think she could outwit a man like Hector Olsen quickly shattered. But she hadn't come so far to give up now.

'I understand why me approaching you here might anger you.'

Hector's face, however, only flushed redder at her acknowledgment. Then, not entirely unexpectedly, he flipped over a nearby table. An expensive-looking vase shattered into a thousand pieces across tile. It was all Dimple could do not to drop to her knees and immediately begin gathering the shards.

This drew a few lingering glances from the crowd. Many of them seemed to recognize Olsen, that this was typical of him, and turned away. Not that it mattered when the music completely overpowered their conversation.

'She's right over there,' Dimple said in a weak final attempt, gesturing in Shyla's direction.

The girl was almost too far to see through the crowd, but Hector faltered as soon as he laid eyes on her. Shyla was young and exactly his type. Hector stumbled a bit, but quickly righted himself. He seemed to have completely forgotten Dimple was there, choosing instead to stagger in Shyla's direction.

'She wants to work for me?' he slurred, smug. 'I think we can make something happen.'

Dimple felt immediate guilt for sending the man after Shyla, even though she knew the investigators were posted around the room for situations like these. She reminded herself that Olsen was drunk and high and Shyla was surrounded by people. All Dimple needed was for the man to approach her and cause a big enough scene for Dimple to slip away. Surely the investigators would pick up on the fact that another brown woman involved in *Insomnia* being approached by their suspect was something to make note of.

Saffi would pick up on it immediately, but her attention would be too focused on Dimple to acknowledge it. She would have to rely on Atlas and Eli to jump to the correct conclusion.

Heart pounding, Dimple watched as the dense crowd parted for Olsen. His attention didn't waver from Shyla, but no one else seemed to catch on to his intentions. The man stopped inches away from her and only then did she look up. They seemed to exchange words, Olsen's voice growing louder and more agitated as their conversation went on. From the corner of her eye, Dimple caught movement.

Atlas. He was heading straight for Hector. The crowd impeded his speed, though, and he was a second too late. Hector Olsen's fist was already raised. Dimple's blood ran cold. He swung forward, knuckles connecting with Shyla's face, the resulting crunch loud enough to be heard over the music. Just like that day on set filming *Insomnia,* Shyla Patel fell. It had been Chris Porter's character who'd pushed her off that ledge. And all Dimple could do – both then and now – was watch. Moonlight illuminated the scene in front of her, like a spotlight. Halfway through her descent, Shyla Patel transformed into Irene Singh. The ledge morphed into that same unforgettable staircase.

It wasn't until the crowd erupted into screams, Shyla disappearing into it, that Dimple snapped back to reality. She could just make out shouted demands to restrain Olsen. Dimple stood frozen, unable to do anything but witness the horror she'd orchestrated. Shyla's unapologetic laugh flashed through her mind. The two of them poking fun at Chris Porter in Dimple's trailer between takes. Joint disbelief over the main character's carelessness. Complaining about the late nights and early mornings. Dimple had nearly forgotten that a man like Olsen, so used to attacking under the influence, would have perfected his aim in those conditions.

'Someone call the police!'

Dimple was out the door before sirens could be heard.

26

August 8, 2026

Saffi stood outside the party, watching as paramedics tended to Shyla Patel's broken nose. Twin streaks of blood were dried onto her cheeks. On the other side of the grounds, Hector Olsen sat in handcuffs, unfocused as an officer read him his rights. Andino was speaking to another cop some paces to her right. The rest of the partygoers were either on their way home or eagerly watching from the other side of the police tape, trying discreetly to record. Saffi had already confiscated several phones.

'It's gotta be him, right?' Taylor asked from her left as he studied Hector Olsen. 'His predisposed violence toward brown women leaked into his anger at being denied as the director for *Insomnia*.'

Saffi didn't reply. Because if what she thought had happened was true, then Dimple Kapoor was a far worse woman than she had thought possible. Considering Dimple's history with abuse, though, Saffi found it hard to believe. So had she been wrong all along? Was Olsen the true culprit? Or did Saffi just not want to believe that Dimple Kapoor was capable of this level of carnage?

Violence perpetuated violence perpetuated violence.

Saffi's phone buzzed in her pocket and she accepted the call, lifting it up to her ear. 'Where are you?'

'Who's that?' Taylor asked incredulously.

'Martinez,' Saffi replied. 'The intern.'

He frowned. 'Why is Mia calling you?'

'She's on assignment for me.'

'What?' Taylor exclaimed.

Saffi ignored him, walking a few paces out of earshot. Taylor watched with suspicion. 'I'm guessing you lost her?'

A missing Dimple could only foretell bad things. Either someone was dead or dying. Or being punched, apparently. One rarely played with fire without getting burned.

'No, actually,' Martinez's voice was hushed and slightly out of breath, 'I followed her.'

Saffi's stomach dropped. 'What? Where are you?'

'Around the time Hector punched Shyla, Dimple left the party. I followed her to this alleyway nearby. I think she's getting changed. I'm going to see where she goes from here.'

'No – that's not what I asked you to do,' Saffi said firmly. 'Send me your location and go home.'

'But I *saw* her put something in Hector's drink,' Martinez insisted. 'She was the one who made that woman trip – that's when she did it. I think she might be . . . I don't know. But maybe I can find out.'

Come to think of it, Olsen did seem out of it and not just because he was drunk. But Shyla Patel was a cautionary tale. The last thing Saffi wanted was for another innocent girl to get caught in the crossfire.

'I said no,' Saffi said. 'I'll take it from here.'

There was a beat in which Saffi was sure she would disobey, but then she sighed deep and low. 'Okay, you're the boss.'

Relief crashed into Saffi like a train. 'Let me know as soon as you're home.' And the line went dead.

Great. Saffi hadn't expected the girl to have such a talent when it came to tailing. She resisted the urge to rub her temples. The last thing she'd wanted was to place this burden on someone else. Especially someone so young.

As she returned to Taylor's side, Saffi thought back to the crash from earlier, to the waiter who'd helped clean it up. Then to when she had seen Dimple snatch a glass of Scotch from the same waiter and pawn it off on someone else. All strange behavior that she couldn't characterize until now. It was clear that Dimple Kapoor was capable of far more than what people gave her credit for. Saffi should've realized by now that backing Dimple into a corner never worked the way she expected it to.

Then again, the girl had *seen* Dimple drug Olsen. And she should be sending Saffi her location any minute now. Whatever Dimple was off doing, Saffi would be finding out.

As soon as Saffi returned, Taylor pulled her aside, his grip on her arm firm and unyielding. She shook herself free once they were alone.

'What?' she snapped.

'Why would you put Mia on assignment?' he asked. The hurt in his tone revealed what he really meant. *Why didn't you tell me?*

Saffi rolled her eyes. 'You and I would've killed for an opportunity like this when we were interns.'

'She could've been hurt!'

'All three of us were there.' Saffi frowned. 'She was completely safe.'

'Shyla Patel wasn't safe, was she?'

Saffi opened her mouth to argue but then paused. Once again, her assumptions of Dimple Kapoor were clouding her judgment. For some godforsaken reason, she had been under the impression that Dimple wouldn't hurt someone like Martinez. As though Dimple wouldn't demolish anyone and anything that stood in her path. Shyla was a prime example. This was exactly why Saffi's father had taught her not to inject personal biases into investigations.

Another horrifying thought wormed its way into her mind. What if Dimple had been counting on Saffi to intercept Olsen? What if the real reason Shyla had gotten hurt was because Saffi had been distracted? She felt sick.

Again. She was doing this again. If she wasn't careful, history would repeat itself and Saffi would be responsible for yet another innocent's death.

Priyal. That was who Martinez reminded Saffi of.

'I didn't think,' she admitted.

Taylor kept his stern disapproval fixed on her for another second before sighing and uncrossing his arms. 'You're right about one thing, though. We absolutely would've killed for an opportunity like that as interns. But you and I both know we wouldn't have been ready.' He placed a comforting hand on Saffi's shoulder. 'She really looks up to you, you know? Even before you got here, she wouldn't shut up about all the cases you solved while abroad.'

Heat rose in Saffi's cheeks. She shrugged off Taylor's hand. 'What's your point?'

'My point is, she could use a mentor.'

Saffi froze. 'You'd trust me with her?' Seconds ago, he'd been chiding her.

Taylor gave her a confused look. 'You're one of the only people I'd trust.'

He said it as though it was obvious. She felt embarrassed all of a sudden. That was when her phone chimed. The location of the alley, a much more pressing matter.

'Martinez says she's on her way home,' Saffi relayed. 'But there's something I need to check out. Will you come with me?' She hoped he wouldn't ask any further questions.

Taylor, like he always did, seemed to sense that. 'Sure.'

Martinez hadn't been wrong, the alleyway wasn't more than a ten-minute walk from Olsen's mansion and they made the trip in five by running straight there. But when they arrived, adrenaline running high, there was nobody and nothing in sight. Saffi scanned for moving cars and found none, upturned every piece of trash and cardboard and found not even a strand of brown hair.

'Some of these houses might have cameras,' Taylor tried.

Saffi scoffed. 'Unlikely any of them see as far as the alley.' These celebrities had entire jungles for backyards; it was probably difficult enough for their cameras to cover the full extent of their property.

'It doesn't hurt to check.'

But Taylor had no idea the golden opportunity that had slipped from their fingers. If only Saffi had been paying as close attention to Dimple Kapoor as Martinez had been. But no, that in itself was the problem. The only reason she'd managed to get so close was because Dimple had been focused on Saffi. They were held prisoner in each other's orbit. Saffi had effectively shot herself in the foot.

Her phone chimed again, this time with a message confirming that Martinez had made it home. She clutched it tight, close to her chest. At least her intern was safe.

[illegible] what was
[illegible]
[illegible] Dunkirk [illegible]
[illegible]
[illegible]

[illegible]
[illegible]
[illegible]

27

August 8, 2026

Heart pounding and head in another dimension entirely, Dimple made it to Olsen's mansion in one piece only because she'd planned her route so extensively beforehand. With her wig securely in place, clothes swapped out, and gloves pulled on, she made the arduous trek uphill. Her knuckles strained with the firm grip she had on the bag she'd stashed in one of the bushes outside the party. Olsen's mansion wasn't too far from the party – about a thirty-minute walk – but she hadn't accounted for his neighborhood to be on an incline. Regardless, the burn in her calves was a welcome distraction from her mind.

The area felt oddly familiar, an eerie sense of déjà vu washing over Dimple in a tidal wave. She felt chilled to the bone. It wasn't until she stopped in the middle of the road, warm summer breeze ruffling synthetic hair, that she realized.

Hector Olsen's house was two away from the Singhs' mansion.

The very breath was stolen from Dimple's lungs as she looked over the exterior of what had once been Irene Singh's home. This view from outside the gate was vastly different from the interior. While Dimple had come to countless parties here, she'd never lingered over the expansive driveway or sloping rooftops. All she could ever think about from out here was how high the electricity bill must be and how much it must cost to keep the water on. From within, it was much easier to feel a part of that world. But there was no one inside now, according to the FOR SALE sign stamped into the front lawn.

This addition felt more permanent than death. Although, one way or another, Dimple had always known that night would be her last in Irene's presence.

The universe had decided that only one of them could bring their goals to fruition. All Dimple had done was what anyone would do to ensure she won in the end. She allowed herself a few additional seconds, head ducked, before continuing up the road.

Like all men with too much to hide and the untempered desire to show off, Olsen had fortified his mansion with a gate. Dimple didn't know the code to enter, but she didn't need it. The security cameras were aimed at the road, so Dimple found a secluded area and tossed her bag over the fence. California building code made it so fences couldn't be taller than six feet without a permit, which meant this fence wasn't more than a couple inches taller than her. That and the jagged stone worked in her favor, allowing her to fit her shoes into the grooves and wrench herself over to the other side.

She felt overexposed. As though anyone could take one glance at her and know she didn't belong. But the rest of the neighborhood didn't seem awake enough to take note of her unwelcome presence. And, looking up at the huge house, immaculate lawn, and expensive cars, she didn't feel so out of place. It didn't feel so out of reach. Dimple could have this one day.

That day wasn't today, though, so Dimple tried her best not to stand out. She didn't gape at the pristinely pruned rosebushes or the luxury cars and didn't rush like she had something to hide. A camera pointed down from the porch, but like most smart cameras, it was connected to the Wi-Fi network. In all the parties Dimple had gone to, it hadn't been difficult to find someone who'd been to Hector Olsen's house and finagle the network password from them. By the time she walked up to the front door, Dimple had already turned off the house's security system from her phone.

For all her preparations, there was a moment in which Dimple feared the key she'd swiped from Hector's pocket wouldn't work, as though the door could somehow sense that she had no business here. She didn't have to worry for long. The lock clicked, allowing Dimple to step into a dimly lit marble foyer that probably cost more money than she'd ever had in her life.

Dimple took a moment to adjust to the darkness. Something was flashing too bright in her periphery and she had to squint to find it. A second security system installed next to the door. She deflated. There'd been a chance Hector would have an additional round of protections in place, but she'd been hoping otherwise.

Closer inspection found a timer stamped across the screen. What had started as one hundred and twenty seconds now read one hundred and ten. The familiar image of Irene's crumpled body, blood steadily leaking from her head, flashed behind Dimple's eyelids. But instead of sending her into a panic like it usually did, it reminded her of all she'd been through to get to this point.

The code had six digits – perfect for that of a date. It could be a random number. Part of her wanted to try 123456 to see what would happen. But Hector Olsen was far from an uncoordinated man. He matched his ties to his suits and his suits to his shoes. From the movies he directed to the women he married, he made his choices meticulously and grew upset when they did not measure up to his expectations.

The alarm beeped, now counting down from seventy seconds. Dimple had, of course, looked into Hector Olsen's life in preparation for this. He had many important dates. His wedding anniversary with his most recent ex-wife, Laila. His estranged children's birthdays. His own birthday even. But there was only one date he never failed to celebrate. One that he seemed to hold in the highest regard.

With thirty seconds remaining, Dimple punched in the day Hector Olsen had won his Academy Award for Best Director. Her heart stuttered in her chest when the screen flashed *Alarm Disabled* with twenty seconds left on the timer.

As much as she wanted to celebrate, she forced her feet to keep moving.

Every hair on her body stood upright, the prickling feeling of being watched that she knew couldn't be more than a figment of her imagination. Olsen was currently between wives and his many children lived with their mothers, but Dimple still darted around on her tiptoes. She couldn't make out much with the lights off, but the house was certainly excessive in nature, especially for a solitary man. He had more rooms than Dimple could think up reasons for. But no room mattered as much as the one she was looking for.

Dimple scoured the house for Olsen's bedroom and found five possible options. She'd been about to turn back when she entered what was easily the largest room in the entire house. All confusion left her at the sight of it. Like most of the mansion, the floors were pale marble, but at the center was a loud tiger-print rug under a California king bed with matching silk sheets.

Dimple scanned along the wall for doors. There, the bathroom, and to the right was his walk-in closet, which was the size of her bedroom.

Setting her bag aside, Dimple got to work emptying the

bottom drawer of his dresser. She stuffed those clothes into the other drawers as neatly as possible before emptying her bag onto the ground, scattering her supplies across the tile.

She rifled through the closet for the suit he wore to Irene's party. It shouldn't have been quite so difficult to find a red tiger-print suit, but Dimple was beginning to sense a theme in Olsen's belongings. Instead, she picked a suit at random, designating it to be the one he wore the night he'd pushed Dimple. She laid it flat on the ground.

Then Dimple took the vial of her own blood she'd extracted from her forearm weeks ago and splattered it onto the suit as meticulously as she could with shaking hands. Saffi had seen the bandage – she would see right through this. But she wasn't the one Dimple needed to convince. While that dried, Dimple finally found the suit from Irene's party and crumpled it into a ball, shoving it into a flame-resistant bag. She didn't have any way of obtaining Irene's blood, but that didn't matter. All Hector had done to her was push her down the stairs.

Once the blood had dried, Dimple shoved the second suit into the bag and zipped it. She placed that in the dresser and shut the drawer. There was still the matter of the bloody vial, though, which she took to the sink to clean. There was nowhere to dispose of it, so her pocket would have to do for now.

The police were surely already at the party by now, hopefully arresting Hector for assault, but that wasn't the issue. The issue, as always, was Saffi. *Fingers digging into her throat.* She would have no problem pinpointing Dimple's involvement in this. It didn't matter what Hector had done, all of Dimple's hard work would be for naught if she was caught breaking into his home.

Regardless, there was one last thing Dimple had to do. The

sight of Olsen's fist connecting with Shyla's cheek replayed on a loop in her mind. The brief flash of fear Dimple had caught in the other woman's eyes had been so intimately familiar. That Dimple had been so instrumental in putting that expression on Shyla's face left a sour taste in her mouth.

She'd only ever felt resolve like this once in her life, and that had been the day she came home from school to find her house burned down and her aunt and uncle dead.

The paramedics had informed her that they'd burned alive in a drunken stupor, too out of it to feel anything. It only occurred to Dimple now that they'd probably only said that in a misguided attempt to comfort a grieving child. Because surely even drunkards couldn't sleep through being burned alive. Dimple liked to imagine that with all the alcohol running through their veins, the flames scorched even deeper than it would for anyone else.

Sick of wallowing, Dimple crept downstairs and searched for an outlet she could put to use.

One last fire. Just one more, and then she could finally live.

28

August 9, 2026

Saffi stared coolly at Dimple Kapoor, who flashed her a smirk too quick for anyone else to catch. If it weren't for the fact that they were in a police station, Saffi might've throttled her. She wouldn't be happy for long. Saffi would make sure of that.

'Here I am,' Dimple announced, as though she was doing her a favor just by being there.

'A returned call would've sufficed.'

'But you know how much I prefer talking face-to-face,' Dimple said.

So she'd come here to gloat. For what, Saffi still wasn't sure yet.

'Where did you disappear to?' Saffi asked, leaning against the only free wall in the precinct.

Several hours after the party and Saffi had caught no sight of Dimple until now. Her dress was a beacon, bright enough to be seen from space. The most lethargic cops moved around her without complaint. A few even stopped to stare, blinking rapidly as though to make sure they weren't dreaming.

'It got hectic, so I left,' Dimple replied. 'Can you blame me?'

'After what you did to Shyla Patel? Yes, I think I can.'

That wiped the manufactured emotions from her face. 'That shouldn't have happened,' Dimple said somberly.

It was the closest thing to a confession Saffi had ever gotten. And it sounded like Dimple meant it. Then again, what would Saffi know? Dimple could say the sky was falling and sound entirely sincere about it.

The problem was that this time, Saffi wanted desperately to believe her.

'I apologize, it wasn't my intention to abandon you,' Dimple said. 'But I'm here now, aren't I? I am as committed to this investigation as you are.'

'Hard not to be in your case.' Saffi gave her a once-over. She was in the same clothes she'd worn to the party, but she seemed more disheveled than usual, hair frizzing up as though she'd been wearing a hat. Whatever she'd been doing between the party and now, it couldn't be good.

She drummed her fingers impatiently against her biceps. A phone ringing cut through the background hum of the police station. The night shift meant everything was unusually somber, so odd sounds were especially disarming.

They were taking forever to get Olsen here. Even Dimple had already finished up whatever the hell she'd been doing. This was one of the rare occasions that being a private investigator felt completely useless. They had no legal jurisdiction, so there was nothing to do but wait.

'Don't make that face,' Dimple said. Saffi could tell by her tone alone that she was amused.

'What face?' Saffi muttered.

'Like you're about to give up when this is the most fun either of us has ever had.'

Saffi turned to glare at her, blood boiling. 'If you think this is enough to make me give up –'

'That's better,' Dimple interrupted, her smile much softer than Saffi had thought it could get.

Dangerous games.

Thc actress shifted, her dress moving with her, and something caught Saffi's attention. Her hand darted out without thinking. Dimple's burning touch circled her wrist, but it was too late. Saffi already had a vise grip on the cylindrical object in Dimple's pocket. Something else bumped against her knuckles – the lighter.

'Let go,' Dimple said, voice firm. Was that a touch of panic Saffi detected in her tone?

'You first,' she replied.

Their bodies were angled in such a way onlookers wouldn't be able to tell anything was amiss. Dimple smelled like honey and burnt plastic. When neither of them relented, Saffi raised her eyebrows. Dimple's grip on her wrist was tight enough to bruise bone.

Then, all of a sudden, Dimple relaxed her hold. Saffi didn't trust it for one second, but this was her chance. She retracted her hand from Dimple's pocket as quickly as she could. The actress was just as fast. Both of their hands clamped around the plastic vial, but Saffi tugged it up to the light.

Empty. Although, she had a feeling it hadn't always been. Probably sensing that she'd lost, Dimple swore under her breath. Saffi twisted her wrist and freed the plastic cylinder from her grasp.

'You should've gotten rid of this like you did the rest of your disguise,' Saffi said.

As though subconsciously, Dimple smoothed out her hair. Before she could reach for it again, Saffi tucked the vial away into the inner pocket of her suit jacket. She would look into it later.

It was then that a clamor of noise erupted from the front of the precinct. They whipped around and Saffi caught glimpses through the window of paparazzi camped outside. They seemed to know better than dare to enter, but their lenses watched carefully. Dimple, also seeming to notice this, turned her back to the window. Saffi stepped in front of her to further obscure the view.

'I don't know who tipped them off, but I have half a mind to arrest them,' an officer mumbled as he shut the blinds.

Just then, the front door burst open, bringing in overlapping shouts and the sound of several camera shutters. Saffi watched as three separate officers dragged in an erratic Hector Olsen. He kicked and bit and threw himself around, attempting to break free. That would explain why it had taken so long to transport him.

Saffi studied the man closer, unsurprised to find that his movements were still erratic. She aimed a pointed look at Dimple over her shoulder, who only shrugged in response.

Olsen sharpened the second he noticed Dimple. 'It was her – that bitch! She did this to me!'

He lunged forward, but the officers' hold on him was unrelenting. Dimple stepped closer to Saffi, seemingly shocked, but excessively so, clearly playing it up for the others present. The brightness about her, though, spoke volumes. Getting a front row seat to this show had to be at least part of the reason why she'd decided to make an appearance.

'You're saying *she* broke that girl's nose?' a bored police officer asked, rolling his eyes.

Dimple stiffened.

'She made me do it – !' Olsen tried again.

'Yeah, yeah,' the officer said, helping the other officers shove Olsen into a holding room. 'Save it for your lawyers, man.'

As the officers moved him out of the way, Saffi watched as Andino and Taylor returned, summoned by the chaos. Andino had a scowl painted on and made a face at Saffi that she read as: *Can you believe this?* Taylor, however, was studying Dimple with a frown.

Saffi opened her mouth to greet them, but sirens cut her

off. Three officers ran past them, which she tracked with her eyes.

'What's going on?' she asked out loud, not expecting an answer.

An officer must've heard. 'House fire in Beverly Hills,' he called over his shoulder.

It took a moment for the location of the fire to click in Saffi's mind. That and the fact that it was a *fire*. Saffi glanced over at Dimple, who looked a little too smug for her own good. She thought of the red lighter always tucked into the actress's pocket. Of the mysterious vial stashed in her own. And of the lingering smell of burnt plastic.

She had a feeling she knew exactly where Dimple Kapoor had run off to.

29

August 13, 2026

Several days after the party, police and lab reports were finally shared with Andino and Taylor Private Eye.

'They found Olsen's suit soaked through with Dimple's blood,' Taylor said, flipping through a file.

The three of them were sitting in the break room together. If it weren't for Saffi straightening out and organizing their papers, they would be strewn haphazardly across the floor for anyone to walk over. They couldn't afford that. While Olsen's house had burned to a crisp with zero salvageable security camera footage, somewhere in these stacks had to be enough information to convict the rightful perpetrator. Right now, the police were convinced that Olsen had burned his own house down – probably with the help of an accomplice – in an attempt to hide the evidence. It didn't help that they'd been in the process of securing a search warrant before it all went up in flames.

Saffi figured that the bloodstains left behind on the suit had to be new – that Dimple had been planting the evidence when she went missing – which forensics would be able to determine. The problem was the fire. It had tampered with a lot of the evidence, allowing discrepancies to be explained away.

'Is this really everything?' Saffi asked.

'No,' Andino said. 'There's a file they're still refusing to release to us.'

Saffi frowned. 'Why?'

'It's the police. They're always pulling shit like this.'

When bureaucracy and high-profile people were involved, there was no use asking for reasoning. They'd never get a straight answer. However, if there was even so much as a minor detail that could connect Dimple to the fire, Saffi would be able to spot it. 'I need you to work on getting that file for me.'

Andino let out a long sigh but gave her an affirmative nod. Suddenly, Taylor was on his feet, pacing and biting his nails in tandem. Saffi stopped to watch. She'd never seen him so agitated.

'Is he okay?' Saffi asked.

'He's been antsy since we got back from the station,' Andino explained as he doodled something in the corner of his notebook.

Taylor didn't reply straightaway, continuing to work a line into the ground. After a beat he said, 'Hector Olsen, a prime suspect in our case and known domestic abuser, punched the supporting actress of *Insomnia*.'

'Correct,' Saffi said.

Taylor, still pacing, continued, 'This all happened at a party that we've been waiting weeks for – that we've been training Dimple Kapoor for. But right before it happens, there are issues with her wiring. Then she disappears entirely and shows up at the police station hours later. Which is exactly when the police get alerted to a fire at his mansion. Please tell me you see where I'm going with this.'

Saffi blanched. There was no way.

Taylor hurried to justify himself. 'I'm not saying she's guilty of anything, but isn't it a little too convenient? It's possible she realized Olsen was her attacker and decided to take matters into her own hands. Fear makes you do stupid things.'

'What, like arson? You're out of your mind!' Andino exclaimed. 'Saffi, tell him he's out of his mind.'

Saffi and Taylor exchanged looks. He seemed uncharacteristically conflicted, his brow furrowed. 'Look,' he said, 'I know she's your friend.' Saffi was ready to disagree on principle alone, but she let him continue. 'But you can't let that cloud your judgment. You have to admit there's something weird going on, right? And I can't keep letting you hang around her with this bad feeling I have.'

Saffi bristled. As though he was *letting her* do anything. Did he think she was an idiot? Had he never once stopped to consider that Saffi knew what she was doing? It suddenly became clear that Andino and Taylor still saw a naïve twenty-year-old girl when they looked at her. They expected her to act the same, speak the same, love them the same.

This entire time as she'd been lying to them about just how many steps ahead she was, the chasm between them had been growing further apart. Maybe Andino and Taylor hadn't been able to get to know this new version of herself because *she* hadn't let them. They still wanted to protect her and Saffi couldn't even feel any warmth in response to that because it wasn't really her they wanted to protect.

'You're out of your mind, Taylor,' she said. With a pang of loss, she felt the distance between them expand yet again. Maybe out of reach for good.

He immediately deflated, but Andino already had a comforting hand on his shoulder. And just like that, Saffi's worst fears had been confirmed. Six words from her was all it had taken for Taylor to backpedal.

She was horrified. She liked to think that she would be different in his position, but would she? Didn't she also seek approval from them without even realizing it? Hadn't she kept most of her theories from them out of fear that they would disagree and accuse her of falling back into old habits?

Dimple was right, but only partially. It was all three of them who were holding one another back. For the first time, Saffi felt only relief at the thought that she would be leaving again when this case was done with. It would be for the best.

'No, you're right,' Taylor said. 'I was jumping to conclusions. Sorry.'

'You had a theory and got trigger-happy. Happens to the best of us,' Andino consoled. 'That's what we're here for, right, Saf?'

She mumbled her support, but her mind was elsewhere.

Saffi already knew that winning wouldn't be as simple as getting her coworkers on her side. The only concrete evidence she had was Martinez's testimony and the vial. She'd been able to send it to a lab for testing – calling in a favor from an old contact of hers – and they'd confirmed it. Blood. That was what had been inside. There weren't enough traces of it to confirm whose blood it was, but it was a start.

With the lack of substantial evidence, Saffi had also gained a new deadline. She needed to prove Olsen's innocence and Dimple's guilt before his court date. Olsen had managed to pull some strings, because of course he had, and got the date pushed back indefinitely until he finished directing his current project. As much as she was glad for the extra time to build a case, she didn't think it fair that he got something so close to a free pass. If it were Dimple facing his fate, Saffi knew she wouldn't get even half of the same consideration.

Saffi only wished it didn't feel so dirty to essentially help Olsen evade consequence yet again. He didn't deserve to be put on death row for a crime he didn't commit, but he had hit Shyla Patel, hadn't he? Along with his ex-wives. Why should a man like that be allowed to roam free? In the safety of her own mind, where no one was around to judge her, Saffi ranked Olsen as a much worse offender than Dimple Kapoor.

'It's awfully quiet around here.' Three heads turned to the door, where Dimple Kapoor herself entered. The sound of her heels clicked alongside Saffi's heartbeat. 'Where are the interns?'

'Speak of the devil,' Saffi mumbled.

Dimple hesitated for a beat. 'Oh, were you talking about me?'

'We give the interns some time off in the summer when classes are out.' Taylor changed the subject with a hint of panic.

He wasn't the only one surprised at her sudden appearance. Saffi hadn't seen the actress since the police station. She looked well, glowing almost, clearly not losing any sleep. Andino, of course, was ecstatic at the sight of her. His pupils might as well have transformed into cartoon hearts.

'We never got time off,' Saffi muttered.

'Eli's idea,' Atlas replied, as though it needed any explaining. 'I hear a couple of their friends are going to Punta Cana.'

'What are you doing here?' Taylor said abruptly. He then seemed to realize how that sounded and amended himself. 'Not that you're not always welcome.'

Dimple rested an arm across Saffi's shoulder. Saffi wouldn't be surprised if a permanent brand was now singed into her skin. She should have pulled away. She did not.

'Sorry to intrude. I thought I'd come by and say hello. I never got the chance to thank you for arresting Hector Olsen.'

Andino and Taylor exchanged looks, but for once, Saffi got the impression that they weren't at all on the same page.

'Is something the matter?' Dimple asked. 'If an outside perspective might help, I'm always willing to listen.'

Taylor opened his mouth to speak, but Saffi's glare cut him off. That hadn't been enough for Andino, though, because he answered, 'We were just discussing Hector Olsen's trial.'

Dimple's attention snapped to Saffi, but only for a moment before darting away. 'But I remember seeing him at the police station. Is he not already under arrest?'

'Was that before or after he accused you of framing him?' Saffi muttered. The twitch of Dimple's mouth revealed that she'd heard her.

'It's more complicated than that,' Taylor explained. 'He paid his bail, so now we'll just have to wait until the trial, which has been delayed indefinitely.'

'That doesn't sound very just,' Dimple said with a frown. Her voice trembled ever so slightly, glancing around as though terrified Olsen would pop out at her from behind a closed door.

Saffi could tell Taylor was carefully studying Dimple for signs of dishonesty, visibly distressed when he found none. He probably felt like he *was* losing his mind. She couldn't blame him. Even Saffi struggled with it and she'd known Dimple to be a liar from the very moment she met her.

'I know,' Andino huffed. 'We don't get paid until the trial's concluded.'

Saffi frowned. 'Is that seriously your only concern?'

Andino rolled his eyes. 'Don't tell me you've grown soft, Saffi. At the end of the day, this is my job.'

Saffi didn't know why his nonchalance irked her so much. She'd witnessed Andino's lackluster attitude the entire time she'd been in America. Hell, him being impatient to the point of negligence was the whole reason Saffi had been called to help. He never failed to bring up her past failures but came so close every day to making the same mistakes she had. And she was the one cleaning up his mess while he remained blissfully unaware. Maybe she should just let him fuck up the case, let him see what it's like.

Dimple was watching their back-and-forth very intently.

'What *are* you doing here?' Saffi asked.

If Dimple was annoyed that her reconnaissance had been cut short, she didn't show it. Saffi really should've known that something as simple as a change in subject wouldn't be the end of it. 'The trailer for *Insomnia* came out today,' she said. 'Have you seen it yet?'

Saffi and Taylor shook their heads, but Andino remained suspiciously unmoved. She'd almost forgotten that Dimple's movie was due to come out soon. September, they'd said. That was only a month away.

Dimple graciously accepted the remote handed to her by Andino and clicked a practiced series of buttons. The TV in the corner of the room that Andino and Taylor usually set to the most ridiculous channels imaginable suddenly went dark. Chilling music washed across the room. Saffi turned to Dimple, suddenly eager to compare the woman on-screen to the one beside her, but Dimple pinched her in a pointed demand to pay attention. Once Saffi looked up, though, she couldn't look away.

There was no other way to describe it – the woman on-screen was beautiful. She was caked in dirt and blood with the most twisted, demented grin on her face, and she'd somehow never looked better. Saffi wasn't one to subscribe to the concept of fate, nor to the notion that a person could be born to do something, but as she watched Dimple's face flash across the screen, Saffi got the distinct impression that Dimple was always meant to do this. To be put on screens and billboards. To carve out space for herself in this godforsaken world, damn anyone who stood in her path.

Suddenly, it all clicked – everything Saffi had scoffed at about actors and the film industry. When it culminated in projects like these, it made sense why so much time, effort, and money were put into them.

Distantly, Saffi realized there had been a conscious and wise effort to leave Chris Porter out of the trailer. But that only meant Dimple got double the screen time.

By the time the TV faded to black once again, every hair on Saffi's body was standing on end. If she thought about it for more than half a second, she would realize that she had virtually no understanding of the plot. Somehow, she didn't want to linger on that.

'That was incredible,' Taylor said in that easy, genuine tone of his. 'You're very talented, Dimple.'

'It's been trending,' Andino muttered, attempting to sound casual.

'Has it?' Dimple asked as though she didn't already know. 'It's been selected for the Toronto International Film Festival next month as well.'

But there was something odd in her tone, so Saffi turned to face her. When their eyes met, all the breath left Saffi's lungs at once. This entire time, it was clear that Dimple had been looking only at her. Her expression was like nothing Saffi had ever seen before – guarded, like a soldier preparing to be struck down, but also eager. For some godforsaken reason, despite critical acclaim and thousands of fans falling at her feet, Dimple Kapoor wanted Saffi's opinion.

She cleared her throat. 'Not bad,' she said. Dimple relaxed at that, her shoulders unwinding.

Privately, however, Saffi still thought the trailer felt subpar when measured up against the performance Dimple had been putting on these past months. The one-woman show Saffi had front seat tickets to. She supposed she should feel lucky.

Almost two weeks later, after running into dead end after dead end, Saffi had come to realize that the biggest gap in her evidence was that Dimple herself had been a victim. But the best way to catch a liar was to allow them to incriminate themself. If Saffi could somehow prove that Dimple had lied about Hector attacking her, she would have a shot at convincing a jury.

She'd been in the middle of digging through her bag for a clean shirt when her office door burst open. Taylor came rushing inside – never a good sign.

'What is it?'

He didn't speak right away, watching as Saffi turned her duffel bag upside down, shaking the contents free. All of her worldly possessions spread out across the floor. She was constantly moving from one hotel to another so she had no permanent address, but seeing the small amount of floor space her few possessions seemed to take up was a little jarring. Saffi dug through the mess on the ground until she finally found a plain white button-down without any stains on it – her last one. She would have to walk over to the laundromat soon.

Taylor didn't seem all that interested in the way she began reorganizing her bag. Instead, he picked up a folded piece of card stock that had fallen out in the chaos. Saffi felt herself flush when she realized what it was.

'This is from three years ago,' Taylor muttered, staring down at the birthday card. 'You kept this?'

Saffi placed her newly folded clothes back into the bag and snatched the card from him. She slipped it back where it belonged, unable to look at Taylor. The sound of the zipper was excruciatingly loud in the otherwise still office.

'I wasn't sure you were getting them with how often you move around,' Taylor said sheepishly. 'I was worried I was pouring my heart out to some confused stranger.'

'Well, I did. And I read them too, asshole. *Happy birthday, have a great day* hardly counts as pouring your heart out. Neither do the stupid little pictures you drew on the back,' Saffi said. 'You really should consider taking an art class.'

Taylor blinked in surprise. 'I didn't draw those.'

Saffi frowned. 'Then who did?'

'Atlas,' Taylor said as though it were obvious.

And, in retrospect, maybe it was. Saffi had never seen Taylor doodle anything. He'd always been better with words. Andino, on the other hand, was prone to spacing out, drawing lopsided clouds at the corners of his papers. However, Saffi had been under the impression that Andino knew nothing about the cards Taylor sent her every year, written entirely in his handwriting. She felt a little guilty now for not realizing it sooner.

'Well, here's another one for the collection,' Taylor said, holding out a card. 'Happy birthday, Saffi.'

Saffi accepted it automatically, uncomprehending until she realized what day it was. Twelve fifteen in the morning on August 25. On the back of this card was another messy doodle, this time of a palm tree. Or, from some angles, a toilet cleaner brush.

'It's not a collection,' Saffi muttered. 'Is this what you came here for?'

'That and to let you know Atlas and I found a bottle of whiskey for the occasion, just like old times,' Taylor said. 'Okay – maybe not exactly like old times. We splurged. I'm a little too old for bottom-shelf hangovers.'

The next morning Saffi woke up in the break room with a pounding headache. Her back ached from sleeping on the floor and the sunlight peeking in through the blinds felt like laser beams. She couldn't remember it being this bad when she was twenty-one. Somewhere in the distance, Andino made the sound of a dying animal.

Feeling generous, Saffi dragged herself to her feet and poured three cups of water, handing one each to Andino and Taylor, which they accepted gratefully. Only when she drank the entire thing did she feel semi-coherent. She checked the time on her laptop, recoiling at the brightness, but was quickly distracted by the title of a trending news article.

'Shit.'

Her tone must've given something away because both Andino and Taylor slowly rose to their feet, coming to read over her shoulder.

Hector Olsen, 'Ladies Killer': Literal or Figurative?

More than an article, this was clickbait, its success hinging on its ability to agitate the masses. They were publicly accusing the man of not only assaulting Shyla Patel, but of killing Irene Singh and attempting to kill Dimple Kapoor as well. No reputable publication would ever get away with that. Leaked by an 'anonymous Hollywood insider.' Including intimate details about Olsen being dragged into the police precinct that sounded oddly like this 'insider' had been in the room with them. It didn't feel like a coincidence that the moment Dimple Kapoor found out about Olsen's trial being pushed back, so did the rest of the world. And no one was happy about it.

'I told you the public would find out,' Andino murmured, as though it weren't his beloved idol who had leaked it in the first place.

'Shut the fuck up,' Saffi seethed, trying to remind herself that he didn't know. Because of her, neither of them did.

Taylor, who'd been squinting down at his phone and rubbing his temples, added, 'Social media is a battlefield right now. There are talks of protests. Nobody thinks it's fair that his trial is being pushed back. Maybe this is a good thing if it means he'll get prosecuted sooner?'

Saffi wondered if this many people banded together against Olsen when he beat his ex-wives. Why was it that when Dimple Kapoor spoke, suddenly the whole world listened? Again, Saffi had been nothing but a pawn in her grand scheme.

'Oh great,' Andino said. His work phone was pressed to his ear. 'The Singhs left a voicemail.'

'Let me guess, they're demanding we push for the trial to happen as soon as possible?' Saffi asked.

'It might work now,' Andino said.

'I know,' Saffi replied, no matter how much she wished she could argue.

'Olsen won't be able to call in any more favors,' Taylor added. 'Not with so much media coverage focused on him.'

'This is great,' Andino said. 'The case is practically closed, we'll all get paid, and you'll be free to run off to wherever you want.'

But that was far from Saffi's concern. With this leak, Dimple had effectively put an even shorter time limit on the investigation. Saffi had, at most, until the end of September to find something undeniable; something that would make any judge stop in their tracks. Because with the way things were looking now, a jury could very well convict Hector Olsen for Dimple Kapoor's crimes.

But would that be so bad?

Saffi bit the inside of her cheek as hard as she could. The metallic taste of blood grounded her. Of course it would be. She'd already promised herself that she would never put anyone else unrighteously on death row. With the new year looming closer, so was her father's next senate election. After five years abroad, she couldn't announce her return just to ruin things for him now. Though part of her wondered why she was so worried about his opinion when he'd never offered her anything but criticism in the first place.

Why are you so eager to leave your family behind? Do you hate us so much? he'd said when she'd shared the news that she'd gotten into Harvard.

When she'd told him she wanted to be a private investigator, not a lawyer, it was *Clearly you have no appreciation for the things I've taught you.*

But this nasty, vindictive part of her sounded suspiciously like Dimple Kapoor, so she promptly shoved it aside.

ACT III

Execution

30

September 1, 2026

Five days before *Insomnia*'s premiere at the Toronto International Film Festival, Dimple Kapoor found herself on the receiving end of far more pity than she could withstand.

'I always knew he had it out for you. The way he would look at you sometimes – I only wish I had said something earlier.'

Dimple had already forgotten the name of whomever she was talking to, not that it mattered. This was definitely the first time they'd spoken on the phone, and possibly the first time they'd said more than a few sentences to each other. This influx in pity was an unforeseen consequence of the article about Hector Olsen she'd anonymously leaked last week.

On her couch, scrolling through her notifications, Dimple listened with one ear. She tried not to flinch when Irene Singh's face took up the screen. Ever since the public found out her death was no accident, there'd been a whole new resurgence of love for her.

Even more disturbing was the small yet vocal group that vehemently denied any and all claims of Irene's death, swearing up and down that she had, in fact, gone into hiding somewhere in the Cayman Islands.

'Don't blame yourself. You couldn't possibly have predicted this,' Dimple replied.

'How are you doing?'

'I suppose I am shaken up.'

Dimple smiled at the messages under the most recent photo Priyal had posted of her. Fans seemed to enjoy her recent magazine cover shoots. Perhaps she ought to say yes to those opportunities more often.

'Oh, you poor thing.'

It was obvious they'd only called so they could sell their story to the press later on. *Up-and-coming actor Whatever Their Name Is has shared that their close and personal friend, Dimple Kapoor, is 'shaken up, but hanging in there' in light of recent events.*

Having gotten what they wanted, the unknown caller quickly made their excuses and hung up. Dimple watched the likes of her most recent post steadily increase. She refreshed the page and the number doubled.

The only genuine call she'd received had been from the owners of the café next door to her first Los Angeles apartment. Every lie that had slipped from her lips while speaking to them had made her stomach twist with guilt. She'd already abused too much of their kindness and so she tried her best to avoid their efforts to reconnect.

In addition to screening phone calls, Dimple had been extraordinarily busy. Between the new lead role she'd landed and promotional work for *Insomnia,* Dimple hardly noticed as the leaves browned and wind picked up in preparation for a cool Los Angeles fall. There was too much to worry about – for one, the knowledge that her newest movie would be filming at the same lot Hector Olsen was working on. This proposed trouble, but also a unique opportunity.

Amidst the chaos, however, it had been rather calm. Perhaps a little too calm. Hector Olsen's trial – moved up to the middle of the month – was still too far out for Dimple's liking. And it would be just like Saffi to pull the rug out from under her at the last moment.

Dimple slipped on a pair of her favorite heels and took the stairs out of her apartment complex. The weather outside today was too nice to ignore. She decided she needed a walk, desperate for the opportunity to clear her head. The wind ruffled her hair and she breathed in the herbal aroma wafting over from the biryani place nearby.

It reminded her of walking by Irene during lunch breaks on set. Dimple stuffed her hands in her pockets and walked briskly in the opposite direction. She could feel people stare as she passed – perhaps they'd recognized her – but Dimple kept her head ducked.

Months ago, when Dimple Kapoor had fallen off the balcony at a party and been subsequently hospitalized, the Hollywood whisper network had been under the impression that she had a substance abuse problem. Now, however, since every media site was pushing the idea that not only had Dimple Kapoor been attacked, but that Hector Olsen was the culprit, it was another story altogether.

Suddenly, partygoers swore up and down that they remembered Hector Olsen following Dimple Kapoor out to the balcony. Several posts even claimed that they'd witnessed him leaving the party in a blood-soaked suit. And these claims weren't just limited to the anonymity of the internet. Nearly every single one of Dimple's acquaintances had been reaching out to her with similar sentiments.

Hollywood was rich in many things, but none so much as scandal. It was imperative to grasp for any stake you could in the fiasco of the moment; that way your interviews for the subsequent documentaries, memoirs, and the like would be secured. All this worked in Dimple's favor. It was glorious, the power of a single seeded thought. It didn't matter what Saffi did, nor did it matter that the trial had yet to take place; the world now considered Hector Olsen a guilty man.

Insomnia churned on regardless. Their scheduled premiere at the Toronto International Film Festival was days away and, realizing that there would be no pleasing everyone, Chris Porter was banned from participating in any promotion after being released from his rehabilitation. This resulted in a drastic increase in Dimple's own interview time and, suddenly, she was the only lead. It wasn't exactly a terrible feeling.

A car sped past, sending Dimple's hair flying. Her phone buzzed in her pocket, and she scrambled to check it. It was only a text from Priyal. She tucked it away.

Chris Porter, eager to rehabilitate not only himself, but his reputation as well, had gone as far as to set up a foundation for victims of DUIs. The producers of *Insomnia* had publicly announced that a sizable donation of box office proceeds would go to that very foundation. And just like that, public opinion was cemented in the positive. Julie had told Dimple privately that the producers had only agreed to the donation in the first place because they projected that the movie would bring in enough revenue to make up for it. Now, days away from her first-ever red-carpet appearance, Dimple felt as though she were walking on air. It was likely the reason she ended up here, at the front steps of Andino and Taylor Private Eye.

Steeling herself, she pushed the doors open.

To say the PI agency was a chaotic mess would be an understatement, but Dimple hardly blamed them. She figured they must be busy these days in preparation for Hector Olsen's trial – or in Saffi's case, her attempts to derail the trial. The floor was littered with memos and rubber bands. The trash cans were piled high. All three PIs were locked in their respective offices with their blinds drawn. The printer seemed to be smoking.

The conclusion of Hector's trial, however, wouldn't be the

end of things. It certainly wouldn't be enough to dissuade Saffi, and that was what worried Dimple the most. What, short of death, would stop her? If nothing but death would do, how could Dimple kill her? Everyone seemed invincible until they weren't, and the quality of a performance hinged on its conclusion.

Deciding she wouldn't find her answers lingering in the hallway, Dimple knocked twice on Saffi's door. When she heard no answer, she pushed her way inside. Compared to the rest of the building, Saffi's office was as neat as ever. Even more so, perhaps. The few square spaces of surface not stacked high with files and memos were sparkling.

'Did I say you could come in?' Saffi huffed, typing rapidly on her keyboard. She sounded tired.

'And here I thought I was always welcome,' Dimple said, coming to sit on the desk, beside Saffi's elbow.

Predictably, Saffi exited out of her tabs quicker than Dimple could read them and swiveled around to face her. The only evidence of her lethargy were her dark circles. They'd always been there, but they were much more prominent now. And yet the show must go on.

'The opposite, actually,' Saffi said. 'What do you want? Thanks to the stunt you pulled, I'm very busy.'

Her false disinterest was futile. Dimple remembered how Saffi had looked at her after watching *Insomnia*'s trailer. Like a moth to the flame. Seeing it for the first time, Dimple had thought, *This is what it's all for.*

A thought wormed its way into Dimple's mind. One could call it an impulse even. Before she could think twice, she was saying, 'I rather think you could use a break.'

Saffi fixed her with an unimpressed look. 'What part of *I'm busy* do you not understand?'

'Not now,' Dimple countered. 'Next week.'

Saffi's brow twitched slightly as she turned her mind over the importance of the date. 'Toronto International Film Festival,' she eventually concluded. 'You want me to go to the goddamn TIFF. You're joking.'

Dimple wanted to see Saffi outside this office for once. Canada had abolished the death penalty, and Dimple found herself curious how Saffi would act when there was nothing holding her back. When there was even ground between them.

'Never,' Dimple said. 'You should feel honored. Not everyone has the privilege of being invited.'

'I feel cheated, to be honest,' Saffi said, leaning back and crossing her arms. 'What's the point of knowing a famous actress if the best time she can offer me is some film festival? Where's my Oscar invite?'

'It's not just some film festival,' Dimple replied. 'The sheer number of critics that show up to these things – it could make or break any debut. In many ways, it's even more important than the Oscars.'

Those dark eyes bored into hers unflinchingly. Despite knowing Dimple's full truth, Saffi hadn't once been afraid of her. Dimple straightened.

'And you want to take me with you?' Saffi asked.

'Of course.'

'What about – ?' Saffi held her hand up to Dimple's hip, severely underestimating Priyal's height.

'Priyal is already coming as my assistant. You're my date.'

With a deep sigh, Saffi rubbed her temples. 'You're too much,' she murmured under her breath.

Dimple inclined her head. 'And you deserve the most.'

She didn't miss the way Saffi studied her computer screen as she considered it. Dimple had piqued her curiosity.

With a final push, Dimple asked, 'What are you so afraid of?'

Saffi scoffed. 'You're the one who should be afraid. You have no idea what I'm capable of.'

'Was that a threat?' Dimple asked, eyebrows raised in genuine surprise. 'That was almost cute, Saffi. Even if you killed me, I'd just come back to haunt you.'

'You really think they'd let you out of hell?'

That startled a laugh out of Dimple. As she looked down at Saffi's smirk, she felt even more resolved. After seeing *Insomnia,* even Saffi wouldn't be able to deny that the end justified the means. She could die knowing she'd been in the wrong all along. The more Dimple felt this desire, the harder those phantom fingers pressed into her neck. It was becoming difficult to breathe.

Saffi turned back to her computer, worrying her lower lip between her teeth, and Dimple got the distinct feeling she was going to decline.

Just as the disappointment was settling in, Saffi said, 'I'm not paying for a plane ticket.'

Dimple was already heading for the door before either one of them could change their mind. 'I already have everything we need; I'll forward you the details. All you have to do is pack.'

'Hold on, I didn't say – !'

Dimple only paused to wave goodbye before shutting the door conclusively behind her. She leaned back against it, glad everyone was too busy to take notice of her in such a state. A strand of hair chose that moment to break free of its artful placement, and she hurriedly tucked it away.

It wasn't just Saffi. The premiere meant the world would see her as a lead for the first time. Even if the film flopped at the box office stage, the way Dimple looked, spoke, and acted would be immortalized like this forever. Frozen in time for generations to come.

Proof that her mother's death hadn't been in vain, and it was close enough to taste. She almost wished her aunt and uncle were here so she could shove it in their faces. Although Saffi was right, hell rarely extended the courtesy of a day pass to its inhabitants. Dimple banished them from her thoughts. If anyone's meaningless existence deserved to be forgotten, it was theirs.

'Oh – hello,' a familiar voice said.

Dimple straightened at once. Atlas had a half-eaten granola bar in hand, jaw slack in surprise. When she nodded politely at him, he immediately returned the gesture.

'What are you doing here?'

'Oh, just visiting,' she replied vaguely.

'By the way, have fun at TIFF. You'll have to tell me all about it,' Atlas said.

'Actually, you can ask Saffi. She'll be coming with me.'

Dimple, admittedly, only said it to see what kind of reaction it would elicit from Atlas. There was a brief flash of jealousy that amused her greatly.

'Will she, now?' he asked, thoughtfully. 'I have to admit it's strange how much the two of you have hit it off. You couldn't be more different. I'm surprised her terrible attitude didn't put you off.'

'I find it rather endearing,' Dimple replied.

'Fair enough. That's how Saffi treats the people she respects.'

Dimple blinked up at Atlas, caught off guard.

'Right?' he laughed. 'It's no wonder she has no friends other than us.'

Us. Dimple contemplated that for far longer than necessary.

'Can you do me a favor?' Atlas asked suddenly, wrenching Dimple from her thoughts. 'Look out for her, will you?'

Atlas had such an earnest gaze, another one of the rare reminders that he and Saffi held more than just contempt for each other. She thought of a photograph, three foreheads brushing, huddled around paperwork. He had no idea the weight of what he was asking, nor whom he was asking it of. Nor did he have the self-awareness to know that he was part of the reason Saffi needed looking out for.

'I will,' Dimple said. 'I promise she's safe with me.'

31

September 5, 2026

Saffi stifled a yawn into the crook of her elbow. She was flying to Toronto the same day of *Insomnia*'s premiere. Planes always made her sleepy, but that fact was only exacerbated by how late she'd stayed up the night before. She'd gone to speak with Hector Olsen, knowing it would bother her for the entirety of their trip if she waited. Besides, it had taken weeks for her to convince Olsen to meet with her in the first place and she refused to let the effort go to waste. If she'd known how irritating the man could be, she might've stuck to exchanging emails instead.

'I'm the best director in Hollywood and this is how they repay me?' Olsen had ranted. 'It's like everyone's forgotten how many of my movies have won Oscars! I've created the careers of ninety percent of the actors working in Hollywood right now!'

Refusing to meet him in his room, Saffi had reserved one of the conference spaces at the upscale Beverly Hills hotel he was staying in while he looked for a new house. Although, it might've been more effective to interrogate him at a police station. If only the bureaucratic mess of paperwork it would require didn't put her off.

No, it was better to stay off the books. A mutually consensual discussion, nothing more. And if the man ended up confessing his sins to her, well, it would only be to her benefit.

'Mr Olsen, if we could please stay on topic –'

'Do you have any idea the work I've put into this industry? This film is going to be the best thing to grace cinema in fifty years! But just because I like to have fun every once in a while, I'm suddenly a threat to society? I've spent every waking hour of the past few months on that set. Just ask my assistant!'

'That's great, Mr Olsen,' Saffi had replied absently. 'Now, the party where Dimple Kapoor was targeted –'

Olsen's eyes had darkened at Dimple's mention. 'You can tell that little bitch to shove her lies –'

'And what, exactly, did she lie about?' Saffi asked.

'She *wishes* I touched her – I didn't even go to that party,' he seethed.

Saffi had paused at that, straightening up considerably. 'What do you mean by that?'

Olsen shifted in his chair, as though uncomfortable, but continued in a much more subdued tone. 'Are you deaf or stupid? I said I didn't go.'

Saffi clenched her fists. 'Mr Olsen, this is a serious claim you're making. You do understand that if you were not at the party, there is no way you were to blame for Dimple Kapoor's fall? What's more, the real killer could be framing you. Why didn't you mention this before?'

'That's what I've been saying!' Olsen shouted. 'It's the ethnic bitch with the long hair – she did this to me!'

He slammed his fist down on the table with a loud thud and Saffi felt the vibrations against her elbows. She didn't flinch, refusing to give him the satisfaction. Men like Olsen were used to lording their power and stature over others. But no matter what he might think, Saffi was the one who held the power there. She could, however, somewhat sympathize with the plight of being the only one who could sense something off about Dimple Kapoor.

'How would you explain her blood on your suit?'

'It wasn't me! Those are custom-made – very expensive,' he scoffed, clearly put out that Saffi was unaffected by his antics. 'Dry clean only. I've never even spilled water on them.'

She heard the frustration creep into her voice. 'If not at the party, then where were you that night? Is there anyone who could verify your whereabouts?'

And because nothing could ever be so easy, Olsen suddenly closed in on himself. Saffi could see it in the way he angled away, crossing his arms. If he was refusing to tell her what he'd been doing, then Saffi figured it must've been something equally as damning – if not more. But if she could figure out what he was hiding, then maybe she could at least get him locked away for another, more appropriate reason. Killing two birds with one stone. If Olsen became too defensive, however, there would be no reasoning with him.

'This information could exonerate you. If you're found guilty, you'll be put on death row. And that's exactly what whoever is framing you wants to happen.'

Saffi had played the Dimple card in the hopes that it would get him riled up enough to admit something. It had been far from helpful.

'I don't care what that bitch says, I didn't lay a hand on her,' Olsen growled, fists clenched so hard they trembled. 'Don't tell me she's still holding a grudge? It was just a little something to get her to loosen up – what she gave me was worse!'

Saffi stilled, pen frozen above her notepad. She'd been almost certain that she'd misheard. 'Excuse me?'

'What?' he asked, suddenly defensive. 'She'd never been drunk before. I did her a favor! Usually, girls love that shit.'

Saffi's throat ran dry. 'Are you telling me you drugged her?'

'I didn't *drug* her, it was just a little alcohol. And it was years ago! It's not like I –'

Saffi hadn't realized she had her hands fisted in Olsen's shirt until he'd stopped speaking, his breath cut off by her tight grip. For a moment, all she could do was stare down at his horrified expression and watch in fascination as his face began to redden. His hands scrambled weakly against her hold. If this was what it took for him to learn that it was not she who should fear him, but the other way around, then so be it.

'Where were you the night of the party?' Her tone was hushed and angry.

When he didn't immediately answer, she shook him and repeated the question. The color of his face was approaching tomato and Saffi was beginning to think she was going about this the wrong way. Olsen was showing no signs of confessing. She let up the slightest amount and he choked out – 'Laila.'

His ex-wife.

The one who'd tried to sue him for domestic abuse and lost. It wasn't difficult to put two and two together. Revenge for the attempted lawsuit or even thoughtless violence, whatever reason Olsen had for being with his wife that night didn't matter. What mattered was how unlikely it was she would be willing to testify on behalf of her abuser.

Just as Olsen began to relax, Saffi tightened her grip on his shirt collar once again. 'Don't get the wrong idea. You may not be guilty of murder, but you've done much worse. If I can promise you one thing, it's this: So long as I live, I will not let you walk away a free man.'

Olsen's lips turned blue and Saffi let go of his shirt. He'd slumped in his seat and hadn't spoken another word. Despite that minor setback, she'd left the hotel with a sense of accomplishment. Even though the world still believed Olsen to be a liar and even though he would never speak another candid word to her again, Saffi couldn't help feeling like it had been worth it. A man so stupid he'd confess something like that in her presence simply could not be the same killer she had been going toe-to-toe with this entire time.

It bothered her that she didn't get the chance to speak with Laila Olsen before the flight. Still, Saffi didn't like the idea of letting a murderous actress leave the country unsupervised. It wasn't that she expected her to run, but Dimple Kapoor was a menace enough by herself in America. Who knew what she'd get up to in Canada? No, it was important to keep her close.

Extremely close. The airplane seats were uncomfortably tiny. Dimple had taken the middle seat, but Saffi had a feeling the troubled expression on her face wasn't discomfort. Her attention dropped to Dimple's hands. They were crossed over her chest, fingers digging into her biceps. Years of harsh touches – was it also the only way she knew to hold herself?

'What – are you scared?' Saffi asked, but the look Dimple gave her was enough to both confirm her suspicions and stop her line of questioning in its tracks.

'Don't say a word,' Dimple warned.

'There's no way. If you're scared of heights, why did you throw yourself off a balcony?' Saffi hissed. It made sense, given her history, but she had assumed she'd found some way to move past it. That she'd been terrified and done it nevertheless spun Saffi's mind in circles. What was it like, to want something that badly?

Dimple's expression said she knew exactly how much this revelation had made Saffi question herself, and that it amused her.

On the opposite side, Priyal had both earbuds in and

her eyes closed. The flight attendants performing final checks indicated that it wouldn't be long before takeoff. Dimple's biceps now had red marks where her nails were digging in.

'Relax, will you?' Saffi said. 'You're gonna break your arm.'

'I *am* relaxed.' Dimple said it so convincingly, Saffi would've thought she was telling her the sky was blue.

This was the first real sign Saffi had seen of what lurked underneath the mask of Dimple's manufactured emotions. She wanted to see more. She wanted to see her break. Saffi wanted to know what it took to push her over the edge – what it took to get her to push someone else over the edge.

She reached over and pinched the actress nearly hard enough to draw blood. Dimple let go of her arms, but not before shooting Saffi an irritated look.

'That thing you said to me – about Andino and Taylor holding me back,' Saffi began.

That had Dimple's attention immediately. It was a weighty thing, receiving every ounce of the actress's focus. 'I have to admit, I'm surprised it stuck with you,' she said.

If anything, Saffi hadn't been able to forget. 'What did you mean?'

Dimple seemed to consider it for a moment, turning it over in her mind. 'They don't let you be great.'

Saffi raised an eyebrow, unsure if she should be offended. 'I think I'm starting to see where your ego stems from.'

Dimple continued as though she hadn't heard. 'Where do I begin? You reported the miscarriage of justice when it was far from your fault. Despite the fact that enough evidence was presented for a jury to convict someone, you made sure the correct verdict was reached in the end. But look how that turned out. You blame yourself. Atlas and Eli blame you as well, and you let them. Even though the only reason you're here is to fix their mistakes. And you have the gall to ask how they're holding you back? They're doing so because you're letting them. The only way to move on is to stop letting them.'

Oh. That was – Saffi didn't know how to respond. Everything from her brain to the tips of her fingers felt numb.

Still, intentions didn't matter as much as people thought they did. It was a point her father had emphasized as soon as she'd been old enough to understand it. The courtroom was no playpen. Every misdeed had consequences – whether natural or lawful.

She cleared her throat. 'Didn't realize you hated Andino and Taylor so much.'

'I don't hate them,' Dimple countered immediately. 'I like them fine. Before meeting Atlas, I'd never had someone I could talk about all my favorite old films with. And Eli is perfectly polite and gentlemanly. It's an odd thing to come across these days. But it's not about anything they've done to me. It's about what they're doing to you.'

Saffi swallowed. 'Careful, Kapoor,' she said. 'It's starting to sound like you care.'

'How many times have I told you to call me *Dimple*?'

Saffi should've felt horrified, but the flipping in her stomach wasn't of discomfort.

'You really could have so much more,' Dimple said, but her voice sounded distant. As though it were coming from the plane's intercom. 'Where's your hunger? Why work with Atlas and Eli when you could open your own agency? Why save face for your father when you could run for office yourself? All you have to do is want.'

Was this why every moment with Dimple Kapoor felt so grand? Why every breath she took felt like it should be recorded in history books? Simply because she believed it.

Despite what anyone said or did to her, she believed it and so it became true.

Saffi shook her head. 'I do it because I care about them,' she argued. 'And because they'd do the same for me. It's selfish to go about life only living for yourself.'

'You think they'd do the same for you?'

'Of course they would.'

Dimple gave her a sad look. 'What you're describing is unconditional love. And it does not exist.'

But even an ocean away, Saffi's parents still worried about her. They accepted that she wouldn't call, text – hell, even email – and settled on a postcard every few months. They met her in the middle. If not unconditional love, then what was that?

'It's not real,' Dimple said, 'and I will prove it to you.'

'That's ominous,' Saffi muttered. 'If you kill my family, I'll make you regret it.'

Dimple looked at her as though it was the silliest thing she'd ever heard. 'It's a wonder the way your mind works. Such extremes you go to. Relax, Saffi. What would murder prove?'

But Saffi couldn't relax. Not when she felt like she'd just been trapped in a burning building.

'Why *Dimple*?' she asked suddenly. Another question that had been on her mind for some time. If she was going to burn anyway, she wanted to make the most of it. 'As your new name – why *Dimple*?' It wasn't uncommon in some parts of the world, but there had to be a reason she had chosen it for herself.

Dimple studied her curiously. 'You're full of questions today.'

'Only because you're full of answers.'

That response seemed to amuse her. Dimple sighed, leaning

back against her seat. There was a flash of red and Saffi looked over just in time to see the lighter. How the hell had she gotten that past security? Saffi turned to check if anyone was watching, but the flight attendants had disappeared. It was then that she realized the plane had already taken off. Neither of them had noticed.

Saffi watched as Dimple weaved the lighter between her fingers. A few times she looked like she might ignite the flame, but she always stopped herself short. There was no need for it, really, when Dimple herself was fire personified.

'Don't you get tired of setting fires?' Saffi asked. The lengths Dimple had gone to just to hold on. To her career, to her image, to the damn lighter. 'Don't you wonder what life is like when the smoke clears?'

This drew her attention, molten brown irises looking at Saffi as though seeing straight through to her core. 'Don't you get tired of running?' she asked, which was fair enough. Because of course Saffi did. That didn't mean she knew how to stop.

They made a funny pair: the fire starter and the evacuator.

There was so much more Saffi wanted to ask, but she was beginning to realize that somehow, to some extent, Dimple had begun to understand her in return. And Saffi wasn't so sure this was a trade-off she was willing to make.

It was never a good thing to be known.

Cutting through the silence, Dimple finally answered. 'When I was sixteen, I was hiding out in the attic and I found these journals that my mother used to write. She was very depressed while she was pregnant with me and it seemed like, other than sleeping, writing was all she had the energy for. She used to say that she was absorbing all of my sadness so that I could be happy for the rest of my life. That was why she'd always refer to me as *Dimple*. She never did get the chance to decide on a name before she died. I suppose that one day I decided I wanted to be Dimple forever.'

'Isn't that unconditional love?' Saffi asked.

Dimple gave her a sad smile. 'My mother was taken from this world and my aunt and uncle were allowed to live. Isn't that proof enough that this universe is too cruel to allow for the existence of something so pure and altruistic?'

Saffi had nothing to say in response.

32

September 5, 2026

Dimple had frozen in place when she finally unveiled her dress for the premiere.

They'd checked into the hotel a few hours ago. Saffi, clearly exhausted, went to her own room while Priyal took off to explore the city. Dimple, on the other hand, had spent her free time trying to expel the lingering paranoia from her mind. She had a plan in place, but at the same time, she kept thinking back to their conversation on the plane. To the promise she had made to Saffi.

It isn't real and I will prove it to you.

The words were easy enough to say, spurred on by the challenge of putting on a good show, but there was a chance Saffi would never understand. Dimple could go through all the trouble of enlightening Saffi, and she'd only despise her for it. Would this be the thing that finally extinguished the fire that drew Saffi's gaze? The thought unsettled her more than it should have.

The dress, though? The sight of it alone was enough to wipe her mind clean.

'Stunning, right?'

Dimple's head whipped around to stare, awestruck, at Priyal. She should've noticed something was amiss. Priyal had returned to help her get ready for the main event, but instead of chatting her ear off like she usually did, the girl had been oddly quiet. So quiet that Dimple worried their time apart had strained their easy companionship.

She'd handed Dimple a particularly bitter dark roast coffee and stood off to the side with her lips pressed together. Now, though, Dimple could see that she'd been suppressing a smile. The awkward pose she'd taken up was because she was attempting to record her reaction. Dimple subconsciously twirled a strand of hair, switching stances to highlight her good side.

'It's –' She cut herself off, unable to supply a fitting response.

It suddenly struck her how precious this gift was. Dimple dared not breathe as she separated the tissue paper with trembling hands. She pinched the dress between two fingers – gingerly, delicately – and lifted the red dress to the light. The brand name stitched into the inside collar was the same as the one embossed all over the tissue paper.

Salomé.

'How?' Dimple breathed.

'Salomé sent it,' Priyal explained, grin stretched so wide it looked like it hurt. 'They want you to wear it for the premiere. It's from their new collection – it's not even out yet.'

Dimple held the dress up to the light. The gown extended down to her feet and when she spun around, the skirt fanned out, bouncing. Priyal was almost giddier than her.

'It's beautiful' was all Dimple could manage, swallowing around a growing lump in her throat.

Priyal crossed the room and pulled her into a tight hug. Moving the dress to her free hand so as not to wrinkle it, Dimple wrapped an arm around her assistant.

'I'm so proud of you,' Priyal whispered into her ear. 'You've come so far. I'm so lucky I got to go on this journey with you.' She sighed wistfully. 'I wish I was an actress so I could dress up too.'

Dimple, still reeling over the dress, almost missed the undercurrent of Priyal's words. This was the first time she'd ever spoken about acting in conjunction with herself.

'What are you doing? You have to get ready!' Priyal said when Dimple began folding the dress to put back into the box.

'First, we're getting you ready.'

Priyal frowned. 'What? Did you not hear me?'

But Dimple was already gathering Priyal's hair so she could brush through it. She forced Priyal to look at herself in the mirror.

'You don't have to wait until you're cast in movies to be a star,' Dimple said. Her assistant seemed to be at a loss for words. 'Besides, it won't be long until you're walking the red carpet, will it?'

'I'm sorry!' Priyal blurted. For what, it wasn't clear.

She looked close to tears and Dimple let go of her hair. Great. She found a tissue box and snatched a couple free, waving them at Priyal.

'Why are you crying?' Dimple asked when Priyal's sniffles turned into full-blown sobs.

'I just – I don't want to leave yet. You barely needed my help when I started working, and now that you do, I have to quit.'

'Priyal,' Dimple said, nearly laughing. 'I didn't expect you to work for me forever. This was always going to happen. Your career comes first.'

'You knew – ?'

'Of course I knew. And I'm happy for you. I know better than anyone how it feels when your dreams finally come true.'

Priyal was no Irene or Isaac – she didn't have a mansion or a backlog of blackmail. She'd worked for her success and deserved it.

'I'm sorry I didn't tell you.'

'There's nothing to apologize for.'

'Honestly, I didn't think it would happen this quickly,' Priyal said. 'When I first met her, Julie said I had a lot of potential, but she didn't have the room to take on any more clients. She also said that my portfolio was so *piss-poor* that she couldn't recommend me to any of her connections in good faith.'

Dimple winced in sympathy but had to hide her laugh with a cough. That sounded exactly like Julie.

'So, while I've been working for you, we've also been working on my portfolio.' She gave Dimple a sheepish look. 'I signed with an agent and everything. But I promise I never let it get in the way of my job! I didn't expect to like working for you so much.'

It wasn't anything Dimple didn't already know.

'That's wonderful,' Dimple told her earnestly. 'And you're booking roles now?'

Priyal nodded. 'I don't even really need a side job anymore.'

It had taken Dimple far longer in her career to be able to pay her bills through acting alone. She couldn't help feeling a little envious.

'But I can stay longer!' Priyal insisted suddenly. 'Now that your career is taking off, you need my help more than ever.'

Dimple shook her head. 'That is completely unnecessary. I assure you, I can manage.'

'But –'

'I'm more upset I didn't get to celebrate the news with you,' Dimple said, cutting her off. 'We'll just have to do that after the premiere.'

Priyal shook her head rapidly. 'No, this is your moment.'

'I'm not so emotionally stunted that I don't know how to share.'

That drew a laugh from the girl. She looked up at Dimple, something not too far off from her usual grin back in place.

'I'm so lucky I met you,' Priyal said wistfully. 'You're the first friend I ever made in LA, you know that?'

'Me too,' Dimple answered without thinking.

'You don't have to lie, Dimple,' Priyal said lightly.

But Dimple had been telling the truth. The embarrassing, unfortunate truth. In all her years in Hollywood and for all her successes, Priyal had been the closest thing to a friend she'd ever had. Now Dimple would be losing her. But before she could embarrass herself any further by explaining just that, Priyal clapped her hands and stood.

'Okay, enough, we need to get dressed. The red carpet is waiting.'

Dimple's bangles clinked as she posed for reporters. It was costume jewelry, but Dimple's mother had left to her a set of solid gold bangles that looked nearly identical. When she'd been a kid, she'd dreamed about finally turning eighteen years old, tugging them onto her wrists, and walking right out the door. That day never came, of course. Her aunt and uncle had long since pawned them to pay off one debt or another. It didn't matter. By that point, Dimple had already given up on expecting anything from anyone. She'd bought these bangles with her own money, and one day she would buy a set made of real gold, just like her mother's. And she'd have nobody to thank but her own hard work.

Jerome Bardoux was here as well, but he refused to pose for photographs, choosing instead to head straight inside the theater. Priyal stood off to the side, shooting Dimple a thumbs-up every time she looked her way. Every once in a while, Dimple's attention would snag on Saffi, who stood beside Priyal, almost hidden in a corner, dressed in her usual black suit. For once, she wasn't ludicrously overdressed.

'You're already trending,' Priyal whispered as Dimple made her way back to them. Dimple's heart soared. She had a good feeling about the night.

The three of them were directed inside a beautiful theater. Soft lighting paved the way toward their seats. It was mostly empty as of now, occupied only by those who had either worked on or acted in *Insomnia.* Dimple found where some of her co-stars were seated and was about to join them when she realized who was positioned beside her.

Shyla Patel.

Dimple froze. Shyla's nose sat just as regally on her face as before and her black eye had completely healed by now, but every time Dimple blinked, she saw twin rivers of blood gushing down her face.

'Dimple – hey! It's been forever!' Shyla beamed. 'Are you getting my texts?'

'What texts?' Dimple replied, voice strained.

'Oh, never mind, then,' she said. 'Anyway, I have so much to tell you!'

It took every ounce of Dimple's effort to keep her voice from shaking. 'You seem well.'

'Uh – look who's talking! Your dress is incredible – *Salomé, right*?' Dimple barely had the time to nod before Shyla barreled on. 'This is your first film festival too, isn't it? What do you think so far?'

'It's very overwhelming.' She felt nauseous, her dress constricting as her breaths grew shorter.

Dimple had to make a decision. Priyal and Saffi were standing politely beside her as she spoke, but the three of them stood out for not taking their seats. Where Saffi seemed content to watch her flounder, Priyal came to her rescue.

'Sorry, my feet are killing me,' she said, flopping into the seat beside Shyla.

Shyla laughed good-naturedly. 'Tell me about it.'

As the two of them lapsed into easy conversation, Dimple gingerly took her seat beside Priyal. She couldn't have orchestrated a better arrangement. No one would bother her with Priyal flanking her left and Saffi a solid presence to her right. She felt herself finally begin to relax, breath evening out.

The room got progressively louder as more people entered: the general public who had paid for the opportunity to see the premiere, and celebrities and influencers who'd been paid to promote it. Dimple could've sworn she saw a couple attendees attempting to snap sly photos of her. She did her best to ensure they got a flattering candid.

'Everyone seems so excited,' Priyal whispered giddily.

Dimple turned to Saffi, hoping to gauge her reaction, but she seemed more interested in the theater's tall ceilings than the proceedings around them. An inherently selfish sinking feeling found a home in Dimple's chest. She wanted Saffi to see her. She wanted to be the last thing Saffi ever saw.

Before she could dwell on it, the lights dimmed and murmurs hushed as the theater plunged into darkness. The screen remained stubbornly black long enough that Dimple feared something had gone wrong. It suddenly occurred to her that she had virtually no idea what all these people would be witnessing in a few short seconds.

Dimple had seen many actors rise as fast as they fell. Most of the time, they never recovered, fading into obscurity in the best-case scenario and ridiculed for years in the worst.

A pinch to her wrist made Dimple's head snap up. She let go of her biceps, trying to remember when she'd started digging her fingernails into them.

'What did I tell you?' Saffi whispered. 'I'm the only one you should be afraid of.'

Dimple blinked at her as the words registered. Her hand slipped into her pocket, closing around smooth plastic. Plenty of actors came back from a flopped movie. None came back from death row.

Dimple turned back to the front just in time to see the screen fade from black. Chilling music sounded around the room, making the hair on the back of her neck stand on end. Her heartbeat thumped to the rhythm. She felt as though she were watching through the eyes of a hundred people as her face flashed across the screen.

33

September 5, 2026

It wasn't until warm theater lights brightened to life that Dimple realized her vision was blurry. In a blink, something trickled down the side of her cheek. She quickly wiped it away with the back of her hand. There was nothing but the ringing in her ears, the thump of her heartbeat.

Her character had died on-screen and yet Dimple felt born anew. Months ago, cradling a candle in her hands, this was what she had wished for. It was so much better than she could've imagined.

Someone nudged her from her left. Priyal, sniffling and laughing. It took Dimple a moment to realize why she'd been alerted. The rest of *Insomnia*'s cast and crew were standing, looking out over the crowd. The ringing in her ears cut out, replaced by thunderous applause.

Dimple shot to her feet. Hundreds of faces stared back at her when she scanned the audience. The whole theater was on their feet, facing her as they clapped. Her lungs felt too big for her body, her heart an endless abyss. Her palms pressed together on autopilot, giving the audience thanks. Bright camera flashes. The shutter of a lens. She couldn't recall if she'd remembered to smile. Only when she registered that her cheeks hurt did she realize she'd been doing it all along.

Small fractions of her soul scattered across the theater, taken into the audience's memories. How this movie made them feel, the atmosphere, maybe even Dimple herself. Even if she died tomorrow, she would live on through them.

When Dimple turned to her left, Saffi was already looking back at her, eyes ablaze. She gave Dimple a tiny, almost imperceptible nod. Something loosened in Dimple's chest. She could've sworn the applause only intensified after that.

It was unclear how long she stood for, but it was enough for her legs to turn to jelly. Dimple could remember standing and knew that she was sitting again now, but had no recollection of what had happened in between.

She blinked and an announcer was walking onto the stage. Another blink and Jerome Bardoux was beckoned to join him. It was the first time Dimple came to realize that the director was a bit of an actor in his own regard. The persona he put on now was in stark difference to that of on set. Barked orders and frowns replaced with fake laughter and over-politeness. Dimple saw Shyla shake her head in her periphery.

Even as Jerome began explaining the process of creating the movie, Dimple felt the scrutiny of a hundred people fixed on her. This time, she knew it stemmed from more than her anxiety. She tried her best to keep her expression frozen in place.

Her co-lead's name, shouted out by an audience member in the form of a question, broke Dimple abruptly from her trance.

'Why hasn't Chris Porter joined the cast for promotions? After all the work he's done to recover from his addiction, it would be nice to see some support from his co-stars instead of outright shunning.'

Dimple's head snapped up and she scanned the audience for the culprit, but came back empty-handed. She did, however, notice several cameras trained on her.

She immediately turned back around. A hundred ants crawled across her skin. Dimple clenched her fists in her lap, barely able to keep from shaking.

Money, it seemed, solved all the world's problems. The producers throwing away box office proceeds. Chris employing people to start a foundation on his behalf. Just like that, it became everyone else who was the issue.

Onstage, Jerome's facade broke. He couldn't speak and began picking so harshly at his fingernail, he must've drawn blood. He always seemed like such a natural on set, it hadn't registered to Dimple before now that he too was new to all of this. *Keep it together,* she tried to convey to him. Every single one of the cast straightened and adopted a poker face. With a glance in their direction, Jerome mirrored them. Hopefully no one else had been studying him close enough to notice the lapse.

'We are all very proud of Chris,' Jerome said carefully. Dimple got the feeling that the public relations team had helped him with this statement beforehand. 'I'm sure you've seen how vocal he has been about the rest of the team working with him behind the scenes to get him the support he needs. And as you know, a portion of box office sales will be going toward the foundation Chris created in order to help victims of DUIs.'

'But what about the rest of the cast? Like Dimple Kapoor. Weren't they dating? Why hasn't she made a single statement about the situation? It really says a lot about –'

The volunteer was finally able to wrench the microphone away. 'Next question,' they said breathlessly, cueing a few awkward chuckles from audience members.

Meanwhile, Dimple's heart thudded even faster, the pit in her stomach opening so wide, she feared it might collapse in on itself. Her hands were visibly trembling now. She could feel every camera lens trained on her. Every hair on the back of her neck stood upright. She understood now why Jerome had cracked. If this was how she felt in the safety of her seat, how much worse did it feel onstage? To stand up there and pretend to be virtuous in front of all these people?

The next audience member began reciting their question, but Dimple was hardly listening.

How had everyone forgotten that Chris was a killer when his character in the movie they'd just watched met such a gruesome and fitting end for that very same reason? All it took was checking into a fancy rehab – more akin to a resort than anything else – and he was in better standing than ever before. Dimple was blamed for not making a statement. Dimple was blamed for not offering Chris enough support in his recovery. Dimple was blamed for associating with Chris at all when he himself faced no consequences.

She couldn't stand another minute of it.

Ducking forward, Dimple stumbled her way out of the theater. She didn't bother looking back at the crowd, too afraid of what she might find there. Or rather, too afraid that her face might betray her own turbulent emotions.

The back exit that she took led to an empty hallway. At the end of it was a bathroom sign. She nearly tripped over the fabric of her dress as she made a break for it.

Shoving the heavy door open, Dimple flung herself back against it, blood-red dress spilling over white tile. The glacial climate inside the bathroom compared to the temperate theater sent a shiver down the entire length of her body. Short breaths echoed across the small space.

The first thing that came up when searching her name online were photos of herself on the red carpet. Priyal had already reposted some of the best ones. Dimple looked into the mirror at her left. Her hair frizzed up in odd patterns, her mascara smudged. She might as well be a completely different person than the woman on her screen.

There was already a video of her during the standing ovation. Her fingernails dug into her biceps as she watched. It was her face. It betrayed her every emotion, despite how hard she'd attempted to control herself. How hadn't everyone immediately clocked her for the fraud she was? Dimple's stomach dropped. Had she similarly given away her true feelings while Jerome discussed Chris? Was that how the audience member had clocked her disregard? There weren't any videos of that exchange yet – nor of her stumbling out of the theater – but that only made the itch under Dimple's skin worsen. This wasn't how she wanted to be remembered.

She paced the length of the bathroom before stuffing her phone back into her pocket and wrenching the sink tap on. This was all wrong. She was supposed to show Saffi – to show herself – that everything she'd done had been worth it in the end. That all you needed to achieve greatness was the drive to do so. That she was finally done with setting fires.

The water was cold when she shoved her hands under the spray, and it did nothing to soothe the invisible ache deep within her. Soap foamed and water splashed, running up her sleeves until they too were wet.

A damp stain formed at the front of her dress.

This was too familiar.

In the mirror she saw a pair of innocent brown eyes. Falling.

Falling.

Dimple shouted, fist coming up and slamming against the mirror with all her force. The action came of her own volition, yet she gasped when the glass cracked, spiderwebs creeping up in every direction. Something tickled. Blood, probably, trickling down from her knuckles onto her fingers, dripping onto the floor.

It had been months since she'd relapsed. Of course Irene would choose now of all times to trouble her again. Was Chris haunted by his mistakes? Dimple doubted it. She tried to see her reflection through the cracks, but it was too distorted to make out.

The bathroom door clanged open, and Dimple inhaled sharply, cradling her injured hand to her chest. She hoped whoever it was wouldn't immediately pinpoint the blood on the floor or the cracks in the mirror, giving her time to clean up.

Her wishes went unanswered.

They cursed, their footsteps echoing as they edged closer. In the back of her mind, Dimple could recognize them by gait alone, and if not that, then surely by their voice. But with the mirror so distorted, her mind could conjure up whatever sick fantasies it desired. Suddenly, she was a child again, just as aware that the blows would come as she was that she couldn't stop them.

Dimple could sense the arm coming for her and reached out to intercept it, slapping it away. She was unable to repress the violent shudder when she finally made contact. It wasn't until the hand closed around her wrist that Dimple registered its gentleness. She opened her eyes, met Saffi's gaze, and breathed. Which made no sense – Saffi was the last person she wanted to see in this context.

'Are you done with your meltdown?' Saffi asked. Dimple's blood was smeared across her palm, but she didn't seem to care.

Dimple attempted a scoff, but it came out as more of a choke. Saffi leaned over to inspect the stalls, likely checking that they were empty. A wave of shame washed over her. She should've thought of that – what was wrong with her?

'Can I help you?' Dimple asked, attempting to yank free, but Saffi only held on tighter.

Gradually, her heartbeat began to slow. There were no ghosts here. Only Dimple and the sickening twist of humiliation in her stomach. She didn't know who to blame. The heckler in the audience or her traitorous, unfortified mind?

Saffi seemed content with her findings. 'You look terrible,' she commented, studying Dimple's bloody knuckles. 'Did that guy really get you this worked up?'

How Saffi could stand to look at her like this, she would never understand. Had the fire in her finally been put out? Dimple was too scared to check.

'I came in here to make sure you weren't up to anything,' Saffi said when Dimple didn't respond. 'But clearly you're as much a danger to yourself as you are to anyone else.'

Had Saffi been checking for dead bodies along with living ones? The thought was amusing. Surely Saffi didn't think Dimple would be stupid enough to allow herself to be caught red-handed. Not even in this state.

'Well,' Dimple said. 'Have you reached a satisfying conclusion?'

The ceramic of the sink dug into Dimple's back as Saffi pressed her against it, but the pain hardly registered in her mind. This close, Dimple's nose was nearly pressed against Saffi's neck. She smelled of the ocean. So little time in California and already it had made its mark on her. Then Saffi pulled back, armed with damp paper towels.

'What are you –' Dimple cut herself off with a hiss when Saffi began cleaning her knuckles. It was humiliating. She didn't pull away.

'Not sure yet,' Saffi admitted, carefully extracting a piece of glass. 'I am pleasantly surprised to see that you're capable of guilt, though.'

‘And what would I have to be guilty of?’

‘Would you give it a rest?’ Saffi sighed. ‘I’m getting bored with this game.’

For some reason, that irritated Dimple. She pushed off the sink, stepping into Saffi’s space. Their eyes met like stone striking stone. That was once how people fashioned tools, wasn’t it? One stone was always stronger, sturdier, but it was used to turn the other into a weapon. Between the two of them, who was the sword and who was the forge that shaped it?

‘You’re lying,’ Dimple shot back. ‘You love this.’

‘There’s nothing I hate more than hypocrites,’ Saffi said.

‘I am not a hypocrite.’

‘Yeah?’ Saffi asked. ‘Then why are you letting other people weigh you down? Where’s *your* hunger?’ She punctuated her words with a sharp jab at Dimple’s chest.

There wasn’t the roaring campfire that had been reflected in Saffi back at the theater, but it wasn’t entirely put out either. Wisps of smoke curled against coal black, occasionally joined by a flicker of red. Dimple wanted to set them ablaze again and again until the whole world burned. This time when the icy phantom fingers threatened to choke her, the electricity of Saffi’s touch was enough to incinerate them.

‘Right here.’

Dimple grasped Saffi’s collar and pulled her down into a bruising kiss.

34

September 5, 2026

Saffi hadn't expected Dimple to touch her so gingerly. Only the tips of her fingers grazed her jaw, as though afraid – of what, Saffi didn't know. The press of Dimple's mouth, however, was something else entirely. Saffi wasn't sure if the bruising force of it was what sent tingles through her lips or if Dimple Kapoor was simply incendiary.

This was . . . What was this? Saffi's mind floated somewhere high above her, disconnected from her body. She couldn't think, couldn't breathe. Somewhere off in the distance, the voice of reason reminded her, *These are dangerous games.* But this felt a lot like winning.

There was a tipping point, the building electricity between them stretching thin, but Dimple began to pull away before lightning could strike.

No.

It couldn't end there, not when Saffi still didn't have the answers she so desperately needed. Fingers tangled in Dimple's hair, pulling her back in.

Somehow, the waxy residue of lipstick and venomous lies had never tasted sweeter. She could feel Dimple's pulse in her neck, thumping like a drum, even faster than Saffi's. The tips of her fingers, one hand brushing the underside of Saffi's jaw, the other her arm. It raised a trail of goosebumps. Suddenly desperate to see Dimple's face,

Saffi pulled back, breathing heavily and coming apart at the seams.

'What the fuck,' Saffi breathed. It wasn't a question, so there was no answer.

They stared at each other. Saffi wasn't sure what her own expression held, but Dimple's was wiped blank. How did she do that? Seconds ago, she'd come alive under Saffi's fingertips and now she was as cold and lifeless as stone. She wanted that Dimple back. The fiery Dimple that consumed everything she touched. If not for Dimple's bloodied hands, her short breath, her smudged lipstick, Saffi would have assumed she was unaffected. Her racing pulse could not lie.

Saffi grasped both of Dimple's wrists, putting an end to the featherlight touches that sent sick flutters through her stomach. She kept her grip loose, easily broken if need be, and while Dimple tensed, she did not pull away. Her knuckles, while they had stopped bleeding, still looked painful.

Regardless, as Saffi's fingers pressed deeper, the way she'd wanted to for months now, the same too-quick pulse greeted her once again. Saffi was no closer to understanding this woman than she had been eight months ago. The thought sent an unexpected thrill through her.

Perhaps the answers lurked where Saffi spun them around and pressed Dimple to the door, trapping her wrists on either side. Or maybe where she ducked down and brought their lips together again. If they did, Saffi was too distracted to notice. Dimple tugged, tempting Saffi's grip, but this time she didn't budge.

'Die,' Dimple gasped.

Saffi replaced the command with one of her own. 'Then kill me.'

As though following through with her request, there was

a thud and Dimple flew forward, knocking painfully against Saffi's forehead.

'Shit,' Dimple said under her breath, throwing her weight back against the door.

It took half a second to realize what was happening, but Saffi caught on just in time. She slammed the door shut and locked it. Their gazes met briefly before darting away. The bathroom was a mess – the mirror still broken, drops of Dimple's blood splattered across the floor.

Without a word, the two of them began cleaning up. The mirror would have to remain – there was nothing they could do about that. When Saffi unlocked the door, they left before the woman waiting outside could get in a single complaint.

Dimple walked ahead of Saffi. She'd cleaned her knuckles under water and the cuts weren't as bad as they seemed, but it still looked an angry mess. Saffi caught her wrist, hoping it would be enough to convey the words she couldn't say.

Somehow, it was.

When they finally made it back to the hotel, cold and tired, Saffi had been certain that whatever happened in the bathroom would be left there. If she thought about it for too long, reminders of *she's a killer* and *guilty by proxy* would flash in her mind until her head spun.

But then Dimple paused in front of her door and Saffi dared to hope. When a warm hand wrapped around her wrist and tugged her inside, she knew she hadn't been wrong.

'What –' she began, but Dimple shoved her back so hard that her head ricocheted against the door.

'Don't say a word,' Dimple snapped.

Saffi obliged without question.

'This is so idiotic,' Dimple murmured as she leaned in.

Saffi couldn't help but agree.

The dress Dimple wore had to be worth more than Saffi could imagine. With how pedantic she was, Saffi half expected Dimple to change the second they stepped inside. Instead, she barely touched the dress, giving the privilege of unwrapping her to Saffi alone.

Unwilling to let such an opportunity go, she took her time. She let the dress hang off Dimple's shoulders like a curtain, like a waterfall, and admired the view. Then from her waist, her hips, her thighs. Each time it slipped, each time Saffi's hand uncovered a new expanse of smooth brown skin, it sent a new thrill through her veins. Saffi's fingertips pressed harshly into it, bruising and unrelenting. Dimple burned like coal and she stoked the flames.

With no barriers between them, nothing stopped them from melding into one. Lips pressed into lips, teeth into skin, fingers into flesh as warm lamplight cast deep shadows across their bodies.

If Saffi had stopped to consider, she might've realized that it no longer felt like a game at all. And that was more dangerous than anything.

35

September 6, 2026

Dimple woke up alone the next morning. There was no trace of Saffi in the hotel room – not her clothes, her voice, not even her scent. Dimple would've thought she hallucinated the night before if not for her bruised knuckles. They twinged as she flexed her fingers. Some part of her had thought this might be the exception to Saffi's habitual desire to run, but clearly the instinct ran deeper than she'd initially thought.

She sat up slowly, ignoring the migraine pounding against her skull in protest. Both of them had been sober the night before, but that only meant that there was no excuse. The state of her mind then might as well have belonged to another person. They were a pair of scene partners too caught up in their respective roles. The performance rewiring their brains until they'd forgotten who they really were.

Or perhaps Dimple had finally lost her mind. Either way, her chest was left hollow, her veins ice-cold. She could still feel the bruising press of Saffi's fingers, but it only served as a reminder of something that could never happen again.

Having gotten up much earlier than usual, Dimple went through the motions of her morning routine slowly. Priyal wanted to explore more of the festival so their flight back to California wasn't until the next morning. When

Dimple returned from her shower, the fog dispersing into the polar vortex of the room, she found a plastic coffee cup sitting on the desk and a new note scribbled onto the notepad.

Last minute news from a job I booked! Had to catch an early flight back to Cali – sorry!!!

Priyal <3

Dimple felt an irrational pang of hurt at the message, which she quickly tempered. Acting jobs were often impromptu opportunities. Priyal had no choice but to take it. However, wasn't being here with Dimple her job as well? At least for the next two weeks? And hadn't Priyal been the one who wanted to stay in Toronto longer?

It was unreasonable to dwell on it, though, so Dimple expelled the bitterness from her mind.

Priyal's drink of choice today was pink. Dimple took a sip and then another. It was very sweet, but not bad overall. She'd been opening the curtains when the early-morning light hit the note just right, revealing mismatched lines of indention. Dimple picked the paper up and held it close to her face. It looked as though someone had previously written a note with too heavy a hand. Before she could dismiss it as something a past guest had written, Dimple spotted a word that looked eerily close to her name. But Priyal hadn't written Dimple's name in her note and the trash can was empty, so where did that come from?

There was only one other person who'd been in Dimple's room since yesterday.

She pushed back the curtains and held the paper up to the

sunlight, trying to decipher the indents. Priyal's blocky writing made it difficult. She gave up, setting the note aside, and scanned the room instead. If Saffi wanted Dimple to read her message, the note had to be somewhere accessible. And if she hadn't wanted Dimple to read it, she wouldn't have left evidence behind.

Dimple double-checked the trash, but it remained stubbornly empty. She reached for a cabinet, pausing when she realized the layer of dust above it had a handprint pressed into it. Dimple lined her fingers up with it in contemplation. There was the possibility of this being some kind of trap, but her curiosity was too great to ignore. Before she could change her mind, Dimple yanked open the cabinet door and came face-to-face with a locked safe.

Of course.

Six digits – perfect for that of a date. Dimple wasn't so deluded as to think it would be something as silly as a date important to either of them. No, Saffi was far pettier than she was sentimental. She would know Dimple wouldn't be able to hold back her curiosity. There was only one six-digit code that incriminating. A juvenile trap, and Dimple was certain she'd never had an impulse this self-destructive before. But she had to know. Hesitantly, she punched in the code to Hector Olsen's security system.

The buttons flashed green.

Dimple reached in to retrieve the message. She'd been half expecting it to be a trap – or worst of all: empty – but was pleasantly surprised when there was only the familiar crinkle of memo paper. Another performance, another gift.

She brought the note up to the light. The penmanship was messy almost to the point of illegibility, but Dimple could make it out in the end. Saffi's trademarked smug tone came forth as she read.

Dimple,

So you know the code to Olsen's security system. I wonder why that is.

I should be on a plane back to California by now, but I've been thinking a lot about what we've talked about. Aren't you the one always telling me to ask for more? So, I've decided I want to make you work for it.

Prove me wrong. And show me how to move on.

-S

The note left a hollow feeling in Dimple's chest. She traced the words with her fingertip. Being known was never a good thing. Fussy children were put in their place. Killers were put on death row. And Dimple had once been both at the same time.

She had thought of several different methods to kill Saffi – a push down the stairs, over the balcony – but in the end, she'd done exactly the opposite.

Somewhere in the back of her mind, Dimple had known all along that she wouldn't have been able to go through with it here. It felt like a disservice. Besides, she'd made a promise to her.

The show must go on.

Dimple shredded Priyal's note. Then, thinking twice, she burned the entire stack of memos, letting the ash gather in the trash can.

It wasn't until she walked back to the desk that she realized she'd left Saffi's note unmarred. Dimple ripped a line down the middle. Panic suddenly seized her, but it was too late. Still, she found herself tearing off the corner of the note – the part that read *-S* – and slipping it into her pocket. Only then did she burn the rest of it.

Saffi did not yet know that once Dimple Kapoor accepted a role, she embodied it until the end. With a steady resolve, Dimple lifted the hotel phone and dialed the familiar number of a well-known media company.

When Dimple finally left her room hours later, just before breakfast came to an end, she realized that the Do Not Disturb sign had been posted outside her door. An odd warmth blossomed in her chest, but it was quickly replaced with guilt. She stared at the sign for a moment, hesitating, but removed it from sight before she could dwell any longer.

The elevator dinged, opening on the ground floor, and just as Dimple began making her way out, she brushed shoulders with a familiar man.

'Jerome?' she asked in surprise.

He didn't answer. Uneven patches of stubble graced his chin and his posture was slouched. He swayed where he stood and smelled strongly of bourbon. Dimple resisted the childish urge to pinch her nose. Everything in her veins told her to duck away before his attention shifted to her.

She chanced a look outside just as the elevator doors began to close again. Half a beat from making a run for it, she changed her mind after seeing the curious onlookers in the lobby. They were craning their heads for a better look, which was cut off when the doors shut. They'd likely already photographed Jerome in this state and the last thing Dimple wanted was similar treatment. People were already upset with her for ducking out of the theater early last night. Rumors of a bad breakup with Chris were spreading like wildfire.

Breakfast was almost over anyway. Room service was expensive, but it wasn't as though Dimple didn't have the money now. She resolved to stand at the opposite end of the space and hope Jerome didn't look her way.

A few seconds of only his heavy breathing reminded her that neither of them had pressed any buttons.

'What floor?' Dimple found herself asking. Jerome's head snapped up, but he didn't respond. Dimple's voice had come out hoarse the first time, so she cleared her throat and repeated the question.

Jerome dragged his stare over to the row of buttons. He looked for a few seconds before reaching a hand up and aiming for the topmost one. The first couple times he missed entirely, but he hit close enough for it to light up on the third try. The elevator lurched and began to rise just as Dimple caught a flash of red – his hand. Fear spiked in her chest. Just what had he been doing?

But upon closer inspection, Dimple realized that it was the fingernails of Jerome's left hand that were bleeding. He had picked at them so harshly – and didn't seem to be stopping now.

'Have you been drinking all night?' she asked. She was tempting fate, so she kept her attention on the man's limbs, trying to keep the judgment from her tone.

Jerome didn't look at her this time, only grunted, but Dimple couldn't let it go. What would he confess if confronted by someone in this state? He was already adding unnecessarily to the drama as it was. The rest of her questions, however, could wait for when they were no longer trapped together. She allowed her floor to pass without complaint, riding with Jerome to his destination.

The elevator dinged again, and Dimple followed Jerome out, making sure the doors didn't close on him as he stumbled. He charted the way to what she hoped was his hotel room, using the wall for balance. He didn't even bother to ask why she was following him. Perhaps he'd forgotten that she was there.

The topmost floor was reserved for suites. Dimple could tell by the fewer number of doors – more square footage for each room. It was nice up here, the furniture newer, the windows taller. It could've been her imagination, but even the carpet seemed brighter, the wall sconces shinier. Dimple wondered why only Jerome had been given a room on this floor. Dimple was the lead actress. If not her, then who? She couldn't help but wonder if Chris Porter would've been put on this floor were he there with them. The thought left behind a sour taste.

Dimple almost bumped into Jerome, who'd come to a stop in front of a door. 'Is this your room?' she asked.

He grunted again.

'Are you going to tell me why you're behaving this way?'

Jerome ducked his head, shoulders shaking. Dimple frowned and moved to stand in front of him. He looked like he might be throwing up – or about to. She began scouring the floor for a trash can when Jerome let out a low, choked sound and Dimple realized he wasn't sick. He was crying.

She hovered in front of him, watching horrified as tears escaped. His sobs only grew louder, echoing up and down the hallway. Dimple winced, glancing over her shoulder to ensure they were still alone.

'Give me your key,' she hissed.

Jerome didn't respond, so Dimple scanned his pockets, fishing the card from the right one. She opened the door and shoved him inside, allowing it to slam shut behind them. The room was at least twice the size of Dimple's. He had a dining table, for god's sake. She allowed Jerome to flop onto the bed while she stood in direct line with the exit.

'What's the matter with you?' she asked again.

Jerome let out a chorus of broken sobs. Dimple scanned the room for tissues, freezing when she spotted a bottle of champagne, a bouquet of vibrant flowers, and a box of chocolate-covered strawberries on the desk. A thick, folded piece of card stock told Dimple that it was compliments of the Toronto International Film Festival organizers. Her fist clenched impulsively, crinkling the paper.

She hadn't been expecting an answer, so when Jerome slurred, 'I shouldn't have done it,' she was more than a bit taken aback.

'Done what?' Dimple asked, turning to face him.

'*Insomnia*,' he said, through hiccups. 'There were signs everywhere.'

'What do you mean? Everything's gone better than we could've imagined,' Dimple said with a frown. 'I heard there might even be an Oscar or two in store for us.' Actually, it was Priyal who'd told Dimple that and it wasn't clear if she had a source or if it was her usual overeager self. It was very rare for this genre of film to be acknowledged by the Academy, but apparently its reception at TIFF and the general excitement surrounding it were spelling good things for the future.

'Irene died,' Jerome snapped, and Dimple took an instinctive step backward. 'Chris killed someone. And no one cares.' He picked up a pillow from his bed and threw it as hard as he could at the wall. Dimple's heart thudded. She inched closer to the door, noting that she could use the chair as a shield or weapon if needed. 'We keep pushing and pushing, and for what? The movie's good but so what? Once everyone finds out what we did, it'll all be over. We should repent now before it's too late.'

Dimple, who'd been about to reply, shut her mouth with a

click. Rage built up inside her until it threatened to consume her whole.

Jerome had been the one to reach out to Dimple the second he found out Irene died. He was the one who insisted they move forward despite Dimple's protests. And when Shyla had spoken up, he'd been the first to bring up saving face by donating a portion of the proceeds. He had no right to act this way now. Not when he got champagne and flowers and chocolate-covered strawberries and Dimple got blamed for Chris Porter's mistakes. He hadn't thought twice about coercing an innocent woman to take on the role of a dead one. If this was all it took to send him spiraling, he wouldn't last a second with even a fraction of Dimple's nightmares.

Like this, he was a liability. Dimple knew from personal experience that his breakdowns would only get worse from here. She thought about the wrap party on set and how carelessly he'd spoken about his manipulations.

People already felt far too comfortable publicly berating Dimple for the things she wasn't responsible for. If it were to be discovered that she'd taken on Irene's role – willingly or otherwise – both she and Bardoux would go down together. His blatant disregard toward her was almost more enraging than his hypocrisy.

Jerome went deathly still atop the covers. 'We're all going to hell,' he said solemnly, the anger draining from him. 'Every single one of us.'

That was the one thing he was right about.

Dimple tossed the hotel memo pad and pen at him. It bounced on the bed and hit him square in the forehead.

He made a sound of protest. 'What was that for?'

'Why don't you try writing all this down?' she suggested. 'It might help you feel better.'

He shook his head. 'No, no, no, no one can find out about this.'

Dimple pulled her lighter free from her pockets and flicked it to life. 'So we'll burn it after,' she said.

Jerome's expression lit up. That was all it took for him to grasp the pen and paper and begin scrawling out his secrets. Dimple leaned against the desk, watching him. There was a balcony to her right, the sun shining brightly through the glass doors. Dimple contemplated how easy it would be to coerce him outside – to push him over the edge.

As much as she wanted to, Dimple wasn't a monster. She did what she had to in order to survive. And Jerome didn't need to die to ensure her well-being.

All she needed was the email he'd sent her long ago and the note he'd just finished writing. Dimple was patient, she didn't mind waiting for him to pass out, snatching the note from his limp hands. Her contacts in the media could take it from there.

Whether Jerome remembered any of this or not, it made no difference to Dimple. She'd already landed her next lead role. And considering that it was Jerome Bardoux's confession in his own handwriting that would cement Dimple Kapoor in public opinion as a victim of his manipulations, he would have nobody to blame for this but himself.

36

September 8, 2026

As soon as Saffi turned her phone back on in California, she began working tirelessly to convince Olsen's ex-wife to meet with her. It took two days of going back and forth, but eventually, Laila Olsen relented. The meeting was set for today, less than a week before Olsen's trial.

For a testimony, Saffi was willing to promise her anything and everything short of her own lungs. Even then, maybe she could afford to live without one of them.

With how much work there was to do in California, Saffi never should've gone to Toronto in the first place. But there were so many emotions warring for attention, and she didn't know what to do with them. It seemed like Saffi had been making mistake after mistake lately and all she could think about was when the other shoe would drop. At the same time, she couldn't stop making them. Like watching a car crash, except she was driving both cars.

The cab pulled into the gated community and Saffi was out of it before the wheels had stopped rolling. There was no time to waste.

With how frazzled Olsen's ex-wife seemed, ponytail lopsided and blouse halfway untucked, she didn't seem to notice Saffi's urgency. They were around the same age and Saffi was startled to see that she was wearing blue-colored contacts. Neither of them offered a hand to shake.

'Sorry, they're still renovating a few rooms, so we'll have to talk in the garden,' the ex-wife huffed. 'They told me they'd be done months ago, but here we are.'

'Lead the way,' Saffi said.

It turned out that when she said *garden,* she meant a full-blown park. Saffi was led around into a backyard of lush green grasses, tall trees, and wildflowers. The two of them took a seat at a circlet of green cushioned chairs near the water fountain.

The woman had lived at Olsen's mansion in Beverly Hills until their divorce, working a few odd acting jobs on the side, but most of her wealth now came from the split itself. Either the ex-wife didn't think far ahead enough to worry about running out of money or Olsen's wealth was simply extensive enough that she didn't have to. You'd think after so many divorces the man would learn to sign a prenup.

'Can I get you anything?' the ex-wife asked. 'Tea? Snacks?'

'No,' Saffi said. 'I'm sure you already have an idea of what I'm here for?'

Laila Olsen dropped her gaze to the cobbled ground. She nodded grimly. 'I do.'

'If you testify in Hector Olsen's defense, he'll have no choice but to corroborate your story,' Saffi explained simply. It was most respectful, given the circumstances, to lay all her cards out in the open and let the woman make the decision for herself. 'He'll have to admit to it. That's all you'll need to get justice for yourself and all the women before you.'

Laila Olsen didn't say a word, staring down at the hands clenched tightly in her lap. Before she could speak again, Saffi's phone started buzzing with a call. She immediately declined. That should've been enough of a hint regarding her availability. When it started up again seconds later, she turned it off with a huff of annoyance.

Saffi continued, 'Don't you want justice for what he's

actually done? Olsen is a vile excuse for a man, but he isn't a murderer.'

'He almost was,' Olsen's ex-wife said so softly it gave Saffi chills. 'That night, I was scared he would become one.'

Saffi didn't know what to say to that. The urge to give up and let the man be convicted came back with force. Olsen deserved it. But Saffi had more to think about than herself. It wasn't as easy for her to turn off the care she had for the people in her life as it seemed to be for Dimple.

'He put something in my drink. I couldn't defend myself.'

And this was why Olsen had to be punished for the crimes he had actually committed. Even now, people called his ex-wives liars and gold diggers. But when Saffi looked at this woman, she realized that the last thing on her mind was what the world thought. All Laila Olsen cared about was finally being free from the man who haunted her.

There had to be another way. Taylor would try putting himself in the ex-wife's shoes to see where she was coming from. Andino would declare this route a dead end and spend his time looking into something else. Saffi's father would stay far away from personal matters, choosing instead to wear her down with the power of the law. Dimple Kapoor, though, would probably suggest killing him and being done with it.

Although, that wasn't exactly true. Dimple never took unnecessary risks – she wouldn't kill unless she was certain it would get her what she wanted in the end. She was capable of using other methods, just as lawless as murder.

'Laila,' Saffi found herself saying suddenly. The other woman looked up at the sound of her name. 'Look, I know this isn't fair. None of what happened to you is and I'm sorry for that. I know you want Olsen to be punished for what he did – and he should be. But you'd be doing Irene Singh a disservice if you allowed Olsen to take the blame for this.'

'I know I shouldn't take advantage –' Laila began, but Saffi cut her off.

'When did I say that?' she asked with a smirk. She felt so much like Dimple in that moment. 'You're forgetting that Olsen needs your testimony. That means you can say anything you want under oath and if he wants to avoid life in prison, then he'll have to agree.'

Laila's eyebrows rose in understanding. 'Anything,' she echoed.

'Anything.'

She seemed to be considering it.

'Speak to your lawyers,' Saffi said. 'I'm sure you'll be able to come up with a story you like.'

Laila's expression was open with hope and Saffi knew she had won.

'What do you need from me?'

37

September 8, 2026

As the cab pulled back into the parking lot of Andino and Taylor Private Eye, the first thing Saffi noticed was that Andino's car was missing. It struck her as odd. The three of them had always had a similar work ethic, going so far as to sleep at the office most nights. Given that the moon already hung high in the dark, starless sky, Saffi dared to hope the man had gone to get dinner.

As soon as she stepped out of the passenger side of the vehicle, the cool night breeze biting at her cheeks, she could tell something was wrong. Taylor was waiting for her at the agency's entrance with a grim expression. Heart sinking, Saffi rushed over.

'Hey,' Taylor greeted her, but there was something solemn in his tone.

'What's wrong?' Saffi asked as they stepped inside.

She glanced around. The office seemed eerily empty for only one person being gone, especially after months of chaos. That was when she realized.

'Where are the interns?' she asked. They were supposed to get back from their trip last night.

Taylor swallowed. 'Mia never went with them.'

Saffi's heart dropped the moment she heard his tone. She knew exactly when the last time she'd been in contact with Martinez was, and it left her feeling uneasy.

'Her friends assumed she'd just missed the flight, so

nobody realized until they got back that she has been missing this entire time,' Taylor continued.

'So where is she now? Is she all right – ?'

'Saffi,' Taylor interrupted. 'The police released the confidential file. They found a body in the remains of Hector Olsen's home.'

Her heartbeat rushed in her ears, Taylor's voice becoming muffled.

'The DNA match came back positive. It was Mia.'

If a *DNA test* was necessary to identify her, that meant her body must've been burned beyond recognition. Saffi bit her cheek hard, tasting blood. She never should've gotten the girl involved. She'd come back to prove that she'd grown from her mistakes, not to make them again.

'This is all my fault,' Saffi said in a voice that felt far away. 'I'm so sorry –'

'No, *I'm sorry*,' Taylor said, and he did seem genuinely so. 'I didn't want to tell you all of this at once because I knew you'd blame yourself, but I also knew you'd hate being kept in the dark.'

'There's more?' Saffi asked.

A numbness was already creeping under Saffi's skin. Emotions, she could bury deep where they wouldn't see the light of day. There was always more work to be done, and by the time she got a moment to herself, the pain would have lost most of its sting. There was an article already pulled up on Taylor's computer, waiting for her. She bent down to read it.

MURDER INVESTIGATION OF BELOVED ACTRESS IRENE SINGH ENTRUSTED TO A FRAUD

Last month, it was revealed that beloved actress Irene Singh's death was no accident (see: Hector Olsen, 'Ladies Killer': Literal or Figurative?). Another one of the victims of this ongoing investigation includes actress Dimple Kapoor (see: 'Dimple Kapoor Hospitalized: Substance Abuse Rumors Gain Traction'). Much to our collective relief, she managed to survive the attack. However, the prime suspect, Hector Olsen, is walking free, protected by his wealth and status.

You must be wondering – is this truly the state of our justice system? How could anyone knowingly let this happen? Well, it should come as no surprise because this is nothing more than history repeating itself.

Due to the police's refusal to look further into the circumstances of their daughter's death, the Singhs hired a private investigator to look into Irene Singh's case. However, it has been brought to our attention by an anonymous Hollywood insider that this investigator has a truly upsetting track record. If you're wondering just who could be so inept that they would let a killer run rampant for almost a year now, you don't have to look any further than Saffi Mirai Iyer, who, ironically, has a reputation of being one of the world's best. You see, Iyer has a dark past of her own. In spring of 2020, she was responsible for putting an innocent woman on death row. The victim has unfortunately since passed, but –

Saffi stopped there, feeling cold all over. *Betrayal,* she realized distantly. She'd known all along what would come of this, and she'd gone and done it anyway.

She had asked Dimple where her hunger was, and it seemed Saffi had to be consumed in order to prove it had never left. Compared to the gut punch that was Mia Martinez's death, this was almost a relief. The other shoe had finally dropped. Still, she couldn't deny that some part of her had wanted to trust Dimple Kapoor. The same part of her that had been shocked at the events leading up to Shyla Patel's broken nose.

Saffi never seemed to learn.

She could practically feel Taylor trying to think of a way to cut the tension. *See what happens when I try to mentor someone,* she wanted to say. The article had been released a couple hours ago, around the time she'd left for Laila's home, and was now widely circulating. Saffi wondered if Dimple felt bad at all. If she was even capable of guilt or if Saffi had been wrong about that too.

'I tried calling you, but it didn't go through,' Taylor said finally. It wouldn't have made a difference if Saffi had picked up the phone, but regret settled in, nonetheless. 'It's too late to take it down,' he added. It was disappointing to hear, but he knew she didn't want coddling. 'We contacted the police and they agreed there's nothing we can do about it now that it's gone viral. For now, we've been trying to minimize panic and get the real facts out there.'

He'd known Martinez for longer – how was he holding it together so well? Saffi felt like the very ground beneath her feet was crumbling away.

When she didn't respond, Taylor asked, gently, 'Do you have any idea who could've leaked this?'

But Saffi found herself hung up on something else entirely. 'Where's Andino?'

If he too knew about the article and about Martinez's death, why would he have left? While he was far from a comforting presence, he was also one of three people who'd been close with both Saffi and the interns. The empty space to her left felt weighty.

Taylor recoiled. 'Come on, I know you don't always see eye to eye, but he wouldn't have done this.'

'That's not why I'm asking.'

Taylor then sagged. His clothes were heavily wrinkled, his movements sluggish. Maybe he wasn't holding it together as well as Saffi had imagined. 'Atlas was here,' he said. 'He was the one who told me about Mia and the article. I watched him *cry*, Saffi.'

His distress was understandable. She and Taylor were alike when it came to emotions in that they both tended to repress them for as long as possible. Andino, on the other hand, never seemed capable of holding them back. He had always had a complex about expressing anything other than anger in front of others, though.

When his family dog had passed away back in college, he'd refused to leave his dorm for an entire week. Saffi and Taylor had resorted to leaving meals and notes they'd taken in class outside his door. Even with emotional movies, Andino would hole himself up in the bathroom until he got ahold of himself. If not for the red-rimmed eyes, they would've been none the wiser about the state he'd been in.

'I didn't know what to do. And then he got this weird look on his face and –' Taylor cut himself off, seemingly thinking it over. 'Well, he went into your office.'

'Why would he do that?'

'I don't know. He didn't say anything before he left, but for now he probably just needs some space. I'm sure he'll be back soon and you can ask him yourself.'

That was when the phone rang, startling them both, and Taylor picked it up, introducing the agency in a practiced speech. He nodded a few times.

'Laila Olsen,' he explained after hanging up. 'She said she no longer wants to testify.'

'Of fucking course,' Saffi said, rubbing her temples.

'Care to explain what that's about?' Taylor asked, frowning even deeper.

Saffi waved him off.

'I don't appreciate both of you keeping things from me,' Taylor said, all traces of pleasantry wiped from his face. In any other circumstance it would've left Saffi with at least some morsel of regret, but numbness had begun to overpower her senses.

'It doesn't matter anymore, does it?' Saffi replied. 'It's a miracle the Singhs haven't called yet.'

'They did,' Taylor said. 'They no longer require our services.'

'Has no one considered that maybe they should leave this to the experts?' Saffi snapped.

'We'll fix this,' Taylor tried, but even he didn't seem convinced.

The phone rang again, and Saffi answered it before anyone else could. 'What?' she snapped into the receiver.

'Saffi?' a familiar voice asked.

The whole world came to a stop. 'Mama?' Saffi hadn't thought it possible, but the numbness magnified.

'It's been so long since I've heard your voice.' Her tone was wistful. It said, *I've missed you.* It said, *How could you?* It said, *Something is broken here.* It said, *I don't know how to fix it.*

Saffi opened her mouth several times in succession, but no words escaped. If she couldn't feel the phone digging into her palm as her grip tightened, she might've thought she was dreaming. Taylor took that as his cue to exit, leaving Saffi with some privacy.

'I know,' Saffi replied softly. But she meant, *I missed you too.* She meant, *I'm sorry.* She meant, *I don't know how to fix it either.*

There was a beat of silence. Then, 'Why didn't you tell us you were back in America?'

The article. 'Did you see it?' If they had, then they would know she'd been in America for nearly a year now. That the postcard from France had been faked. They would know exactly why she'd left all those years ago and how close she'd come to destroying her father's career.

No, she hadn't *come close*. It was official. With her crimes now publicized, Saffi had single-handedly destroyed his life's passion.

'It's difficult to ignore,' her mother said. 'Everyone's been sending it to us.'

Red-hot shame burned through Saffi. 'You weren't supposed to – I didn't want you to –'

She didn't know how to finish that sentence. Hushed whispering on the other end of the line. Her father must be nearby. Saffi braced herself for questions she wouldn't know how to answer.

'You know this will affect his campaign,' her mother began slowly. 'He's Arizona's only Indian senator, you know they're looking for any excuse to make his life difficult. Even if they don't remove him from office, he'll never be reelected. This will be his legacy.'

This was exactly the kind of thing Saffi used to dig up about her father's political opponents. It had been so easy to judge them when she was younger. *If you're going to run for office, at least use a more secure format than email to accept bribes. Maybe check your children into rehab instead of waiting for them to get a DUI.* She'd seen enough of them to know that this was the kind of scandal no one ever came back from.

'I know. I know, that's why I left. I was trying to protect you from my mistakes –'

'Protect us?' her father's voice cut in. He wasn't angry, no, never angry. He was the prosecutor, forever molding your words into weapons against yourself. 'How can you say that when your carelessness killed someone?'

'A jury convicted them –'

'With evidence that you gathered,' he said. 'And instead of facing up to the consequences, you decided to deceive us for five years.'

She should've known better than to try and explain. It was him who'd first introduced her to the concept of good and bad, of just and unjust – far beyond the expectation of a father's teachings.

But Saffi knew better now. The law was far from just. If it was as righteous as her father claimed, then Hector Olsen wouldn't be walking free. Chris Porter wouldn't have gotten away with a slap on the wrist. Saffi and Dimple wouldn't be suffering more than anyone else in their shoes would be.

'I thought I raised you better than to blame others for your own actions,' he said.

'You can't control what she does,' Saffi heard her mother say in the background. She sounded so tired. 'Children grow up to make their own mistakes.'

'I raised her,' her father said. 'I'm not a hypocrite. I'm willing to accept my part of the blame in this.'

'What can I do to make this right?' Saffi asked, unable to keep the desperation from coming through in her tone.

Her father had never been one for punishments that didn't teach something. If she broke her mother's favorite vase, she had to pay for it. If she called someone names on the playground, she had to apologize until she was forgiven.

'You don't get a plea bargain after evading arrest,' her father said. 'You should have thought about that before running away. What were you hoping to achieve?'

But he was supposed to know the answer. He was supposed to tell her how to fix everything, just like he always did.

'I didn't want to drag you into it,' she said.

'Don't you see how much worse it is now? Maybe if you would've faced the consequences then, things would've been different.'

Saffi scoffed. 'Can you seriously say you would've wanted me to be at the center of a scandal like that?'

'I would've been proud to see I raised a daughter who owned up to her mistakes.'

Proud.

Saffi's father had never once said he was proud of her. Not when she got into Harvard. Not when she graduated top of her class. Not even when she'd gotten her PI license. The one time he chose to say it, it was in reference to some alternate, idealized version of herself. The filial daughter that she never was and never would be.

'And what now?' Saffi asked, voice thick with emotion.

Her father took his time responding, as though consulting his notes. 'You've had five years, Saffi. It will take time for us to process.' Like a goddamn fax machine. 'It's not just about you. I have the campaign to think of. My phone hasn't stopped ringing once in the past hour. I don't even want to know what the media's saying.'

Your Honor, the prosecution will rest and request a brief recess. It shouldn't have surprised her, but Saffi hated when her father treated her like an extension of his job. When she was younger, she'd been a glorified paralegal. Now she was opposing counsel who had just brought up a point he hadn't been prepared for. Considering how good he'd been at destroying his opponents – both politically and in the courtroom – Saffi wasn't sure she wanted to stick around to see what his plan of action would be.

Saffi didn't cry. She didn't get angry either. The numbness had never left, and she was beginning to think it never would. Her father, the very man who'd taught her the meaning of justice, had declared her immoral. Judge, jury, executioner, he was all three in one. And she wasn't even the first item on his agenda. A single thought ran through her mind.

Dimple had been right.

There was no such thing as unconditional love.

*

Saffi felt stripped raw by the time she joined Taylor in the hallway.

'Atlas isn't picking up my calls,' Taylor said.

He didn't mention her parents, somehow sensing that she didn't want to talk about it, which Saffi was grateful for. It probably helped that there were other things to worry about. Because if Andino was screening even Taylor's calls, it couldn't just be grief keeping him away. Saffi kept inadvertently glancing around in search of him. Instead, her attention landed on a red envelope sitting on a table beside the office's entrance.

'What's this?' she asked, picking it up.

'It came in earlier,' he said. 'I think it's for Atlas, he opened it.'

The handwriting on the front was the most beautiful cursive Saffi had ever seen. There was no return address, but it was definitely addressed to Saffi Mirai Iyer, not Atlas Andino.

'Could you maybe commit mail fraud later?' Taylor asked, sounding uncharacteristically strained, but Saffi ignored him in favor of ripping the thick envelope apart. She didn't need to – it was already open – but it felt good.

Inside was a small square of paper. It was heavy, good quality – unlike the hotel room's memos. Saffi unfolded it while Taylor, now curious, watched. If Andino were here, he'd make some sort of quip like, *That's your eviction notice.* Except Andino had already looked through this, hadn't he? Right before he'd stormed out.

She scanned the text, written in the same neat cursive, and immediately crumpled the paper in her fist, understanding dawning on her. She knew where Andino had gone.

My Dearest Saffi,

I'm sorry.

-D

38

September 8, 2026

Shooting for her latest film had long since wrapped for the day, but Dimple had stayed behind to speak with the director, making her the last one on set now. Rarely did anyone want to linger too long, the director rushing out the door as soon as their conversation was over. Clearly, he was no Jerome Bardoux. But Dimple couldn't help it, she had concerns regarding her character arc. Although the writing wasn't quite as strong, this film needed to do just as well as *Insomnia.* No, it needed to do better.

Dimple found herself missing her old coworkers. Even Chris Porter, to an extent. They'd all gotten along relatively well, all eager to do a good job. For many of them, *Insomnia* had been their first film of such caliber. However, Dimple was beginning to realize that those environments were rare.

'Are you sure you're not upset about me leaving the festival early?' Priyal asked. She'd dressed up today – done her hair and makeup as though she had a red carpet of her own after work.

'I'm quite certain,' Dimple reassured her for the third time. The two of them were in Dimple's trailer, just about ready to go home for the day. She was waiting for Priyal to finish editing some photos on her laptop first. 'You have to take every opportunity you get in this business.'

'Sure, but I don't want to hurt my friends in the process.'

The sincerity in her tone made Dimple pause. 'While I

appreciate that, you didn't hurt me.' Priyal wasn't capable of it.

She breathed a sigh of relief. 'Good. I promise it won't happen again.'

'The good news is, you'll only have to worry about it for another two weeks.' It was a miserable thought. Soon, Dimple would have to take care of her own social accounts. She would have to buy her own coffee. She'd spend most of her days alone. Because the thought of hiring someone else, of giving yet another person the chance to grow close to her, was unthinkable. She'd been trying not to dwell on it, throwing herself into her work instead.

'Right,' Priyal said. 'But we'll still hang out, won't we? Maybe we'll even see each other at the same events.'

Dimple tried to imagine it. She'd already spent some of the most important days of her life with Priyal by her side. How different would it be with her there to promote her own work? Where once Priyal's brilliance was used to further Dimple's career, what would happen when she used it to further her own instead?

Priyal had always been endearingly charming. Dimple's co-stars had taken to her immediately. In a world where Priyal herself was a star, how quickly would Dimple fade into the shadows?

'Of course,' Dimple replied.

Absentmindedly, she brushed a finger over her knuckles. They were nearly healed now, just a few days later. As though they'd never bled in the first place. Dimple almost wished she'd been left with some sort of scar, but it seemed she was eternally cursed to carry invisible wounds.

'Hey, even if I'm not invited, can I still come with you to the Oscars?'

'What on earth are you talking about?' Dimple asked,

taking a sip of her drink. Matcha again. It left behind a strong aftertaste, but she'd found herself growing to like it.

'Obviously *Insomnia* will be nominated. Especially after it did so well at TIFF.'

Dimple set aside her drink. 'Sure, Priyal. If we get nominated, you can come with me to the Oscars.'

With that answer, she seemed to be content. 'My phone's been buzzing for ten minutes, do you mind if I take a break?' Priyal asked, stretching.

Dimple waved her off, instead picking up her script. It wasn't until Priyal gasped a few moments later that Dimple thought to wonder why, exactly, her phone had been so active.

'Saffi is – ?' Priyal asked. 'Oh, Dimple.'

So the article had finally broke.

Dimple didn't dare read it, but she knew it had to be done. With Saffi's credibility destroyed, this was the only way Dimple could keep her promise. Saffi would never look at Dimple the same way, yes, but maybe in turn she would finally see everything and everyone that had been holding her back from her true potential. The proof was right in front of Saffi, if only she looked. Dimple's career had never been better, the public adored her. The effort had been worth it in the end.

There were no steps forward but this one. If Dimple could go back and do it again, she would. The show must go on.

'Didn't you say she was your friend?'

Dimple attempted to discern Priyal's expression, but she was facing away from her. 'That was a cover for the investigation. I had no choice but to go along with it.'

It was clear that Priyal was shaken up by this. Dimple wondered if she was reconsidering stepping into the spotlight now.

'But you were so convincing,' Priyal said.

'I'm an actress, Priyal,' Dimple replied easily.

'No, I've seen you act. It wasn't like that.'

'People reach strange heights when it comes to life-or-death situations.'

'That sounds terrifying,' Priyal said, although she didn't sound completely convinced. 'I wish I could do something to help.'

'There's nothing you can do,' Dimple said simply.

'And the killer – do you think it's – ?'

'Hector Olsen? I do.'

'But he hasn't been convicted?'

Dimple shook her head. 'Not yet.'

'Thanks to *her*.' Priyal said it like a curse.

Dimple didn't respond. Hadn't she already done enough damage to Saffi's character?

There was a knock at the door, which was odd considering they were the last two people left on set. Priyal was still reading the article, so Dimple went to answer it. If the news had broken, then there was a very good chance that it could be a lingering cast or crew member attempting to comfort her.

But when Dimple opened the door, it wasn't a coworker waiting for her. It was the cool barrel of a gun pressed hard against her forehead.

Dimple stilled, hand frozen on the doorknob.

'Who is it?' Priyal called out.

'Priyal,' Dimple began, meeting her attacker's gaze unflinchingly. 'Hide.'

'What?'

It seemed that she finally turned to face the door because she gasped. Something heavy enough to be a phone clattered to the ground.

'Hey,' Priyal said, voice wobbly. 'What's going on?' From her peripheral, Dimple watched the girl slowly rise to her feet and press herself flat against the wall.

'I wasn't expecting you to have guests,' Atlas Andino said, cold as stone.

'What are you doing?' Dimple asked, at a complete loss. Clearly something had changed between him asking her to take care of Saffi and now, but she couldn't for the life of her figure out what. Atlas pushed inside, forcing her to walk backward. 'What is it you want?'

'The truth,' he responded.

He didn't act like a madman. It wasn't as though his speech was slurred. He seemed resolved and that was almost more terrifying. This was nothing at all like the man who'd once looked at her as though she were the sun.

Dimple's heart was startlingly still. Empty. She couldn't die like this, in the trailer of the film she had yet to wrap. There was so much left to do – awards to win, promises to keep, legacies to create. She'd only just started living.

The door slammed shut behind Atlas. When Dimple's calves hit the couch, she sank dutifully into the cushions. The barrel of the gun followed her down.

'You act innocent, you sign autographs, you bat your eyelashes,' he said. 'You've been laughing at me this entire time, haven't you?'

Dimple's blood ran cold. He knew.

The gun pressed harder against her temple. 'You manipulated me!' As though it was her fault he was so malleable.

'You know what the worst part is?' he asked, laughing. 'I believed you. I stood up for you against the people I love because I thought you were a good person.' He scoffed. 'At least I was right about one thing. You're the best goddamn actress I've ever seen.'

'You're the killer, aren't you?' Priyal asked shakily. 'It's not Olsen, it's you.'

'Don't be an idiot,' Atlas said, gun trembling against Dimple's forehead. 'That honor goes to your friend here.'

'Priyal, *leave*,' Dimple tried weakly.

'Move and I'll blow your friend's brains out,' Atlas said as though he were reading the weather report.

Priyal didn't move an inch. 'What do you want?' she asked a bit hysterically. 'Money? I'm sure we can get it for you – however much you want!'

'Tell her what you've done,' Atlas ordered.

'Atlas –' Dimple tried.

'Tell her!'

'I don't know what you're talking about.'

All her life, Dimple had been haunted by impossible decisions. Suffer her aunt and uncle's abuse or become a murderer. Cover up Irene's death or subject herself to being forgotten. Protect Priyal's image of herself or die. Dimple was tired of setting fires only to put them out later.

'Fine, then,' Atlas sneered. 'Should I tell her? Where should I start? How about when you killed your competition, Irene Singh?' The ghost of his smile flickered in front of Dimple's eyes. Months ago, they'd been comparing notes on their favorite films.

'Or how about when you killed an innocent waiter? Why – just because he figured out what you are?' Atlas continued.

Isaac Klossner was far from innocent. Saffi wouldn't have gotten the details wrong like this. Dimple's blood thrummed in her veins. Atlas had looked at the sun so long, he'd lost his vision.

'Or maybe when you framed Hector Olsen for murder and burned his house down?'

No mention of her aunt and uncle. Even now, Atlas looked at her through a lens. In many ways, Dimple only existed through Saffi. The true, unfiltered version of her. It left her a little smug, the thought that someone like her was only comprehensible through someone like Saffi.

Dimple then realized, horrified, that the only way Atlas had come to know this information was through Saffi. Either she'd told him, or he'd gone through her files. The former was incomprehensible. The latter was unforgivable.

'Are you listening?' Atlas snapped.

'Yes,' Priyal responded immediately. 'Whatever you say, I believe you. Just let us go, please.'

She didn't believe him. Dimple was a bit awestruck at the extent of her assistant's loyalty. Priyal would sooner believe that a madman had broken into her trailer to spew made-up nonsense than think for a moment that Dimple might actually be a killer.

'Worst of all, though, is what you did to Mia,' Atlas said, all his attention back on Dimple. 'She was just a girl! What kind of monster are you?'

Dimple blinked in confusion. 'Mia? What?'

'Don't play dumb. They finally identified her body – it was so badly burned, they had to use DNA testing to figure out who she was.'

The eyes she'd felt on her at Olsen's house – they had been real? Dimple shivered, sick to her stomach. 'She's dead?'

'You really are an incredible actress.' Andino huffed a humorless laugh. 'If I didn't know any better, I'd believe you.'

'I didn't. I *wouldn't*. Ask Saffi if you don't believe me.'

If Mia had been there, that meant Saffi was the one who'd sent her after Dimple. She didn't care much what Andino thought of her, but Dimple felt she was losing her mind. For a brief, hysterical moment she wondered if she really had planned the girl's death. But she couldn't have, not if she had no idea Mia had been there.

'I saw the letter you sent her,' Atlas said. 'Did you know that saying *sorry* counts as an admission of guilt?'

Dimple felt her blood simmer, and then boil. Rage overtook her. 'That wasn't for you,' she spat.

No, Dimple wouldn't choose anymore. This time, she would forge her own path. Dimple kicked with all her strength, which Atlas wasn't expecting. She took the opening to reach for the gun, pointing it away from her face, but Atlas managed to gather his bearings enough to latch onto the handle with a death grip. Wrestling with him, she tried to loosen his hold, but it wouldn't budge. Thinking fast, she lifted her knee and caught Atlas in the stomach.

She expected that to be enough for him to let the gun go. Instead, his hand instinctively clamped tighter and engaged the trigger. A gunshot echoed across the trailer.

Priyal shrieked as both Dimple and Atlas fell to the ground with the force of the rebound. The gun clattered somewhere in the distance. Dimple immediately lunged for it, ears ringing. She'd expected Atlas to follow, but when her fingers closed around the cool metal, she realized she no longer had a pursuer.

Heavy weight in her palm, Dimple rose to her feet. Atlas was kneeling, mouth hanging open as he stared at the back wall. Dimple followed his gaze, stomach already flip-flopping before she landed on the scene awaiting her.

It took a moment for it to sink in. Blood splattered all the way up beige walls, some of it even reaching the couch. Dimple's stomach lurched. Come to think of it, there was a metallic scent permeating. The source: a small figure curled into herself against the wall. Her shoulders rose and fell with each pained, shallow breath. Dimple couldn't tell where Priyal had been shot, but there was already enough blood loss for it not to matter.

The scene shifted for a moment, and it was Shyla Patel lying at the bottom of a ledge, stage blood splattered all around her. Isaac Klossner, two stories down. Irene Singh at the bottom of a staircase.

'No.' The voice was so small and hoarse it took a moment for Dimple to realize it was she who'd spoken. 'No, no, no.'

She dived to the ground, holding the girl's face between her hands. That was when she remembered that she was still holding the gun. She couldn't put it down, though. Atlas hadn't moved since she last saw him, but it was clear now what he was capable of. Dimple settled on angling it away from either of them.

'You'll be okay,' Dimple said nonsensically. 'Everything is going to be all right.'

'He was lying,' Priyal rasped, almost incomprehensible. 'Right?'

Dimple froze. Something had given her away. But then she realized this was Priyal in a haze of blood loss and adrenaline. She had no idea what she was saying.

'Yes,' Dimple agreed. 'Yes, he was lying. Look at him – look at what he did to you.'

Priyal coughed again.

'Let me see,' Dimple demanded, trying to keep the panic from her tone.

After a moment's hesitation, Priyal uncurled. Her hands were covered in blood and there was a large pool of it in her lap. So much that Dimple still couldn't tell where the wound was. The hysterical part of her lamented the loss of Priyal's new clothes – the new image she was finally embracing. She pulled a blanket from the couch and instructed Priyal to apply pressure.

'It hurts,' she said.

Dimple pushed the blanket harder against the wound. 'I

know, but you need to keep this here.' She couldn't tell if Priyal understood, but she did lift a weak hand to at least hold the fabric in place.

She scanned the room. It had to be somewhere nearby. *There.* Priyal's phone on the ground beside her. Dimple reached for it.

'I'm scared,' Priyal said softly.

'There's no need to be scared,' Dimple insisted, trying to unlock the phone, but her fingers were slippery with blood. 'Everything is going to be all right.' Priyal didn't answer. Dimple cursed when she looked up and realized her eyes were closed.

'Hey!' She shook Priyal lightly by the shoulders. 'You need to stay awake, okay?'

Priyal murmured something incomprehensible.

Her eyelids slid closed again. Dimple took in a sharp breath. When the girl didn't rouse, she shook her. Then harder when that didn't work.

How many times had Dimple seen the life bleed out of a body? And yet this felt like something out of a nightmare. But when she pressed two fingers into Priyal's pulse and found nothing there, she knew Priyal wouldn't be able to wake up from it.

Half an hour ago, they'd been talking about going to the Oscars side by side. *How did one win in a world that favored the cruel?* Dimple had long since come to realize that the ones who deserved it never won in the end. Perhaps the only solution was to become undeserving.

Dimple didn't know how long she'd knelt there in front of Priyal's lifeless body. It could've been seconds, it could've been hours. With her free hand she'd tried igniting her lighter but was trembling too much for it to work. With a shout of frustration, Dimple tossed the thing aside. It landed in a pool of blood.

Priyal Tiwari was dead, and it was all Dimple's fault.

Although, despite holding the smoking gun, Dimple hadn't been the one to shoot her, had she? Dimple turned to face Atlas, who was still kneeling on the ground. He hadn't moved an inch since the last time she'd seen him.

'You did this,' she accused, rising slowly to her feet.

He didn't protest. Dimple's arm was lifting before she realized what she was doing. The barrel of the gun pressed firmly against Atlas's temple. He didn't so much as flinch.

She tilted it to a better angle, catching a distorted reflection of herself in its silver exterior. Never had Dimple seen herself like this, set ablaze. Atlas had killed Priyal, and Dimple was going to make him regret it.

There was a bang, but it wasn't that of a gun. The door to her trailer swung open and someone else came barreling inside.

39

September 8, 2026

The scene Saffi had walked in on was a bloodbath. Someone gasped, maybe it was her, maybe any of the other occupants of the trailer.

She shut the door behind her. Andino had seen the letter and gone to her office. Saffi wasn't sure what he'd put together, but it was clear that he'd realized Dimple Kapoor wasn't as innocent as she seemed. He had always been one for direct confrontation.

Dimple didn't jump at her presence like Andino did, but the clench of her jaw gave away her surprise.

'Saffi,' Andino choked out. 'Be careful.'

There was so much blood. Priyal appeared to have bled out and Dimple Kapoor was the one holding the gun. None of the puzzle pieces fit.

'What the hell happened?' Saffi found herself asking.

Dimple very pointedly did not look in her assistant's direction. 'You wouldn't believe me if I told you.'

She was right. Saffi didn't believe her. Andino was a lot of things, but he wasn't a killer.

'I didn't mean to,' Andino choked out.

The room spun.

'Oh, so now that distinction is important?' Dimple asked. 'After you gave Saffi so much grief about putting that woman on death row? And me about Mia? At least we weren't the ones holding the smoking gun.'

Martinez. So it was true. 'Did you know – ?'

'No,' Dimple insisted with so much vehemence, Saffi almost took a step back. 'What I don't understand is why you had her follow me when you knew.'

She didn't finish, but Saffi could understand where she was going. When she knew how dangerous Dimple was. When she knew the bounds of her ambition. When she knew her attention would be focused solely on Saffi. Less than an accusation, it was a plea of desperation.

'I did have her tail you,' Saffi admitted hoarsely. 'But only at the party. I tried to send her home after. She told me she left.'

'So she lied,' Dimple said after a beat. 'Sounds like someone I know.'

'Saffi, what?' Andino asked. 'You sent Mia after her?'

His words barely registered. It was such a bizarre development, standing here discussing their equal share in someone's untimely death. Both accepting their part of the blame. Except it wasn't really that strange, when she thought about it. To be known, maybe it wasn't as terrible as she'd imagined.

Saffi had Dimple's attention on her and suddenly her feet were planted firmly on the ground. 'I know you're upset with me right now, Saffi, but you must understand I have my reasons.'

'He killed Priyal,' Saffi said simply.

Dimple blinked at her easy acceptance.

'I'm not upset with you,' Saffi said. 'Mia Martinez's death was just as much my fault as it was yours. And the article – you were keeping your promise, weren't you? In your own fucked-up way.'

Many people had been brutally honest with Saffi throughout her life, and she'd always accepted it as best she could. It was much rarer to see someone stand unflinching against her own brutal honesty. To lay bare the truth and receive the same in return. What was that if not justice?

Dimple's eyes sparkled and she took a step closer. 'You understand. You see it, don't you? That we're the same. I know you do, I can read it on your face.' She laughed in disbelief. 'Saffi, it doesn't have to be you or me anymore. It can be you *and* me.'

Saffi opened her mouth to voice her confusion before she realized that wasn't true. She knew exactly what Dimple meant. It didn't feel like they were on opposite sides anymore, not really. They felt more like accomplices.

'What the hell is going on here?' Andino mumbled with a humorless laugh.

Saffi looked at him and then to Dimple. It suddenly occurred to her that this was Dimple Kapoor without her mask. There was no trace of lie or deception in the small space between them. Saffi had wanted so desperately to see this side of her, and rightfully so. The embodiment of fire itself. This was Dimple Kapoor driven to murder. It was fascinating.

'Don't kill him,' Saffi said.

Dimple sighed something weary, but she did turn away from Andino. 'If that's still how you feel, then I clearly haven't kept my promise.'

Then she did something completely unexpected. Dimple walked over and pressed the gun squarely into Saffi's palms. It was cold as ice and clean despite the fact that Kapoor's other hand was covered in blood. If she hadn't wrapped Saffi's fingers around the handle, she would've dropped it on instinct.

At her visible confusion, Dimple leaned in. 'You asked me how you can move on,' she whispered. 'This is how. Let him go.'

'I can't,' Saffi whispered, horrified. She tried to push the weapon back into Dimple's hands, but she refused to take it.

'It's your choice,' Dimple said.

When she stepped away, leaning against the wall with her arms crossed, Saffi realized that this was Dimple's way of returning the power to her. She would let Saffi deal with this however she saw fit, whether that meant putting a bullet through Atlas's heart or through Dimple's. How long had it been since someone had trusted her judgment so completely?

When Saffi didn't get right to work, Dimple made an over-the-top gesture for her to get on with it.

The amount of stubbornness in this room would only pave the way for disaster. Letting Andino live would mean turning Dimple in. She'd be choosing the man who did nothing but remind Saffi of her worst mistake – the same mistake he'd also been about to make before she'd shown up to help. The man who'd cared more about a delayed check than he did about bringing the right criminal to justice. The one who, even now, after killing an innocent woman in cold blood, refused to see Saffi's perspective. The one who'd asked for Saffi's help and then, in turn, been jealous of her skills. A hypocrite. The one thing Saffi hated more than anything else. When had Andino turned into one? Or maybe he'd been one all along, and she'd just been too blinded by the memory of the boy who wrote *minus ten for excessive arrogance* at the top of all of her essays and doodled cacti on her birthday cards.

Seeing her approach, Andino gave a sigh of relief and began rising to his feet, but Saffi clamped one hand down on his shoulder and forced him back to his knees. Andino's mouth opened and closed in horror, but he couldn't seem to figure out what he wanted to say. It wasn't a bad view, entirely. She'd never been in the position to look down at him before.

'What the hell are you doing?' Andino asked, equal parts anger and fear.

If he had found out about Saffi's crimes for the first time today, just like her parents had, would he have reacted similarly? Saffi could imagine it. Him cursing her and cutting her off. Very rarely did someone understand another's predicament unless they too had been subjected to it. Dimple seemed to be the only exception.

'How did you piece it all together?' Saffi asked. 'Not even Taylor could.'

Andino's eyes flicked down at the gun in Saffi's grip. She wasn't pointing it at him, but he seemed to recognize the implied threat. 'That's because you gaslit him,' he replied.

'You helped,' Saffi said. It was true, even if he'd been unaware at the time.

'Don't act like you weren't playing both of us.' Andino glared up at her. 'Eli was right, and you let him think he was losing his mind. What – were you afraid we'd take the spotlight from you? Afraid we'd solve the case faster than you ever could?'

'I work better alone,' Saffi said.

'You were working alone when you put that woman on death row,' Andino spat.

'And you were working alone when you killed Tiwari.'

'Fuck you,' Andino said. 'You're aiding and abetting the woman who killed Mia!'

Saffi saw red. She'd been the one holding this damn investigation together, the one who'd been hunting the right suspect when Andino had been more than happy to write things off as an accident. To think he had the gall to bring up Martinez when he'd just killed Tiwari in cold blood. She lifted the gun and pointed it to the underside of Andino's chin. Her finger wasn't on the trigger – even now she couldn't fathom actually hurting him – but the fear in his eyes as he was forced to look up at her was gratifying.

Saffi felt twenty-three again, standing in the middle of an airport in Arizona. This, without a doubt, felt like it should be a momentous occasion. Once again, she had the naïve notion that Taylor would burst through the door, the only chance in hell they had at understanding each other.

But Taylor did not come. It was foolish to think he would.

'Answer the question,' she demanded. 'How did you figure it out?'

'I saw the letter she sent,' Andino said, suddenly compliant. Dimple made a sound of disapproval in the background. 'It came at the same time the article was released. Seemed like too much of a coincidence. It got me thinking about what Eli had said, so I logged in to your computer.'

Saffi blanched. 'How did you know the password?'

Andino huffed something close to laughter. 'It's the same from five years ago. You think it's so clever, don't you?' he scoffed. 'You told us once when you were drunk.'

Even if that was true, it wasn't easy to remember. Her father had instilled the importance of cybersecurity into her from a young age, so her password was a stochastic combination of letters and numbers. No dates, no references, no correlation to anything in her life. It was this reminder of exactly how many years Saffi had known Andino – reminders of exchanging drunk secrets and laughing until odd hours of the morning – that left her feeling ill. She angled the gun away from Andino's face. Still held in place, but no longer a direct threat.

Sensing an opportunity, Andino began speaking rapidly, low enough that Dimple couldn't hear. 'Saffi, listen to me. This isn't like you. You have a gun and the killer you've been chasing all year is right behind you. I know you feel guilty for what happened to Mia. This is your chance to make things right.'

But Saffi hadn't learned nothing from her conversation with her parents. She shook her head. 'No. There's no making things right.'

'Of course there is – what are you talking about?'

In all her years of knowing him, Saffi had never been able to get through to Andino. But some part of her still wanted to try. Maybe now that she was finally starting to understand what she really wanted – who she really was – it could be different. 'Five years ago, I left thinking I was doing the right thing. Not for myself, but for everyone else. And I'm so sick of it. I'm so sick of living for other people when they wouldn't do the same for me.'

'Then don't do it for anyone else,' Andino said, a tinge of desperation peeking through. 'Do it because it's the right thing to do!'

'Says who?'

'She's killed people,' Andino said.

'So have I,' Saffi said. She almost glanced over at Tiwari's lifeless body but stopped herself. 'So have you.'

'She killed Mia!'

'You keep saying that as though her death was more punishable than Tiwari's,' Saffi said.

Andino didn't respond, which was an admission. To him, one innocent life meant more than another. It was a selfish sense of justice that was more similar to Dimple's than he probably realized.

'If I let you go, what will you do?' Saffi asked.

'Don't pretend like I'm a complete stranger,' Andino said. 'You know what I'll do. And you know why too.'

Of course Saffi knew. Andino would turn Dimple in for killing Martinez along with all of the evidence Saffi had stacked against her. It was the same thing Saffi had done five years ago after finding out that the woman she'd put on death row had died needlessly. But all that had resulted in was suffering on her end. She'd done the right thing and had been punished for it too. The same would happen to Andino.

'There's not enough to convict her,' Saffi said. 'There is, however, enough to convict you.'

'That's a risk I'm willing to take.'

Of course it was.

'You could help me,' Andino tried again. 'You haven't done anything wrong.' His eyes darted down to the gun in her hand and then back up, quick as a bullet. 'Not yet.'

'I want to move on,' Saffi said softly. It was the first time she said it out loud. Her fingers curled tighter around the cool metal in her palm.

'So do I,' Andino said, now full-on pleading. 'Why can't we move on together?'

'Because I'm starting to think you're the one holding me back,' Saffi snapped.

Andino's face shuttered. 'Wow,' he said, and there was enough emotion in it to drown her. 'I can't believe that's how you –' He cut himself off, shaking his head. 'You're the one who invited a serial killer into the place Eli and I built together,' he said, shaking with barely restrained anger. 'And you don't even care because we've always been disposable to you, haven't we?'

'No,' Saffi protested. 'No, of course not.'

'But you think I'm holding you back?' It wasn't a question, not really.

Saffi answered it anyway. 'I didn't mean it like that.'

'Then kill her.'

'I can't.'

'What happened to you?' Andino asked. 'The Saffi I know would never let go of justice for anyone.'

'What is justice?' Saffi asked. 'Letting a serial abuser walk free because he has enough money for bribes and enough friends in high places? Or is it letting someone guilty of manslaughter walk free because he has enough money to check into rehab and start a foundation? The truth is, you don't know what justice is, Andino. And you don't know me either.'

If he did, he would realize that Saffi wasn't doing this for anyone else, nor was she doing this to hurt him. For once, she was doing something for herself.

'How could I possibly know you?' Andino asked. 'You've been lying to me just as much as Dimple has. Has anything you've said since you've come back been true?'

Saffi opened her mouth to respond, but Andino cut her off. 'You know what, don't answer that. It'll probably be another lie anyway.' He pressed his forehead into the barrel of the gun with so much force, Saffi had to take a step back. 'Go ahead. Kill me. I'm done *holding you back*.'

'Andino,' her voice came out weak, the words getting stuck in her throat. 'God, what the fuck? Since when do you have a death wish?'

'This is what you want, isn't it?'

'*No*.' Her grip loosened on the gun. She pulled away, just a bit, and there was a red mark left behind on Andino's forehead. He tracked her movement. 'I'm trying to help you, you idiot. They'll lock you up, you'll never work as a PI ever again, and Andino and Taylor Private Eye will go down just like Stronghold did. Is that really what you want?'

But Saffi could tell from his blank expression that Andino hadn't heard a word she'd said. The gun was the only thing that had his attention. She should've expected it – of course someone as stubborn as him would never accept defeat. But he moved faster than she could predict, one arm outstretched, reaching for the weapon. Without thinking, Saffi pulled the trigger. She didn't even hear the bang. One minute there was scuffling; the next, her ears were ringing.

Andino crumpled to the ground.

Red, pouring from his mouth. Convulsing. Then, quicker than the gunshot itself, it was over. Even holding the smoking gun, Saffi could hardly believe it.

Seconds passed. Minutes even. Then she was on her knees, clamoring over to him. Something warm and viscous soaked into her pants. His blood, Saffi realized. She tried calling Andino's name and was met with no response. She pressed two fingers to his neck. Still warm, but no pulse.

Swallowing around the urge to vomit, Saffi pulled back, trembling from head to toe. She'd seen too many corpses to count, but this couldn't compare.

This lifeless body belonged to the man who'd doodled palm trees onto the back of her birthday cards because he didn't know how else to show he cared. The one who, five years later, still remembered the ridiculous things she'd said while drunk. For someone so stubborn, it didn't make sense for him to go down so easily.

Saffi was acutely aware that she was hyperventilating, but somehow that knowledge only made it worse. Her lungs had stopped cooperating with her. The numbness from before consumed her whole, leaving her a deep, soul-crushing, bottomless pit of nothing.

This was murder. Whatever she'd thought she'd known before paled in comparison. Saffi had gotten her wish. She was one step closer to understanding Dimple Kapoor.

40

September 9, 2026

Saffi felt a strange sense of déjà vu as she sat in the hospital waiting room. The same hospital where she'd met Dimple Kapoor for the first time. It seemed fitting to be back here again. Except Andino and Taylor had been with her at the time. And now Saffi was alone.

Nobody would relay to her what Dimple's condition was. That likely meant Dimple was in a position where she'd be unable to give consent for visitors. Knocked out, in surgery, in a coma, dead, the possibilities were endless.

Either that or Dimple didn't want to see her.

But shooting themselves had been Dimple's idea. One with crime scene knowledge and the other with the ability to construct a compelling narrative. Together, they left that trailer framed as victims. Saffi had tried to avoid all the important arteries, bones, nerves, and vessels when she'd shot Dimple in the leg, but now she second-guessed herself. What if she'd aimed wrong? Or misremembered? Saffi's own injury had been entirely uncomplicated. The bullet had grazed her arm. A few stitches and she was fine. Apparently, Dimple had missed, which Saffi didn't believe for a second. No one ever played with fire and expected to come out of it unscathed.

And yet, here she was.

With her phone checked in to evidence, Saffi couldn't monitor the situation with Hector Olsen. She'd already given her statement to the police, but it didn't seem that any of the news channels playing on the hospital's TVs had picked up on it yet. Early this morning, they'd snuck into Olsen's trailer, which had been unnervingly close to Dimple's, and planted the evidence. Smeared blood, the gun. Still, a part of Saffi was worried they'd overlooked something.

She pulled on loose threads of the old scrubs she'd been given to wear. She was slowly but surely losing her mind.

Just as she'd been about to go ask the nurses, yet again, if there had been any updates, the waiting room door swung open. She sat up abruptly, wincing when her arm protested the movement. Part of her expected Dimple Kapoor to be standing there like a beacon, uninjured and captivating as ever. If not her, then at least a nurse to tell Saffi she could visit her.

Instead, there was Taylor.

Saffi rose to her feet. She'd never seen him look so lost, so manic. He scanned the room before landing on her. Before she knew it, she was being pulled into a bone-crushing hug. It pulled at her stitches, but Saffi didn't care. Taylor was warm and she'd been so, so cold until now.

When she pulled back, finally able to read every emotion on Taylor's face, Saffi felt the urge to throw up come back in full force. Because she hadn't just killed Andino. She'd robbed Taylor of his other half. She could see it in the pull of his mouth, the furrow of his brow, the tension he now carried in his shoulders that she feared would never go away.

'Are you okay?' Taylor asked. He held both of her forearms in a gentle grip. It suddenly struck her how awful it was that he was asking her that question.

'You're shaking,' he said. Saffi looked down. As it turned out, she was. 'Do you need to get looked at?'

That finally broke her from her trance. 'No,' she said. 'I've already been cleared. But Andino –'

Taylor shook his head, cutting off her words. His lips were pressed into a thin line. One push and it seemed like he'd fall apart. Saffi knew a man in need of a distraction when she saw one.

'How's the situation with Olsen?' she asked instead.

Taylor breathed in deeply, the man's name alone enough to bring that rare dark glint to his eyes. 'He's in custody until his trial. No bail.'

Saffi raised her brows. 'How the hell did you manage that?'

'Even if his trial is in a few days, I wasn't going to let the bastard walk free for another second,' Taylor declared. 'I'll make sure he rots for life. And then in hell afterward.'

Saffi felt sick again, Taylor's words too similar to her father's for her liking. If he knew what she'd done –

'Tell me something,' Taylor said, pausing to collect his thoughts. 'Was it painful?'

Just like that, she was transported back into the moment. Andino choking up blood. Crumpling to the ground. It happened so quick, he hadn't even been able to vocalize his pain.

'I don't know,' Saffi found herself saying. Because who truly knew the pain of death until they felt it? If it was anything at all similar to the pain of causing another's, then she feared for what was to come. 'It happened faster than I could comprehend.'

'Good,' Taylor breathed in relief, but it didn't last long. A complicated expression overtook his features as he seemed to mull something over. 'Why didn't you tell me where you were going?'

The question caught her so off guard, she pulled away. Taylor's expression was grave.

'I didn't know what to expect,' she admitted. 'I didn't even really know where I was going. I just knew Andino could be in trouble.'

'After both of you disappeared for hours, I had to find out from the police that my closest friends were shot. And that one of them is dead,' Taylor said. 'How do you think that felt?'

Saffi was silent. She'd never been on this end of his anger. There was nothing she could say in the face of it that didn't feel like a cheap mockery.

'I thought you coming back meant we could all be together again,' Taylor said. He let go of Saffi in favor of pacing. 'Don't you think I get sick of always being in the middle? You're too stubborn to admit you care about us and Atlas is – *was* – too stubborn to admit it hurts him, but what about me? Both of you have hurt me too! Do you even care? Do either of you think about me at all?'

'I thought you would come,' Saffi blurted. It was a childish sentiment, but she needed him to know – *of course* she'd thought of him. 'It felt like such a big moment, I thought you'd burst in and save us, like you always do.'

Taylor stopped pacing. Saffi braced herself, but his words were far from accusatory. 'You know, before you left, Atlas and I were going to ask you to start the new business with us. To be a partner.'

Saffi froze. 'What?'

When she'd heard from the other side of the world that Andino and Taylor had created an agency of their own, she hadn't been surprised. They'd always been Andino and Taylor – Atlas and Eli – a duo. Saffi was the outsider. The coworker they were kind enough to indulge every once in a while. She tried to imagine a place where Andino, Taylor, and Iyer Private Eye could exist. Even in a world where Andino lived, it felt fantastical.

But was that why there was an extra office waiting for Saffi when she came in? All set up as though they were always expecting her to come back?

'You're not the only one who had expectations,' Taylor said. 'The difference is that I was happy with what I got. I looked at you after five years and I saw that my friend – my family – was still there.' He met her gaze. 'Clearly, that wasn't enough for you.'

But wasn't this the clearest evidence that the three of them were better off alone? Taylor had lost Andino and then managed to get Olsen custody without bail. He would accomplish even more without Saffi holding him back. Without her failing to live up to his already low expectations. The painful thought slotted into her mind so easily, she'd had to have known it all along. Yesterday was the last time Saffi would ever speak to Andino, and this would be the last time she ever spoke to Taylor. Even in death, they were always paired.

Taylor had mentioned the kids needing a role model, but really there was no one better than him. He was the best chance they had at a better fate. Maybe, years in the future, Saffi would see all three of them standing side by side at an agency of their own. Doing what Saffi, Andino, and Taylor never could.

And then she was struck by the sudden reminder that *Mia Martinez was dead.* Saffi had managed to doom both herself and the generation after.

Something fell atop Saffi's cheek and when she reached up, she realized it was a tear. Her vision was blurry. Still, she could see that Taylor had turned away from her, his shoulders shaking with effort. The tears didn't stop after that, only gaining momentum.

You always cried the hardest watching someone else trying not to.

41

September 9, 2026

Dimple awoke to a pounding migraine and bright white lights. This was too familiar. She closed her eyes for a moment, collecting herself before trying again. It only made her headache worse, but Dimple needed to find her. She turned to her right.

Nothing.

Then left.

There was someone there, but not Saffi, like Dimple had been hoping. Instead, it was Julie sitting in a black chair. Noticing that she was awake, her manager rose and came to stand beside her, arms crossed.

'Good news,' Julie said. 'Bullet didn't hit anything vital. You passed out from blood loss, though, and they had to do a transfusion. You might need help walking for a while, but other than that you'll make a full recovery.'

'What are you doing here?' Dimple's voice came out hoarse.

'You're the one who put me down as your emergency contact,' Julie said, eyebrows raised.

There was a question in her tone, one that Dimple didn't waste her energy answering. The hospital staff had forced her to complete the form after she'd fallen from the balcony. Not expecting to ever need to put them to use, Dimple had put down Julie and Priyal.

'Just so you know,' Julie said, pushing up her red glasses,

'I would've come either way. You've been through a lot this year, haven't you? Poor girl.'

In all the years they'd worked together, Dimple had never heard Julie say something like that. Still, she'd somehow managed to make *poor girl* sound like corporate lingo.

'I've been meaning to ask if you want to hire a security team,' Julie said. 'You can afford it.'

Dimple tried to shake her head, but it only made the migraine worse. 'Priyal –' she began but her throat closed up before she could say anything else.

Julie nodded knowingly, taking a seat at the corner of Dimple's cot. 'Did she tell you she was planning on quitting before she – ?'

'Yes,' Dimple said. 'I don't want another assistant.'

Julie folded her hands together and made a motion as though resting them atop her desk before remembering where she was. Instead, she placed them in her lap and stared at Dimple consideringly. She seemed to deliberate back and forth over something before asking, 'Do you know why I pushed you to hire Priyal?'

Dimple sucked in a shaky breath. 'Because I am useless when it comes to social media.' It was an almost exact recitation of what Julie had told her when Dimple had asked her the same question.

'You're forgetting that you could barely afford one at the time,' Julie quipped. 'I could've forced you to learn how to use the applications yourself. With how driven you are, I know you would've done it. No use in wasting the money.'

'Then why?' Dimple asked.

'Because, Dimple, you were depressed. Don't give me that look – it's true. You'd been in the industry for five years and made plenty of enemies, but no friends. You were lonely. And I happened to know a girl who needed work, yes, but who was also lonely. I thought you might be good for each other.'

When she'd killed her aunt and uncle all those years ago, Dimple had relived their abuse in her nightmares for a long time afterward. Sometimes, on her worst nights, she still saw them now. With Irene, Dimple felt only guilt when she watched her bleed out in her nightmares.

With Priyal, however, Dimple just felt numb. She hadn't cried. Images of Priyal's body didn't haunt her every waking moment. There was just . . . nothing. Perhaps someone like her wasn't capable of emotions any longer.

'Priyal had been in LA for a couple years already and she had no friends,' Julie continued. 'She was worse off than you even, since she wasn't getting any roles.'

'You've always liked taking in strays,' Dimple commented absentmindedly. Julie glared at her, but she didn't refute the point.

'I wasn't in the position to accept more clients, but I figured I could help her in other ways. Help both of you.'

'That's –' Dimple couldn't suppress the flash of indignation in response to that. 'You overstepped. That's not your job. You're my manager, not my mother.'

'Do you wish I hadn't done it?' Julie demanded. Dimple faltered, closing her mouth. 'That's what I thought. And don't give me that, Dimple. Look at where we are now. I've always been more than just your manager and you know that. I care about you, and I want you to succeed. I didn't want to drop you, so I did what I thought was best.'

Dimple had nothing to say to that. Priyal was dead. If she'd never worked for Dimple, that wouldn't be the case.

No, the worst part was, if Dimple could go back and do it all over again, she wasn't sure she'd do anything different. Would she have landed a lead role had it not been for Irene's death? Would she have gone to her first film festival or continued to book the roles of her dreams? Would Julie have kept her as a client?

Would she have met Saffi?

'The thing about life is that you never know how long someone is going to be a part of yours,' Julie said. 'When you get to my age, you start realizing that when you meet someone you genuinely care about, you have to seize every moment you get with them and make them count. Priyal is gone, but you'll always have the good memories to look back on. She shaped you as a person. That piece of her that lives on inside you will never die.'

This was too much. Dimple could still see Priyal's limp body bleeding out right under her fingertips. That was the only version of her that she could seem to remember.

'But my point is, you and Priyal were better off for having met each other. And I think you'll be just fine not hiring another assistant,' Julie said, eyes twinkling. 'You know me, I won't ask any questions, but there's someone who's been waiting in the hospital for the entire time you've been unconscious.'

Saffi. Ignoring the pounding in her skull, Dimple rose slowly to her elbows.

Julie's arms hovered nearby, as though afraid Dimple would fall. 'Lean back, you need to rest.'

Something cold pressed into her hand.

Dimple's confusion must've shown because Julie explained, 'It might be a little watered down now, but you must be thirsty.'

Tentatively, Dimple took a sip. Cold and bitter with a hint of sweetness.

Iced coffee.

Dimple heaved, suddenly unable to inhale enough breath to fill up her lungs. She hiccuped. It was almost a relief when she began sobbing.

'Oh shit, what now?' Julie muttered. 'Don't tell me you're vegan and I forgot to make it oat milk or whatever the fuck?'

Dimple found herself laughing through the sobs. She wiped at her tears, but they just kept falling. Her chest seized and it felt like her heart was ripping in two and she couldn't articulate why, not even to her own mind.

Matcha had been growing on her.

42

September 13, 2026

Dimple hadn't been able to bring herself to see Saffi while she'd been bedridden. It reminded her too much of their first meeting, opponents of a war that had felt as important as their entire lives. This new era they were ushering in demanded a fresh start. But she'd heard from Julie that Saffi had never once left the hospital. And so as soon as Dimple was cleared to leave her bed – albeit in a wheelchair – she'd arranged for them to meet in the place she felt was most fitting.

Now their arms pressed together on the roof, a warmth hotter than the sun. Their reunion hadn't been the one Dimple had been expecting, though, not with the nurse running over Saffi's foot with Dimple's wheelchair.

'You should need a license to operate those things,' Saffi had muttered. But then she'd laughed, proving it had all been worth the wait.

They were alone now, though. A cool breeze ruffled Dimple's hair, sending it flying back.

Production for her film had been put on hiatus, so she didn't have to worry about that just yet, but there was a chance that Dimple would be left with a memento. A visible scar on her thigh, her first one. Much more pressing, however, was Olsen's trial, which was still set for tomorrow. Even with all the damning evidence, it would likely last a while.

'What are we supposed to do now?' Saffi said.

Dimple gave her a look. 'Anything. You know that.'

'You have your films,' Saffi said. 'One day, you'll be at the Oscars. But what about me? Nobody will ever hire me again after that article – thanks to you, by the way.'

Dimple considered it. 'Is that something you would like? To be hired for cases again?'

If it was, then Dimple would find a way to make it happen. But she had a feeling that wasn't what Saffi truly desired.

Saffi paused to consider. 'The most fun I've had in years was trying to catch you. But now I don't know if I have anything I'm passionate about anymore. Not like you do.'

After a moment's thought, Dimple took her hand. Saffi didn't protest, but she did watch with furrowed brows. Dimple dropped a tiny paper into her palm. The corner of the note she'd kept from the hotel – the part that simply read *-S*.

'Have I taught you nothing?' Dimple asked. 'There's nothing you can't ask for. And nothing you can't have.' Up here, so high above the bustling city, it seemed especially possible.

Saffi pinched the paper between her fingertips, holding it up to the sky. 'Have you ever considered that a universe where we can both be happy at the same time may never exist?'

'Then we'll build one, together,' Dimple said. 'We've achieved far more impressive feats.'

Saffi shook her head, looking out over Los Angeles, but she was smiling. 'It still weirds me out how much of an optimist you are. I wouldn't even know where to begin.'

'I didn't either. You know about my college years,' Dimple reminded her. 'This is the most exciting part. Life can take you anywhere from here.'

'It really is.' This time when Dimple turned, it was Saffi who dropped something into her palm.

A torn bit of paper just like Dimple's, but it read *-D* instead. From the apology note she'd left Saffi. Traded and then traded back.

'No more setting fires,' Saffi said.

Dimple reached into her pocket, pulling out her lighter. She'd cleaned it of all traces of blood, but sometimes she was almost certain she'd seen a lingering remnant somewhere along the surface. Dimple weaved it through her fingers one last time, igniting the flame. The fire was as beautiful as ever, but Saffi was proof that it wasn't the only all-consuming thing in this world.

Her aunt and uncle, Irene, Isaac, Mia, Priyal, Atlas. All gone so that Dimple could finally have everything she wanted. With Saffi by her side, there were simply no more fires left to set – nor any left to put out.

'No more running,' she said, holding the lighter over the roof's edge.

When Saffi nodded, a determined look in her eyes, Dimple finally let go. It soared, but neither of them paid any mind to where it landed. Perhaps, someday, someone else would find it – make better use of it than Dimple had.

This was an end in some ways, but mostly it was a beginning. *The thing about life is that you never know how long someone is going to be a part of yours.* It wasn't entirely true. From the first day Dimple had met Saffi, she knew that she would be a thorn in her side for a long time to come. Now she was glad for it.

A year ago, Dimple had viewed her life in two parts: before and after her aunt and uncle. Then, with the addition of Irene and Isaac it split into three. Now she felt a new fissure begin to form. And, for once, it wasn't one created by death. This one, brought about by Saffi alone, felt like a rebirth.

Dimple didn't know what was to come. Perhaps the pieces of her life would continuously fissure and break apart and come back together. And perhaps by the end of it, her life would be an endless cracked mosaic of time. But wasn't that the fun of it?

Acknowledgments

This whole publishing journey started one day when I decided that I was tired of writing about the traditional main characters. I wanted to write about villains instead. Maybe it's because the narrative allows for them to be as unhinged as they want, and that really speaks to me. Whatever it is, Dimple Kapoor was born from that. And what a roller coaster of a journey it has been. I never would have imagined this story would turn into what it has. Back then, I was a university student still convinced that I would be going into the medical field. Writing, as much as I loved doing it, was supposed to remain a hobby. Something I did in the shadows, something I would never speak to another soul about (dramatic, I know). Unexpectedly, I ended up writing a book that I loved too much not to share. This story has taken over my life in the best way, and what a blessing it is that I have so many wonderful people to thank for that.

To Amy Bishop-Wycisk, my superstar of an agent: You helped me achieve my dreams beyond my wildest imagination. Thank you for being the champion this book needed (and for always making sure I'm sitting down when you tell me the big news). Thank you to Jenny Chen, my editor, who understood the very heart of this book from the start and continued to ensure that these characters and this story mean as much to you as they do to me. I owe the world to the team at Bantam Dell: Cindy Berman, Saige Francis, Diane Hobbing, and Jean Slaughter. And to my wonderfully talented cover designer, Carlos Beltrán. Thank you immensely to Katie Greenstreet and the Paper Literary team, to Allison

Malecha and Tori Clayton, and to Grace Long and the team at Michael Joseph for helping bring this story to a new audience.

To my family: my mom, my dad, and my brother, who were immediately on board when I told them about this crazy dream of mine. Thank you for always believing I would do great things, whether it be curing diseases or writing about villains.

To my dearest friends, who both feed into my delusions and keep me sane. Lainey, my day one. You've been here through practically every stage of my life, even the really, really embarrassing ones. Thank you for being my first and loudest cheerleader. Maya Rose, the other half of my brain cell. Nobody has sat through more rants about these stupid characters than you. Thank you for always being my twin in delusion. Maya, my favorite person to scream about writing (and, well, everything) with. Thank you for suffering alongside me. Lia, who has always pushed me to be more unhinged, thank you for being a sounding board for my chaos. This story would not be what it is without you. Tayo, my writing buddy, my reading buddy, my fellow deadline girlie. Half of the reason I get things done is because of you. Thank you for your invaluable advice and for cheering me on every step of the way.

To my sorority sisters at Kappa Apple Pie: Jade, Jenna, Laynee, Rushi, and Sanj. Thank you for your endless support <3.

I feel it would be remiss if I didn't thank the star herself, Dimple Kapoor (and let's be real, she would be extremely offended if she wasn't at least mentioned), for teaching me to hold on to my dreams with both hands. You changed my life, girl.

And, of course, thank you, dear reader, for picking up this book.